ISBN: 9798990070509 (Paperback)
ISBN: 9798990070516 (eBook)

Any references to historical events, real people, or real places are used fictitiously. Names, characters, and places are products of the author's imagination.

Cover design and art by Christian Storm.
Book design by J.T. Rath

First printing edition 2024

www.jtrath.com

I0770267

INFINITUDE

J.T. RATH

Prologue
2477 | Unknown location

Purple tendrils of lightning stretched across the darkened sky, reaching for something distant and out of grasp. Slowly, almost indiscernibly, the legs of light dissipated.

One…two…three…four…

An aging, tired woman sat and counted the seconds it took for the light to dwindle. This was a new weather phenomenon within the last twenty years. She couldn't remember the science behind what she was counting to measure. Maybe it was how much power was in the strike itself.

Sixteen…seventeen…eighteen…nineteen…twenty.

At that count, the light had finally faded from view and the woman came back from her trance-like state. This type of storm was rarely accompanied by rain, usually just wind and lights, but today it was drizzling. She stood and walked across the crumbling floor of the room, toward a hole where a window used to be.

The weight of the future sat uncomfortably on her shoulders. She felt ten years older; aches in her knees pulsed and there was the strange sensation of her right arm falling asleep.

It was never cold anymore, even during storms with moisture. Trembling slightly, she extended her sleeping arm out in the rain. The first droplet woke the appendage up and the feeling of a second, third, and fourth drop soothed her. Even the rain wasn't cold.

My, how much this earth has changed… it was a thought she had often these days, usually coupled with a secondary, contradictory sentiment: *But has it really? It still turns day after day.*

She brought her dripping hand into the longstanding building's walls and observed the heavy drops of rain slide across her wrinkled skin. Time, much like these strings of liquid, moved ever forward.

The room was silent except for the constant, soft humming of the machine behind her. For what felt like the thousandth time, she turned to look at the man she loved, still not moving, but very much alive. The humming machine monitored his vitals courtesy of a thin band across his forehead with two metal links pressed against the temples.

Returning to her seat beside him, she gently held his arm and pressed its inserted glass panel. A handful of numbers and lines decorated the readout. His pulse was steady, as was his blood pressure. No change from the previous hundred times she had checked, but it was a force of habit at this point.

It had been so long since they'd started this journey. Since he had begun his mission.

Hope had been there a long while ago, now it had all but disappeared. Somewhere deep inside her mind, she believed he may still be trying to save them, but the majority of her spirit knew he was lost.

Somewhere. Some *when*.

At that moment elsewhere…

The world had gone to shit and the rest was on its way to hell. Previous cultures had preemptively mused about what the apocalypse would look like…what might lead to the fall of man. He guessed they had never been too far off, but wasn't sure if they ever predicted it would look quite like this.

Instead of battling for resources: space, food, water, fuels, the human race and the world was being brought to its knees through pure evil. There was no agenda other than power and rule. Peace was an ancient idea, spoken in whispers, and the meek around the globe were dying out.

The only reason he'd survived was by fighting back and hiding. He had the scars to prove it.

But he was done fighting. Even he knew when he needed to get the fuck out of *here*, out of this *time*. That moment was fast approaching. The world's final governments had all crumbled within the last year and the Regime was carrying out their will with no resistance. For the first time in human history, every being had given up hope, himself included.

A miniature scraperdrill fumbled in his fingers and fell to the floor as he lost his concentration.

"Son-of-a-bitch." He cursed softly to himself. For several months he'd been building a Warper. A time machine. All time travel had been banned by the Regime several years past and the punishment for those caught was severe. He'd heard rumors that recursive torture was being used, where you relive the day and pain of your torture over and over again. That was not something he intended to experience first-hand.

If it came to it, he'd end his own life with his sidearm, Zorex. The squared, gray barrel was made of a heavy metal and it dealt as much stopping power as one would assume from appearance alone.

One of the final components, a simple spring, slid into place. Carefully, he pressed its middle. It was taut. There was something about building he found comforting and even in these dire times, he couldn't deny enjoying himself.

There wasn't much left to do. The time to leave was coming soon.

Around him, the air grew abruptly and perceptibly dense. For a brief moment, he felt he may be sick, but it wasn't caused by body or mind. An aggressive blue flash burst inside his bunker. With no thought, Zorex was up from his side and pointed at the light.

Shit! Did they find me? Mentally, he readied to turn the gun on himself if the Regime burst through the door. Instead, it was a man – or some *apparition* of a man.

Half there.

Half not.

This distantly familiar stranger looked drugged and ragged. His eyes were drooped shut, he could barely hold his head up, and it seemed as if something or someone else was speaking through him. How did he know this man? Was it his mind playing tricks on him? Whatever this was, the man was not in full control of himself as he spoke,

"Titus, you must go back before it began…"

The apparition was fading in and out.

He knows my name.

"The lines are all different, this isn't what you think. You know who I am. You have to end it." It seemed he was struggling against whatever held him. Whatever had control managed one last statement before it disappeared in another blue flash, clarifying to Titus what he must do.

"You have to end it…to prevent it."

Chapter 1 – Aiontis
2404 | Unknown location

I am a historian and I need drugs. Why those are my first thoughts in *this* place, I'm not quite sure, but both materialize as absolute fact.

"This place" isn't immediately obvious, though it does feel familiar. *When* is this place? It feels like I'm in the present, but I also sense a wandering, visiting element.

Fuck it. I need drugs. Specifically, Jinx. But it's 2404 – I know *that* somehow – and Jinx has been banned for over twenty years. They don't make the stuff anymore.

I wake as if I were just in a deep slumber, but I don't feel rested. Like I was already up and I'm just more awake now.

Odd. Perhaps that's a side effect of not having a lick of Jinx in my system? I get up from the floor (why the hell am I on the floor?) and look out the window of my 151st floor apartment. Now I recognize my setting.

Omaha, Nebraska. United States of America.

Modern day America isn't what it used to be, but we're in a better place. No longer the main superpower of the globe (or even the second, third, or fourth), our nation has done a lot better when we're not carrying the weight of the world on our shoulders. That's a lot of responsibility and, knowing what happened in the past, it was nearly the country's downfall.

Now a mostly modernized nation, even cities like Omaha are bustling, sprawling downtown locales. Farming has been taken over by science in terms of production and takes up just a sixteenth of the total space it needed in the 20th and 21st century.

I like Omaha. I like that it's in the middle of the nation. I generally enjoy its weather. There's enough to do. There are good jobs, crime is low.

Below me I watch the tiers of air transport vehicles (ATVs for short) zooming from one place to the next. Yes, they're "flying cars". Talk about disappointing technology. Flying cars were invented and semi-perfected in the 2100s after automated cars had become the norm. I'm not sure what officials decided it would be a good idea to allow the general population to "fly" their transportation, but the result was catastrophe for the first few decades. If you thought people were bad at driving, just wait until you put someone in the air with a powerful propulsion system.

All that's automated now. For the better I suppose, but I have always wondered what it would be like to actually drive a car or fly an ATV. Guess that's the historian in me: always distracted with the past.

Now that I'm up and walking around, I'm more grounded, but still airy. As if I'm half here and half not. A half elsewhere.

Across the marble floor is my bar cart. Maybe a bit of the hard stuff will bring me back to life. The stopper cork on the bottle squeaks in delight as I pull it out. *Me too, bottle. Me too.* I pour some gorgeous golden liquid into my favorite glass and take a small swig, letting it sit in my mouth for a moment. The swallow hardly burns, but just enough. I roll the pour around in this glass, a crystal pyramid that's been hollowed out and flipped over. The bottom of the glass is the point and is always perfectly balanced. Obviously, it always reminds me of the Pyramids of Giza, but it's also just damn cool.

I pull the last traces and it burns more this time, tasting wonderful. I can't tell if I feel better – or different – yet. My thoughts strangely turn to my wealth, as if I'm taking in this apartment's opulence for the first time. My fortune doesn't come from being a historian, obviously, though there is value in that profession these days. I'm what one calls a Historian Consultant. I study humans or, more specifically, human nature, and the paths that we as a species have taken to collective failure or success. After the near downfall of the U.S. nearly 100 years ago, my line of work was created. It's a wonder it took our race that long to create a workforce like it, but if I've learned anything in this role it's that we're collectively not always the fastest of learners.

Being a Historian Consultant may sound like awfully qualitative work and there is a lot of that. Generally speaking however, it's based on sophisticated models of data, strategy, and statistics. As the profession progressed, it became highly regarded within society and there's a certain code all Hiscons (slang jargon for the role) abide by and must swear an oath to:

"I hereby dedicate my work to guide, teach, and inform the human race toward prosperity, fulfillment, and survival. I will do this with my mind and my heart and the full history of the human race as my foundation."

Wow, did I just say the fucking Hiscon oath out loud? Alone in my apartment? Something's definitely off, and an odd sensation hit my tongue with the word "survival".

Why?

I'm not sure, but I do take that oath to heart. I adore history. Always have, even as a child. There's something about recognizing past events, especially the BIG ones, that blows my mind. I go down rabbit holes easily:

What led that group or individual to make *that* choice?
Did they assess the risks?
How are two or more events linked?

History is so incredible because you can literally *never stop asking questions*. Being a Hiscon is the single most interesting job a human can have. My humble, biased, opinion of course.

If you're wondering how much one of the most important professions of the modern era gets paid, my answer is: not enough, but we're not exactly skirting by either. My wealth largely comes from "Ancestral Growth Accumulation", or AGROW. It's an economic phenomenon stemming from the fact that the planet, in large, has become far more stable than past centuries and millennia.

Because of this, most collective families have been able to build their wealth over the course of several generations, assuming they don't have a bad apple along the way that blows it all. People are generally having fewer children as the population of the world was becoming a big concern (that's better now, though not fully solved) so with less children and more wealth to pass on, AGROW became a realized truth. Some families are even wealthy enough to hire Hiscons to guide some of their bigger life decisions.

So, who's my family? Where do I come from?

Aiontis Breaker, Hiscon in the 2400s.

Chapter 2 – Aiontis
2404 | Omaha, Nebraska

The whiskey isn't cutting it. I still need some Jinx.

Easier said than done, idiot. Sometimes I hate the way my subconscious talks to me.

It's going to be a process getting my hands on some – a *long* process – and I'm not sure why I need (or want?) it so bad. Sure, I dabbled with the shit back in my younger days, but I never felt "addicted" to it, per say.

Though here we are.

Jinx can be some nasty business if your genetic makeup is especially susceptible to its influence. Luckily, I'm more immune to it, but it still packs a mean punch…in the best of ways.

Unlike most drugs, Jinx is a somnolence inducer and only activates once you're asleep. It makes the user incredibly tired within a few minutes (depending on dosage) and puts them to sleep for anywhere from three to seven hours.

For some, that's reason enough to take it and part of the reason it was banned. Insomniacs became increasingly addicted and it quietly became an epidemic where a large chunk of the population became dependent on it to function in society.

Once you're asleep, Jinx gives you the incredible ability to *mostly* control your dreams. Sounds fucking crazy, right? It's as nuts as it sounds. Your subconscious still picks the themes and moods of dreams – sometimes even the locations – but once you're in there you have most of the control. Perhaps unsurprisingly, controlling your own dreams is an immense responsibility. It essentially gives you a second life with rules defined by you.

You're probably able to see why people became so hooked on it. Even worse, people had a hell of a time separating reality from their dream "selves", hence the aforementioned subset of the population that was extra susceptible to Jinx's pull.

It started as a pharmaceutical technology – meant well enough to try and help treat sleep disorders. The dream controlling was an unintended side effect and then it quickly turned into one of the most profitable street drugs ever over the span of only a couple years. The stuff became more potent with experimentation and the government shut it down in 2390.

You want to know the "side effects" of a societal group that can't discern reality from their dreams? Spikes in rape, murder, theft, suicide, you name it. It never quite got to the same levels of the opioid epidemic that occurred in the 2000s, but that's largely thanks to Hiscons. Once the pharmaceutical companies determined the effects of Jinx (they called it something different obviously, but I can't remember for the life of me), Hiscons were brought in to make recommendations.

The opioid crisis several hundred years ago was continuously supported by doctors, politicians, and pharma companies. Thanks to that historical example (among others), Hiscons predicted the trend of Jinx being even worse. The government stepped in and made companies shut down the research, but it was too little too late. The formula was already out on the streets, but at least it was a lot harder to acquire.

So yeah, it was some nasty business and those that didn't end up getting arrested or killed for confusing reality were usually lethargic sloths as a result, often becoming morbidly obese and unable to support themselves. How could they? They were sleeping 10-20 hours per day. There were very few people in the population who could regularly take Jinx with a balanced approach.

I was one of those people, or at least I was the several times I took it. It was definitely fun to be the master of your own domain in your mind, but I always felt there was something missing in the midst of it. I could never place my finger on it, but the dreams always had a, dare I say, *boring* quality to them. Perhaps my imagination just wasn't up to par or I wasn't talented at creating fully rounded experiences, but everything was just so *easy* with Jinx. Like a videogame with all the cheat codes turned on. Wanted that girl in your dreams? Walk up and have her. Wanted to be rich and famous? You got it, no questions asked. Go to the moon? Have a great trip! Perhaps others were able to create more conflict, but luckily my inability to do so was probably the defining reason I never became truly hooked on it.

"Yeah, says the guy who suddenly needs it ASAP." These words hang in my empty apartment, dripping with mystery. This fact alone is weird and I still don't have any idea what I did last night or why I feel…*off*. Frighteningly, it's as if I have a concentrated episode of short-term memory loss, and given my keenness toward Jinx right now, I'm forced to beg the question: *is this reality?*

The haunting thought sends shivers up my spine and I eliminate it from my mind. This is *definitely* reality. That whiskey tasted way too damn good to be anything my own head could come up with to trick me. Plus, none of this feels easy right now. I'm in the present and I'm not dreaming.

Now, what the fuck do I do about this Jinx problem? Unfortunately, there's only one option and it sounds like a pain in my ass.

Chapter 3 – Aiontis
2404 | Omaha, Nebraska

I should probably mention that time travel exists in 2404. In fact, it's been around for about thirty years. Much like ATV's, it's a disappointing technology.

Almost immediately after the announcement by CERN, the governments of the world agreed to red tape the shit out of it with regulations. To be fair, a significant reason for that reaction came from the outcry of Historian Consultants worldwide screaming that this was unprecedented territory for mankind, and would be the single most disruptive technology in our earth's history.

Obviously, scientists were terrified of the prospect of time travel from having watched too many sci-fi movies and hearing about all the implications to the "space time continuum". The problem was that they couldn't explain exactly *what* would happen – it was all theory. Theory with a lot of strong scientific observation, mind you, but the time warps, bending, or doom they read or saw in their science-*fiction* failed to materialize after rigorous experimentation.

Of course, there were only small things they'd test for the "preservation of the timeline", so no one really knows what would happen if you went back and assassinated a world leader or something gargantuan like that, but we do know what would happen if you eat a doughnut last Thursday instead of a banana: nothing! The answer is literally nothing happens and things in the universe are not as dependent on other actions or reactions as we liked to believe.

Neither Hiscons nor scientists were wrong to be concerned, but it effectively neutered the whole idea to little more than a tourist attraction. There was a lot of money to be had with granting a human the ability to travel back in time so, naturally, several companies began offering up the "product" and specific experiences. The woman who invented time travel, Emma Dexter, became history's first female trillionaire and one of only a handful of trillionaires worldwide. She sold the technology to said companies for exorbitant sums, often at the disgruntled scoffing of the scientific community, but hey…if I'd invented time travel? You can bet your ass I'd want to make money off of it. And her wealth wasn't all greed; she set up several charities, scholarships, and even schools with the funds, many of which are large institutions today. I'm jealous, really. She got her cake, got to eat said cake, and made an impact while doing it.

Anyway, "time travel" basically became akin to taking a vacation…one that only the very wealthy could afford.

Wanted to go on that flawless tropical trip with "perfect" weather? The company would look back at recorded data, pick a date range for you and book it.

Love the fashion of a certain era and want to experience it first-hand? Pick a date off the calendar and have at it!

Missed that one big concert in the desert with a certain performer and thinking about going to get your rage on? The opportunity is all yours…for the right price.

Almost miraculously, there hasn't been a significant underground creation of time travel capabilities largely because the entire process

A) Uses a *lot* of energy and
B) Features a very specific radiation emission that's nearly impossible to cover up

And that's not to mention that there've been a handful of instances where someone tried to go via the "Hack Market" and…well…let's just say the results weren't pretty.

Perhaps you've put two and two together by now, but in order to get my hands on some Jinx, I'm going to have to go back in time. It's no longer available during the present, but if I go back before 2390, I should be able to gain access to some easily. Then, once I have this crazy craving out of my system, I'll hopefully feel normal again. *I hope?*

A shower sounds fucking amazing right now and I pee while the water heats up. Something about peeing in the shower always grossed me out. The toilet flushes automatically once it determines I'm through and I enter through the membrane shower door into a humid, warm space. One technology that's certainly gotten better in the last couple hundred years is showers. Variations still exist and the basic models are around, but for connoisseurs like myself, I've basically got a whole room dedicated to mine. Small, heated droplets suspend themselves in the air throughout the room and I have three different heads I can walk under for varying sensations. No matter where I'm at, I'm getting clean and I'm always warm. It's a great place to relax and barely uses any water thanks to a recycling drain that cleans it so I don't ever feel guilty for spending 20 or 30 minutes here.

Today unfortunately, it seems as if I'll need to keep it short. In an attempt to wake myself up, I shift the water to cold, which really changes this room into a torture chamber of sorts, but one that awakens the senses at least. I feel a little better, but the odd premonition that I'm only "half" here still hangs like a haze above me. *I've got to figure this out.*

As I get dressed to actually join society, I ponder how I'm going to get away with finding, buying, and taking Jinx while I'm back in time. It'll be easier said than done because all time travelers are heavily monitored while they're back in time. Some argue it's an invasion of privacy, but much in the same way that crime is illegal in the present, it's illegal in the past. Probably even more so. And laws are retroactive so Jinx is banned *today* and *back in time.* Usually, you don't even get to commit the crime in the past because of the active monitoring from this "end". Each company hires monitors that keep tabs on the guests and if they're about to possibly kill someone, or, you guessed it, take illegal drugs, they pull them back instantly. Which is not a pleasant experience physically, mind you. It makes sense why they do this, and you're forced to sign a waiver of privacy beforehand, making it all legal, but it complicates things for me.

What's worse is this hankering – this *pulse* – for Jinx is getting worse. It's been an hour since I've woken up and it's consuming my thoughts. Strangely and almost frighteningly, I feel like going back in time to take some Jinx is my destiny. And yeah, that's just as fucking stupid as it sounds, making me the world's most grandiose addict.

"Home: power down" I speak into the ether of my

apartment. Everything that was once on goes into a low-consumption "rest" mode. The smartglass windows covering my walls activate their shaders, protecting my unit from getting too hot, saving on cooling costs. Perhaps unsurprisingly these days, the entire globe is much more concerned with saving energy and leaving small footprints. It's one area where humankind seemed to have learned its lesson, with the help of some Hiscon algorithms.

Before I leave, I'm sure to check my iNsert on the underside of my wrist. No one – unless they're truly old fashioned – uses wallets, watches, or phones anymore. It's all loaded into the small glass plate in your arm, mini projector in your eyelid, and microscopic speaker in your ear. Invasive, sure, but incredibly efficient and useful.

I've got my credits loaded and I'll need them for taking the time trip. The clock tells me it's 10:30 in the morning. In an unsettling way, it feels a lot later. The iNsert also reveals I have three missed calls and a slew of messages, but I ignore them for now. I'll review them once I'm on the MagRail.

Lastly, I double check (out of habit) that I have my X-34 in its interior holster. It may be a small firearm, but it'll still mess up someone's day when given the opportunity. As my finger grazes the icy metal, that feeling creeps back in my gut. Today feels big, important. I imagine it feels like what us Hiscons refer to as a "D-Day" or "Defining Day" in history.

This is bigger than the Jinx fix…
Hell, this feels bigger than me…
But what the fuck *is* this?

Chapter 4 – Aiontis
2404 | Omaha, Nebraska

Some fucker just buzzed me as I emerged onto the launch platform. They must have been off autopilot illegally and I nearly lost an arm for it, but hey, at least it's a gorgeous day.

My ATV is parked on the 100th floor, which always gives me a small sense of vertigo. No matter how advanced technology is, high is high. Though…I do guess they have SaverShields to catch anyone should they fall.

I select a command on my iNsert and stand near the platform's edge, hoping some other jackass doesn't think they're talented enough to manually fly today. A few moments pass and a stiff, warm breeze cascades around me. It feels wonderful and pulls me back from reality for a moment. Despite all the odd head games I've had this morning, despite all the technology around, sometimes you realize the Earth still turns.

The sun…the stars…the oceans…the weather…it all keeps going and barely feels the effects of time. So strange and fascinating. Perhaps that's just the historian in me?

With a quiet hum, my ATV parks nearby and opens its door. As I have so many times before, I step into the vehicle and start typing in a destination on the console.

"Hello Aiontis. Where are we headed today?" the vehicle asks in a feminine tone.

"Hi Betty. Have something I need to do in New York. Let's head to the Omaha MagRail please."

"Are you feeling alright, Aiontis? I'm sensing perspiration and a lack of quality sleep." One of the more annoying things about superficial AI is they're quite nosy. But sometimes it's nice to feel like some…*thing* cares. I smile.

"Yes Betty, I'm fine. Just feeling a bit off today. Thank you for asking though."

"Of course. I see you've got an X-34. Are you planning on using it today?" She asks about my sidearm. Like I said: fucking nosy.

"Not if I don't have to. Just there in case I need it." I pause to see if there will be a follow up question. "Betty, can we be on our way please? I want to catch the next MagRail."

"Right away, Aiontis. Any music today?" She begins to pull the ATV into traffic.

"It's a short trip, but sure. Surprise me."

Music starts playing and I tune it out. Instead, I watch out the window as we pass through the Omaha architecture, looking at all the other people and vehicles going about their day. It's amazing what this city has emerged into as a true central hub of America, really only dwarfed by Denver in terms of sprawling downtowns from adjacent states.

I swipe a panel on the window and it pulls up some of the day's news and weather. No wonder it felt so great outside, it's a perfect 22°. And yes, that's in Celsius; the U.S. finally came around to the metric system about 100 years ago.

The top news stories are mundane or, at the very least, not all that different from the norm. There's been an ongoing conflict in Africa for five years so far. It's not incredibly violent or large so America mostly ignores it. Several financial articles scroll across my screen. A rather lengthy article about an advancement in artificial intelligence. A related article about said AI being incorporated into an android. A new film review. Some sports results. And a piece about Hiscons helping the U.S. to anticipate the next 50 years of growth. It piques my interest.

The U.S. Government is tapping into the wealth of knowledge and skill from some of the nation's best Historian Consultants (Hiscons) in order to determine what the next 50 years for the country could look like.

BLAH BLAH BLAH

The request details are highly classified, but a high ranking official within the Paulson Administration tells us the analysis will be centered around infrastructure, population, and potential pandemics.

BLAH BLAH

It's a significant undertaking, utilizing no fewer than 15 Hiscons across the states and stemming from various specific fields of Hiscon analytics, statistics, algorithms, data, and forecasting.
"This is a really exciting endeavor for the Administration and it shows they are forward-thinking. Hiscons have never been used to predict 50 years out and certainly not by a world government. This should be looked at as a positive, whatever side of the aisle you're on."
That could be just what the Paulson Presidency is looking for as her approval ratings have been slowly declining as of late.

BLAH BLAH Political bullshit…

50-year trajectories are not a common occurrence and could spell trouble for a profession that values its accuracy. Hiscons mainly focus on using past events and behaviors combined with data to help make decisions, map out their consequences, or determine forecasting. That forecasting is usually limited to 10 years however. Top Virginia-based Hiscon, Jamee Thent tells us why.
"In the Hiscon world, anything past 10 years is —"

BLAH BLAH BLAH

It begs the question if the results will actually be worth it and if the answer is yes, will other countries of the world follow suit? 50 years from now in 2454, where will we be? How close to the forecast will we come?
Quite literally, only time will tell.

"Did you enjoy that article, Aiontis?" Betty's voice startles me.

"Hmm? Oh yeah. Sounds really interesting, I mostly skimmed it, but from what I can tell that's going to be a difficult undertaking. Kind of wish I was on that project though."

"That would be nice, sir. We're arriving at Omaha MagRail

now."

"Thanks, Betty. Appreciate the ride."

"My pleasure, Aiontis."

I exit the ATV onto a platform, much lower than the 100th floor I started at, to the hustle and bustle of the Omaha Central Station. I glance at my iNsert and send Betty home, my ATV quietly zooming off into traffic.

Inexplicably, I feel lonely now. I'm out in public at the busiest place I've been all day, but imagine that if I closed my eyes, I'd open them and everyone would be gone. I test my theory and take a few deep breaths. Another brief flow of wind comes behind me and through my shirt. Once more it feels incredible on this pristine day, but I'm scared to open my eyes.

"Get the fuck out the way, man!" I'm forced to look as some other jackass – there's apparently a lot of them out and about today – bumps into me.

Clearly everyone is still here.

"Standing there gawking like an asshole…" he mumbles as he continues walking.

And I wish they weren't.

The iNsert component in my eyelid tells me it's 10:50am. The next Omaha-to-New-York MagRail leaves at 11:07. Just enough time to grab some coffee.

High, rounding walls come together at the top of the large dome in Omaha's premier transit station. Much like the evolving city around it, this building represents what used to be a smaller metropolitan in what was a predominantly farming state, now boomed into a significant central hub for many surrounding states. On the ceiling of the dome, part of this history is painted across several gorgeous murals. I always get distracted by them when I walk in. There's something about their artistry that captivates me more than just the historical aspect. It's like I can see the brushstrokes and their congealed peaks of paint from all the way down here.

People pass on my right, left, front, and back on this apparently very-busy day. In the distance, I see a woman, face in half panic, sprinting to what must be a soon-to-leave connecting rail. Her automatic suitcase can barely keep up, wheeling behind her at top speed and narrowly avoiding taking some pedestrian's knees out. I smile at the scene, silently hoping it does collide with someone just for the laughs.

There isn't much of a line at the quaint café tucked away in the center of the space, directly under the dome. A few tables and chairs are occupied with people working away on their iNserts doing an assortment of activities. As I arrive at the counter, my iNsert begins to interact with the café's interface and the menu appears on virtual boards above, complete with handwritten chalk letters for perceived authenticity. A simple drip coffee, black, is what my eye focuses on and the iNsert confirms the purchase. The café interface goes away and my coffee is ready on the counter.

Coffee is one constant throughout time, I've decided. It's not the *only* constant, but it's always been there as a beverage of choice. It seems like once any human reaches adulthood, beginning to drink coffee is a (very enjoyable) rite of passage. Even in most science-fiction stories and adventures, coffee – out in the deep dimensions of space – is still there to start your morning.

"OMAHA to NEW YORK. Departing in 10 minutes. Platform 17." The womanly voice from the station's audio system makes the announcement. Here and there, people experience various levels of anxiety from the notice. They turn away from their iNserts quickly. Some head to the restroom before the trip.

I'm calm, all things considered. I've done this trip many times before and I know it only takes a few minutes to get to Platform 17. I push aside the lid of my coffee cup and blow on the dark brown liquid. Shiny waves ripple outward to the edges and the rich, nutty flavor fills my nose. I take a small sip and it tastes just as good.

Perhaps all I needed was a damn good cup of coffee?

Through the crowd, taking slow sips, I make my way over to P17. Ahead, I spot the lady who was rushing to her train, clearly stressed out. On the floor beside her lies her suitcase, wide open, with clothes strewn about and a pedestrian on the floor cursing at her and the bag.

"Oh…I'm sorry sir! I just needed to catch my MagRail!" She pleads with him. "Are you ok?" Meanwhile, her suitcase is twitching on the ground, wheels still spinning rapidly as if it were upright.

"That thing ran straight into my nuts! Do I look alright?"

I can feel myself stifling laughter so I just keep walking, not wanting to add to her embarrassment, but dammit! I wish I could have seen that happen.

Once you go deeper into the station, it's louder and windier, with the *WUSHHHHH* of the departing or arriving trains forcing air movement. Comparatively they're pretty quiet against older, more primitive systems, but those were also ten times slower. There is something pretty incredible about seeing a MagRail launch toward its destination. It reminds me of those ancient sci-fi films where they jump to "hyperspace". Especially now that the technology has been perfected over recent decades; they're faster, more efficient, and safer than ever.

P17 is up ahead to my left and there's already quite a few people waiting there. I cross the platform's "threshold" meaning my iNsert has communicated with the station to purchase my ticket. There's a small buzz near my wrist and I glance down to see the screen displaying a purple MagRail ticket, *"OMA – NYC"* printed underneath the logo.

Beneath me, deep in the concrete of the floor, there are vibrations from the incoming train and not long after, its *push* of air through the barrier membranes and onto the Platform. This particular rail must have come from Los Angeles because it's busier than normal. LA to New York is a long commute when you factor in stops, but some people make it work. Many get off here in Omaha.

The safety membranes act as a one-way gate, allowing the passengers to depart if they need, but not allowing us to enter. Eventually the last passengers needing to get off do so and the membrane wall turns translucent, indicating we can walk on. I take a quick sip of coffee, cross the threshold into the air-conditioned train, and look for a window seat.

I must have gotten lucky on this particular section of the Rail because it's nearly empty, sans three or four others who are busy working away with their iNserts.

Perfect for me. I still feel uneven and questionably "off",

even with the coffee. My fucking ridiculous craving for Jinx hasn't subsided and I'm just ignoring it as best I can. I worry that I look like a fucking junkie, even if I know I don't.

Something in the back of my brain reminds me I have a bunch of messages left on my iNsert so I'll distract myself with those on the trip to New York, which should take just over half an hour.

As I sit, my seat begins "adhering" to me – a necessary safety precaution of traveling at high speeds on a MagRail. I've never studied the technology behind it, but it was one of the biggest…learning curves…people had to get used to. Your seat, particularly on launch and approach, seals you into itself to prevent you from absorbing the high G-forces that accompany the acceleration and deceleration. In the event of a crash, this mechanism can kick "on" within less than a nanosecond across the entire train. Although MagRails are some of the safest forms of transportation in history, this technology has saved countless lives.

But damn does it feel weird…

Before I start scouring through my backlog of messages, I watch as the station turns into a streaky blur one moment and outside to the warm Omaha sky the next. Towers and buildings zoom by incomprehensibly until we're out in the plains of neighboring states…not so much plains anymore, just *less* developed structures than downtown Omaha.

I still only have three missed calls, but it seems the number of outstanding messages has increased since I left my apartment. I look at the most immediate one,

11:05am – Hello sir, I've made it back home. Safe travels! – Betty

I delete it, glad my ATV made it home and without any additional prying in her alert. The next several are more concerning. They're from the same person who called three times.

As I read the messages, each with an increasing degree of alarm, my blood runs cold. For a brief moment, my anxiousness toward getting a Jinx hit settles.

"What the fuck…" I whisper slowly. The messages are from a close friend, Thomen.

3 days ago — Aiontis, haven't heard from you in a week or so. Thought we were going to meet up this week to chat about a Hiscon opportunity. And get a drink. Mostly get a drink. Let me know…

1 day ago — Hey friend, hope everything is ok. Haven't seen you online or anything for a while. Off the grid is very unlike you. Verria is worried about you. So am I.

2:37am — Aiontis, your neighbor called me a few hours ago, said they hadn't seen or heard you in days, maybe weeks. Getting really worried, just please give me a call or message. Need to know you're okay…feel like the next step might be the police.

The messages themselves are concerning, but the thing that terrifies me most is that I can't remember a damn thing about the past month.

Chapter 5 – Titus
2477 | Unknown location

*Y*ou have to end it to prevent it…
You must go back before it began…
The lines are all different, this isn't what you think…
You know who I am. You have to end it…

Once heavy, the air around him was settling; as if it had suddenly lost humidity. It was colder, though Titus couldn't tell if that was the chill down his spine or the actual temperature of the room.

His head was swimming with confusion. The man who – with a flash of blue light – had appeared and disappeared was one he strangely remembered, but couldn't place. *Why is that?* And it was an odd sense of remembrance…felt more within his body than in his mind.

The incredible theatrics that had accompanied the visit were unlike anything he'd seen before. Certainly not the type of time travel his Warper was able to perform. Though, that mystery seemed to be the least of his worries at the moment. What had the man meant about "ending it to prevent it"? Why had those messages been so cryptic?

He said that I should "go back before it began".

"What's '*it*'?" Titus asked aloud. The question sat unanswered in the silence of his bunker and frustrated him.

Why had this man come and done this? He had his plan of escape ready to go. The Warper was nearly complete. Within a couple days' time, he would pick a time to travel back to, make a new life, and be free of the Regime forever. His Warper was a one-way ticket, rigged to self-destruct after he was on the other side. Or, more accurately, other *time*.

But now…now all this had been placed at his feet. He was exhausted. This world was going to shit, hell…it was already there, and he didn't have time for this.

A dilapidated couch that often doubled as his bed stood

against a far wall. Its tan, faux leather hide was cracked and ripped in a few spots, but it gave him momentary relief as he sat down, swallowed in its embrace.

Despite his anger, there was a knot in his stomach and he was tired. A wave of fatigue crashed over him. He knew what the knot in his stomach was…something a forgotten stranger had explained to him long ago. You learned to recognize when it was happening to you.

A D-Day. A Defining Day. One that would shape history forever. Before the gentle wisps of sleep took him, he believed he had just been thrust into the midst of one.

And as much as he wanted to forget it, Titus knew he would have to unravel the mystery. Just after this nap…

Chapter 6 - Aiontis
2404 | Omaha, Nebraska

*W*hy the fuck can't I remember anything? It is a question worth asking aloud, albeit, to myself.

"Why the fuck can't I remember anything?" I look around to see if anyone heard me. Then I look around to see if anyone is following me. Why? "You're losing it, man."

The more I ponder on today, the more it all comes across like a dream. I don't remember how I got "here"; it feels like I *dropped in* on today, like how a dream starts you right in the middle of everything.

How does that even make sense?

I can't emphasize enough how terrifying it is to begin questioning your reality, knowing full well that you're not in a dream. I imagine it's what Alzheimer's patients must feel like when they come out of hazes.

I know I'm *me*, but why can I only come to terms with long-term facts?

I recognized Betty, my ATV.

I know who my friends Thomen and Verria are.

I know I'm a Hiscon.

But what did I do yesterday?

What work projects am I on?

Why do I want Jinx so bad?

"Holy fuck!" I exclaim, loud enough to attract attention, but luckily everyone's too deep in their iNserts to care.

The Jinx.

One of the side effects of heavy usage is the inability to distinguish true reality from the one you make in your dreams. Somewhere along the line I must have gotten hooked on the stuff and now I'm creating this nightmare. That *must* be it.

But why would I go and get hooked on Jinx? It makes no

sense. I never liked the stuff and, to be blunt, I'm doing well in life. I don't need it. A darker thought enters my mind:

What if someone is drugging me? What if they've been drugging me for a while? I panic for a moment as the worst-case scenario takes me further. *How long have I been here?* I imagine myself sitting in a dark, dank room, hogtied to a chair with a steady IV of Jinx flowing into my system.

Like I said, worst-case scenario.

I'm spiraling. I stare out the window observing the outside world pass by, and take some deep breaths. In through the nose… chest rising… out through the mouth… abdomen pressing lightly against my stomach. It helps and I even laugh as I realize that my brain must be really good at creating dreams because the outside blur of everything looks incredibly accurate. If I'm truly on Jinx, there's only a handful of things I can do.

For starters, I could just stop participating and wait for it to ride itself out. I'd likely just stay on this train perpetually and eventually wake up, but who knows how large of a dose I had?

Or I could check my iNsert vitals monitor and take a blood sample. Betty mentioned that my vitals were abnormal; I'd assumed it was from bad sleep and the Jinx craving. Maybe it was already in my system. Though… if I was creating this dream, I could always *tell* the reading to be positive. Which brings me to my last idea.

I could try and create something in the dream. Something substantial that would leave no question about whether this was real or not. It wasn't completely fool-proof but certainly as close to a guarantee as I was going to get.

Checking my vitals is the easiest and quickest option so I navigate to my iNsert's biometric menu and initiate a diagnostic. I attempt some more deep breaths, thinking it will affect the outcome if I'm in a calmer state. The MagRail turns slightly and sunshine covers my face, warm and bright. I close my eyes, waiting for the signal when the diagnostic is complete.

There's a small pulse in my arm and a barely audible beep. My eyelid iNsert displays my heart rate, blood pressure, cholesterol, sleep quality, and a variety of other things that all seem to be checking out. My heart rate is obviously a little high, but nothing concerning. With my gaze, I scroll downward through a list of various tests to the "Foreign Substance" one.

NEGATIVE

Had Jinx been in my system, it would have shown up there. I question the results and almost start running them again, remembering that if I'm actually on Jinx, I could be subconsciously controlling the test outcomes too.

Fine.

Fuck it.

I'll try to make something in the dream. I spend a few moments, sunshine layered on my face, thinking about what I could create that's easy enough, but noticeable. A string of music plays through my mind. *I'll put a live band on this train.* I imagine it: a synth-guitar, DJ, synth-drums and wait to hear it. Nothing appears. I look down the aisle behind me. Nothing still.

Frustrated and weirdly disappointed, I shift to another idea. Outside is still rushing by at a breakneck pace. Everything up close is a connected blur, while everything far away passes slower. I'll craft a skyscraper, straight up from the ground.

I envision it in my mind – a tall, spiraling, black structure – but again nothing appears. I notice we're getting close to New York. The trauma of this train ride has made it fly by. *Or was I controlling the time of it?* A few moments later and there's still no skyscraper. Not even a deformed base or semblance of a bastard creation.

I'm not in control.

"Holy fuck."

I'm not on Jinx.

Chapter 7 – Aiontis
2404 | New York City

Somehow with this revelation, my first thought is that I need to message Thomen back. Maybe he knows what's going on?

His messages conveyed he was even more confused than I was, but it's worth a shot. I construct the note with my eyelid iNsert.

Thomen — not sure what's going on. I can't remember anything from the past few weeks. Woke up this morning feeling…weird…heading to New York now. Need to time travel. Hard to explain. I'm ok, please don't call police.

-Aiontis

We are pulling into the New York station. I brace as the gel-like seat absorbs me during the massive deceleration. It's amazing how dealing with G-forces really takes your mind off things, even if only for a moment.

New York's station is bustling with people, per usual. It isn't as clean as Omaha's because it is much older. It was reconstructed out of one of the old Subway tunnels and honestly not much has changed from my historical knowledge of that archaic, but impressive system. I pass through the membrane and exit into a hot, smelly, concrete tunnel aged with human interaction. Paint is chipping off benches, holo-ads have cracked smartglass, leaving pockets of dead pixels, and the floor grips like it has a layer of adhesive to it.

Welcome to New York…

Behind me, those that had been waiting to board are settling in and the MagRail, always on precise time, blasts-off out of the tunnel, leaving those of us that linger to get smacked with a wave of putrid air. I'm standing in the middle of the platform, bystanders ignoring and passing me all around, and my world is spinning. I feel sick. There is a pulse from my iNsert, a reply from Thomen.

"Holy shit man. Finally! What do you mean you need to time travel? Call me. I can come get you. Maybe take you to a hospital?"

Thomen is a good friend…from what I can remember. For now, I have to ignore him. Hypothesis #1 where I am already on Jinx and this is all a dream has not panned out. It's time to double down on going back in time and getting some of the stuff. I can't explain why, but it feels like the right move. Call it a "higher purpose".

The next couple of hours were a weird slog. I made my way up to the main level of New York City (the ground floor, once a bustling metropolis, is now somewhere you do *not* want to be). Almost immediately, my stomach roared in protest, so I opted for some lunch; it was…food, I guess. My mind was elsewhere. After, I walked toward the whole reason I was here: Tyme Corp. – one of the big corporations that offers and sells time travel – figuring the fresh air would do me good. It ended up being tremendously windy, even raining for a short bit, and I regretted going by foot. Thomen kept messaging me and I switched my iNsert to DND. Damp and annoyed, I realized I faced a bit of a conundrum: *how the fuck was I going to take Jinx once I travelled back?*

Remember all those rules I told you about? Yeah, explicit drug use – particularly use of *banned* drugs – is one they enforce. The second they notice me trying to buy some; they'd pull me back to the present and probably slap me with a fine and a ban. I hadn't thought this part out and I'm less than ten minutes away from Tyme Corp.

"Fuck!" For what was likely the fifth time that day I curse alone and out loud, attracting attention. I stop along the towering walkway, far above the ground, and lean against its glass paneling.

Beneath me, I catch the fleeting yellow shimmer of the SaverShield and rows of walkways and buildings. ATVs zip in straight lines, ascending and descending as needed, and the world

– as it does – goes on. That feeling that something much bigger is going on creeps up on me again, causing anxiety.

What the hell is actually happening?

The rain has stopped, but the wind keeps up. I'm probably in a skyscraper-crafted wind tunnel, so it feels more violent than usual. Normally I'd be cold, but now I just feel…*overwhelmed*. My coat's length rips in the wind, tugging me with it. I open its app on my iNsert and adjust the length, turning off the rain-proofing I needed a half hour ago. The tugging stops and I laugh when I notice where it has been pulling me: straight toward Tyme Corp's tower. I glance upward to whatever eternal being is orchestrating this and throw a hand up,

"Alright, alright. I'm going."

Within a few moments, I stride into Tyme Corp's opulent main lobby, still no more sure how I'm about to pull off what I actually need to do. Inside the lobby is a lot of glass – walls, floors, tables, a coffee shop, the front welcoming desk – and a unique water feature to display the time. Water shoots straight along the lengths where hour and minute hands should be, eventually colliding with the edge of the clock and recycling back into a pump. Crystal blue digital roman numerals subtly line the edges, completing what is a highly impressive and sizable piece.

I've become easily distracted staring at it, wanting one for my own abode, though preferably smaller.

"Hello sir!" A voice sneaks up from behind with a gracious hand on my shoulder. I startle and turn to see a gorgeous woman with shoulder length dark hair and piercing blue eyes. Caught in between my dumb gazing at the clock and the nerves from the day in general, I don't have much to say. She smiles and brings up her mobile iNsert, "Admiring our time piece?"

"Hmm? Oh…yes!" I smile back, finally engaging like a normal fucking human. "It's very captivating. Kind of amazing how it all works!"

"Yes, it seems to attract a lot of attention ever since we installed it a year ago." She pauses briefly, clearly wanting to get to the meat of things but still offering up good customer service. "What can I help you with today, sir?"

"Well, I'd like to travel back in time, but with a few

modifications to the trip…" I am going to try something to see if I can get around the monitoring.

"Of course. We have special packages where we can provide you vacation rentals and target specific historical events like sports, politics, concerts, and more!"

I wince slightly. Those aren't exactly the modifications I need. "Yeah…I'm sorry what's your name?"

"Oh my! So sorry, my name is Andrea."

"Andrea? Nice to meet you. I'm Aiontis. I was looking for some more…sensitive modifications."

Based on her reaction it is clear that her mind instantly goes to some kinky sexual assumption and she's likely sick of serving those creeps. I quickly backpedal.

"You see, I'm working an investigation of sorts." Her interest comes back with a raised eyebrow. "Do you mind if we sit down? Do you have a desk?"

"Yes, we can sit over here." We approach two side-by-side stools. She types something on the iNsert tablet and a glass table rises from the floor. I decide now is a good enough time to continue.

"I'm a Historian Consultant…" I start as I pull up my Hiscon credentials and swipe them over to her iNsert. "I'm investigating specifics on drug use. In particular, *banned* drug use and how we can learn from our past mistakes. Jinx is a key focus in this assessment."

"Oh! I see. Perhaps I should go and get my manager?" She gives a nervous glance back. It is an annoying, yet understandable, reaction as I've barely started explaining.

"If you need to, that's fine, but I think we're able to reach an agreement on this between the two of us." A sleazy line, and I hate saying it to someone as nice as Andrea, but a necessity. She appears apprehensive, knowing the pressure is back on her to secure the transaction. And I know her interest is piqued.

"Ok. What specifics are you needing?" There isn't anyone around but she speaks in a quieter tone.

"Simple." I have to sell this with complete confidence. "I'll need to actually take Jinx and not be monitored or recorded. I need to experience it for myself to properly assess its effects and log my vitals." It's a risky request. Definitely against company policy. Hell, it was against federal policy.

"I…" she starts, clearly knowing it is against the rules.

"Look, I know it's a big ask. Don't put yourself in danger here if you feel uncomfortable." I want to earn her trust.

"Sir, I respect what you're trying to do, but that breaks so many rules and measures that our company and the country has surrounding time travel that I can all but assure you it's not possible." I can tell she feels bad letting me down like that, as if I've asked her out and she is declining politely. "There may be some wiggle room around actually taking the Jinx, but turning off recording and monitoring measures is not only illegal, it's dangerous. I'm sorry."

"No, no. It's ok." I reassure her. I am already forming another plan in my mind, but it isn't a good one. "You mentioned there may be wiggle room on actually taking the Jinx. What does that process look like?"

"I'm not sure, it's such a unique ask. I'd likely have to escalate to my manager, and her manager, and her manager's manager. We'd have to validate your credentials, your research, conduct interviews…I imagine we could have an answer in a month."

Fuck. Fuck, fuck, fuck. I contemplate it, but instantly feel a searing pain in my head: a splitting headache combined with an awful wave of nausea. Andrea notices.

"Sir, are you ok?" She looks genuinely concerned. The pain subsides. I know what it is telling me. The fucking universe or something…*why me?*

"Yeah, yeah. Sorry. I've been getting really bad headaches lately. They're called 'ice pick' headaches, I guess. Long hours at work."

"Would you like some water?"

"Yes, that would be nice, thanks."

She returns a few moments later with a lemon-infused glass of water. I take several refreshing swigs.

"Andrea, let's go ahead and start that process. I'd still like to travel back today though. It'll allow me to scope out the location and time period a bit more and part of my research I can do without having to take the drug." I lie.

"Excellent!" She states, clearly relieved. "I'll write up a special request and escalate it along with your Iliscon credentials. If you'll follow me, we can quickly get you set up with a Warper room."

"Sounds good, thank you."

As we take the elevators up, we continue chatting. I'm only half contributing, wondering how crazy I am for doing what I'm about to do. Andrea drops me off on floor 57.

"Here we are, sir."

"Please, call me Aiontis."

"Well, here we are, Aiontis. Please enjoy your trip. I look forward to working with you more in the coming weeks." I can't tell if she is flirting or just really good at customer service, but it doesn't matter either way.

The only way I am going to pull this off *today* has consequences.

I'll be permanently stuck back in time.

Chapter 8 – Aiontis

2404 | June 7th | New York City

"Hello sir." A peculiar man with glasses greets me as the elevator doors close, taking Andrea down to her next customer.

He wears some sleek, blueish hologlasses, a fashion statement with this day and age's eye-repairing technology. The mop of dark hair atop his head is a mess and he seems squirrely, though oddly endearing even only in the few seconds I've known him. I extend a hand.

"Aiontis." He shakes it nervously, almost comically.

"Dustin." He nods to the Tyme Corp. name badge built into his uniform. It features a goofy picture of him, clearly not ready for when it was taken. "Andrea sent me a little bit about your circumstances. Very unique indeed, but we're happy to help with any Hiscon research within our boundaries! I understand that today you'd like to only go back for some preliminary research." He pauses, waiting to see if I have anything to say. I don't. "Was there a specific date you were looking for?"

"Hmmm. I actually hadn't determined the date yet. I assume you know I'm researching Jinx, specifically? So, I'd have to go back before it was banned in…"

"2390." Dustin finishes before I can.

"Ah, you a historian yourself?"

"Modestly. When you're a Warper Technician, it tends to be something you pick up naturally." He adjusts his hologlasses. "We could shoot for 2389? Today is June 7th and we could just send you back by whole years?"

I ponder when would be the easiest time period to get my hands on the drug. Probably well before 2390.

"I think I'll need to go back further, Dustin. Let's say…2380? We can keep it June 7th. Does that work?"

He nods. "As long as it's not before 2377, we can do that!" He laughs at his own joke far too hard.

It reminds me of something I forgot to explain – stupid of me – and it's perhaps the most important rule of time travel as it exists now: you cannot travel back before 2377, the year that Emma Dexter invented the capability itself.

Why? I honestly haven't a clue and the science around it is still in its infancy. The most solid and widely accepted theory is that time travel, as we understood it within pop culture, was always inaccurate and that an initial "portal" or "landing pad" had to be established. In this case, Dexter's successful experiment in 2377. That portal is defined as Time = 0. Since you cannot go back before "0", you can only go in between the present and it.

Many people have tried to go back before "0", but none return. In a way, I guess that doesn't confirm or deny the fact that one *could* go to a time before 2377, but at the very least it means that you don't have the technology to come back. Some have even planned to go to 2376, live for a year, and take the technology back to present day to prove that you can, in fact, go *before* "0".

None of them have ever returned either. So…yeah…it quickly became another time travel rule that you must select a period between 2377 and the present.

Luckily for my need today, that rule doesn't matter much, but trust me when I say that Hiscon's would give one or two valuable appendages to go back as far as they wanted.

"Ha! Good one." I reply to Dustin who's still, somehow, cracking up at a joke he's likely delivered over a hundred times. Weird dude.

"Ahhh." He calms down. "So, June 7th, 2380 then? You're sure?"

"Yep." I'm ready to get on with it. "That'll work."

"Great. Just follow me over this way," He leads with an arm down a hallway behind a clear membrane. "Now have you Warped with us before?" I have, but it had been a while. And much like the rest of my memory at the moment, the details were fuzzy.

"Long time ago." I answer.

"Awesome. You should be in our system then." We turn a corner down the plain-looking hallway. "You'll need to sign some updated agreements and disclosures, but it shouldn't take more than ten minutes."

I remain silent while we walk to his office. The walls are plastered with some old-school shifters: thin glass posters whose images change on a loop. Some images even have subtle motion, like a calm waterfall. There are mostly old photos of some of the world's most famous cities. Dubai, London, New York, Sydney and others. I laugh as a motivational-poster transitions onto one; a baby with a clenched fist and a look of determination on his face. It reads: "You got this. You've got all the time in the world!" Dustin notices my laughter.

"Hmm?" He glances from the documents he's been organizing to the old image. "Oh! You recognize that? It's what they used to call a 'meme'. I love them." I chuckle again.

"Yes, they're entertaining. It's a pity they didn't really live on past that period."

"Right?!" Dustin exclaims. I settle back into the silence, looking around at the shifters. "Ok…should be done." He motions the documents to my iNsert. "You're just going to sign where I've highlighted if you'd like to read them, or just confirm all with your biosignature."

I confirm all. It's not going to matter anyway.

"Have you eaten or drank anything recently?" Dustin inquires. I think back to the sandwich I had for lunch.

"Yes, about an hour or so ago."

"Ok." He gives me a small, thin strip of translucent material. "Take one of these, it'll help settle your stomach and maintain your body's center of gravity. Some people get really shaken up when they Warp."

It tastes awful, but Dustin offers me some water to wash it down.

"Alright! We're going to June 7th, 2380, all your documents are updated and signed, and I'm assuming you just want to go back to New York City?"

"Yes, that's fine." I'm eager to get on with it. Despite the medicine I'm starting to feel as shitty as I was this morning and I can tell it's the lack of Jinx.

"Splendid. Is three hours enough time?"

"Sure." Again, it didn't matter.

He pulls a circular, black dot out of his desk and peels something off the back of it.

"Very important. This is a Tyme Corp. tracker. It monitors your vitals and presence within time so that we don't lose you. It also allows us to understand if you're committing any acts against our policies. Any violation will require us to pull you back immediately – an unpleasant experience, let me assure you – and fines or jail time may be served if the violation is severe enough.

"Removal of the tracker is also against policy, but also nearly impossible without our proprietary equipment. Without it, you'd be stuck back in time, so don't try it." He smiles at me and swings his arms somewhat wildly. "But of course, I just have to say all that. You're a Hiscon! You'll be fine!"

I smile back. Poor Dustin. I hope he doesn't get in trouble for any of this.

"You ready?" He asks as he stands and motions to a membrane doorway next to his desk.

"Yep. Let's go."

The next room is dark and filled with a ton of expensive equipment, all parts of the Warper. I imagine it's what archaic computers looked like at the beginning, filling up full rooms with their cords and motherboards. I wonder quietly if this technology will ever be portable.

Dustin places the tracker on the back of my neck on the left side. It is cool to the touch and the proprietary adhesive *sucks* my skin.

"Stand right here in the center next to this podium. You'll hold these rods that will conduct electricity through you and center the Travel Pulse Sphere around your body. It's important to not let go, you will feel a mild tingle, but that's it." I nod and grab the rods tightly.

"The room will get dark, eerie…kinda scary. Trust me, everything is fine. That's just the Dark Particles doing their thing." I nod again.

"Ok! See you in a few moments, Mr. Breaker." He turns and leaves me in the dark room.

"Goodbye, Dustin."

The room, already dark, somehow begins to *glow* darker. The oxygen in the air instantly feels lighter and heavily purified. I've always pondered if this portion of the travel is viewed as the time *between* time. There's no sign of the room as I knew it when I walked in. I just feel me and the dark.

The tingling sensation begins in my hands and as soon as it starts, it's over.

I sense a final pulse of darkness.

I know my eyes are open, but the light entering them now is as if I were on the inside of an old television set, facing outward. It builds from the center as a dot, and grows into a full picture that races toward me.

Within moments (or longer…shorter…it's hard to tell when you're in *between* time) the light, and the image that accompanies it, fills my entire field of view. I'm no longer holding on to any rods and I'm very clearly in the middle of a city, high up on one of its walkways.

New York City, 2380.

Ain't time travel grand?

Chapter 9 – Titus
2477 | Unknown location

A robust bead of sweat rolled across Titus' warm, wrinkled forehead, eventually overcoming its surface tension and dropping onto the couch cushion.

"Arrragghhh!" With the exclamation, Titus sat up, breathing heavy, disoriented. As his chest heaved, he assessed where he was, slowly calming down.

"Damn!" The shirt came off, drenched in sweat and grimy from his day of building the Warper. After a half dozen deep breaths and closed eyes, he was back to normal. He took the shirt and wiped the ancient furniture, absorbing most of the sweat that remained.

Though he was calmer, he was still shaking – and his thoughts were darting in a thousand directions – from the dream he'd had during his nap. *How long was I asleep?* Surprisingly, he'd only been asleep for an hour. It had felt like days.

Sitting on the warm couch, he closed his eyes to concentrate. *What had the dream said? What had happened?* It was clear this was part of the mystery…somehow. He grabbed his note tablet from the work station where he'd been tinkering earlier and propped it against the back cushions. Slowly, he paced around the room as he tried to recall as much as possible about the dream – *no…vision* – that had just haunted him.

"I fall asleep instantly. The dream is here, in this workspace. Just as it is now."

The tablet converted the audio into bulleted notes as he spoke. After a pause, he began again.

"The lighting is different…all hues of blue…the same that man was using when he showed up. It's dark; the blue light doesn't offer much visibility.

"I get up, as if I'm truly awake, and go to the Warper. I check its log. It's set to June 7th, 2380. Someone did that. I hadn't yet programmed the date. I hadn't even figured out which date I wanted to escape to yet, but it wasn't going to be *that* far back."

Another pause…thinking through the implications of the date.

"First question, why 2380? What's in that year? Continuing recollection…I keep the date at 2380 and turn around to my workspace. It's exactly as it is now except for two things: "Zorex is lying atop the desk, not on my hip, and there's a device I'm not familiar with beside it. It's a small sphere, clearly made of components from this workshop. Nothing immediately foreign about it."

The room grew silent, with a canyon of thoughts needing to be traversed before he could continue. *That sphere…it's the key, but what is it?* The dream had barely faded from his memory, thankfully, though he knew he must capture it quickly.

Focus, Titus. Breathe, and focus.

His iNsert, aged and scratched, showed his heart rate. He watched as it slowed. 100…95…80 a few moments later…70…60…55. He calmed, breathing normally. Thinking clearly.

"Begin drawing…" the tablet started to sketch what he described with accurate detail. "A sphere, no bigger than my palm. It has a digital readout with a date. The date is the same as the Warper's: June 7th, 2380. The sphere is translucent, and feels like a polymer of some sort. There are mechanical components inside, and there's a flat strip on the backside that is a dial of some sort.

"I stroke my finger across it and the date changes backwards…*far* backwards. In the mid-1900s. I reverse the movement back across the strip and it returns to the date in 2380." Almost at once, he recognized what this device must be, but believed it impossible. The understanding came with a key question.

"Is this a miniature Warper? More specifically, is this a mobile time travel device? Question – a terrifying one: how could I select a date as far back as the 1900s? The scientific restrictions of time travel prevent it." The tablet recorded the powerful questions.

Discouragement hit Titus in the chest. It was just a dream

after all. What he articulated and what he saw drawn wasn't possible. The science was fantasy and it certainly wasn't going to be made from components in this bunker. *So much for taking it seriously...*

Once more, the hollow concrete walls of his deep bunker fell into silence. The weight on his shoulders was heavy. He was hungry. All around him were spare parts, tools, and trinkets he'd gathered to build his own Warper. This bunker had been his home for the better part of a year as the world above was ripped apart. He wondered what it was like up there, but knew he didn't need to. The answer was that it was desolate, ruled by humankind's worst product: the Regime.

The insides of his head pounded, not painfully, but as a signal. Where his logic wanted him to give up, his heart and thoughts knew there was more.

What if they figured out a way to travel back further than 2377? Some unknown presence was screaming back at him: *You must go back before it began.*

Could that man, the half-stranger, have traveled forward? *The rules must have changed?* The presence again answered: *The lines are all different, this isn't what you think...*

One question he hadn't yet considered came forward and he asked it aloud for the recorder: "What's the significance of Zorex on the table? It's always on my side." Some deep recess of his brain pushed forward a reply: *You have to end it to prevent it...You know who I am. You have to end it...*

Titus felt as if his feet had been cemented to the bare, cold floor. Somewhere within him, a violent sensation was birthed. *You have to end it to prevent it.* Without knowing where it came from, he knew he needed to kill that man. He was no stranger to violence, but liked to avoid it if able. This...this calling was pungent and certain however.

That man must die.

And I'll need to go back in time to do it.

That's what the dream was for. What these schematics were for. They were how to build a portable Warper. Or at the very least, try.

Sitting on the couch was the sketch of his memory. He walked to the tablet, and studied what was there. Surprisingly something so powerful wasn't all that complicated, at least on the surface. Aside from it being impossibly small, he couldn't discern what made it *different* from the technology of a Warper.

"It must open up a controlled TPS as opposed to it being a portal on larger models." A Travel Pulse Sphere was the ether one would be absorbed by to actually complete the time travel. "It looks like there's two zettacapacitors for energy storage…that's a lot of reserve electrical power."

He rotated the drawing a few more times, puzzled that something was missing.

"There seems to be no sign of a Dark Particle chamber." Knowing that was impossible – Dark Particles were the only reason time travel actually existed – he concentrated on his memory of the now-fading dream once more. In it, he turned the sphere over in his palm, feeling the hum from its immense electrical energy. The casing was clear, but frustratingly ever-so-foggy, like a window that let you see what was on the other side, but not the intimate details.

His dream-self rotated the sphere and observed it from the top. There it was: the faint eerie glow from a Dark Particle chamber. If one were to describe the soft light emanating from it, they'd describe it as black which, up until a hundred years or so ago, would have made no scientific sense. Though still, it was a common characteristic of these particles to "glow" black.

Titus was shocked by how small the chamber was. "How could the chamber in the middle be that trivial and encased? The Dark Particles would have no room to activate in this scenario." The tablet recorded the question among his long list of many. Confused, Titus was unsure of what to do next, but knew that his recollection of the dream wasn't done either.

Back in his memory, less intense now than it was a few moments ago, he remembered walking to his tool desk…*already been there*…seeing Zorex and the sphere lying side by side…*got it, still not sure what it means*…picking up the sphere and studying it…*this is where we left off*…and setting the dial to 6.7.2380…*what's with* that *date?* He took the sphere, twisted it a quarter clockwise turn and something happened. The whole sphere began to glow black, as if he was holding a much larger Dark Particle…*whoa, now I'm definitely confused…*he grabbed Zorex from the table, holstered it, and gave the sphere an additional clockwise quarter turn. Briefly he caught the glimpse of the pulse waves from the TPS and the dream ended.

Immediately, Titus repeated all this to the tablet, taking notes furiously, but keeping up with his quickened speech. In a rush, the answer came to him.

"The sphere *is* the chamber. That quarter turn releases the particles, with a second releasing the power that activates it." *I have it.*

What all seemed impossibly mysterious only an hour ago was slowly revealing itself as, in fact, simple. A hundred scientific questions rattled through his mind, but there was so much adrenaline pumping through him that he just wanted to get to work.

Zorex weighed heavy on his hip, powerful and lethal. Able to take a life. It was distracting for now and he took it off, placing it on his workbench, consciously noting he was fulfilling the imagery of his vision.

Eight hours passed and, other than a small break to eat and go to the bathroom, Titus had worked straight through. He was unsure of the time of day, but that didn't matter since he'd be leaving soon. Leaving for good, and going to kill the strange man (another surge of finality assured him this was his objective), far away from the Regime. And with a new, portable Warper device.

Now, he had two means by which to time travel, and he was faced with determining what he should do with the larger Warper he'd created. The thing, a hulking presence in the room, seemed ancient now that he held one in his palm. It was the difference between computers of the 1950s and those of the late 2090s. Part of him believed he should leave it active, in case this portable Warper, which was likely the first of its kind, didn't work. Or if he was forced to return to this time.

This place.

If the Regime was here when he returned, he would put Zorex in his mouth and be done with it, but he could at least throw them off his scent by programming a fake date in the large Warper. One far away from June 7th, 2380. As he shifted the date with a cold, metal dial, he felt disappointment. He'd worked hard on this big hunk of equipment – spent months finding the scrap and pieces to put it together. Securing the Dark Particles had nearly cost him his life. And now he was abandoning it before ever using it. For good reason, but still…it stung.

There was a coldness in this space. He looked around the bunker that had been his home for that last year or more. It was barren. *This is no way to live.* It was designed to survive, and that's what he had done. Now it was time to leave.

He visited his bathroom one last time, washing his hands in the rusting metal basin. The water was cold and clear, surprisingly, so he splashed it on his face once he'd rid his hands of the grime from his workshop.

The refreshing liquid invigorated his rough skin and he repeated it a few more times. He reached for a dirty towel beside the sink and dried off, revealing his face in the small, cracked mirror.

The image of a monster stared back at him. His first run in with the Regime had been a violent one, filled with death and blood. He'd come away from it, but not without the mental and physical scars to remember it. There were long, straight serrations across his face. It was his alter ego when he went out into the world. One that gave him confidence, but also made him less human.

One that was a killer. He would need it now.

Titus approached the bench, as if in his dream. Zorex and the Warper sphere sat beside each other. He grabbed both, giving a quarter turn to the sphere allowing it to emit its dark glow.

The Scarred Man. That was what he called himself. That was the name that had his enemies cowering in fear.

He gave the sphere a second quarter turn and was gone.

Chapter 10 – Aiontis
2380 | June 7ᵗʰ | New York City

My feet, once floating, find solid ground.

"Oh fuck…" I dry heave as my lunch nearly comes up. I battle to keep it down and win. Time travel can be disorienting as shit, no matter how many controls Tyme Corp has in place.

The clock has started: I've got three hours, no time to dick around. I have a lot to do and I imagine that Dustin is quite punctual.

Carefully, I reach and find the tracker on the back left of my neck. Getting rid of it will have to be swift and it's going to hurt like hell.

I'll have to cut it out.

Ignoring the incredible fact that I'm back in time by over 20 years – and all the fascinating observations of the immense (and some subtle) differences – it's this point that I focus on:

Am I ready to be stuck here? Do I believe this "mission" is more than just a drug fix? I'm still utterly confused, but the hounding of something larger at play overwhelms me, especially in the moments since I've come back to 2380. An intense purpose and commitment to getting these next objectives met fuels me and in these periods of doubt, I have an inexplicable amount of dread. The universe is, quite literally, telling me something.

Focusing back to the task at hand, I begin to perceive the shocking and sometimes comedic differences of the early 2380s. New York is largely the same with towering skyscrapers, established walkways, and scores of rows of ATVs shuttling around. 2404's version is even more vertical (probably by about 30 stories or so), but the city hasn't changed much in a couple decades.

The fashion is laughable – though I'm sure every person looking back says that – but something about the late 2370s and early 2380s brought back "retro" overly-futuristic clothing. It was as if we were trying to live up to the visions of old-school sci-fi tropes hundreds of years in the past. Aesthetics over function. Every 70 years or so since the early 2100s, this type of fashion seemed to make a comeback and burn out quickly as it arrived. Tall collars, slim sunglasses, tight and fake-looking clothing often made of material that doesn't breathe…it was all a bit much.

Digital stamps were a big thing back then. Often referred to as Datats (aka "Data Tattoos"), these were temporary designs someone could get implanted in their skin rather painlessly. Each one was composed of thousands of microscreens that would digitally display an image, creating the effect of a vibrant tattoo. Users could change their image or its color whenever they wanted, and even add animations. In 2380, there was a big trend to put these on faces and necks – a trend I'll never quite understand – and it looked just about as bad as it sounds. Personally, I always found Datats interesting and contemplated getting one when I was younger, though never on my face. They were low risk and easy to remove, but eventually the larger companies started moving toward subscription-based payment plans. After that, they had a slow demise and back (or forward, rather) in 2404 they're still around, but the industry is much smaller than it used to be.

Like most things, they couldn't stand the test of time.

And I was running out of it.

The tracker has to go first. I'll need a knife and some medical equipment to clean up the mess and keep me from losing too much blood. I picture briefly bringing a knife to my neck to free the tracker and it sends a shiver down my spine. I'll need some booze too. For disinfectant, of course.

Within twenty minutes I've got everything I need. That's the benefit of having an Amazon hub store nearby. You're able to purchase nearly anything (except a firearm…yes, America finally fixes its gun laws, though only after unprecedented tragedy) and receive it within five minutes. That bit of history makes me double check for my X-34 on my hip, for some reason thinking it may have not survived the journey. It's still there and I'm surprised Dustin didn't ask questions about it earlier.

Oh well, better for me.

I take a swig of the mediocre whiskey I bought, enjoying my

second helping of liquor for the day. It's not remotely as delicious as my private collection, but it'll do the trick. I maneuver to the lower levels of the city, aiming to find somewhere private. Without much effort, I spot a dilapidated building – a smaller skyscraper – that seems abandoned.

I enter its atrium, dusty and untouched for God knows how long. It's like a time capsule and, strangely, bathed in sunlight. Most of the tall glass panels that sit high above me have been knocked out, leaving an archaic skeleton that looks as if it's barely holding it together. In the center is an old fountain, obviously no longer working and void of a single drop of moisture. As I lay out my things along the fountain's edge, I bask in the warmth of the sunlight.

The weird thing about time travel is that you begin to think about immense stuff. Right now, I'm thinking about how crazy it is that I'm feeling sunlight that's about eight minutes old right *now*, relative to *this* time. In 2404 though, this specific sunlight is long gone. It's warmth and benefits transferred into other energy within the universe. How will its energy spread over the next twenty years? Have I encountered it before?

Wild. That's all I can conclude before I realize I don't have time for rabbit holes like this.

My nerves start to build.

What comes next isn't going to be pretty.

Chapter 11 – Titus

2380 | June 7th | New York City

The dirt, dry and coarse, pressed into his palms as he stabilized himself. Even with one knee and one hand down, Titus felt disoriented beyond comprehension.

He vomited, fully and drastically, onto the ground beside him. It smelled awful, had a concerning white color to it, and offered no relief. His head was still spinning.

"What on earth?" Slowly, against the screaming lack of balance in his head, he brought his eyes to the horizon. In the distance he saw the Statue of Liberty, decrepit and deteriorating. Behind it, the skyline of an older New York City. Definitely one from before the Regime. Quickly, he glanced around, able to observe he was in some sort of old outdoor parking lot before he'd lost balance and fell over on his side. He lay on his back, staring into the cerulean sky, wondering what the hell was going on.

How did I get here?

Why I am suddenly outside of New York City? I was nowhere near it a…moment…ago…?

Titus realized he had no concept of time. Obviously, he was in a different period given New York's mostly pristine exterior. Worse than that, he felt like he had drunk too much and wasn't confident what his last actual memory was. His days in the bunker were blurred together as of late, but all he could come up with was working on the Warper.

Something weighed in his palm. He brushed the dirt off his other hand and held the item in the air, exploring it with both hands. It was a foreign object, but there was *something* about it…

What is this?

It was a nearly translucent sphere with mechanical and electrical components inside. The exterior was a semi-flexible polymer shell that was surprisingly light. On the back he noticed a readout with a set of numbers: 6.7.2380. A date? His intrigue in the numbers paused when he noticed an odd glow when glancing the sphere from a certain direction.

Dark Particles.

The numbers.

Slowly, as if a misty veil had been lifted, Titus remembered he had just time traveled to New York City in 2380. *Why?*

To hunt the man from the vision. To kill him.

Zorex's heft was present on his hip.

There was a certainty about this place. This date. Titus couldn't explain it.

The device he held in his hand was more portable than any other time travel device he'd ever seen. The veil continued to rise. He'd been planning to run from the Regime, but now there was this…mission? Could this be his new start too? 2380 was a far better time than he'd come from, though what he needed now was sustenance to make up for all the food and bile he'd just lost.

Feeling less nauseous, but still lightheaded, Titus sat up off the dusty ground and stood, cautiously testing his balance. He tucked the mystery sphere into a jacket pocket and headed off. Eager to get some food, water, and, if it came to it, start his new life in 2380.

He knew not that he was just a pawn in the plan.

Chapter 12 – Aiontis
2380 | June 7ᵗʰ | New York City

"Arggghhhhhhhhhh ffffffffffuuuccchhhh!"
The expletive came out of my mouth jumbled, but was clear as could be in my mind. I spit out the bunched-up fabric I'd purchased along with the medical equipment and booze. I think it was a sock, but I honestly don't give a shit right now.

Holy fuck, they put those trackers in deep. I make sure I'm not going to pass out before I bring the gory hand to my eyeline. It must have worked because I'm still here. The black disk pinched between my fingers is grotesque with blood on its edges and wires that had woven into my muscle tissue. Those bastards really do some damage with these things.

One moment the tracker is in my view and the next it's gone, as if it wasn't something I'd just violently cut out of my neck. They must have pulled it back, knowing I tampered with it. I'm fully *stuck* back here. In this time. That momentous feeling looms over me once more, seemingly ready to beat me if I continue to doubt it.

I pull heavily from the whiskey bottle, two full swigs taken in with one big gulp. It burns my throat and my eyes, but takes my mind off the dull pain in my neck. I pour a heavy amount of it on the wound sending my nerve endings into another round of *"What the fuck are you doing, Aiontis?"* The liquid trickles down my back under my shirt before I put the bottle down.

Next to me is gelseal that I place on the wound. Instantly, it cools my skin, freezing and sealing the gash while adhering to me. It's refreshing and administers local anesthesia as it assesses my vitals. Once it has settled, I touch around the edges. Luckily, the tracker was small and the chunk of skin I took with it wasn't much larger. The gelseal should be low profile.

Done with my first task, it's on to the second. I leave my makeshift medical station and half a bottle of whiskey in this hauntingly gorgeous atrium, to visit the mid-levels and score some Jinx. More than ever, I'm intrigued to understand *why* Jinx, and *what* will happen when I take it. By now, I'm convinced this is *not* an addict's craving driving me. For starters, I'm not even an addict, more than that, it's this feeling…this feeling that I'm part of a D-Day…or will be…keeping me on this admittedly destructive path. I hate clichés, but truly only time will tell.

Within twenty minutes I'm in the less seedy, but arguably still questionable mid-levels of New York. I don't really need to keep track of time anymore because, well…I have lots of it. I ponder if I should drink in the sights of an older New York for a day or two, enjoy myself a bit before…whatever...*this* excursion is about. The omnipotent feeling is back, answering the lighthearted inquiry for me.

I've never liked the mid-levels of this city because they're almost more depressing than the ground floor, while obviously not as gorgeous and lively as the top ones. Stuck here is "middle" America (literally); the people who are trying so hard and failing to pull themselves out of the doldrum of life. They're doing okay financially, but everyone seems rigid, like they're being pressed by an invisible force against an invisible wall. Faces are friendly enough, but tired. At least on the ground levels you know what you're getting. Here, the hustle is real. The grind hurts. These are the people that haven't felt the benefits of AGROW in recent decades or centuries.

In other words, it's the perfect place to find some Jinx.

A mid-level NYPD ATV cruiser passes by the edge of the sky market I'm walking by. It moves slowly, trying to track down illegal activity among the shadows of the buildings that reach for the clouds. There's odd sunlight in the mid-levels. Not completely gone, but always hiding in the shade or reflected by some surface.

I tense at the sight of the "law", though I'm guilty of nothing…yet…other than committing myself to this past. I take a breath, whiskey still warm on my palate, and try to scope out potential drug activity.

It doesn't take long.

A walking stereotype, the man is leaning within the walkway of an alley, buying-in to the weird fashion trend of dressing in bulk sci-fi garb. His jacket is long and dark, with a high collar crowned around the back of his neck. His face is covered in datats, all of them animated, but too detailed for me to make out from here. I watch an exchange go down and glimpse the metallic gloves he wears too, shining profusely from a block away. I wonder why he wears something so flashy while supplying illegal substances, but hey…drug dealers aren't necessarily Emma Dexters, now are they?

He's across an ATV airway so I search and find a pedestrian bridge. It is full of people, with paint and shifter ads that are chipping or barely working. I focus on the dealer once more and bring up the optics display on my iNsert. It reflects what my eyelid iNsert sees and I press the small screen in my arm where the dealer is. An option list pops up: call, mail, report, track, along with a few others. I select "track", an option that only unlocks after intense legal scrutiny in 2404, and it highlights his outline gold in my lens. I don't want to lose him as I make my way around the bridge.

Something else about the mid-levels is that they smell. I could say something poetic or metaphoric about how it's the smell of hard work and perspiration to make something of one's life, but realistically it's the smell of too many *other* smells – food, body odor, garbage, smoke, etcetera – that combine to create a heavy, dank scent. It's worse as I approach the bridge, one that looks like it may no longer meet engineering codes, and the density of New Yorkers increases. Though, I realize, I am probably adding my own dreadful stench of sweat and alcohol to the mix.

Along the floor is a moving walkway that takes one up a steep angle, over the ATV airway, and back down the other side. As I step onto it, my pace is immediately accelerated, and I begin to pass those who just wish to ride it. To my right, I can see the gold silhouette of the dealer through several walls, still standing in place.

A curious man on the bridge walkway grabs my attention, traveling in the opposite direction. His face is badly scarred, straight across, and he looks tired. His clothes are even more strange, basic and purely functional but with a sense of past fashion that isn't from this time. They're well worn. He seems lost, maybe confused, but also oddly content. In the couple seconds I analyze him, we lock eyes. His are fierce and full of hurt, but they seem to react to mine. *Do I know this man? Is this why I'm here?*

The sensation is fleeting and I'm quickly on the downramp to the other side. There's a shimmer of gold in my eye; the dealer is on the move.

I need to catch up.

Chapter 13 – Titus
2380 | June 7th | New York City

After several hours, Titus had arrived at a part of New York City that he'd only read about in text books: the mid-levels.

On the way he'd gotten some coffee, water, fruit, and a protein pack – each of which had made him feel tremendously better.

The nausea wore off with the coffee and water, plus it felt good to have something substantial (and delicious) in his stomach. It had been a long time since he'd *not* scrounged for food. In 2477, he'd had plenty of money, all loaded to his iNsert, but when the world goes to shit, money doesn't play as big a role as some would believe. It served him well here though, and he was already becoming attached to this much more peaceful era, even if he had no clue why he was here.

These mid-levels, that were supposed to be so depressing, teemed with life and human persistence. Sure, they smelled undeniably odd, but there was a hum that gave him energy. It wasn't the decimated, hopeless world from whence he'd come.

Titus was simply wandering about, taking in the atmosphere, the other people, and the city itself. Soon, he'd move up to the immaculate upper-levels and be wowed. He'd only heard of them as a child and never been to New York City before the Regime.

Because of his clothes, people had been glancing, curious why he was wearing the aged, worn fabric. Eventually, he would need to look the part and buy some new ones, but that could wait. As he walked around the mid-levels, he kept his hand in his jacket pocket, clutching the portable Warper that had sent him here. It felt warm to the touch. Briefly, he speculated where the man he needed to kill could be.

Titus found himself crossing a pedestrian bridge, hovering high above the ATV airway and chasms between skyscrapers. The moving walkway across the bridge helped accelerate the busy foot traffic and personal transportation devices that some had access too. Titus was fine standing patiently on the side of the path to let others pass.

After a few moments, he glimpsed to the opposite walkway, locking eyes with a man whom he knew he recognized, but not *how*. It was the exact same sensation as the blue man from his bunker. The one he had an unexplained destiny to kill. The look he received in return was strange – perhaps he'd been thrown off by Titus' scars – but there was some semblance of history in his face too.

The event was quick, leaving Titus nearly breathless that he'd found his target so quickly. Slowly, his hand moved to Zorex. Every bone in his body told him to kill that man on the bridge. Aggressively, his mind was shouting internally at him.

Don't make a scene. This can be your new life too.
Once the deed is done.

Chapter 14 – Aiontis
2380 | June 7th | New York City

This guy is fucking quick. He must have gotten spooked by the NYPD ATV across the way, and knows how to efficiently navigate through a crowd. In my retina display, he still shines bright gold and I'm ten paces behind him, pushing through the thick mass of people.

The gold silhouette turns a corner, peering back through the crowd, looking for someone he doesn't find. Slowly, I edge around the same corner and see a wondrous site: a massive gap between buildings and their walkways, creating an impressive man-made canyon of glass and steel, hundreds of feet deep. Wondering why the city would have a random blank space on its canvas, I move to the walkway's edge, checking the gold in my eye before I do so. The dealer's pace has slowed. I can catch up in a moment.

Below me, at the ground level of the city, are the haunting pools of the 9/11 Memorial. Realizing I must have lost total track of where I am within the city, I'm taken aback at seeing these from high up and the odd effect they have on the city's design. Even after 350-plus years, they're still sobering and, as history evolved, that event became one of the key moments in human history. One of the most significant D-Days ever.

Perhaps it's the place I'm at or the massive holes in the ground, but deep inside my gut, this feeling of purpose roars louder. It's the final confirmation I need that whatever the hell is happening here is being orchestrated by some higher being(s). *I just hope this is for the right reasons…*

Over on the tree-lined walkway, which is much cleaner than the main street I was just on, the dealer sits on a bench, scrolling through something on his iNsert.

"Hi!" I say, perhaps too breathlessly, as I approach. It startles him.

"Hiiiii….?" He peers at me. I'm probably not his typical

clientele. As I approach, I notice the details of the datats on his face. They're a dark gray "ink" against his whiter skin and they slowly shift to form different versions of skulls from various cultures. At the moment, the gray had settled on a design from Hispanic culture. It was as menacing as I'm sure he intended, yet also hard to look away from.

"Hi. Yes, so look…I'm just going to come right out and say it: I know you're a dealer." He makes a sudden move, to run or to pull out a weapon, I'm not sure. My hands spring outward. "Woah, woah, woah. I come in peace. I'm…not from around here." He's settles down. The skull begins to morph again. "I'm looking to purchase. I can pay."

He stares, sizing me up. I realize that I'm talking to a drug dealer, and one who may suspect me of being a narc, in the mid-levels of New York. I didn't go about this the right way. The presence of my X-34 seems more apparent now.

"What're you looking for, man?" He finally asks. I clear my throat.

"Jinx. Just one or two capsules." This seems to settle him down. I'm not looking for any hard shit that could get him in trouble.

"Ok. I can hook you up. It'll run $400 for one, $500 for two."

Not as bad as I thought, but still fucking ridiculous.

"Why only $500 for two?"

"I don't know you. Consider the first one a risk tax."

"Fair enough." I transfer him $500 through my iNsert. He verifies and reaches for a handshake with those ridiculous gloves. At the end of it, I've got two capsules taped to my palm.

"Pleasure doing business with you." He states, with a hint of *now get the fuck out of here* underneath.

"Likewise."

The skull has shifted to resemble a pirate skull-n-bones. I hope these capsules are actually Jinx and not something that could fucking kill me.

I've planned on taking these in the comfort of a hotel room. Something about that just feels *peaceful.* Within an hour, I'm showered and lying in bed with the blinds of a four-star suite closed. The room is frigid thanks to some effective thermal cooling in the walls and floor. Darkness owns the space except for the glow from my iNsert and a timepiece built in the wall next to my bed.

Partly due to the room environment and partly the fact I've been through some crazy shit in the last several hours, exhaustion seeps from my bones. Regardless of what's going to happen with these Jinx capsules, I could use a good sleep. Who knows? Maybe this whole thing has been a weird dream all along. I'll wake up back in Omaha, 2404 and laugh about it over drinks with Thomen.

Probably not.

Before I slip away, I put the Jinx capsule into the med slot of my iNsert. It dispenses into my bloodstream and exhaustion transforms to a terrible blackness.

Chapter 15 – Titus

2380 | June 7th | New York City

Titus was acting off instinct as he rushed *back* over the pedestrian bridge and around a corner. There was a significant gap in the skyscraper structure of the city that, were he not in the middle of trying to hunt a man, he would have appreciated more.

Full, emerald trees lined the walkway. Nearby, a man with a long coat and metallic gloves sat, occupied with his iNsert and mumbling to himself. Everyone else that Titus could see was walking to or from somewhere; they wouldn't have seen where the man went. His best – and only – choice was the odd person sitting down.

Titus approached calmly, but with purpose. If this wasn't quick, he'd lose his target from the bridge. The man looked up to his new onlooker. Across his face was a gray skull, slightly different from a biological approximation. It startled Titus, shocked to see someone with…datats (*is that what they're called?*)…on their face.

With a chuckle, the man went back to his iNsert.

"Excuse me." Titus said, approaching closer. He looked up again. "Sorry to bother, but did you happen to see a man come through here a few moments ago?"

"Lots of people coming and going." He waved to the crowd of people. Titus went on to describe his brief look of the individual.

"He may not look like he's from around here."

"Yeah. And neither do you." He motioned up and down toward Titus. "What happened to your face?"

"I could ask you the same." Titus responded. He didn't have time for this.

"Fair enough. Yeah, I saw the guy you're talking about. Sold him some merchandise not more than a couple minutes ago."

"Sold him?" Titus was confused. The man cleared his throat,

obviously not wanting to outright confirm his practice to a stranger. Soon enough, Titus figured it out. "I see. What did you sell him?"

"Client-patient confidentiality."

"You're not a doctor." Titus was becoming increasingly frustrated. He flashed Zorex within the man's eyeline.

"Nice piece. I got one too." He smiled menacingly. The skull on his face began to shift. "Whatever. What do I care?" He spit into the grass. "I sold him Jinx."

"Jinx…?" The name rang a bell to Titus, though he couldn't remember what it did.

"Jesus, you're definitely not from around here. Jinx. The sleep prescription drug. Lets you control your dreams." Titus remembered now.

"Did he say where he was going?"

"He didn't, but he seemed eager to take it. Didn't have a problem paying either. If I were him, I'd go to a nice hotel, relax, and build dreams in a cushy bed."

"Ok." Titus' mind was already onto his next mission of finding that hotel. "Thanks." The dealer didn't reply, just went back to his iNsert. Wanting to distance himself from the creepy individual, Titus walked further down the path and found his own bench.

The day remained beautiful and Titus appreciated the sun on his face. Within this massive gap between towering structures of glass and steel, a crisp breeze shook the trees. There was plenty of visual splendor to enjoy within this moment and this place, but Titus wasn't absorbing any of it. He was looking for cameras. If his hunch was correct, his iNsert technology was vastly superior to the security they had in this time period and he'd be able to hack in and track his man.

Why do I want to kill him? What do I know of him? Now resting, his brain asked the natural questions left open with insufficient answers. Even more odd was that this need to kill wasn't violently raw in nature. Titus had felt that before. This felt more akin to a chore, and one that *had* to be done. The mystery around this mission was a haze hovering within his mind.

Frustrated, Titus tried to focus on finding answers.

Something about this man was tied to his memory. An image ripped across his brain, almost too quickly to comprehend. A man…a blue image of a man…yelling at him. In panic. He couldn't tell what he looked like; it had been too quick. Maddeningly, the image wouldn't reappear. Instead, Titus was flooded with memories of the Regime. The times they'd nearly killed him. Tortured him. Killed his friends. Raped him. Destroyed cities.

Gentle tears rolled down Titus' cheeks as he realized the strongest memories associated with the man-from-the-bridge were ones of pain and the Regime. *That* was the connection. This man, somehow in the past, played an integral role in the Regime of the future. That was all Titus needed to know. The man would die.

Dark clouds rolled in front of the sun and the wind became more aggressive. It took Titus a few minutes to hack the camera system and locate his target. Above and around him, leaves chattered loudly as they clung to their stems. Sure enough, the man had entered a hotel nearby – a nice one. Titus found the hotel's security system and hacked it too, following the individual to his room, 777. He sped up the footage to the present to make sure the man hadn't left. He was still in there, likely drifting away in his dreams.

A strong gust shook the trees while the leaves continued to yelp. A few lost their battle and fell to the ground. Back down the path from where he'd come, Titus caught the dealer looking at him, a shifting, smiling skull returning his gaze.

Inside the hotel, there were mostly robotic employees, designed for specific tasks and customer service. Here and there you'd see a human pattering about with their list of to-dos and behind the bar there was a talented gentleman serving up afternoon cocktails. It was a fancy place, with modern styling, a comprehensive color scheme, and eye-catching, artistic light fixtures. Oddly, the furniture came across as aged and worn, either a poor design choice or the last checkmark on a list of renovations.

Titus felt out of place, so he'd make this quick. A few ritzier guests stole second glances, but he was used to that by now. One of the two spiral walkway belts took him up several floors until he reached seven. Technically, the hotel itself was stacked upon many other stories, so 7 was more like 70, but nonetheless, he was here.

Unlike the lobby, these halls were darker, with minimal lighting and striking blue, white, and black flooring. Titus' heart was thumping loudly as he passed the doors. 740…750…755. He couldn't discern if it was excitement to hurt the Regime, or anxiousness about killing an unknown, sleeping man. He steeled his resolve, grabbed Zorex from its holstermesh, and made sure it was in "kill" mode.

After a few swipes on his iNsert, he unlocked the door, an even older technology than the camera systems. His heart hadn't stopped beating. In fact, it was almost like he could hear it now, as if it were powering up…or trying to.

Bwah….bwahhhhh…bwaaaaahhhhhhhhh

"What the fuck?" *Is it coming from inside the room?*
Bwwwaaaahhhhhhhhh

Titus opened the door, flooding the room with light. The sound grew louder and more prolonged. He stepped in to the opening living room.

BWWWAAAAHHHHHHHH

The man was lying in bed, unconscious and unaware of the sound. It was originating from Titus.
The Warper!
Frantically, he lowered Zorex and pulled out the portable time travel device. It was pulsing with a dark aura, even among the dim light from the hall. Titus was confused.
Did I bump it? How do I turn it off? The digital readout was frantically cycling through numbers and symbols Titus had never seen before.

BWAAAHHHHHHHHHHHHH….

The sound was sustained and the numbers suddenly stopped shuffling. Titus didn't have time to read what they were…

"No! No, no, no, n —"

His concern was cut short in the year 2380 by the growing ether sphere one uses to time travel.

Historian Consultant Report
The Battle of Sekigahara, Japan
October 1600

Before I start this report, I'll provide some background. Traveling back in time can be incredibly disorienting. Often, it takes several moments to physically get your bearings, and that's if you *know* where (read: when) you're going.

In this particular case, where I had no fucking idea how I got to a certain place (and later, places), time travel is basically like being reborn over and over again. Okay…maybe not *that* drastic. But "disorienting" is the nicest way I can put it.

Hence, these Historian Consultant Reports (HCRs) on specific time periods and events. I hope they help you, the reader, feel a little better about all this craziness than I do. If these don't suffice, I encourage you to do your own research.

At the turn of the 17th century, Japan had been in a period of war and social unrest for over 100 years. Often referred to as the Sengoku period, it's here that daimyos would often battle in hopes of obtaining more power and influence within the country. In many ways, it was a period of consistent civil war among various territories the island encompassed.

Generals of these territories were known to have massive egos and, rather than display alliance to their people and their land, sought to achieve personal gain and honor. They aimed to be appointed Shogun by the Emperor, who was little more than a symbol at this point in Japanese history.

Alliances between various states were weak and susceptible to corruption and rot. Even the strongest ones would be laced with doubt in a period of frequent betrayals.

The Battle of Sekigahara was a Defining Day (D-Day) in Japanese, and even world, history. Located where North Japan meets South Japan along the Shiga and Gifu prefectures, this battle ultimately led to peace in Japan for nearly 250 years, a much-needed respite for the people of the country. The inner workings of the battle play like a soap opera and are immediately intriguing to Hiscons simply because the outcome of the entire battle hinged on a single decision.

Eastern forces were led by Tokugawa Ieyasu, a well-liked general, who numbered over 80,000 strong. Western forces were headed by Ishida Mitsunari, an administrator to the previous ruler of Japan, Toyotomi Hideyoshi. The need for the Battle of Sekigahara was formed because of Hideyoshi's death, which left a vacuum of power in the country as his son was not old enough to take up the mantle. Ishida, being an administrator, was not a well-respected general, but commanded a force of equal size.

Starting on an early morning in October, the battle was put on hold until a thick fog cleared from the fields and hills where each side was positioned. Once it began, it wouldn't last long. Within six hours, the casualties of the warring groups of samurai totaled over 35,000. It's recorded in history as the largest battle of samurai to ever take place, and also one of the deadliest. It was fought primarily with bladed weapons, but also featured early muskets that caused violent, bloody deaths.

As the battle progressed, both sides needed help. Upon nearby Mount Matsuo, Kobayakawa Hideaki and his sizable army observed. Before the battle, Hideaki had agreed to refrain from fighting until given a signal from Ishida's forces. Unbeknownst to the Western general, Hideaki had also been courted before the battle by Tokugawa of the East.

Below the Mount, the clash raged on, death after death littering the battlefield with blood, sweat, and steam. Ishida's forces sent a signal calling for Hideaki to join the contest and land a final blow on Tokugawa's.

Hideaki and his men remained motionless.

Tokugawa was angered as well, awaiting the extra samurai to help turn the tide. In a bold decision, he commanded his men to fire their cannons upon Hideaki on the ridge, forcing him to make a decision.

Ishida or Tokugawa. West or East.

Hideaki had made his decision. He ordered his soldiers as they charged down toward Ishida's forces, overpowering the tired men quickly. Not long after, Tokugawa and the Eastern forces declared victory, one which had not been guaranteed mere hours ago.

Pivotal alliances and a single decision had made it so.

Chapter 16 – Aiontis
1600 | Unknown location

I've never felt like this before, my body wholly awake, pulsing as if I've had an unsafe amount of coffee. But my mind…it's still asleep. I try to move and find my muscles are slowly waking back up.

"Mmmmgggghrrrmmm" My mouth is under the same spell. I open my eyes. It doesn't feel like I'm lying on a lovely 5-star hotel bed. I smell grass.

What in the actual fuck?

My eyes adjust to the silvery light, crusted over with deep sleep. I'm slowly gaining feeling in my arms and lower legs. My jaw has unclenched. Sluggishly, my vision begins to focus on the environment.

A grassy slope covered in thick fog. It's cold.

Echoing a similar sentiment as my mind, my stomach violently releases its contents; it's the hardest I've ever vomited in my life. I ache for it to put me back to sleep, but I've got a shit ton of adrenaline going through my system right now.

I study my iNsert, trying to get a gauge for what's going on. A graph reports my sleep was deep and strong, up until a few moments ago, then there's an odd blank space in the heart rate monitor. Almost as if there was no heart rate to measure. Now, however, it's soaring. I'm at 170 beats per minute just sitting here.

Gradually, my memory begins to build the pieces. There's a pulsing sense of urgency as it does. I traveled back to get Jinx. Why? No fucking clue. I bought some, went to a hotel, and took it.

"What the fuck did that guy give me?" That's what I get for buying drugs from a random, skull-faced individual. Now I'm likely in a fucked-up dream state of Jinx mixed with some horrific concoction. Sitting, I half expect a pterodactyl to fly out of the fog and rip me in half. Why a pterodactyl? As per usual at the moment, I have no fucking clue.

If I'm truly on some brand of Jinx, I should be able to control aspects of the dream. Recognizing the irony that I've already done this experiment once today (and in a different time, no less) I set my mind to the task. I'll make flowers grow from the ground. Simple.

Except nothing happens. The fog lingers heavy on the hill, the grass still and dewy. Confused, I try again. Still nothing. I check my vitals on my iNsert again and run a blood test. Within moments it reports back nothing in my system. That alone would be enough to make me nervous, but something even more terrifying catches my eye.

In the upper corner of the screen, the date stamp of the test report reads: "XX-XX-XXXX"

Chapter 17 – Aiontis
1600 | Unknown location

When the fuck am I? Was my iNsert damaged? It seems perfectly fine. iNserts have a time-location sensor that reports back the date of *when* the user currently is. It had been working before I took the Jinx; the readout had read 06-07-2380. I'd never seen it provide a readout of entire Xs before.

Unless…

I laugh aloud at the idea. There's no way. Still, I ponder the question: what if the date readout can't register *when* I am because I went back before 2377? It was an impossibility. Wasn't it?

That feeling from before returns. The one that I'm tied up in something epic, something ferocious. Being here isn't wrong. In fact, it's frighteningly right. I start to accept the fact that I'm no longer on Jinx (though I can't say the craving is fully gone either), which means I had to have been ripped out of my slumber somehow. That would explain the vomiting and temporary paralysis.

"Holy shit." I state, wondering how on earth I traveled *back* in time without even being near a Warper. It's just all so preposterous. I don't believe it; this must be some sickening side effect of the drug.

I'm damp from lying in the grass, and cold from the eerie fog. There's so much wrong here…I can't answer *why*, *when*, or *where* I am. It's some of the most crippling fear I've ever felt.

From atop the hill, I hear footsteps coming toward me. They're soft, making small sounds as they kick across wet ground. Whoever it is certainly isn't sneaking up on me, but they may not know I'm here either. I roll onto my stomach and slide down the hill a few meters so I can see.

My heart is thrumming in my chest as my adrenaline runs high. The person crests the hill, of Asian descent, and dressed in full Samurai armor save for a helmet atop their head. *What the hell?!*

"Saitou? Saitou, where'd you go?" I can tell he's speaking Japanese, but yet I understand him perfectly. This gets weirder by the minute. He glances down the hill spotting me, cowering and staring back. "Saitou! There you are." He begins walking toward me. I ease up from his familiarity. "What are you doing down here? Why are you half way down the hill?" I reply with only a stare, unsure if I can even speak Japanese. He slows.

"Is everything alright? It is the morn of battle, do not start acting weird now!"

"Battle?" I reply, apparently in Japanese. He raises an eyebrow.

"Yes. Battle. Get up, Saitou. I have no time for these games. Put on your armor and gather your sword and Tanegashima. We could be called to fight at any moment." I recognize the foreign word from my studies, it's a type of early musket introduced to the Japanese in the mid-1500s. The man, I'm assuming a mid-ranking general, storms off confused by our interaction.

I'm equally as confused when I do a recap of what I've discovered:

I can understand and speak Japanese.

My name is Saitou.

It's sometime around 17th century Japan.

And I'm supposed to be preparing for battle.

Holy shit. It hits me. *I'm in someone else's body.*

Chapter 18 – Aiontis
1600 | Japan

The historian in me is naturally curious about exactly when this is, but I'm not sure I have time for it right now. *Though, it would help to know what I'm getting into.* Figuring that out could be nearly impossible just by guessing; this was during a significant warring period within Japan's history. One that lasted for hundreds of years.

Or I could just ask…

I hike up the hill from where the general had come, unsure how I will "blend in", but at this point, I need answers. The fog is clearing gradually as the sun begins to poke out on this cold morning. It feels like fall weather, but it's hard to be sure. Still, it acts as my first clue.

Atop the hill is a camp of soldiers – smaller than I expected – all busy eating or preparing for battle. They're mostly silent which lends to the eerie feeling I've had since I…landed(?) here. Oddly, I feel as if I know where I'm going, making my way through various rows, arriving at a small tent with multiple places to sleep and various sets of gear. I see what must be my armor, my sword, and my musket.

"Saitou!" I hear rushing footsteps behind me. "Saitou! Where have you been?" A moderately plump individual doesn't let me answer the question before he delivers a barrage of more. "Have you eaten yet? Why are you not in your armor? Did you hear that Tokugawa and Ishida's forces are ready? Everyone is waiting for the mist to clear."

I react to the man's information.

"Did you say Tokugawa and Ishida?"

"Uhh yes, Saitou. That is why we are here."

"And what date is it?" As soon as I ask the question, I know it's the wrong one. The Japanese have had several shifts in calendar types throughout their existence and it's unlikely I'll get a straight forward answer without having to do some heavy calculation. Either way, the man looks confused.

"Uhh…"

I wave him off, "Nevermind. Where are we? Who are we aligned with?" His eyes respond with shock. All these questions must be disorienting for him too.

"Very strange, Saitou! We are on the side of Mount Matsuo. Just outside of Sekigahara. We'll follow Hideaki into battle when the time is right"

All I feel is cold shock. I know exactly when and where I'm at, and it's not great.

I'm in Japan, 1600, around October-ish (if I'm remembering correctly), about to be in the Battle of Sekigahara, one of the largest samurai battles in history. Also, one of the deadliest.

The man just stares. I thank him and walk into my tent. He takes his leave and I sit on a stool, my head in my hands.

What the fuck is going on?

Why am I here?

And why, specifically, here? *Japan?*

I could cry. I've never felt more alone in my entire life. This day started by feeling funny and not remembering how I even got to my apartment in Omaha. Now I'm in Japan over 800 years earlier!

I'm tired.

I'm hungry from vomiting everything up.

I've got some awful cold sweats.

But I knew what I was getting into. I knew I'd be stuck back in time when I went to New York. And I may not have known that Japan was the next destination, but I'm here for a reason. There's still some unknown force at work here; I can feel it. This is all part of some plan, but at this point I have to question what exactly that plan is.

I sit for a while, wondering if I can will this all away. I think about a lot of things, some for brief moments, some for longer. All the life I won't live. The lovers I won't have. The children I won't create. And for what? This weird intuition that came out of nowhere?

I don't know how long I'm there, but there's an abrupt commotion outside. Men, samurai, are scampering about, their armor clinging like a chorus. Interested, I glance out and note the troops standing along the hill's crest, all peering downward. The fight must have begun. A round of musket shots from a considerable distance confirms it.

Almost instantly, I forget about my sad predicament and begin dressing in my armor. Again, I know exactly what I'm doing. Within a few minutes, I have my traditional dou, kusazuri, haidate and other extremity plates on. I place my helmet (kabuto) on, but leave the faceplate. As menacing as it looks, it's ceremonial and impractical. I'm going to need all the help I can get if the fighting finds its way up the hill. I grab my gauntlets (kote) without putting them on yet and strap my sword to my back – disoriented that I know how to do all of this – then sling my Tanegashima (musket) over my shoulder.

Outside, the fog has lifted and it's a crisp, chilly day. The men remain along the top of the hill and the musket fire is more prominent and frequent. Shouts can be heard in the distance. I notice provisions on my way toward the group and stop. I take several scoops of rice, a radish, some leftover fish, and a handful of chestnuts. All of it is delicious and the sustenance makes me feel whole again. I sniff a carafe of some sort: sake. I take a swig, wait, and take another swig to wash it all down. It doesn't have the same burn as whiskey, but damn does it warm me up.

I approach the hill's edge with the other men, chewing some last chestnuts. What I see horrifies me, but I cannot look away. I am witnessing history. Monumental history. A moment that has stood the test of time and relevance for thousands of years. I've never had such an uneasy feeling; one where my mind feels on the cusp of unlocking secrets of mankind because I am here, so many centuries before my own, witnessing a human conflict that shaped the world. It's as if the gut feeling I've been having – this one of incredible significance – has been dialed to eleven.

On the battlefield below, of which I see only a portion from this vantage point, there's tremendous bloodshed. I focus on a few points of the battle, jaw hanging loose in wonderment. Musket fire cuts down an entire line of men, some still alive and writhing in pain. Two larger samurai battle by sword, almost poetically. From this distance, I can't hear their clashes (plus the cannon and musket fire drown them out), but I'm in awe at the vigor of the swords slamming metal against one another. Their might going into every blow, unknowing of who will survive.

One of them pulls off an intricate dodge and thrusts his sword upward, removing the other man's arm at the shoulder. The wound pools blood onto the grass, staining it. He staggers, but faces his adversary, knowing this is the end. With another horizontal thrust his head is removed, rolling backward into the red puddle. The victor charges into another section of the battle, searching for another victim.

I may lose the contents of my stomach once more. The plump man from before comes to my side.

"Saitou, have you ever seen anything like it?" Concern and dread are etched along his face. I can tell he's scared. Many of the other men seem determined and fearless.

"I have not."

For several moments we, and the rest of the army, stand, watching the epic and bloody battle unfold. Patches of fighting leave more dead than alive and those remaining soldiers move on to other patches of conflict. Smoke continuously rises from the musket fire and cannons. One man is hit in the shoulder by a cannon, exploding a corner of his body into nothingness.

"FOR-MA-TION!" A voice howls near us, filled with vigor and anger. There is a clatter of metal, feet on the ground, and shuffling weapons. The soldiers atop the hill, including myself and this plump individual, organize into crisp lines with flag bearers at the endcaps. There's a nauseating silence among our small army, cut only by the screams and cries and blasts of the skirmish below.

Beyond our line walks a man in grand armor, he must be higher ranking than the general I encountered earlier. I'm on the frontlines – a thought that does not give me comfort – and he approaches my position. His armor is rich in deep reds that run a spectrum from vibrant apple to profound burgundy. He does not yet wear a faceplate but his helmet is massive, with large, curved and spiked decorations protruding upward. A sword rests on his back and he carries no firearm. I imagine he doesn't actually participate in the fighting. His gait is filled with purpose, but his face looks troubled, as if he's trying to make a complicated decision.

I lean close to the plump man, mouthing my question with minimal movement,

"Who is that?" He looks stupefied.

"That? That's Kobayakawa Hideaki."

Chapter 19 – Titus
1600 | October 21ˢᵗ | Japan

There was no describing what the last couple hours had been like for Titus. No words that could begin to explain the fear he felt.

He'd awoken in a gray mist, outfitted in ancient armor. Alone in the forest, he believed he might have been deserted, but soon found he was close to a camp of soldiers who wore the same colors and armor as he.

Where the fancy hotel, the man lying in bed, New York City, and the year 2380 had gone, he had no idea. The Warper had apparently triggered without his desire, his world went black, and he "landed" here. After retching up what little contents of his stomach remained, he'd taken time to do reconnaissance and assess what he still had. Zorex and the mini-Warper were present, the latter of which now acting as if nothing had gone wrong. The readout displayed 10.21.1600.

Titus had plenty of questions with none of them nearing anything close to an answer.

How is traveling back to 1600 even possible?
Where am I, geographically?
Was my Regime target transported as well?

Battling the Regime had taught him instincts of prioritization. If you want to survive, focus on what you know *now*. Figure out the rest later, while you're alive.

Titus, immensely disoriented, tried to keep to himself. After carefully entering the camp and realizing he was on the "right" side (whichever that may be) he assessed what was going on. Trying not to move as awkwardly as he felt in the bulky armor, he could tell men were nervous, but brave, and making final preparations for a battle. Some were eating, some were talking, while others were tending to their weapons. By his best guess – based on the weapons and armor around him – he was in an Asian territory, likely Japan. He knew enough about history to be competent, but certainly wasn't an enthusiast. It was a luxury he couldn't afford while trying to focus on surviving the Regime's takeover.

Had others been paying attention, they would have found his wandering peculiar. Eventually, he arrived at a barrack and tent that was empty. There was a sword leaning against a small cot. Intuition told him he'd need it.

After gathering the weapon and eating enough for two meals, Titus was more at ease. No one had talked to him aside from nods, though the tension in the air had risen almost proportionally to the rate the fog had lifted. This was something big.

Around him, there was deep forest and rolling hills in the distance. He was far within the camp and couldn't yet see the enemy, but he knew that across a vast field was whomever they were against. A man in the distance shouted a command and a great commotion began. Soldiers were running to specific placements and readying their muskets. Further back, cannons prepped their loads. Titus did his best to fit in the ranks and still, no one said anything, so he continued to play along. The other men had swords at the ready and horrific looking faceplate armor on.

I'll put a mask over my own monstrous face…

Titus reached to the one dangling from his side and attached it to his helm. He was just now getting accustomed to the additional weight on his head. Questions crept into his mind that he had only seconds to ponder: *Am I really about to fight? What am I doing here?* Running away would get him killed by his own men, so he was stuck.

A general, atop a grand, muscular horse outfitted with small armor plating, galloped in front of the soldier formation and spoke. His voice was assured and thunderous.

"We are here! Where East and West Japan meet, near the city of Sekigahara, to fight! To battle! To win for the heart of Japan and our great nation's future!"

His gaze was furious, filled with passion.

"You fight for the glory of Ishida Mitsunari! Beyond that, you fight for the memory of whom he served: Toyotomi Hideyoshi. The enemy seeks to take power and land and people that are NOT theirs! You will CUT them down with the honorable power of the samurai until they succumb to the true future Shogun of Japan: Ishida Mitsunari!"

Men around Titus thrust their swords briefly into the air, remaining silent, as an act of affirmation. There was a distant clap of what sounded like thunder followed by an explosion of dirt and grass near the middle of the field. Behind Titus, their own cannons, *Ishida*'s cannons, fired a volley that rang his ears.

The battle had begun.

Chapter 20 – Titus
1600 | October 21ˢᵗ | Japan

Much different than previous battles Titus had been part of, this felt antique, with more ceremony. And much more organized. He was used to expecting the unexpected and finding any means to survive, but here it was clear that some of these men knew they'd be dying for their country today.

The samurai charged forward to meet those from the opposing side, while the musket lines remained in place and fired away. Men on mounted horses began curving inward on the battlefield. *Astonishing.* He'd never seen anything like it. *Is this a dream?*

Unbelieving that he was back in 1600, Titus debated his own participation. Soon enough, the decision was made for him. The back lines began to advance and his troop was pushing him into battle. He didn't dare resist for fear of being put down like a cowardly dog. Zorex was secure on his hip and he thought about using it, but what would the implications be? These men had never seen a futuristic weapon, much less a handgun. He decided to refrain unless it was absolutely necessary.

Awkwardly, Titus unsheathed his sword from the hilt on his hip. It wasn't awkward because he'd never done it, but rather because it felt like he'd always known how to.

Ahead, the battle was closing in. He was used to the cannon fire and ringing musket balls by now, but the new sounds of sword conflicts, screaming men, and dying horses was a torture all its own. *Men have always been violent creatures, it would seem.* The battle found him within a few moments and he reluctantly charged forward.

Vibration rang up his arms as his sword clashed with that of an opposing soldier, one who was not a samurai, based on his armor (or rather, lack of it). There was fury in the man's face, and it was brave to strike against something as frightening as Titus was in samurai armor. Still, the attack was weak and his sword was weaker.

Titus shoved the man's blade away with his own in a sweeping motion downward, connecting into his thigh. The soldier screamed as blood cascaded from the wound. With a thrust, Titus cut the exclamation short plunging his sword into the soldier's mouth and out the back of his head. Without a thought, he removed his weapon from its predicament, the shine of the blood contrasting the dark metal of the blade, and continued into battle.

Cannon fire crashed into the ground within meters of him. It had missed hitting anyone, but the closest warriors, including Titus, were dazed. He'd felt the shockwave from the impact and his ears buzzed, enough to knock him on one knee. An opposing samurai, outfitted in similar armor, complete with frightful faceplate and horned helm, charged. His blade was up and gleaming, ready to plunge through Titus' neck.

He hadn't heard the horse coming from behind – his ears were just starting to gather sounds back – and the mounted soldier on the majestic creature shoved a pike through the rushing enemy's chest. With a crunch, the momentum of the impact lifted him off the ground and the rider slammed the body back to earth as he rode away.

Realizing he'd narrowly escaped a horrific death, lost in God-knows-when, Titus got to his feet quickly, and more cautiously moved across the smoking field. After dispatching several opponents, and dodging more close calls, he noticed the army he'd been "placed" in seemed to be winning. The tide of war was slowly shifting in their favor, not by a wide margin, but it appeared that Ishida – whomever that was – had the upper hand on this gargantuan effort, dense with casualties.

At least, for now.

Chapter 21 – Aiontis
1600 | October 21ˢᵗ | Japan

We (the plump man and I) stand and watch the battle unfold from our crest for what feels like hours. Hideaki has since put on his faceplate armor and continues to pace in front of us. Because of his hidden face I can no longer tell if he is troubled, but the fact we remain on the sidelines of this battle is indicative.

There's death everywhere below. I believe I smell the stench of it. Above, the sky is a grayish blue, mostly cloudless day. It provides a much-needed break from all the violence.

I hope that when I look back down, my gaze will be met with the home I know: Omaha, 2404. Same blue sky, hundreds of years in the future, thousands of miles away, but familiar, towering skyscrapers and ATVs flying about. I'll come to find this was a daydream because I got drunk in a walkway park with some friends one Saturday.

I know it's a false hope.

The weight of the armor is still on my shoulders. Uncomfortable, yet strangely familiar.

I still hear the sound of battle. The blasts of guns and cannons.

I'm still here without any idea of why or how. A heavy sigh unloads as I return the battle to my field of view. *Yep, still here.*

Ishida's forces are slowly winning, which is in line with what actually happened in history. This has been at the forefront of my mind, actually. Not only *why* am I here, but *does being here affect history?*

When I say it like that, it sounds like ridiculous science-fiction bullshit – I've been reading too many time-travel books – but I'm genuinely curious if this series of events will be altered. So far, it has not, and as far as I'm concerned, that's a positive worth noting in this hellscape of a situation. Plus, it's the only question I remotely have an answer to.

"What are you thinking about, Saitou?" the plump man asks.

"Nothing really." I feign confidence to sound more like the fearless samurai I'm supposed to be. "Just bored. Ready to join the fight."

"Oh…" His response seems crestfallen. Fine, I'll bite.

"What are you thinking about, er…good friend?" I don't know his name. He continues to stare at the battle below.

"I am frightened." He pauses, wondering if I'll respond, but I don't. "I thought I wouldn't be, back in camp, but now that I see all of this…I can't help but feel like I'm going to die today." I'm not sure how to respond. I've got my own problems to figure out about stuff he probably can't even begin to comprehend, but I have sympathy for him. Truly, I'm scared too.

"It's ok to be scared. That makes you human." He looks to me and nods, appreciating my response. I place a hand on his shoulder for a moment. If I didn't know any better, I'd say I just made a friend in the past.

The tender moment doesn't last long. Men are reacting to Hideaki rushing along the ridge to look at Ishida's army. I can't see what is happening, but a series of tall banners below face our position. It's definitely a signal from Ishida to Hideaki. He stands there, realizing this is the moment his army is needed in battle.

Yet, he does nothing.

Moments pass and the men are getting restless. The more experienced ones realize they've been called into battle and are reacting to their leader, at least for now, ignoring the call. But he's still their leader and they stay in line.

A man on horseback comes from a back trail, wearing the colors and armor of Tokugawa's camp. He's a messenger – a small, nimble man – who's guided to Hideaki. The message is transmitted verbally, though I'm too far to hear what's being said. The messenger leaves as swiftly as he came, back down to the outskirts of the fray.

It's a surreal thing, being surrounded by men that don't know how pivotal this moment in history is.

Nor does the man making the decision himself.

But I know how significant it is within Japanese culture. Kobayakawa Hideaki was courted by both sides before this battle.

Ishida believed he was aligned with him, surely winning the battle if he were to honor that commitment. Tokugawa had secretly approached Hideaki as well, a decision that, if considered, could turn the tide.

That epic weight of importance is back. The one telling me this is all the right thing. The reason I am here. I realize that in spite of my terror, I'm enjoying this. It's a Hiscon's dream to be part of integral moments in history that we've only read about! I wonder what it all means. What am I actually *doing here?*

Hideaki is still pacing, his gaze transfixed on the battle, glancing from side to side. He's taking too long to make a decision; both sides are becoming frustrated. The dead litter the battlefield and his decision will make or break the day.

An explosion of grass and earth shake the ridge, sending debris pluming into the air: a cannonball and warning shot from Tokugawa. A bold way of saying, *"Make up your fucking mind, man!"*. The men twitch and ready their weapons, curious if more rounds are coming. It jolts Hideaki out of his daze. He stares toward Tokugawa's regiments and turns to us, mind made up.

"We enter the battle now! Not for the glory of Ishida or the legacy of the previous ruler, Toyotomi. NO!" The battalion reacts with murmurs and glances. "Instead, we commit to a *new* Japan! One of peace! One of prosperity! We fight to aid Tokugawa Ieyasu!" He pauses after this declaration.

"You will HONOR your commander! For your legs are fresh, your armor unbroken, your swords sharp, and your minds sharper. TO BATTLE!"

I have to say, it's a short, but effective speech and even the plump man beside me lets out a cheer among the raucous affirmation of the leader's command. The front-line collapses as it charges down the ridge where I first woke up. Then the second line, and soon the entire formation.

It's that patch of grass I wish I could fall back asleep onto. Instead, I am a samurai in 1600 Japan heading into one of the deadliest battles in their history.

So yes, the phrase, *"What the fuck?"* is appropriate here.

Chapter 22 – Aiontis

1600 | October 21ˢᵗ | Japan

The participants on the bloodied field collectively pause as our battalion – large and full of energy – rounds the bottom of our camping ridge, Mount Matsuo, and enters the encounter. Ishida's men are either white-faced, as if they've seen a ghost, or blazing hot with anger.

Tokugawa's battered samurai and soldiers receive adrenaline anew, clamoring to get back into the fight with the side-flank of our army against Ishida's.

It's great that everyone else is so dedicated because I'm trying not to lose my most recent meal from all the blood and gore I'm trampling across. Soon enough, my "friend" and I arrive at a patch of skirmishes. My pulse echoes in my ears. Remembering my iNsert, I discreetly turn my wrist to its readout. My heart rate is an insane 185 beats per minute. I am fucking amped. And terrified.

One of Ishida's samurai comes charging toward the two of us, spear in hand. He's menacing, and based on his hollers, probably in the "angry" camp, underneath his faceplate. His aim is focused on my friend as the point of the spear levels with his chest.

With a blur, the portly man who's supposed to be afraid sidesteps the weapon with calm, grabs its shaft, unsheathes his katana from his hip, and opens the man's gut all in a swift motion. My jaw hangs as the wounded enemy falls to the ground, clutching intestines between his fingers. The suffering doesn't last long as the katana finds his heart between his ribs. My friend turns to see my shock.

"What? I said I was afraid. Not that I wasn't talented."

"I...just..."

"Thought a fat man couldn't move like that?" He's smirking under his faceplate, lets out a boisterous laugh and charges elsewhere in the battle.

A musket ball glances off my armor and knocks me to my knees. Instinctively, I remove my katana. *Why did that feel so natural?* I look up to a group of soldiers surrounding me. Most have swords, though their armor indicates they're not samurai, but normal grunts. It would appear I'm on my own at the moment. My wrist vibrates and my iNsert shows 200 beats per minute. I can feel it.

I stand.

A soldier wielding a spear yells and lunges forward.

Opposite of him, a separate shout, with a sword.

The spear tip reaches me first and I step forward, gracefully out of its way. My grip, firm on the sword's shaft, plunges it backwards on my right side.

I feel the resistance as it penetrates the man's armor and his skin.

With the same grip, I yank it out as he falls to the ground, mortally wounded, and swipe the thin, gorgeous blade upward toward the soldier running toward me. The length of my blade enters the bottom of his chin and leaves at the top of his skull.

The four remaining soldiers, shaken by what they've just witnessed, tighten the circle around me. Two brandish their swords, cheap and rusty. My strike – from much stronger metal – cracks one of their blades in two.

The other lunges at me, and I deflect it, grabbing the man with the rusty, broken blade, pulling his arms into the neck of the other. The jagged piece of old steel is engulfed in blood and the soldier grabs his companion, dragging him down to the ground. I stick my katana through his ribs to end it while the remaining two navigate to either side of me.

"Guys, you really want to do this?" I ask, half taunting and half shocked they're still around.

They simply stare, determined to bring me down as a foe. A tremendous blast comes from behind as a musket shot blazes past my head and takes off half an enemy's. While his body crumples, I turn toward the remaining one and bring a mighty blow down on his head.

But he blocks it. His sword is able to withstand the impact of mine. He counters with a kick to my knee that sets me off balance, and attempts to swing at my left side. I block it, but just barely.

For a moment, the fight back has removed me from my adrenaline-haze. *Focus!* I scream internally, wanting to unpack how I can actually swordfight (*seriously, what the hell?*) later.

The brave soldier's next attempt comes as a thrust forward that I deflect away with a ringing clash, returning a blow with a follow through strike. His sword is there to block it. This guy is fucking fast. *Why couldn't the musket have killed* him?!

A flurry of attacks erupts and I deflect each one. He's frustrated and I know that will be how I catch him. For several minutes, I play defense, letting him come to me, protecting against his blows. Finally, he slips – only slightly – on blood smeared along the field. It throws him off and his attack misses me by centimeters.

I punch the side of his head. The blunt impact of my large, armored fist draws blood from his ear and makes him stagger, clutching his head. With a harsh, energetic thrust, I bring my blade across the wrist near his neck and through it. My reddened metal continues through his neck and out the other side, leaving a headless and handless corpse on the ground.

I stand in shock over what I've just done. Six men dead, some truly gruesomely, all by my hand. The feeling of being sick comes back around, though lesser because of my sky-high adrenaline. I glance to my iNsert but it's covered in blood.

I continue my foray into the largest mass of the fighting until I find my friend again, his armor caked with the blood of others, but still alive and eager. He has since removed his faceplate and is laughing again.

"If I didn't know any better, I'd say you're enjoying this!" I run up to join him. He lets out another thunderous chuckle.

"Saitou! I see you've dispatched some foes." He nods to the blood on my sword and armor, "Fun, is it not?" I smile.

"Not even a little bit, but I'm glad you're no longer afraid."

In front of us, a samurai from Ishida's camp cuts down several of our own. He moves swiftly, and with ferocity, but also intense precision. The jabs and swipes he creates seem to have little waste. They are exactly as long and as quick as he intends them to be. Within seconds, four of our men are dead.

He sets his sights on us.

My friend sees it too and the laughter stops. His stance is set and he knows this will be a fight. There's something different about this other samurai, outfitted with stately armor. It's as if he's unnaturally here somehow, but I'm not able to pinpoint why. It doesn't help that ghastly armor covers his face; one with an evil grin that brings back memories of the skeleton-faced dealer many hundreds of years in the future.

With vigor, my friend lunges toward this mysterious enemy. His sharp blade is poised to enter the man's chest, but the villain brings his blade downward to block the forward thrust. Anticipating this, my friend rotates his wrists to bring his sword down, back around toward himself, and above the blocking strike. It's a move full of artistry and I realize it's one that would have killed me had I been across from it.

The menacing samurai simply sidesteps, and the brief bout is a tie with neither man landing a blow. Within seconds, they are dueling once again, while I stand awkwardly by, preparing to jump in at any moment. Truthfully, I don't want to get in the way of my ally.

After back-and-forth trades of deadly near-misses, a grapple begins as the two wrestle, clutching swords, clashing and grinding armor. I hear a sickening snap, thinking it's a bone, but realize it's a chunk of armor breaking.

They eventually let go, readying their swords. Dangling from the enemy's helm is his facial plate.

It takes a moment, but eventually I make the connection and gasp. It seems as if he's going through a similar process as our eyes connect and he notices me in the fervor of the battlefield for the first time.

It's the Scarred Man from the pedestrian air bridge of faraway 2380.

Chapter 23 – Aiontis

1600 | October 21ˢᵗ | Japan

What the bloody fuck is he doing here? Or better yet: *HOW the bloody fuck is he here?*

The mysteries of today keep piling up and I'm exhausted by all the fucking questions I'm juggling.

(Sorry for all the fucks)

The distraction doesn't last long because my portly friend, oblivious to the reactions, charges back in. Where it was clear his talent over other soldiers was significant, here he may have met his match.

Even battling against an enemy who wants him dead, the Scarred Man keeps looking at me. His gaze will break for a few moments as he defends himself, but comes right back. Each time I can almost sense his blood boiling more and more, but I have no idea why.

Who is this man?

How do I know him?

Why does he seem to be getting angrier just at the sight of me?

Is he the only one from 2380 here?

Do I fight him?

If I had a dollar for every question I had since waking up today, I'd be a multi-millionaire. Every time I think I've figured out what's going on – just even a little bit – a new element is introduced.

Still fighting with tenacity, my battlefield friend is tiring. The Scarred Man is toying with him, having been on the defense for their entire skirmish. A bad step forward leads to a whiffed lunge and the Scarred Man catches him off guard, elbowing him in the back of the head, sending him crashing into the ground.

He's up quickly, converting the fall into a semi-roll. Just barely, he gets his blade above his head, blocking a killing blow against the stranger I "know" from 2380. I watch, trying to piece all of it together, as my friend calls out.

"Saitou! Help me!" I also don't know why he calls me that; another question piles on. The other man, blade pressing against the horizontal one in my friend's grip, squints at me once more with pulsing hatred. It's the distraction my friend needs.

He pushes upward on his blade, enough to release the tension, and kicks the man hard. It doesn't do as much as he'd hoped, but does force a stumble, creating a window of opening. Several slashes are aimed at the enemy, so fast they create small, wispy sounds cutting through the air. Each is met with a last-minute defense, and it's now the Scarred Man who tires.

If I only helped my friend, this would be over. I'm apparently a lethal samurai, after all.

Trouble is, I don't know if I'm *supposed* to help him. I have so many questions for this man – who's angered by the sight of me – I can't have him dead.

Fate is going to decide for me. The Scarred Man blocks an incoming downward strike with his forearm and his armor's integrity holds while he pushes the blade away, thrusting his into the gut of the man I've only exchanged a handful of words with.

I should be more shocked – he's clearly dying – and I am sad, but this day is so surreal that I'm not comprehending situations normally. There's pain in his eyes as the blade releases from his stomach, and he sees me, frozen there.

I should be ashamed, but he sealed his own fate. Harsh, I know.

The Scarred Man turns toward me, his blade wearing a fresh coat of crimson. It's my first really *good* look at him and there's still some sense of familiarity, as if I've known him before, not just from 2380.

I take in the full effect of his scars, straight and long across his face. They look painful so I can only imagine how it must have been receiving them.

He takes a step toward me.

Bwah….hwahhhhh…bwuuuuuhhhhhhhh

There's a new sound coming from the battlefield. At first, I think it's a cannon, perhaps misfiring? The Scarred Man hears it too.

Bwwwaaaahhhhhhhhh

His face retreats from anger, morphing into shock. The sound was louder that time and, yet again, I've got no idea what is going on.

BWWWAAAAHHHHHHHH

He throws his sword down in startling fashion, removes his armored gloves and reaches behind him. In his hand is a small sphere, pulsing with…dark…light? That is definitely not technology from the 1600s. In fact, if I didn't know any better, I'd say that's…

"Holy shit…" I say aloud as I realize it's Dark Particles.

BWWWAAAAHHHHHHHH…

The sound is definitely getting louder and originating from the small sphere. What the hell is that thing? Frantically, the Scarred Man, holding the sphere as if it could break at any moment, pulls a gun from the same place he'd retrieved the sphere, also not of this time period. He aims at me.

"Woah, woah!"

No shot leaves the weapon as my world goes black. For an instant. There's that familiar hollow radiance of Dark Particles. I feel drastically different than a moment ago – almost as if I'm in a vacuum. The air is less dense. I'm not entirely sure I'm wearing samurai armor anymore.

There's a distant light that forms a picture without defined edges, but is microscopic in my field of view. It grows and I can distinguish shapes and moving elements, even if being thrown into (what I can only assume is) time travel has me disoriented.

It doesn't matter how I explain any of this to you because, truthfully, it's nearly impossible to describe being shuttled through time. I struggle to even comprehend it, so the idea of words doing it justice is laughable.

How could this day get any weirder and worse? So far I've: woken up in 2404 Omaha with short term amnesia, *chosen* to get myself stuck back in 2380 New York City all so I could take a drug, woke up in 1600 Japan where I'm suddenly a samurai master, and am now floating in the ether toward God knows what.

It's only been a few seconds (*I think*) but the image, growing larger and larger, begins to look much clearer.

"Shit."

I'm, at once, "there". Surrounded by a high dirt wall supported by slabs of wood. There's raw mud and ground below me and a gray, melancholy sky above. I study my clothes, my uniform, and the men around me. There's a sunken, deep fear within their eyes.

I'm in World War I.

Historian Consultant Report
World War I, Europe
September 1917

When Hiscons look back and think about some of the most significant, shaping events in history, World War I is often top of mind. Many would think it's World War II – and they'd be right there too – but The Great War kicked off a series of dominos that are still tumbling today. The ripples from a modern world plunged into war (twice) will likely last for a millennium.

Hitler fought in the First World War. Ceremony and decorum of battles were quickly abandoned and replaced with savagery and the emergence of early guerrilla tactics. Military tools, weapons, and technology were all forced to enter a new, and more deadly, era. The world stage, having had many smaller conflicts for the previous couple centuries, was getting a taste of world politics and what committing to an alliance really meant.

Most think that World War I was started by the assassination of Franz Ferdinand, the Archduke who was next in line for the Austrian throne. They're partially correct as that was the spark that lit the powder keg, but there had been building angst beforehand.

Germany and France had been growing their armies – in a race to see who could be the largest and most threatening – while their attitudes toward each other festered. The Germans were proud and arrogant, while the French despised them. Once Germany began attempting to acquire new territories, particularly in Africa (where Great Britain and France already had several), tensions rose. After the assassination threw Austria and Serbia into war, the tangled web of alliances between nations did the rest, forcing the most significant powers at the time headfirst into what would be a long, bloody, and incredibly violent war.

Battles had to shift from the proper marching, drumming, and banner waving that came before into a new mindset: survival. And thus, life in the trenches – a staple of the first World War – was born.

Trench warfare is best described with two words: anxiety and boredom. Days were long, and nights were longer, often with soldiers sleeping while the sun was out and on duty when the stars shone. Conditions were horrendous, particularly if the weather didn't cooperate. Rain caused trenches to get muddy and pool with water, leading to cases of trench foot. Rats often infested entire segments of the tunnels.

It was a depressing existence, exacerbated by the fact they (whichever side you're thinking about) could be attacked at any moment. Artillery shells could be launched with noisy explosions that would rattle your bones, or even worse, spray shrapnel downward into your trench. A cloud of yellowish-green gas could slowly cascade toward you, causing maximum discomfort on your skin and face, potentially even killing you days later. At any moment, the war could find you.

And so, The Great War went on, mostly like this, for years. It ushered in a new type of violence and fighting unlike anything the globe had seen before, and would lead – almost directly – to the second World War and a multitude of other, unforeseen consequences.

Chapter 24 – Aiontis
1917 | Europe

I try to move and I cannot. Is this some new form of time-travel paralysis? Lovely…this situation just keeps throwing more and more at me. Perhaps worse, my skin crawls with a burst of itchiness and I have a flash-in-the-pan headache, as if someone hammered a chisel a single time on my skull.

"Oy! Williams! Got yerself stuck in the mud did ya?" A pale man sitting on a wall of the trench taunts me. Several others nearby smile and let out stifled chuckles. I look down.

My boots are sunk into the mud nearly up to their tops. No wonder I can't move. I try to pry free again and can only feel my feet inside shifting; the boots aren't coming loose. The itchiness and headache subside as fast as they appeared. Strangely, I can't help but laugh myself.

In a time where they've seen so many of their fellow soldiers die and have been on edge for weeks at a time, the other men take my laughter as a green light to release their own. Together, we join in a chorus of it.

I have no idea who these men are – though I oddly feel like they know *me* – and I am even more confused here in the early 1900s than I'd been in 1600s Japan. But the laughter feels good. Among the bullshit, it's comical to find myself *literally* stuck in the mud.

"Boys, let's help him out." The pale one finally says as the final chortles die down.

"You sure, Taylor? If we leave em' in there, it means we can sleep a bit longer before startin chores." A few men laugh again.

"I reckon that's true, but let's get to it anyway." The same men sigh.

A couple of soldiers on either side lean over the mud and lift me by my armpits. There is no strange sucking sound; my feet come completely out of my boots. They will have to be fished out once the mud is no longer quicksand. I land on solid, but soggy ground in my socks.

The group dissipates, getting back to whatever they'd been doing before a time traveling moron got stuck in the mud. Taylor (or at least I assume that's his name) approaches with a smile.

"Williams, you never cease to amaze me with the trouble you find yerself in." I don't know how to respond given that I've just transported here so I look down at my semi-bare feet. The thick, wool socks are comfy (also a bit scratchy), but the left one has a small hole forming in the toe, with threads of the cream-colored stitching fraying around its edges. By now, their bottoms are soaked. "I think you can get some boots if you go back to the Support Trench. Can't promise they won't be from a dead chap though."

The thought of trying on different shoes from dead bodies sends a spike-like shiver down my spine. I simply nod.

"Thanks."

"You alright, Williams? You seem off. Ya know I was just jokin around righ'?" I concentrate on my facial animations, realizing I'm likely conveying my epic confusion and disappointment (the time travel and someone else's body, not the socks and boots) all over my expressions.

"Hmm? Yeah! Yeah. I'm fine" I have a British accent now. "I'll head back there and look for some. Catch ya later." He nods, gives me a pat on the shoulder and I'm on my way.

It is impossible not to ponder my existence at this very moment. Within the last five minutes I have: been in a historic samurai battle, almost gotten shot by a stranger, been transported to one of the most depressing wars in history, lost my boots (!), and am walking around an unknown trench with soaking socks. I'm not really a crier – I can't remember the last time I had a good one – but all I want right now is to find a nook of this trench and let it out. I'm hopelessly lost in time and seem to be landing in increasingly violent places. I have no inkling who the Scarred Man was (or is?) or if he's here with me now. I'm still confused as to why and how I understood the Japanese language and samurai tactics back in 1600, why I am British now, and exactly how I am being transported through time in the first place. And why am *I* changing bodies while The Scarred Man looks the same (this one is a doozy I can't even begin to unpack...)? Or why the hell did I feel so *odd* when I got here? And why was it so quick?

Naturally, I return to the Jinx because it feels like the most logical solution, but this no longer *feels* like that. It's hard to explain, but between my gut and my iNsert, I know it's not the drug. Could the itchiness and headache have been withdrawals? The question is tabled as I look at the screen on my wrist that still reads "XX-XX-XXXX".

"Lotta good you're doing me now..." I know it's World War I so I've got the dates narrowed down to likely 1916 or 1917 based on what I've seen. In a war this big, does it matter what day it is?

I'm walking aimlessly through a trench, the sky gray and depressing, feeling like it's many more miles away than usual because I'm three meters deeper in the ground. I take respite in the brief intervals where there's wood planks instead of bare earth. Rigid ground is somehow comforting. Eventually, through my wandering, exhaustion overcomes me.

My body aches. I'm cold in my soaking socks. Like many other soldiers during this war, I search for a nook in the trench where I can drift away. Sleep would do me good. I can reset and come up with a game plan.

Nearby, I see the space I'm looking for: a rectangular dug-in slot along the trench's side wall. It doesn't even look wet thanks to the direction it's facing. Getting more tired by the second, I climb into the compact space, seated, and lean my head against the wall.

I think of two things before I drift off:

The subtle smell of the ground around me and...I don't have that nagging, but comforting, sensation of being part of a bigger plan anymore.

I expect I'll dream nightmares.

Chapter 25 – Aiontis
1917 | Europe

Luckily, my dream wasn't a nightmare. More surprising is that I slept comfortably given I was sitting in what is essentially a cold hole in the ground.

I'd like to tell you my dream was some grand premonition about all that is happening to me…that I woke up with answers. What I'd really love to report back is that I woke in my own damn bed, but alas, none of that is true. Instead, I had a normal, perfectly boring dream. I was back in Omaha – in my time – enjoying a casual day at work as a Hiscon. Going into the office, grabbing coffee with a coworker, performing some analysis and studying history…it was all so blissfully mundane.

Waking up in itchy clothes, surrounded by dirt, with a sky that has changed from light gray (noonish) to dull gray (afternoon) is about as depressing as it gets. My feet are still cold and my socks haven't dried much. I should go to the Support Trench to get new boots, but I'll spend a moment more, here in my nook.

It's a common theme to not know what's going on and my questions number in probably the high twenties. I don't know, I haven't counted them. None hang heavier than:

When will I leave 1917(ish)?
Will I *ever* leave this time?
Where will I go next?
How do I escape this?

In a blur, someone sprints past my crevice. Their pounding footsteps and heavy breath disappear around a bend. It startles me, but there doesn't seem to be a commotion otherwise. Perhaps he had to deliver a message or go to the bathroom really badly? Either way, I remember I'm still at war and I shouldn't be the lazy asshole that sleeps in the trench all day. Plus, I *have* a mission:

find warm socks and boots.

I force myself out of this comfortable cut in the wall (if I'm going to be here a while, I should figure out how to claim dibs on it) and stretch. The ground of solid wood planks separates my damp feet from the dirt and my body's tingling blood flow preaches about how cramped I was.

Once more there are footsteps, this time from the other direction. As a man rounds the corner, his eyes are white with fright, and his mouth small. He's worried, anxious. I call out before he gets to me.

"What're you runnin about for? What's going on?"

His pale face responds with one, breathless word. "Gas."

"Gas?" He nods, barely able to speak from sprinting back and forth and the type of fear that puts a lump in your throat. I start running alongside and stop, grabbing him. "So, what're you running about for? Lotta good that's doing!" He catches his breath.

"Need…to find…alarm…"

"Gas alarm?" He nods again. "Got it. Let's look together. Show me where it usually is."

We shift to a light jog and turn some corners, my bare feet pounding against the wood slats. He looks down at them.

"Why're you…"

"Long story. Boots can wait." I cut him off. We stop at what looks like a supply section of the trench. There's a small stockpile of ammo, food, and other reserves (but no damn socks or boots!).

"Alarm is usually in one of these stockpiles hanging on a nail. I've been running between them to find it."

"Ok. Why is no one else fretting about? You seem to be the only one concerned."

"I know, I know. I have a weird sense about these things. I get clammy and tunnel-visioned before a gas attack. Like I'm about to pass out, but I don't…I haven't been wrong before."

"So, it hasn't actually happened yet?" He's disappointed I don't believe him.

"Look mate, I can find this alarm on my own. My squad believes me – they've seen it with their own eyes."

"I believe you." I've seen crazier things today. Like a massive samurai battle. "How much time do we have?"

"Not sure, it doesn't really work like that. If I had to guess, I'd say a few minutes."

"Ok. Think…why would the gas alarm not be here?" He's the one who's been in this war for longer than a couple hours. I need him to think logically.

"Fuck if I know!" He responds, but he's trying to figure it out. "The only reason is because we don't have enough of 'em. So, the alarm would be where the most recent attack came in…" I see his eyes light up and he starts at a sprint again.

"Mind filling me in?"

"The last gas attack came near the front lines, but on the Western side. We're in the center trenches right now and I'd been checking the Eastern ones." Good enough for me. My awkwardly half-dry, half-wet feet smack loudly against the wooden planks and eventually across dirt and mud where the trench has seen damage. If this guy is right about incoming gas, cold feet are the last of my worries.

I begin to get tunnel-vision too…that weird kind where you're incredibly focused, but you feel light headed. The reflecting light from the gray clouds is more intense than moments ago. Sometime within the last few seconds my body and mind recognized that A) I'm in fucking World War I and B) about to experience mustard gas – a chemical weapon – for the first time.

My unnamed friend (this is becoming a common theme) continues to lead me through a complex weave of trench hallways. Barbed wire, coiled like a cobra, perches high above our heads. It's not able to protect against much in this war, especially gas.

"What's your name?" I yell forward. By now, several other soldiers have seen us running, but ignore us.

"What?" He's surprised, but answers. "Thomas!" He doesn't ask for mine, it's clearly not a priority. We continue running to the Western trenches. A line of soldiers marching in the compact narrows slows us down; I have to turn to scoot past them. One man's gaze locks with mine and I'm startled. I've never seen someone look so hopeless or defeated with just a glance. It's more than a thousand-mile stare, it's the type that says he knows he'll never be the same after this war, and he's already not sure if life is worth living past it. The moment is fleeting and I'm back in pursuit of Thomas. For what feels like the twentieth time, he rounds a corner.

"Here it is! There's two here!" He hands me one. I recognize it as a gas alarm rattle, essentially a large gear that loudly "claps" against a thin wood slat as you crank the weighted arm on its side. I watch as Thomas takes his alarm, holding it by the handle, and twirls it above his head. Clap after clap – almost like gunfire but distinctly different enough to know the difference – echoes from the device. My gut contorts, anticipating the attack once more.

How long has it been? He mentioned a few minutes? That feels like ten minutes ago.

"Oi! Pick yours up and do it! We need all the noise we can get!" I must look bewildered, truth is, I kind of am, but I raise my arm and start twirling the device. It's lighter than expected and there's something satisfying in how old-school it is, sitting perched in my hand only inches from the centuries-from-now-tech of my iNsert.

I hear "Gas!" echoes along the trench. People are taking it seriously and prepping for whatever comes. Almost instantly I hear more commotion and artillery shells firing from a distance.

They aren't ours.

I climb a trench ladder, cautiously easing my head over the rounded top of dirt. Artillery lands many yards away, slamming into the ground, showering their craters with dirt. There's something else, once the dust and earth settles: a green-yellow cloud, like a sinister snake, gripping the ground and slithering toward my trench.

Turning around and climbing down the ladder, Thomas has gone. I have no idea where he went. Near where we found the alarm rattlers, I spot a gas mask. Primitive in design, but as effective as it gets for the time period.

More shells hit in No Man's Land. The gas will be here any moment.

I throw the mask over my head, its breathing tube jiggling

wildly, and clip the respirator box to my pants. I notice the weight of my X-34 as the box hangs on the opposite side. I situate the mask on my head to see out of the narrow, glass-plated eye holes. It is wildly uncomfortable on the bridge of my nose, pinching with great pressure, and breathing through the rubber mouthpiece and tube is challenging.

Those are the least of my concerns right now. I wish there were spare, frozen moments to indulge in the grandeur of it all. I am in World War I! Putting on a gas mask to avoid an attack! Just a few days ago I'd have told anyone that experience would be a trip. Now, I'm gripped with the horror of what it was *actually* like.

With my mask on, I run back a few paces, out from under the dug-in cover of the trench. Through the mask I hear an overpowering screaming sound. Not a human, but instead a massive object rocketing across and falling from the sky.

I turn toward No Man's Land as a shell explodes high in the air, releasing gas and shrapnel angled downward into the trench. Miniscule "*thumps*" echo around me as metal impacts the wet ground. Something knocks my head, but it's small. I've avoided the shrapnel (somehow miraculously), but there's a crack in my mask's eye hole. I poke it softly and the glass breaks, falling into the mask with me.

The gas is here, yellow and menacing. It smells like garlic, but quickly turns to something more potent like horseradish. My mask is compromised and I cover the exposed eye hole with my hand while my eye tingles in the thick vapors.

I begin choking and hyperventilating even with the respirator mouthpiece in. The tingling sensation starts to burn and my eyes water with pain. I'm freaking out…losing my calm. My vision, what little of it remains, fades.

The gas has overwhelmed me. It's on my face, my hands, and somehow in my lungs.

I fall backwards and my socked feet leave the ground, still damp, as I pass out.

Chapter 26 – Aiontis
1917 | Europe

Where am I? Why am I so…comfortable? Restless, I shuffle to move and realize I'm lying down. A thin, comforting blanket keeps me warm, and shifting causes discomfort in certain places, outright pain in others.

"Ughhh." There's a pressure over my eyes and they won't open. Panic sets in. Painfully, I reach to my face.

Cloth bandages are wound snuggly against my eyes and around my head. No words escape, but my internal monologue is on fire.

Fuck, am I blind?
What happened?
The gas! Why did the mask fail?

Not thinking, I attempt to remove the bandages, fingers fumbling like a drunk. A gentle hand stops me, guiding my own back down to my side.

"Please don't do that. It'll only make the healing process take longer." An angelic voice with a soft English accent accompanies the touch. She gives a soft, reassuring squeeze. "Just go back to sleep. You need it. You will be fine, but you were hit with a direct gas attack. You need time to heal."

I blindly nod – probably not even in the right direction – and doze off. For the first time since this whole "adventure" started, I feel safe.

Even if I'm in 1917.

Many hours later, I wake again. My stomach growls, but…how do I call for help? I sit up and raise my hand like a child in school with a question. Eventually, I hear a distant giggle and that gentle hand is back on mine, lowering it to my side.

"Can I help you?" I sense she's smiling, which makes me smile.

"Do you have anything to eat? I'm starving. Also, really thirsty."

"Yes, give me one moment and I'll be back with some biscuits and water."

"Thanks." She returns swiftly to me still sitting upright in bed.

"Here you go." A biscuit is placed into my hands. I take a bite and am delighted by its sweetness. Some crumbs break and fall into my lap; I must look like a clumsy dunce. "When's the last time you've eaten?"

I think on her question for a moment, then I laugh. The last time I ate was as a samurai, shoveling down food and sake before an enormous battle.

"What's so funny?" She's clearly amused.

"Nothing. It's been a while, plus I have no idea how long I've been sleeping."

"It's been a little over two days since the gas attack. You were transported here with some other men."

"And where's 'here'?" She pauses before answering.

"I'm not entirely sure. We're in a temporary triage unit, but far back enough from the front lines to not be worried. This war…" Her tone shifts and there's deep sadness in her voice.

"It's brutal." I know my response isn't comforting, but it's true. Her hand rests on my shoulder and we sit in silence as I munch on the delicious biscuit. "Can I have some water, please?"

Silently, she takes the biscuit and guides my hands around a cup, easing it up to my mouth. Something about the motion causes minor pain. I probably have blisters where the gas contacted my skin. Some have likely popped or broken. Despite that, the water is cooling and I can't get enough. She refills the cup from a nearby pitcher (or at least that's what it sounds like) and hands it to me once more, trusting I can drink on my own this time.

"Ahhhh. Thank you." I'm tired again. "Do you mind if I go back to sleep?"

"Of course." She replies, quieter and more somber than

moments ago. "I'll come check on you later." Footsteps depart my bedside.

"Thank you." I say earnestly in her direction. It's the best I can do right now. Within moments, I'm asleep again.

Chapter 27 – Aiontis
1917 | Europe

I know it's daytime when I wake because there's warm sunlight draping my face and arms. All this sleep has done wonders and I feel the best I have in days.

For several minutes, I sit in the balminess, relaxing. It's hard not to consider my current predicament, but I do my best at this moment. At the very least, I'm not on the frontlines of a battle anymore, and that counts for something.

Eventually she returns.

"Are you ready to have your bandages removed?" Her hand lands on mine again, sending a pleasant shiver down my back. I nod, excited that I get to see this stranger's face.

"I'm curious." I start. "I had a mask on…how come I passed out and couldn't breathe?"

Her arms dance around my head, unwinding the cloth. The comforting grip they held begins to loosen.

"I didn't get a good look at it, but the soldiers who brought you here told me the mask failed."

The pads over my eyes fall off but I keep my eyelids closed, knowing the sunlight will be a shock to my system if I open them right away. She continues to explain.

"A gas artillery shell exploded above you and the shrapnel broke a lens of the mask, and ripped the rubber tube to the respirator box. You might as well not have had it on at all."

"Will I be ok?"

"Yes." I can tell she's smiling again. "It did get into your lungs, but there are no signs of respiratory complications. Other than that, you likely have some painful blisters that will eventually go away."

I wipe off the dried eye fluid and slowly let some light in, sliver by sliver. It's vivid, and after several blinks I can begin to focus. I rub my eyes gently and look around.

That sense of purpose…of being involved with something

grandiose and important, comes rushing back when I see her. Frighteningly so.

What does this mean?

She's the most beautiful woman I've ever seen in my life, radiating completely from her eyes and smile. Both are kind – just like she has been to me – and alluring. There's a power within her, perhaps she does not know of it, but for whatever purpose that I am here, *I* know of it.

Those eyes are miraculous, brown, with flecks of green that almost get lost unless the sun catches them. My stomach screams at me, not hunger, not butterflies, but somehow this woman is important to everything going on.

She smiles and laughs. I'm staring and making her uncomfortable.

"Sorry…I just…"

"It's quite alright." Seeing the words come from her mouth with *that* smile is mesmerizing. *What is going on?*

"Have we…met…before?"

"I don't think so, outside of the last few days." She replies, still smiling. "What's your name?"

"Williams." I remember quickly.

"Just Williams?" Shit. I'm not sure I ever learned what my first name was. I tell the truth.

"Aiontis Williams." Her eyes widen with a face that displays: *Huh!*

"That's certainly a unique name."

"Yeah, well…uh I'm not really from around here." She nods with that same skeptical face and reaches under the bed, placing my X-34 on my lap. Then she rolls up my sleeve and taps the screen of my iNsert.

"I figured as much." A different tone comes over the conversation. I can tell she's more frightened than anything. I don't even know where to begin and remain silent. "No one knows but me; I've been the only one tending to you."

That's reassuring, and I have nothing to say.

"I…" I stop, thinking over my words carefully. The best I come up with is, "You wouldn't believe me if I told you."

Bwah….bwahhhhh…bwaaaaahhhhhhhhh

The sound is so subtle I almost don't hear it, but it immediately drowns out whatever her reply was. My face contorts. I've heard this pattern before…

Bwwwaaaahhhhhhhhh

It was right before I transported here from Japan. The Scarred Man held some sort of device…some portable Warper. Unheard of technology. Was he here now? I throw off my blanket, now stifling, and get out of bed.

"What's going on? What is it?" She asks, worried.

"Do you hear that?"

"Hear what?" She's still sitting while I aimlessly walk around, barefoot. I look right, left, up…nothing to indicate anything out of the ordinary. All of the other patients are lying in their cots, sleeping. She's up and looking panicked.

I'm not sure how much time I have.

BWWWWAAAAHHHHHHHHIII

I rush back to the bed and grab my gun. Forgetting it in this time period could have more consequences than I'd ever know. Or not. I honestly don't even fucking know at this point. *Why is this happening?*

"What is going on? I don't hear anything." Now she seems slightly perturbed, as if I'm making it up. I don't have much time with her and somehow, she's involved in this. I look into those deep, powerful eyes.

"Like I said, you wouldn't believe me if I told you. Thank you for taking care of me. I don't know who you are, but you are important." Her smile is contagious.

"My name is Caroline. Now you know who I am."

BWAAAHHHHHHHHHHHHH….

The sound deafens everything around and I'm not sure how

she *can't* hear it. I secure my gun in its interior holster, but otherwise try to spend as much time as possible staring at her.

I never thought I'd say it, but it's good to have *this* important gut feeling back, whatever it actually means.

And all at once, the embrace of a vacuum and Dark Particles takes me.

Chapter 28 – Titus
1917 | September 10th | Europe

Titus began on solid ground, stance firm, with Zorex pointed at the alleged Regime member (*leader?*) he'd been following through time. A smoke-filled, gory samurai battle raged around them.

At the moment he fired the weapon, the enveloping nuisance of Dark Particles and thunderous noise took him, placing him gently into the stream of nothingness in which he would end up somewhere else. Zorex's projectile had missed its intended target and pierced through the helmet of an unaware soldier. The man died from a technology several thousand years ahead of his own time.

Solid ground is where Titus returned, in the same stance, now outfitted differently with a shift of weight on his back. Slowly, he put Zorex away in its holster, now enraptured by the wonderment of all that was happening.

I'm traveling through time without control.

It was all he could think about as he pieced together his location in time. The excursion to Japan as a samurai hadn't been a fluke. What he'd believed a mistake was now made purposeful, but that *purpose* was terrifyingly elusive.

The intricate, blood-stained armor he'd been in was replaced with an olive-green set of fabric coat, pants, and boots. The sword he had cut down soldier after soldier with was now a rifle slung across his back. A plain bayonet hung from his side.

I must be in one of the World Wars?

Confirming his suspicions, the portable Warper read the date: 09.10.1917. Titus didn't know what exact battle this could be, but the cold, damp air told him it had been raining. He was in a room of sturdy wood walls, lit by candles, and dusty, dry ground. Strangely, he was alone, but this looked to be a strategic map room, with a large table featuring a mock-up of the battlefield. A door swung open, and dusky light filled the room before it could shut, temporarily blinding Titus. Two men entered, speaking German passionately, and walked to the table.

Titus understood them without trouble, but remained still, unsure of what he should do. One man looked over, but continued on with the conversation, ignoring his presence.

"Dammit, Alec! Why are we still toying with them? Day after day we sit here and let our troops do nothing while at night, we chip away at them little by little. This cannot go on for many more months!"

"What would you have me do? My orders are simply to hold the line. We are comfortable here. Our barracks and trenches are much more suitable for long-term living than theirs. They have rats and mud and shit. We have electricity, rooms, and beds."

"We also have rats…"

"Yes, but you get my point. If we don't get them, the weather and sickness will."

"You!" One of the men shouted toward Titus who was already observing them. "Come over here, lad." Titus stepped into the candlelight, revealing the scars on his face. Neither man reacted, likely having seen far worse from this war. The man, who Titus guessed was his superior officer, turned to the map.

"This is us right here. And this…" he waved his hand, "…is No Man's Land. Across this way, on the other side of this small ridge –"

"It is *not* a small ridge." The other one corrected.

"Fine, across this *medium* ridge, lies the enemy. We know their tunnel system and trenches are not as sophisticated as ours. Plus, they get a lot of water runoff from this hill here, creating a muddy mess. Thick enough to suck the boots right off your feet!

"I say we flank them on that very hill, acquiring the upper ground. It would be a surprise attack of course, after we send multiple shells of gas their way."

"And *I* say that we follow orders," The other man chimed in, "by sticking here, and waiting them out. There are other battles in this war than our own. A single broken thread to the master plan could cause the whole thing to unravel."

"What say you?" They both looked at Titus. While they'd

been talking, a moment of angry clarity had struck him. For whatever reason, time had placed him on the German side. A Regime of its own, and a precursor to the Nazi's.

It boiled his blood.

He wanted no part of it.

The confusion of it all required him to play along.

"I would storm that hill. And No Man's Land. If the enemy is as weak as you say they are, then what are we worried about?"

The answer caught them off guard, each visibly furrowing their brow in embarrassment for him. One patted him on the shoulder.

"Well…yes…hmm…probably better you're not in charge of the war strategy then. Why don't you get to your post soldier, I'm sure we've kept you long enough."

Titus dismissed himself through the same door, taking in the dull sunlight trying to press through the clouds. The German trenches, while far nicer than those of the opposing armies, were not the definition of luxury. For several hours, he wandered aimlessly, keeping an eye out for the man from the Regime.

Here and there he questioned his own predicament, but couldn't help but be distracted by the war of an ancient time period. The German men, fighting and dying for their country, were doing so in incredibly violent ways. Not all that different than those of the Regime. Proof of this came from the continued phenomenon of no one reacting to Titus' facial scarring. It was almost guaranteed that at some point in the last week, they'd seen worse:

A friend's head blown in two by a sniper.
Some gnarly loss of limb from grenades.
Particles of a man left by incoming artillery fire.

Titus continued like this for several days. During which, he participated in orders and assisted fellow soldiers to avoid suspicion. On his first day, he'd fired artillery shells filled with toxic gas toward the enemy trenches across the expansive, barren terrain. The next day he'd heard reports their attack had been mildly successful. Other hours consisted of repairing trench walls and keeping tabs on No Man's Land through a periscope.

On his second day he called out the location of a soldier to a fellow sniper camouflaged in a tree. The man went down in a spray of blood from the chest, and lay there writhing. Distantly, Titus could hear his cries, but the sniper left him.

Consequences…it was all he could think about after that. In Japan he'd killed many during the battle, but here, there was something disconnected about the death that made it worse. Would that man have died if he hadn't been here? If he hadn't made the callout to the sniper?

It wasn't long before the questions ran deeper. Sitting back in the same room he'd arrived in; Titus lay with his mind twisting in knots.

Have I done this before?
Would that man get shot in every version of this?
How many times have I been here?
Are there versions of this where I'm not here? And he lived?

Morning arrived on the third day with Titus confused, and taking a break from trying to unlock the time travel fiasco he found himself in. As he walked through the trenches – unceremoniously – the portable Warper began its war cry anew.

The guttural bulges of sound could only be heard by him as he frantically walked through the trenches, looking for the face of the Regime.

He must be close.

The pulses of sound were screaming and the Travel Pulse Sphere swallowed Titus in mid-stride, having not found the man he was looking for, unsure of where he would end up next.

Historian Consultant Report
The Old Kingdom, Egypt
2507 B.C.

Close your eyes and let me pose a question.

What do you see when I say "Ancient Egypt"? Pyramids? Pharaohs? Gods? Lavish Egyptians on the Nile?

Many people would answer the same way, presenting one of the most interesting gaps of historical timelines as understood by the general public. Specifically, The Old Kingdom of Egypt, after 3000 BC, is often lumped into the more famous Egyptian narratives but in actuality, it was far different than what we've come to know. In fact, the pyramids themselves were dated to have been built nearly 1000 years before the term "pharaohs" was used to describe Egyptian leaders.

The Old Kingdom of Egypt lasted 400 years, beginning in about 2600 BC through 2200 BC. Often referred to as "The Age of the Pyramids", many would be surprised to know it was much more primitive than what we generally picture when pondering ancient Egyptian culture. Many men and women would work naked or covered by animal hides or papyrus reeds.

Weapons consisted of flint blades, prone to dulling and breaking easily, and bows and arrows were popular, but inaccurate, also featuring flint heads. Copper weapons were optimal, though rare, and shields were built out of the same material as clothing: animal hides and papyrus reeds.

Instead of pharaohs there were kings, often coupled with their own assistant, a vizier. This government and societal hierarchy consisting of kings, priests, nobles, soldiers, scribes, merchants, slaves, and more would lay the foundation for what would come in later centuries. Even some gods changed from what they once were into what we know today. Isis, for example, evolved from Heret-Kau, a protective goddess of the souls of the dead. Others, like Ra, the god of sun, were significant enough to last across eras.

These were not the lavish times of gold decoration, bold makeup, silky linens, or expensive incense adorning the gods, at least not to the degree we're familiar with. Though that's not to say the Egyptian Kingdom was not prosperous during these times. The pyramids themselves pose perhaps one of the greatest mysteries in human history. We've never quite unraveled how they were built, though there are numerous logical theories. More astounding is how primitive a time they were built during, and the massive workforce and organization that would have been required to achieve such feats across the span of 80ish years.

The Pyramids at Giza, certainly the most awe-inspiring of any ever created, are comprised of over 2 million blocks of stone, some of which weigh as much as 30 tons or 27,000 kilograms. It's believed the workforce was 20,000 men – likely Egyptian agricultural workers – but there's claims that number could have been as high as 100,000 at key points in construction.

Wild conspiracy theories surround the massive, still-standing structures, nearly five millennia old. Are they signs of a lost ancient civilization that was more advanced than we believed? Are they gigantic batteries that regulate the earth's energy? Were aliens once on this planet assisting in their construction? Likely "no" to all of those and more, but the excitement around such iconic structures that have lasted for so long, coupled with the lesser degree of understanding we have from this time, creates some intriguing far-fetched hypotheses.

Either way, the Egyptian history you know and love isn't wrong, but instead skewed against how long of a time their era actually lasted, creating an interesting dichotomy between what we know and what's real.

Chapter 29 - Titus
2527 B.C. | Egypt

If the trenches had been an ashen hue, then wherever he was now was excessively gold. Even with his eyes closed, Titus could feel the warmth of the color.

There was an actual heat too. His body felt more naked than seconds (minutes? hours?) ago as a hot surge of wind swept across his chest. When his eyes opened, they absorbed a wondrous view. He stood in a palace, in its great opening that had ceilings rising far above his head.

Out on the horizon was a town, full of brown and tan structures made of earth, a section of a large river with sections of green along its banks, and, in the distance, some of the most iconic structures from the old world.

The Pyramids.

Or…at least part of them. They were incomplete.

It didn't take a Hiscon to know where he was. This was Ancient Egypt and a new wave of terror emerged. This was further back than anything before. His mind immediately skipped to the technology on him: Zorex and the portable Warper. For the first time he noticed he was wearing a loose cloth around his waist and between his legs. Both items, millennia ahead of their time, lie on the ground, dropped during the shift in time.

Titus gasped and hastily knelt to pick them up, another cascade of hot wind hitting him in the face. Scrambling, he ensured there was no one around and took refuge behind a large stone pillar. There were leather bands around his arm and he removed one of them, securing Zorex to his thigh under the uncomfortable skirt of papyrus reeds. Similarly, he ripped a piece of the papyrus apart, creating a small pocket for the Warper.

Before putting it away, he checked the date.

04.15.(2527).

The number startled him for several reasons. He doubted there were calendar months all the way back in Egypt and the parenthesis around the year cemented his fears that he'd now been pushed (taken?) back to a drastically different period of the world: 2527 B.C.

Titus took a deep breath, searching for calm against the growing list of questions. He was absolutely positive he hadn't touched the Warper in the trenches. Something was doing this to him. Or someone?

Or perhaps the Warper was defective? Had he missed a critical component? He'd been in the World War I era longer than Japan. Did that mean he'd be in Egypt even longer? The thought was troubling.

With the two pieces of technology hidden away, he paused to study himself. In ancient eras there was usually a strict hierarchy…what role did he play?

There were rough sandals on his feet, worn, but sturdy, with golden sand crusted across in patches. Other than those and the fabric around his waist, he was naked. He had no shield, no spear, and the clues stopped there.

But he was in this grand building. It wasn't adorned like the Egypt he knew – there was little gold for example – and was instead built of stone, with statues of gods cut in the same material. Unless he was here illegally, it was a clue; he was part of some higher realm of society.

Carefully, Titus went exploring to find his place.

Chapter 30 – Aiontis
2527 B.C. | Egypt

I am taken aback by the heat. It's stifling, particularly when you're transitioning from…well…*nothing.*

Moments ago, I was frantically saying goodbye to Caroline in a World War I makeshift hospital, then in the void of time with nothing but an image of gold far in front of me. Now, I'm on all fours in the sand, hot, grainy, and blinding. I'm nearly nude while the sun beats on my back. Again, there's a searing fire along my skin and a hyper-fast thunderstorm in my head. I'm becoming more and more confident about my hypothesis; these are Jinx withdrawals.

If you told me what I was about to witness as I leaned up off my hands, I would have told you to fuck off. My split second of wonderment is cut short by the internal scream of fear. Sitting on my heels, pushing downward into the sand, I face the pyramids. They aren't just any pyramids; they are incomplete. Probably by a quarter, but incomplete nonetheless.

If World War I had been "progress" toward *my* time in this hellscape of a situation, Ancient Egypt might as well be the universe telling me to go to hell. As this is the third new time period, my mind goes through the usual litany of questions to try and solve the problem.

Dream?

Jinx?

Fake?

Alternate time?

Multitasking, I observe my environment to build the puzzle as much as I can. I piece together that I'm a worker. I have only sandals and a cloth around my waist, actually somewhat surprising for this time period. I should be naked. My iNsert glows in the bright daylight, so I shift its settings to match my skin tone, which seems to have bronzed? Maybe I'm imagining that. It's clearly not fucking important right now.

Other workers around are busy and moving, readying a gigantic block of stone to be pushed up a series of ramps toward the pyramid's top. My jaw hangs agape because I get to witness this (historians have never been able to *totally* confirm how the pyramids were made!), but also because I'm petrified of being stuck in this vicious loop forever.

I sit in awe of the view – it's one of the most spectacular ones I'll ever lay eyes upon – and assess which pyramid we're constructing. I believe it's the Great Pyramid based on how I'm reading the ramp path in front of me. There are thousands of men working at one time, an invigorating experience to take in. Most will be agricultural workers of Egypt, contrary to the belief that these were built by slaves. Some are doing it for the glory of their past ruler, King Khufu, while others are actually receiving payment.

Surprised that no one has come over and scolded me for kneeling in the sand, I join a group of men ahead, prepping their ropes around a series of poles and around the block itself to pull it forward. Slowly, it moves with each man doing their part to contribute to the group.

I'm unsure of my specific responsibility, so I try to not get in the way. After ten minutes I'm sweating, but I'm not as gassed as I would expect. Similar to the way I was birthed with samurai skills in Japan, I have absorbed this worker's stamina. Yet another new body, though a powerful one, to get used to. After another hour, we're still pushing the same stone, but have made it a long way toward the top of the pyramid, easily more than halfway. By now, I understand we're going to the top and every fear I've had throughout this experiment is secondary to my child-like excitement that I'm getting to help build the pyramids *and* going to the top.

That's a Hiscon's wet dream right there!

We summit the peak and secure the stone in its final spot. Sweat beads like dew on my brow and shines on the back of others, but everyone is in good spirits as they trek down to start another block. The sun rests lower in the sky so I estimate it's mid or late afternoon and this next stone may be our last for the day (unless they work at night by torch and moonlight). I pause and soak it in.

From atop the pyramid – or at least its *current* highest point – I can see for miles. The Nile River and the green earth along its banks are to one side, with never ending sand and desert to another. In the distance rests a small town, Giza and Cairo, much different than the cities I know from my time. In the 2400s, Cairo is a pillar of the Middle East, much as it was throughout history, but even more prominently. Skyscrapers dwarf the pyramids where (sorry, *when*) I'm from and it has become a surprising location for a new tech boom.

I can't explain it, but I'm calm. My pulse and breath feel measured and steady. I'm stuck far, *far* back in time, but finally somewhere relatively peaceful.

I'm not a samurai about to enter a horrendously violent battle.

I'm not in the trenches of World War I scrambling for a gas mask.

I'm a worker on one of the Seven Wonders of the World and I just contributed to what will (would?) be the world's tallest structure for centuries to come. Not even the wild time loops I begin to ponder (example: has this brick…*my* brick…always been placed by me?) can shake me of how fucking awesome this is.

With a broad smile, deserving of the gods of this time, I head down the ramps with my fellow men to continue Day One of my work on the Great Pyramid of Giza.

Chapter 31 – Aiontis
2527 B.C. | Egypt

It's Day 7 of working on the pyramid and I'm slightly less enthusiastic about my position. Don't get me wrong, it's always *incredible* when I get to the top, and we've made a surprising amount of progress in just a week's time, but it's grueling, demanding work. Particularly in the heat. Also, I come from a time where back-breaking work is rare. Relatively speaking, we're a bunch of wimps.

My skin feels like hide and I'm tanner than I've ever been – likely because I have "assumed" (that's what I'm calling whatever it is that's happening) the body of someone Middle Eastern – but my muscles still ache the same from long hours. We get food and water at several points throughout the day, though they're rationed because of the sheer size of the workforce.

The men don't talk much so they can focus on their work, and because you're seeing hundreds of new people a day. The mystery behind how the pyramids were built includes some magnificent planning and engineering, but it also comes down to a simple fact: they threw a shit-ton of bodies at it.

I've learned my first stone on Day 1 was a "lighter" one (fuck me, right?) and we're averaging 2-3 stones a day, depending on their size. These workers are dedicated and most are proud to be here, aware they're part of something grand. I wonder if they have any idea just how long their work will stand the test of time? They probably wouldn't be able to conceptualize it.

There are some *gigantic* men, straight out of myths you hear about, and I've also witnessed some tragic accidents. Just yesterday, distant ropes snapped loudly on a ramp nearby, and the stone slipped backwards. It gathered speed with several men behind it and slammed into a stone being pushed up below it. The men caught between were pulverized and several others were badly injured.

I'm not all that worried with being here, but it creeps up

more and more each day. This has already been a week and not a single odd or questionable thing has happened. I'm enjoying the simplicity and relative calm, but in another week, I'm going to be having a mild panic attack.

It's a week later and I'm pretty much freaking out. Everything is so strangely *normal* and it's driving me insane. My iNsert doesn't indicate anything is wrong with me. Hell, it doesn't even register that something is horribly wrong with *when* I am. Stupid, piece-of-shit technology. I've kept my X-34 hidden well underneath my single garment of animal hide, but the thought has crossed my mind about using it. I don't know any of the rules here…what if I "kill" myself? Would I actually die? Would I wake up? Would I be "reset"? What the hell does being "reset" even mean? I can't answer a single one of these. To make matters worse, I've had those bouts of itching and blinding headaches every few days…making me think I'm craving Jinx again.

The only small blessing at this point is the daily work. I've grown comfortable with it, understanding what the end-to-end process is, and small tips and tricks for securing the ropes, pulling them, pushing the stone, etc. We're getting closer and closer to finishing the top of the pyramid, though I estimate it to be a couple months away given how gargantuan these things are. At least with the work, my mind is focused on a task. I dare say I'm enjoying it – perhaps because it's an effective distraction – but there's something so damn cool about building the pyramids.

I don't think that will ever get old.

I woke in the night and climbed the Great Pyramid, passing the "night crew" without issue. The workforce at night is smaller, but they're pushing smaller blocks of stone or rearranging ones that have already been positioned. I wasn't sure I'd be allowed up there at night, but the foreman…manager…whatever they were called back then (I've yet to completely nail down the work-force hierarchy here) just nodded at me as I pointed to the top inquisitively.

Now that I'm at the peak, the moon hangs gigantic in the sky. So big that I actually question if it is the first "weird" thing since I've been here. It is…unnatural. Underneath its blue glow are undulating waves of calm sand. Reflections from the distant Nile give off strips of white against the dark. I've never seen the stars so crisp and articulate and *vast*.

The reaches of space are infinite! I study the light from a particular cluster of stars. The light they emit is likely from thousands, if not millions of years ago. For all I know, they could be dead by now. This thought shrinks the span of my problem…*What's the difference of several thousand years against billions?*

A terror reaches me that I hadn't considered.

What if I keep going backwards?

How would I survive with dinosaurs?

How would I survive if there was no Earth yet?

My gut…my internal dialogue punctures me with reassurance. I realize it is the first time I've had *that* feeling since being here. I've been distracted by the grandeur of the pyramids and the normalcy of the work.

I'm supposed to be here.

On the horizon, there's a small glow of firelight traveling across the sand. As it gets closer, shapes reveal a small caravan of horses and men. Five in total, and they're traveling fast. We've not had many visitors, so I wonder what could bring a group like this at night. They wear more fabric than most and the small outlines of weapons are visible, probably a combination of officials and soldiers.

Knowing I'm going to be tired for tomorrow's shift, I scramble down the pyramid to a height I can spy from. Eventually, they arrive at the base of the pyramid and I work down a little further, hiding under a section of wood ramp. I can't hear them, but I can see well. I figure it's best to not risk it further. My heart pounds like an excited child, but I don't know why. This could be a mundane visit.

The man in charge of night construction saunters over to greet them, waving a hand, then bowing. *Ok, so a King?* The small party certainly appears official. In the middle is a man who remains on his horse and wears an elaborate fur. It looks like a bear or a lion.

Most of the others dismount to talk with the foreman. It looks cordial enough. I scan each of them. *It can't be.*

My eyes strain and I shift in an effort to get closer. Beneath me, a rock slips and tumbles down the side of the structure. *Aiontis, you fool!*

I drop to the ground on the other side of the ramp and slowly peek through the wood slats.

A man with a deep scar across his face reads the horizon. He's tall and muscular, clearly a soldier with the spear he wields. Unconcerned, he turns back to the conversation they're having, but I know that was *him*. The one from New York City and the Sekigahara battlefield.

Does he still want to kill me?

I peek out and receive my second shock of the night. The individual on the horse dismounts. They confer with the Scarred Man quickly before joining the other conversation. This is clearly someone with status. The King's right hand perhaps? Deep in my memory I know that assistants to the Kings are called viziers, but this person is clearly a female…I rack my knowledge for examples of female viziers. There are only a couple and they certainly weren't during this time of the Pyramids.

This is an anomaly! Did historians have it wrong? It's not entirely impossible, but unlikely. Perhaps she's not the vizier? Maybe I'm misinterpreting? With the turn of her head, all those questions flutter away in an instant.

Her. My whisper lingers, laced with confusion,

"Caroline?"

Chapter 32 – Titus
2527 B.C. | Egypt

The past couple weeks had been a whirlwind for Titus and he'd struggled to pull it off. Upon his abrupt arrival, he pieced together what role he played in the hierarchy.

Within a day, he was assimilating to an unfamiliar routine of being the vizier's bodyguard. Strangely, that was a woman. His knowledge about this era wasn't robust, but a woman being in that particular position felt out of place. Was it *true* history, or some sort of fluke?

Until now, every era he'd been shuttled to was factually correct (to the best of his memory), but something about this felt strange. *Could it be an alternate timeline?* He tried to not think about such things as it caused him great stress. In times of mental panic, he returned to the reminder that he was no longer with the Regime. Regardless, he was *so* far back that wrapping his head around it was sickening. The distance from when he'd started this journey to now was over five millennia and he questioned how such a time as simple as this eventually led to something as painful and apocalyptic as the Regime.

The weeks passed and he grew more comfortable, though the terror of being stuck periodically struck him. He kept busy with the daily responsibilities of following the vizier around. She was a kind woman, one who acknowledged and gave respect to those below her, but she was also one with a streak of ruthlessness. Titus believed he was attracted to her, but didn't dare act on it and risk her discovering that he was not from…around here.

No longer than a week ago, he and several other guards had been in her small, elegant throne room as a farmer came to visit her, seeking help with a matter. She listened intently to his story.

"So you see, my vizier, that I am at a crossroads." The man paused, getting to the crux of his tale, "I can no longer supply my cousin with shares of grain as he struggles to feed his family.

It has gone on for too long and my own family is struggling to eat *and* supply the Kingdom with grain."

The dilemma seemed trivial to Titus, but the fact it had risen to face the vizier indicated this man was likely one of the bigger suppliers of grain.

"What were the original terms you set with your cousin?" she asked coolly.

"I…er…never made any official. He told me he was struggling and just needed enough for his family. So, we split rations. Then the ask became greater."

"I see…" Titus could see her thinking. "And what does your cousin do for work?"

"He is also a grain farmer. It runs in the family. His land has seen a blight in recent seasons."

"And why doesn't he and his family work for you then?"

"I had suggested that, my vizier, but he claims to have become ill in recent months."

"Hmmm. Thank you for telling us this. I need time to think…please return at sundown on the second day."

After the man had left, she looked to her guards,

"Track him. Observe him. And report back to me."

Titus remained by her side, and the other men recounted the next day.

"Your royal vizier, it would appear as if the farmer was not telling his entire truth."

The guard went on to explain how they had overheard a conversation between the farmer and his "sick" cousin. The cousin was aware of the vizier meeting but believed the conversation was around acquiring different land to move away from their barren one. The men had been by the land earlier in the day and neither farm was barren but rather fertile and full of crops. They were trying to swindle the King to get more land. The cousin was unaware of the betrayal of the other, having blamed him in front of the vizier, ultimately trying to cut him out of the deal.

"I suspected there was more to the story." replied the vizier once the soldier's debrief had ended. She was visibly frustrated. "Have them both come here at once." Later that day, both men arrived, the one who'd seen her previously wearing a subtle smirk.

"It has come to my attention…" she began. "That I have been lied to. By two men." Her gaze set on the farmer she'd already seen.

"Both of you seek to deceive me for more land, while hoarding away grains of your own. The other of you came to see me, placing the blame solely on the laziness of the other." Shock plastered the stranger's face as he looked at his cousin who was no longer smiling. "You will both pay a heavy price."

"Your highness, I…" One man began to beg. She spoke over him with ease.

"You have sons, I trust?" Silently they both nodded. "Good. You will need them." She turned to her guards and barked the order, emotionless. "Take their hands."

Both men entered a frenzied state of panic, pleading with their vizier. Within moments, two guards had them pinned on the ground with arms extended. Titus was thankful the guards used a copper axe instead of a flint one; he didn't imagine the latter would have been a clean stroke.

Two screams escaped as four hands separated from their appendages, grotesquely leaping forward. Blood pooled on the floor.

"Leave this place." She stated directly, done with the both of them.

Their stumps trailed blood out into the sand. A female servant entered and immediately began cleaning the floor. The vizier got off her throne, knelt down and placed a hand on her shoulder. She said nothing, but the message was clear. *I'm sorry you have to do this because of me, but thank you.*

She walked with purpose over to Titus.

"I wish to see the pyramids. The King requests an update and I fear I have not seen them in too long." She gazed outward across the horizon toward their hulking mass. "I have been impressed with the progress." Her eyes turned to him, hiding more secrets than he could imagine, but full of playful spirit, despite what had just transpired.

"What say you to a nighttime ride, gentleman?" Her smile was directed to Titus but she turned to face the other guards.

"We can travel by moonlight tonight! It will be an adventure!" They grunted confirmation and it was settled.

Nightfall came, casting a quiet, white ember of light on the peaks of the desert's dunes. Titus was enthralled riding a horse against the Egyptian landscape, carrying a torch and following the stars. His steed seemed to be excited as well, pulsing ever forward underneath his legs, throwing back plumes of dark sand behind in his speed.

The wind was slight; a chill against the sand that still radiated the day's warmth. The men rode with their vizier, some releasing hollers of excitement once they were far enough from the city.

Eventually, they rounded the corner of taller dunes to come under the moonlight shadows of pyramids. Their size from a distance did no justice, and even though Titus had visited them virtually as a young boy, their incomplete, but monumental stature was nothing short of jaw dropping.

Ramps extended far outward from the jagged peaks and wrapped around the cores. As they got closer, he could see smaller blocks being pushed up in the night, slowly but surely. Given the primitive lifestyle he'd experienced in past weeks, the construction of these massive clusters of stones was truly historic. There wasn't much *ever* built in the history of mankind that could say it had lasted as long.

The group of horses slowed, breathing heavily from their sprint across the desert. All but the vizier, wearing a large fur for warmth, dismounted. The evening manager of construction waved and approached, but Titus hung back. The other guards knew the man and they exchanged pleasantries as a sharp gust pushed through the small valley between pyramid and ramp where they resided.

Behind Titus, there was a clambering sound. Something falling from higher up on the pyramid…*what is that? A person?* Holding his torch away so his eyes could adjust more to the night sky, he peered toward a cross section of ramp. A stone tumbled downward. *Strange.*

In the back of his head a small voice urged him to go investigate. *But why?* He didn't have an answer, but there was something unspoken, strangely compelling him. It felt like an equation nearly solved.

By now, the vizier had gotten down from her steed.

"Don't be so uptight." She smiled. "There's nothing there."

Titus returned the smile and turned back to the group. Perhaps she was right. The feeling had fleeted like a grain of sand in the wind. But what a strange grain it had been…

Chapter 33 – Aiontis
2527 B.C. | *Egypt*

After several minutes of conversing, the night foreman takes his guests and their horses on a tour of the pyramids elsewhere. Their torchlight grows smaller against the muted darkness of the sand.

I can barely breathe. There's something wrong about what's going on here. What had been some surprisingly mundane weeks were now completely out the window.

"How is *she* here?" I ask myself aloud. It's one thing for me and the Scarred bastard to be shuttling around time – after all, I suspect he has the device that is pushing us through history – but how is *she* involved? An innocent bystander? My gut again screams at me, telling me that's wrong. *How do I know this?*

My feet and arms subconsciously move underneath me, carefully bringing my torso down the side of the pyramid. In a few hours, the sun will rise and I'll be expected to start pushing and pulling huge ass blocks back up the ramps. I contemplate following them and…saying something? *What would I gain?*

"Fuck!" Should I spy on them?

There aren't many options. They didn't know I was here and seem to be on an innocent visit to their King's big production. The best choice I have is to return home and form a plan.

Walking to my sleeping quarters is both incredibly long and yet over within what feels like seconds. Every thought of Caroline pains my heart and I'm fearful we've somehow involved her in this mess. After a couple, less mysterious weeks – I've been pushing blocks all day for fuck's sake – I'm overwhelmed by it all again. The added element of Caroline, as a vizier of Egypt no less, has thrown me down a multitude of rabbit holes that have no discernable (or pleasant) end.

It's cold in bed, partially because of the desert night, but more because of my spirit. If this was ever fun, it's not anymore. Previously I'd been confident that history hadn't *changed* at all, but now I'm unsure and the consequences are unknown. Concepts of the space time continuum, alternate realities, alternate timelines, and existence-ending-paradoxes creep into my thoughts. A crack of light indicates the sun is cresting and soon yellow warmth fills the place where I've gotten exactly zero sleep.

I can only muster a sigh and prep for a day of arduous work. I have no plan. I have no idea what's going on. And I have a sneaking suspicion that time is fucked.

Chapter 34 – Aiontis
2527 B.C. | Egypt

Through the exhaustion and heat, the only thing on my mind that next day was: *Will she remember me?* On a different note…is it even called "remembering" if it's technically *before* she even met me?

To make an awful day's story shorter, it was a useless working session. I was unfocused, tired, and distracted, and my body desperately needed sleep to reset and make a plan. To my own surprise, I slept wonderfully that evening, rejuvenated when I woke. Still confused as shit, but at least I could do some basic problem solving.

Throughout the next day of pushing stone and pulling rope I was determining ways to request an audience with her. It was the only logical thing to do. Perhaps she'd even have answers for me? Something told me she would, but I worried about the Scarred Man. Any audience with her would likely include him. *How had he followed me here? Had he* sent *us here?*

My fellow workers were surprised (and annoyed) when I began chatting them up. I mentioned the vizier and inquired about an audience, but they either shook their head or gave a fearful look and stopped talking.

I'd almost given up asking when a man I'd not seen before came and saddled next to me behind a large stone we were pushing. His skin was leathery and darkened and he was bald, with intense eyes. When he spoke, his voice was like gravel.

"I hear you're looking for an audience with the vizier." His eyes pierced through mine. I grunted against the stone before replying.

"I am. So far, I'm not having much luck."

"PUSH!!! And HOLD!!" Our group's SME (Stone Moving Expert is what I call them) shouted. The men further up the ramp needed time to rearrange the ropes around different pillars. I heaved a laborious push and set my feet.

"What can you tell me about it?"

"Why do you want to meet her?" He inquired.

"Does it matter?" I wasn't about to tell him my story.

"No. No, I suppose it doesn't. She's a very busy lady you know."

"I can only imagine. All I need is 15 minutes. Can you make it happen?" I was growing frustrated in the arid heat. He seemed to be playing games. He let out a hearty laugh.

"MOVING!! ROPES, PULL!!" The stone began up the ramp slowly and we pushed it with less effort this time.

"I cannot get you an audience with her! Who do you think I am?" I stayed silent, displaying my shortening attention span. "She's a very busy woman and won't meet with just anyone. *But*…she does oversee the judgment of most…*significant* crimes."

"Significant crimes?" I didn't like where this was going.

"Sure. If you want a definitive way to get an audience with her, you must earn it." He smiled. "Steal something. Burn something. *Kill* somebody."

"PUSHH!!" I gave a tired, hollow shove.

I could keep explaining how the man overstayed his welcome and wanted to help plan my audience with the vizier. I'm convinced he wanted me to kill someone for him, but I was more focused on *my* plan.

As frightening as his suggestion was, he was right. The easiest and quickest way to see her was committing a crime. I'd have to worry about the consequences later. If she recognized me, perhaps there would be none?

After a few days, I finally had a plan. Killing someone random was out of the question due to both ethical and timeline rationale, so I settled for stealing a local farmer's crops. All of them.

At the expense of my own sleep, I sneak out nightly and traverse to the farm located between the pyramid sleeping quarters and the Nile. Cloth bag in hand, I pick grain stalk after grain stalk by the moonlight. I have no idea who this farmer is, and I don't want to ruin his life. At the end of each night, I take my bag and bury it in the sand, hopefully preserving the crops for later. In a way, I'm doing his work for him (or at least that's what I'm telling myself).

Tonight, is my sixth time in this cycle and I've gotten into a rhythm. In a week's time the "damage" will be significant enough that I can turn myself in to the vizier. As I move through the crops, I'm not as tired as I anticipated. There's a surging energy in the cooler moonlight. Perhaps it's confidence in my plan – or the fact that I actually *have* a plan now – but I'm eager for answers. I need Ancient Egypt to just be a stop on my way back home, not my new home.

"Halt!" My bag of grains drops to the hard ground with a thud. I turn to a blazing torch piercing against the black night. It illuminates two men, one of whom has no hands. The other, younger, holds a heavy stone in one of his.

I believe he intends to use it.

Chapter 35 – Aiontis
2527 B.C. | Egypt

Flames lick the underbelly of the night sky, pulling upward from the torch and shifting shadows across the ground.

Carefully, the young man hands the torch off, the older wedging it upright against his ribs. He approaches, hand still clutching the stone.

"What are you doing in our field?" He begins. Before I can answer, the next question comes, his voice cracking, "Why are you stealing our crops?"

"I mean you no harm, let me explain." I raise my hands with a shrug: the universal sign of *I'm unarmed, please don't kill me.* "I've stolen nothing from you."

"Liar!" His voice cracks again. He's nervous and young.

"Son. Let him speak." There's a weariness in the handless, older man's voice. His son's gaze shifts back from his father, boring holes through me. I nod subtly toward the father and continue.

"All your crops are buried and safe. My purpose, while misguided, is not to harm your family or your business, but to seek an audience with the vizier." At this mention, the father shakes his head but remains silent. The son's footsteps toward me have stopped…for now.

"I cannot explain it, and you probably wouldn't believe me if I did, but I must meet with her as quickly as possible. Aside from breaking into her chambers or murdering someone, *this* was the best I could come up with. And it doesn't result in me dying." *I hope.* A whisper of wind blows sand into my eyes, stinging them. I rub them clear while the other two hold their arms to block the particles. Yet another subtle sign I am not from around here.

"I wouldn't be so quick to meet that woman." There's anger in his voice as he lifts his stubs. "She's vicious. Gods only know what she'll do to you for this."

"She took your hands?" I sense myself nervously gulping like a cartoon. "Why?"

"It's a long story and you're still in our field, grains in hand."

A silence emerges between the three of us, threatening to either end in some sort of peaceful resolution, or a violent burst. The son readies his stance. My pulse quickens.

Finally, the older man speaks.

"Take us to where you're storing our yields. If what you say is true, then you've done our work for us and I see no issue. If you're lying, my son will kill you."

I breathe a sigh of relief. "Follow me."

My stash isn't far and within ten minutes we arrive at my marker of stones in the shape of a triangle. I dig by torch and starlight for another ten minutes and retrieve several bags. The older man's eyes widen.

"By the gods! You're more efficient than my son!" He looks into one of my earlier yields. "Smart you buried them, but another week and some of these would have started to spoil."

Another silence permeates among us. The son has been cautiously quiet, but his death grip on the stone remains intact.

"What do you think, son? What should we do with this man? What's fair?"

"I think we should beat him and take our grain back."

Fucking really? I keep my mouth shut.

"Yes…yes. You would say that. That's because you're young and stupid." He pauses solemnly, staring at his stubs. Looking closer, I see they're still healing. Whatever happened to them was recent. "I was stupid once too. Very recently actually. And I paid a great price for it. I cannot claim to be any wiser, but I believe my vision to be clearer." He looks at me and measures me up. His curious stare reveals he knows I'm strange, but the confusion on his face says he doesn't know how.

"This man has done us a great service. We shall reward him by granting his wish to seek an audience with the vizier. Come, grab these sacks with him and take them back to our field. In the morning, I shall report the theft and he can explain the rest to her."

The son's face reveals an odd mixture of dismay and relief. The stone drops with a thud onto the sand, creating a small crater. Better sand than my head. He and I pick up several bags each and begin the trek back.

"Thank you." I say to the older man.

"Don't thank me yet. Pray to the gods the vizier has more mercy on you than she did on me."

Chapter 36 – Aiontis
2527 B.C. | Egypt

I miss the next day's work shift. Consequences of that decision are unknown, but it doesn't matter right now. The father, son, and I travel into the town and approach the king's palace. It's a coffee-colored, grand structure adorned with a long staircase to a vast opening.

It feels even hotter today…or perhaps those are my nerves. Beside me, the older man is nervous too. The last time he was here, the vizier changed his life and it doesn't escape me that he's making a great sacrifice by coming here. I hope it does not result in more punishment.

To build upon our story, he has tied my hands together with rope. It's for show more than anything, though I could tell the son wanted the bind to be tight. He still doesn't trust me…I suppose I can't blame him.

We approach guards at the top of the stairs and the father reports the crime. Several minutes later, a scribe, who looks strangely like a weasel, greets us.

"You have a crime to report, I hear? Speak then."

"This man," the father gestures toward me as I keep my head down. "We caught him stealing our crops in the night. He'd been doing it several nights in a row before we confronted him."

The scribe eyes the stubs where his hands used to be.

"I have brought along my son as further evidence. He was with me the entire time and I understand the trust the vizier has in me has been…*compromised.*"

"Is this true, boy? Or is your father about to lose his head this time?" A gross smirk unveils on the scribe's face. A man with false power who perceives it to be real.

"What my father says is true. We confronted this man last night and caught him in the act."

Just as we rehearsed. Good.

"So be it. The vizier will see you when the sun is highest."

With that, he scampers off.

I'm no expert in telling time with the sun, but I know it is mid or late morning, so we'll be waiting for an hour. We find a shady spot on the steps, where others also wait, and sit. People stare, likely because I'm the most well-behaved captive they'll ever see. Internally, I'm beginning to grasp this moment.

Will she recognize me?

Do I explain that I'm from the future?

What if the Scarred Man is there?

Am I walking into a situation I didn't fully think through? (this one is rhetorical and the answer is, yes…yes, I am).

The single solace I have is the unknown, driving feeling I've had so many times throughout this journey. A gut reaction, but something so much more decisive than that. However, given my current circumstances, I question if it's trustworthy anymore.

Time passes quickly. Lost in my thoughts, I hardly hear the weasel-scribe's command,

"She will see you now. Follow me."

The three of us trail through a short series of hallways further back into the palace. We arrive into a larger space, where the in-progress pyramids are dramatically and reverently in view of a throne that sits alone in the middle of the room. The pyramids are small from here, but no less impressive. Their scale against the horizon tells you all you need to know.

We circle the space, approaching from the front. She sits, adorned in a dress that fits her form. It's a rare fashion for this period as most citizens don't wear fabric, but rather papyrus-based clothing or leather.

My breath hitches as I see her up close for the first time. It's Caroline, but a much *different* one than I met as a nurse in World War I. This Caroline has a fire behind her eyes and power the other did not. Where I saw kindness before, I now see responsibility.

Her gaze tracks the scribe and the handless man behind him. They narrow.

"Back again so soon?" She speaks to him. He doesn't answer. "For your sake, I hope this time isn't a lie."

The scribe begins to speak.

"Your grand vizier, this man and his son claim to have caught the criminal stealing their crops at night. They believe he has been doing it for several nights in a row."

"Is this true?" She asks.

"It is, my vizier." Says the father, with a shake in his voice.

"I was asking the criminal." Her tone is harsh. "You've proven not to be trusted."

I look into her eyes. For the briefest of moments, I think I sense a connection, but it is fleeting.

"It's true." I answer. "I did it so that I may have an audience with you; I could think of no other logical way. This man and his son have been honest and have done nothing wrong."

She is disoriented by my answer and stares…with anger or confusion I can't quite tell. Her gaze still rests on me when she replies.

"Very well. They may leave. You have my attention." The father and son leave quickly and unceremoniously, their footsteps disappearing as they leave the room. I wait a little too long in the silence before speaking, unsure of what to say.

"Well? We know you're not mute. Why must you steal crops to meet with me?"

"I'm struggling to know where to start…I'm not sure you'll believe me."

"Let me be the judge of that." Her patience is wearing thin.

"Ok…" I take a breath. "You and I have met before. In the future." Despite my pause, there's no reaction from her. "I was injured in a great war many, *many* centuries from now and you took care of me. Your name was Caroline."

"That's an odd name…"

"It suits you there." I reassure her. "However, I'm not from that time either. I'm from even further in the future, at least five thousand years from now if my calculations are correct." I pause once more to see if she has any questions or reactions. Her face remains stoic, but her eyes indicate that her brain is moving at hyper speed.

"I'm not sure why, or really even *how*, but I've been jettisoned through time for the past several weeks. This time period is the furthest back I've been by a considerable amount. It's also the longest I've been stuck.

"I'm a lost traveler, my vizier. A *time* traveler, but lost nonetheless. My only guiding light is the notion that somehow, I must speak with you."

I feel those were the right words to say, but I understand how crazy I would sound in *any* time period, nonetheless an ancient one.

There's an uncomfortable silence, and I hold my gaze on her. Sweat builds upon my brow and under my arms. Her piercing brown eyes reflect the flecks of green I saw in Caroline's, studying me for recognition. My intuition screams that there's something there…some sort of unbreakable bond.

"I do not know you, traveler. I am sure of it." Her gaze remains on me as she takes a deep breath. "Though for some reason, I feel a connection to you."

I hold back a smile, shocked this plan is working. It's the only one I have. She continues.

"But it's one which I fear. Your story is either foolishness or from a cursed god. And this connection is some sort of curse as well. Guards!"

From an adjacent room and behind the massive pillars to her side, several men emerge with spears and armor of animal hides. I scan them quickly, panicking that I've made a mistake, and spot the Scarred Man, appearing the same as he did in Japan, save for the clothing.

Our eyes meet and his fill with flame. For a brief second, he motions toward me, but remembers his place. He cannot break his cover.

"My vizier," I begin my best plea, "I know you feel it too. I cannot explain it – what's happening to us – but I know I was supposed to come here and talk to you. My only request is that you sit down and speak with me." It's a last-ditch effort.

"I cannot. This dark spirit surrounding you is only conquerable by death and burying you very deep in the desert."

She turns to the Scarred Man.

"Kill him."

Like a hulking mountain, mottled flesh in a thin strip down his face, he approaches, turning the spear in his hand. I freeze, unsure of what to do next. Maybe death is the answer, but I'm still naturally afraid of it. What I'm certain of is that he wants to kill me and – however he plays into this equation – he believes it's the thing he must do right now.

My intuition is gone as I look to Caroline, the vizier. There's no sympathy, but there's something in her eyes.

The spear raises as he approaches. With a gnarl of a toothy smile, he thrusts it forward.

I feel the copper tip pierce my chest and enter.

Then the world goes blank.

Chapter 37 – Titus

2527 B.C. | Egypt

When Titus rounded the corner and saw the man, here in Egypt with him, it was all he could do to not lunge for him. Intuition prickled the back of his neck, battling the instinct to kill a suspected Regime member. He awaited his vizier's orders.

"Kill him." She ordered. *With pleasure.*

Their gaze was locked as he approached, the man's face betraying his panic and desperation. Briefly a thought raced across his mind, wondering if he killed this man if it would end everything.

Would he be sent back to his time period?

Would he be able to choose one of his own liking?

Would he be shuttled elsewhere?

Before any answers came, the spear leapt forward, his hand firm and solid against its shaft. His own eyes saw the spear begin to pierce the man's chest. There was subtle yet definitive feedback from the blade making contact against a surface.

In less than an instant, the spear disappeared along with the vibration of impact. In fact, most all *feeling* was gone.

There was nothing to hear.

Nothing to see.

Nothing to smell.

No taste.

No touch.

He wondered if he was dead…brain function was the only thing left available to him. In many ways, it felt like his brain was on fire, buzzing differently than he'd ever felt, firing more synapses than he could conceive. Failing, he tried to let out a shout.

This was the void. He was in some nebulous ether, floating or drifting or just *being.*

Confusion set in. He'd not heard the miniature Warper prepare a Pulse Sphere. This was different from the black chasms he'd been using when shuttling from one time to the next. Those at least had some sense of *physicality*. This was true, frightening, nothingness.

This must be death. I'm certain of it.

But then how had he died?

Titus didn't know how long he remained in limbo. It hadn't felt like any determinate amount of "short" or "long" …it just *was*. Eventually though, a sensation outside of brain function began to form. There were two other people? Beings? And a conversation.

It played half like a memory and half like a dream in his mind, coming all at once, the contents of which shifted his mission entirely.

Chapter 38 – Aiontis
~ ~ ~

I know I felt that fucking spear tip enter my chest, right above my heart. It was a searing, jolting pain.

And just like that, it was gone.

And when I say *gone*, I mean that it didn't just stop and I was left with an ache or a lingering sensation. I mean that it ceased to exist.

All my senses have. I can't feel a damn thing, but I can think like I've never been able to before. Trust me when I say that I'm doing my best to describe all of this, but it's ambiguous…near impossible. Knowingly perhaps (or just a lucky guess), I've entered a higher realm of thinking.

My mind can perform multiple trains of thought at one time. It's on overload; equal parts enthralling and terrifying. Quickly, the questions pile up.

I have no idea why I'm here, how I got here, or, more importantly, where "here" is. My best assumption is that I'm dead and it's definitely an educated guess given that I just felt and saw an ancient Egyptian spear enter my fucking chest.

Is this what death is? Nothingness and a super-brain?

I heard no indication of a potential shift through time from whatever device the Scarred Man was carrying. The deep, guttural bass that had been present before didn't happen this time. Not to mention that whatever situation I'm in right now is far different than traveling through time. This is hollower. Deeper.

I settle on the fact that I died, and this is what happens when you die.

That is, until "it" all comes to me.

When I say "it", this is precisely where it gets tricky to explain what happened (or is happening?) but the revelations are startling. I sense two other entities around me. All at once we begin to have a conversation and it is over, as if I was given an entire memory all at once.

As if time does not matter.

"Who's there?" I begin, *feeling* something out there; the only sensation I have.

"Huh? Who said that?" It's a rough, hoarse voice without a body.

"I asked you first." Silence lingers for a while.

"My name is Titus."

"Who are you, Titus?" I struggle to phrase the question better and there's another quiet as he determines his answer.

"What do you mean?" A pause, as if he's determining whether the next bit of information is relevant. "I am from the year 2477."

I'm not sure why the next question feels appropriate, but I ask it anyway.

"Do you have a scar along your face?"

"Yes." There's a tinge of shame in his answer. I'd say a chill goes down my spine, but I can't feel my spine right now. Now I know who I'm trapped here with.

"Who are you?"

"My name is Aiontis Breaker. From the year 2404." Somehow that answer is all he needs to know.

"It's you. I just killed you… in Egypt." He becomes angry. "Then how am I here? What tricks are you using? What tools does the Regime have?"

"The Regime?" For some reason that phrase sounds faintly familiar, but I'm certain I've never heard it before.

"DON'T PLAY COY, YOU COWARD!" The scream echoes as if we're in a chamber. It's unsettling.

"Aiontis. Titus. Please calm yourselves and pay attention. We haven't much time." The disconnected voice is one I've never heard before, tranquil and commanding. Almost not human.

"The fuck?"

"Who's there? Another Regime member?"

"My name is Odyssian and you are in *between* time, in the Bulk. It is a realm you do not understand, but where my kind lives. I am an evolved being, several epochs in the future."

Somehow, my brain is actually comprehending this, even if only minimally. As if he knows my question, he continues.

"You are both experiencing what it is like to have evolved brain activity and power, equivalent to that of newborns of my species. While exciting, I'm sure, I cannot keep you here long or else it will do permanent damage. And…other reasons."

"We're in the fourth dimension?" I ask, suspecting.

"Yes, that is correct. If you are a dot on a canvas, think of me as a line. If you are a line, think of me as a cube looking down on you."

"So, the Regime has determined how to manipulate time *and* dimensions?" The Scarred Man's (now Titus), question still shows anger, but curiosity too.

"For an advanced AI, you're certainly not keeping up like I expected." Odyssian retorts. "Neither of us have anything to do with the Regime."

"Excuse me, an advanced what?"

"An android, Titus. A very sophisticated one at that."

"I'm certainly not." A lingering, awkward pause. "I've experienced pain, joy, anger, ecstasy…I know I have. I would know if I was a machine."

"As I stated. A *very* advanced AI. That's precisely the answer you'd give if you were human, isn't it?"

A new uncomfortable silence falls over our unique, strange group.

"I'm from a future…" Titus stops himself. "A *time* where the Regime is all powerful. They've laid waste to the world. I'm here to kill that man. I know that to be true, but I don't know *why* or *how* it became my mission."

"Your memory of him is lost because you are damaged. The Regime permanently altered your ability to store memory, which affected your system's capability to hold on to pieces of it from your life before them. Your…mission…was coded into you."

I think back to the implant I painfully removed in an abandoned building. It was the only reason why I kept my memories…but only from Omaha. I still have that significant gap about how this all started. And the Jinx…

Odyssian continued, "And that man you've been chasing has no relation to the Regime. At least not in the way you think he does. He's a significantly strong memory for you – one that seems to have made it across the chasm of time travel – because he's your master."

"My WHAT?!"

I have a similar reaction, but I respond with silence.

"Your master. Later in Aiontis' life and earlier in yours, he purchases you as his personal android. All androids have biometric sensors linked to their owners. These are nearly impossible to override and likely why you were *recognizing* Aiontis in different time periods."

"Why would I do that?" I ask, unaware that I would even have that strong of an interest in owning a near-humanoid.

"For protection, mostly. Though you two form a strong bond."

It's as if his words unlock a floodgate of memories I've not found yet, and I experience them all at once. Titus and I conversing together, laughing, traveling, even eating together…these are all things we'll do in the future. If we ever get back there.

"I remember now. How can I remember things that haven't happened yet?"

"They *have* happened, Aiontis. Just not in the flow you normally experience. Here, time is not only a straight line."

"Why do my memories of him seem broken? As if there's interference." Titus asks, now having a similar breakthrough. There's a shake in his voice.

"I've tried granting you the same access to these moments, but – as I feared – you've been damaged. That scar you carry…it's more than just physical. I believe the Regime damaged your internal systems."

"When they were trying to get information on you…?" Titus seems to remember how he got the injury now, the revelation coming toward me.

"But why would they want information on me? Who is the Regime?" I ask.

"We'll have time for that later. Right now, there are more pressing concerns and we've already wasted enough pleasantries."

"I thought you said time moves differently here? How are we wasting it?" I challenge.

"Yes, well…" the mysterious Odyssian pauses. "One can still find a need for haste if the stakes are high enough."

Ignoring the need to move forward, Titus keeps asking questions.

"It was Aiontis that came to me…before I jumped back. It was a strange vision…you said 'You have to end it, to prevent it'. Then I received the idea for the portable Warper in a dream. And the mission to kill him."

"Yes," Odyssian took over. "That brings me to my main point. Aiontis did visit you, but he was not the one who transmitted you the idea of the portable Warper and certainly not the one who wanted you to kill him."

"Then who did?" I ask the question for the both of us. I also don't remember ever visiting Titus, the Scarred Man.

"His name is Ryveliant." The name carries a heavy weight, and a hint of intimidation. "You two are caught in the middle of a war."

"Why would Ryveliant send him the idea of a portable Warper?"

"Because it's the first step toward the creation of the Regime."

"How could it be if I created it in 2477? The Regime has already been around for several years." Titus asks the question that's on my mind as well. Even with the extra brain functionality, I'm beginning to lose track.

"As I stated, time does not *only* flow in a single direction."

"And why are we being shuttled throughout time? Japan, World War I, Egypt…what do they have in common?"

"I am shuttling you through time. Ryveliant is hunting you. Those moments share no commonalities other than they are key moments in human history and thus, are easier to attach and subsequently travel to."

So that's why the portable Warper has been going off on its own. This is bigger than I ever could have imagined, but my questions continue to mount. Before I have a chance to ask any of them, Odyssian speaks.

"You must go!" There's a swiftness to his voice. Fear too. "We will speak again. Work together and stay alive! I will do what

I can in this realm."

There's panic there now.

In a moment, I feel dreadfully human again, with my feet firmly on concrete and the Golden Gate Bridge in my sights.

Historian Consultant Report
The Great Faultline Disaster, San Francisco
May 15th, 2098

The general consensus immediately following The Great Faultline Disaster (aka the GFD, or "The Big One") was:

"Our models were wrong."

A sobering and disappointing statement, sure, but it was also – most importantly – based in truth and shouted to the human race that, as much as they thought *they knew Mother Earth, the margin for error could be substantial.*

The resulting series of earthquakes was a prolonged barrage of intense shaking all along the state of California. Often grouped as the San Andreas Fault Zone (SAFZ), it was this complex series of faults (that include more than just the San Andreas fault) which caused high-intensity shaking from San Diego up to San Francisco – 500 miles away.

It began with the Southern San Andreas Faultline suffering its long overdue "big" slip. The magnitude of this earthquake was a 9.1, the second largest earthquake in American history and the largest in Californian history. Uniquely, the intensity of this earthquake wasn't higher than a VI (strong shaking, moderate damage) in the densely populated Los Angeles and San Diego area. Intensity is a separate value than magnitude measured from I to X+ using the Modified Mercalli Intensity Scale. The reason for moderate damage with a quake so big was twofold:

1) It originated over 100 miles inland from Los Angeles
2) It was a deep quake registered to be 25-30 miles beneath the surface

It still did plenty of damage to Southern California, causing billions in physical and lasting economic damage while killing over 800 people and injuring 4,000 more. But it was the unforeseen "resetting" of other fault lines along the coast that dwarfed those tolls.

The most recent model at the time, the Uniform California Earthquake Rupture Forecast #9 (or UCERF9 for short) had placed a 14% likelihood on an earthquake of 8.0 magnitude or greater striking the Southern California region in the next 30 years (the report was published in 2091). That was double the 7% likelihood that UCERF3 in 2014 had stated, but still a low value regardless.

In San Francisco, it had the likelihood of a similar event at just 10%. What the report had failed to consider was how much the minor fault lines (e.g. Hayward, Calaveras) are interconnected with the more prominent ones (e.g. San Andreas). Explained simply, their projections failed to take into account what would happen to the other probabilities if a large-magnitude quake happened. The "ripple effect", if you will.

The answer, as it turned out, was that the likelihood of similar events on other faults tripled, quadrupled, and quintupled in mere hours after the 9.1 Southern San Andreas quake.

The result was a series of quakes all occurring on Thursday, May 15th 2098, that rattled and decimated most of the Californian coast. In particular, the Hayward Fault, which runs directly under the San Francisco Bay, had decades of built-up tension released – violently – due to the ripple from the Southern San Andreas. The Greater San Francisco area that encompasses San Francisco, Southern San Francisco, Oakland and more neighboring areas, was home to over 17 million people in 2098. The quake from the Hayward rupture was a smaller 8.5 magnitude, but closer to the bulk of the population and only 6 miles underneath the surface. It registered a IX on the Intensity Scale which classifies itself as violent shaking and heavy damage. Many older buildings and historic districts were leveled. The Golden Gate Bridge all but collapsed, hanging desperately by its cables.

Once it was all said and done, over 4,200 people lost their lives, with 3.4 million injured in some way. Millions were displaced and there was over a trillion dollars of lasting *economic damage. It was the worst natural disaster in American history.*

Because of The Great Faultline Disaster, the San Francisco region was never the same again.

Chapter 39 – Titus
2098 | San Francisco

S alt circulated through the air, invisible flakes touching everything in sight. On the concrete beneath, with water pooled in no particular pattern and drying around the edges, the sun reflected into Titus' eyes. Coming from pure nothingness – *the "Bulk" he had called it?* – it was blinding and he had to shield his eyes and readjust.

Rubbing his eyes and looking elsewhere, they opened to find the glassy water of a bay. The ocean. Dark blue, massive, with moving white edges as waves transferred their energy. Land was in the distance, green and fertile, sprinkled with the browns and grays of buildings and glass. Above him, navy shifted to the fervent turquoise of a cloudless day.

On his left was an archaic representation of the America he'd only heard about in history books: The Golden Gate Bridge. In 2477 it was occupied by the Regime and weathered…dilapidated. Here, it was magnificent and proud. An enduring red-orange against the gang of blue. It wanted to steal his attention, but failed. Titus' mind was elsewhere.

I am an AI. I am an AI? He was unable to determine if it was a question or statement. All of the freedom…the extra computing power…he'd had in the Bulk was now gone. His standard, apparently artificial, brain function felt limiting, like a boring baseline.

The revelations from the conversation were there, grouped in a bunch, and he could hardly choose which to focus on.

I may be an android.
Highly advanced beings are controlling all of this.
We're caught in a war.
I was in the 4th dimension.
The man I've been hunting is actually my master.
We were once friends.

Challenging the notion that he was simply an advanced machine, the game-changing nature from this collection of thoughts was enough to make him cry. But he did not. Instead, Titus stood, taking in the manmade wonder before him. Seeing *past* it, lost in circling thoughts while the warmth and beauty of the day went unnoticed.

"Are you Titus?" a voice eventually asked. A middle-aged African American man, with graying stubble, entered his field of view. The voice was one he recognized, but the appearance was not. Though his biometric sensor (apparently) told him all he needed to know.

"Aiontis?"

"Yes. I'm the man you were hunting." He shrugged and looked down his body. "This isn't what I normally look like, but I also don't really know how this all works." Titus stared at him, unsure of what to say. "You…you look the same as I remember though. Or as I *will* remember you? This whole thing is fucking confusing."

Titus returned his gaze to the bridge. It was a comforting sight, and this man's confusion wasn't his responsibility. Even with a flood of memories together, he didn't know what to trust now. Aiontis – this strange person he knew a lot about instantaneously – let him have his silence.

Chapter 40 – Aiontis
2098 | San Francisco

I have another headache that screams for an instant and vanishes. The itchiness is less severe this time. Is that the return to normal, dreadfully dull brain function, or still the Jinx? My vision of the stupendous Golden Gate Bridge blurs and settles. It's a towering mass against a bright sky and the metal gently bounces light off in a hodgepodge of directions.

Cresting waves and a whistling breeze play in my eardrums. I'm excited to once again *hear* things, as opposed to experiencing a conversation all at once in that place…the Bulk. *How long was I in there?* I wonder, as if it matters. I suspect the answer is probably something unbelievable like "zero seconds" or "infinite minutes".

I'm in the middle of some wharf. It's damp and the areas where seawater pools color the concrete darker. I turn my hand a few times. I'm black. I've been mostly unable to see myself in past eras, so this is my first *official* confirmation that I'm indeed changing "persons" (as I already believed) each instance I get pushed through time…by Odyssian, I should add.

In front of me, stands a tall man, still as a statue and gazing at the Bridge. There are muscles etched under his clothes and a slight trace of the edges of a scar along the sides of his scalp. I know already that he's Titus and emotions nearly overcome me.

My friend.

My companion.

All these memories Odyssian gifted me that I haven't had yet, but I know are real…I long to have a reunion with this…android, but very real member of my life. Though, I try to imagine what he's feeling right now. We were both given a lot to unpack, a staggering amount of information that changes our narrative. But Titus…he learned he isn't real, or at least not *organically* real, and I can't pretend to even begin to know what that's like. I fight the urge to rush and greet him, instead spending time thinking through what to do next. Or if there's anything we *can* do.

One key explanation was provided: the *why* behind all of this. Those sensations that have been peppering my gut in each era must be side effects of quasi-control by a being of the fourth dimension. And we're being pushed through time to avoid…what was his name…Ryveliant? An image conjures of some massive being, furious in persona, hulking and brooding in a dark room. It's a laughable assumption given I have no idea what a 4th-dimension being looks like.

I also know *how* – to a certain extent – that the portable Warper (not to mention, the mission to kill me) was an idea given to Titus by Ryveliant and somehow is related to this fearsome Regime of which I have little knowledge. Though it seems they've done a number on Titus…and had he mentioned that *I* visited him to tell him about something? I begin to lose the threads of the timeline and wonder *when* I'll do that (or if I've already done it?).

One key question remains however (okay, let's be real…I still have like 20 fucking questions, but this is a big one): *why us?* If we're caught in the middle of this timeless conflict between beings that are millennia away, then why Titus and I? In that vein, I've never felt smaller in my life and yet we're key players to the outcome?

Or maybe we're not, I hypothesize. If these beings are as advanced as they say, perhaps there are hundreds…thousands…millions of 3rd-dimension beings being shuttled back and forth through time? Pawns on a 4-dimensional chess board. I wish we had gotten more time with Odyssian because my head spins at many of the concepts he introduced as if they were grade school mathematics.

Thinking about it too long is making me angry. *Why the fuck would he have pulled us into the Bulk if there wasn't enough time to explain everything?* In the back of my mind, this seems misplaced, but given my nauseating level of confusion right now, I'm going to let myself have this one.

Titus hasn't moved an inch; in this way he really *does* seem like an android. Twenty minutes have passed and it's time to put things in motion. What exactly those "things" are, I'm not sure, but at the very least we need to figure out why we're here. My eyelid iNsert is still displaying XX-XX-XXXX like a cruel, very unfunny joke. I approach, unsure of how he'll react,

"Are you Titus?"

Our initial pleasantries are awkward and he seems more interested in the Bridge than talking to me. Perhaps he's broken?

Fuck him. I need to figure out when we are. It's obvious we're in San Francisco, but there aren't many clues as to what era it is. This wharf is deserted and the city is too far in the distance to judge. My attire feels unremarkable, meaning that it likely came from the early 2100s. Sticking with that assumption forces my insides to constrict. I feel hot and there's clamminess on my brow and palms. Odyssian had mentioned that bigger events are easier to attach to and there's a pretty damn big fucking event in San Francisco around this time:

The Great Faultline Disaster.

The sole of my shoe scrapes as it turns in wet concrete. I'm leaving. Titus notices and calls out apathetically.

"Where are you going?" He asks. I face him, feeling my lips move, but not focusing on what I'm saying.

"Look, I know you're going through an extra layer of shit right now. I can't imagine how you feel, but I know you're my friend. Or eventually you will be. Right now, we've got to get going."

"Why?" He says with a lingering openness. Almost as if he's ready to talk about everything in the Bulk now. *Too fucking late.*

"I believe we got pushed back – or forward, I guess – to the Great Faultline Disaster." He searches his brain for knowledge of the event.

"It's exactly what it sounds like and we're about to be in the hardest hit spot."

That's enough to convince him as his face contorts, forgetting all the bullshit of the 4th dimension, Ryveliant, and Odyssian. With his scar, it's a frightening look. Perhaps for the first time, I'm truly feeling empathy for my friend and the pain he must have gone through – android or not – to get that mark. He removes the portable Warper from a pocket and reads a date.

"May 15th, 2098."

"Shit."

"How much time have we got?" He asks.

"That's what I'm going to find out."

Leaving the sight of the Bridge in our rear view, we cross the thin concrete path connecting the wharf to land.

An indescribable sensation pummels my cerebellum, suggesting my equilibrium is off in a fun-house sort of way. The path before us undulates, almost indiscernibly, cracking along the edges.

I use the expletive again. "Oh shit."

It's beginning.

Chapter 41 – Aiontis
2098 | May 15th | San Francisco

"Run!" I yelp, setting my own feet to the task. My hands instinctively rise to keep balance, but it's a challenge. I focus on placing each foot *flatly* on concrete as I propel forward.

CRRRRAAAAAACCCCKKK!

The sound like an elongated firecracker pierces the guttural bass of rumbling and I gasp while the wharf pathway breaks and crumbles from its connection to land, leaving a two-meter (and growing) gap. I'm not liking the alternatives of staying on this disintegrating platform or falling into the ocean water of the bay. Jumping it is.

Behind me are the heavy footfalls of Titus gaining ground. I wonder if he'll pass, but he's deliberately hanging back. *Letting me jump first. Awesome.* The petty thought flashes as the concrete strip spiderwebs beneath my feet. I'm running in false quicksand, outputting enough effort that I should be sprinting, but only getting a clumsy jog out of it.

My lower half tenses and prepares to convert forward momentum into my leap. Titus speeds to my side, heaving my beltline upward and outward. Feet scraping on concrete suggests he jumps not a second after.

His throw takes me by surprise, and is effective. I crash onto the other side, gravel and dust kicking into my mouth and eyes, thankful to be on solid (though shaking) ground. His landing is more graceful, and he helps me up.

"I think your intuition was correct, Aiontis."

"What gave you that idea?" We exchange a smile.

"What next?" He questions.

I look around. Near us are small shops, vibrating and spitting out panicked patrons. Further out there's mostly just e-parking stalls and grassy hills. Leaves on nearby trees shiver on their quaking branches and I can hear the internal damage to the wood with periodic snaps.

"This is a really bad event, Titus." I begin to explain. "All of California is going through it right now, but the earthquake here is so close to the surface that it's going to get very intense." I pause and point around us. "We're actually in a safer spot, out in the open like this."

"Do we just wait? What if Ryveliant comes after us?"

Titus' question gives me anxiety. I hadn't considered that at all.

"Can he come after us? Is that how it works?"

The ground's movement gathers intensity; we're both in a deep crouch. I remember this earthquake is long and has very few breaks. The aftershocks are nearly as bad as the initial rupture.

"And what about tsunamis?" He asks, looking toward the waterline right next to us. Fate hears him as the tsunami alarms along the coast begin to blare over the rumbling.

"If I remember correctly, there isn't a tsunami threat with this quake. The plate and fault movements are all land-based. Tsunamis come from ocean-based fault movements."

Titus nods and we're disrupted by another fearsome sound: cars crashing. The crackling parking lot nearby is in chaos as drivers frantically take control of their self-driving cars to escape the situation. Along the road that winds between the now-snapping trees on the hill, there's a multiple car pile-up.

A man, with puffy eyes and red skin, gets out of his car shouting obscenities. He's crazed by the event, clearly in a panic. There's a gun, and he points it at another driver. Even over all the other sounds, I hear the gunshot as he executes the defenseless person.

In tandem, Titus and I have both our weapons drawn. Mine, a trusty X-34 (it's crazy to think I still have it) and his is some model from the future I've not seen before. The man, afraid and angry, glances around for more people he can kill. I'm not sure why he's having such an unhinged reaction, but after he pops off a couple additional shots at random, he spots us: challengers who also have weapons.

Before anyone can do anything, Mother Nature takes her turn and, with a yearning growl, opens a crack in the earth, swallowing the man up. Titus and I sprint to the commotion, weapons ready, to find the gunman lying at the bottom of the crevice, 15 meters deep. There's nothing we can do to help, and I suddenly realize what our plan should be,

"We need to get in a car."

"Why? What good is that going to do?"

"Things get really bad here. If we can get inland, or even a couple states over, we'll be safer."

We spot an electric SUV that's motionless. Cautiously, we approach from either side with weapons drawn, prepared to commandeer it if we need to. There's a woman in the front seat, hunched over and unconscious.

A new tremor forces us to catch our balance on the car and rolls her to the side, revealing her face. Even through a nasty gash on her forehead, I can tell it's *her.*

The fourth dimensional beings are at work in some weird way.

"Caroline?" I ask.

"The vizier!" Titus exclaims.

We know we're in the right spot.

Chapter 42 – Aiontis
2098 | May 15ᵗʰ | San Francisco

Our eyes lock through the windows. They're both of bewilderment. Chalk this up as one more question that I forgot desperately needs an answer:

Who is this woman and why does she continue to appear?

On the driver's side, Titus thrusts open the door, and slides his arms underneath her. I hustle to the other side and pull on the back-half's gull wing door. Another shake rattles us, and Titus nearly drops the woman. It's a not-so-subtle reminder that we need to promptly evacuate, so he efficiently lays her down, closes the door, and I'm already in the passenger seat typing away at the navigation instrument.

"Ok, either way this is going to be rough. We can go north along the Golden Gate *or* head east through the city to the Oakland Bay Bridge. That eventually puts us most inland out of the two options." I'm scrolling swiftly across the touchscreen. Titus has the car started with its quiet, electric hum and the quake's vibration forcing my torso against the seatbelt repeatedly.

"Do you remember where the quake hits? That should define our choice." He makes a good point.

"It started in Los Angeles and San Diego about an hour ago. San Francisco had virtually no warning before it made its way up the coast through the network of fault lines. The San Andreas is the fault responsible for most of this, but it's the Hayward that's causing what we're seeing now." I rummage through the rest of my Hiscon knowledge and make a decision.

"We should go north."

"Across the Golden Gate Bridge?"

"Yes."

Titus doesn't need to be told twice and punches the vehicle into reverse, avoiding scattered debris, then shifts into drive. I hold up a finger before he goes any further, swiping to a performance screen. I select "Absurd Approach" that shoves all the vehicle's energy into going as fast as possible.

A violent rattle pushes the whole car upward and Titus' foot slams the accelerator. We're sucked into our seats, flying up the tree-lined hill. Several cringey whines echo inside the vehicle as we trade paint with parked vehicles along the way. Most of these people are too paralyzed with fear to make any moves, or are on foot, running for safety.

My vision starts to tunnel under the seamless acceleration and I catch Titus checking the map for the best path. With nearly equal, but opposite force, he brakes, putting the vehicle into a slide around a turn. Another rumble throws us in the direction of our momentum and we slam hard into an abandoned parked car. The crinkle of malleable metal is disheartening, but doesn't faze Titus. In the back, our mystery woman remains unconscious, getting tossed around more than I'd like. Reaching back, I search for a seatbelt and wrap it around her torso, hoping it will help.

With constant and aggressive accelerations and decelerations, Titus is on course to the freeway to cross the bridge. Outside, all I see is fear and pandemonium. Fires from ruptured gas lines and small explosions are beginning to spread. Buildings over 50 years old have lost chunks of concrete, brick, and glass, or collapsed completely. These are all relatively small one- or two-story structures. A knot in my stomach tells me downtown is a different picture.

There's an exit off the freeway ahead, opposite the direction we're traveling. It's packed with cars. There's an on-ramp that looks better, aside from a handful of abandoned cars waiting it out along the road's shoulders.

"On-ramp is clear, go that way." Titus nods and stomps onto the brake with a yank of the wheel. I'm surprised he can drive this well, but I don't question it. The soup of my brain pushes to one side of my skull and then I'm being sucked into my seat again. Even the g-forces of ATVs aren't *this* drastic. Beneath us, the crackled road shakes and passes beneath our dusty tires. The long on-ramp has seen better days. Near the top, I spot a woman running.

"What is she doing?" Titus asks the question I'm thinking.

She's distraught…not seeking help, but rather crazed with panic. There's snot and tears down her face and her eyes are huge in her skull. Her run is sporadic.

Without warning, an oil tanker (ironically an electric vehicle) looms over her. It's a behemoth, chasing her down. She's too slow and the runaway vehicle plows over her, swallowing her in its undercarriage with a mist of red gore.

"Hoo-leee fuck!" I exclaim, bile building in my throat. Titus swerves just out from the front of the truck as it continues to barrel down the ramp, showering sparks along the side as it re-acts to the wall. Flames appear on its back half, coupled with dark smoke. Neither Titus or I have to say anything – it's clear there's a new bond between us – as he hammers the accelerator even further.

A thud sends a wave of force and heat and boisterous sound through our cabin. Behind us is a fireball that swallows the road in a layer of napalm.

I sigh when we finally get on the freeway. They've opened up both directions of the bridge heading north.

Most people are driving far over the speed limit, but Titus is even more aggressive. He's weaving effortlessly through traffic, getting angry and frightened honks every few moments. From the bridge, I try to see downtown and can barely do so through all the smoke from fires along the way. It doesn't look good. I remember somewhere around 4,000 people die today and a sub-stantial number of those are from this region. An additional three million are injured, some permanently.

Orange keeps flashing in my view, the Bridge begging to be admired. I grant its wish, focusing on the thick, aging cables. I wonder how high they rise as we make our way across its deck. While there are some cracks along the road, I'm impressed how well it's holding up given its age. Briefly, that thought sends an-other wave of nausea pulsing: we're driving across an old sus-pension bridge in the nation's largest earthquake.

We make it across, thanks to Titus and some stupendous driving. This side is much less affected – and nearly abandoned aside from the other cars on the road – than where we came from.

"Keep driving north and stay out of any towns or cities." I hear a shuffling and moan behind me.

"Ugh…where am…what the hell…hey!" I turn and see a panicked woman, with Caroline and the vizier's features, staring at two men from the future who have technically carjacked her. "Who the FUCK are you two?"

"I'm er…uh you were unconscious and we needed a ride. It's happening…the big one. We'll give you your car back, don't worry. We're just trying to escape the area."

"The big one? What?"

"There's a huge earthquake going on right now." Her anger subsides and she remembers how she got the congealing cut on her forehead. Her hand finds it, but then her face drops, with wide eyes.

"Oh my god. We have to go back!" She yells.

"Excuse me?" Titus' whips his neck to glance at her.

"My son! I was heading downtown to pick up my son when this all started." I'm staring blankly, unsure of what to say. She screams it for me, "We have to go back!"

Chapter 43 – Aiontis
2098 | May 15ᵗʰ | San Francisco

A shot of hot jealousy hits behind my eyes, but I know that isn't fair.

"Your…son?" I stammer. She furrows her brow. Clearly, I'm the weird one right now.

"Yes. My son. And who are you two anyway?"

"We're the ones who just saved you, miss…?" Titus answers her. By now he's slowed the car to the side of the road on some grass.

"I'm Rachel." She answers, "And you two would be? For the third time."

I extend a hand back. "Aiontis. This is my friend Titus." I can see her brain processing the weird names, but she doesn't comment. A violent shake jolts the vehicle.

"Look," she starts, with passion. "I've got to get my son. He's on a class trip and only ten years old. If we're all dying today, I don't want him doing so alone. So, either get the fuck out of my car, or turn around and haul ass, but I need an answer now."

Titus and I catch eyes, stifling a smirk. Clearly there is some of the vizier in her.

Without answering, Titus audibly hammers the gas to the floor and we're on our way back toward the Golden Gate Bridge. From this distance, I can see it swaying and vibrating…hanging on for as long as it can to remain a pillar of American exceptionalism.

The street is rougher and far more cracked. It feels like we're off-roading, but at high speed. My hips are getting sore from the seatbelt resisting momentum. I glance back to see Rachel wearing a grimace, but she says nothing. She's toughing it out.

We approach the bridge a second time, its hulking, orange towers welcoming us into an event that will forever shape this city. Going south is proving to be more challenging than north. Traffic is flowing against us, but Titus' speed doesn't let up.

Other cars' horns blare then recede into echoes as we pass either screaming "Get the hell out of the way!" or "You're going the wrong way!".

Being in a vehicle, driving at high speed, on a suspension bridge, during a massive earthquake is a sensation that I'm not sure is describable. I feel a plethora of random movements across my body, not knowing if it's g-forces from weaving between oncoming traffic, or the shaking bridge slicing from side to side in the air. The balancing functions of my brain are on overdrive.

Though I'm not driving, my view stays on the road. Ahead, also weaving through traffic, is a sporty 2-door traveling the opposite direction. I can hear the deep rumble of the quake, even suspended above the earth, and the creaking moan of the bridge. The path before us looks less like a road and more like a wave. It tosses the sports car into the air like a child's plaything, heading straight for our windshield. I have no time to react or shout or piss my pants before Titus cranks the wheel to the left. Millimeters away from my passenger seat, our vehicle trades molecules of paint as the sports car slams down in a thunderous shattering of mechanical parts.

"Oh my God…" Titus says.

"I know. That was close."

"No. Look." Rachel points upward from the back.

One of the massive main cables that runs parallel to the bridge is hanging by a thread, about to disconnect from the south tower. Attached to its underside are all the vertical cables used for actual bridge suspension. For a brief moment, the world seems to go silent. A brutal pop fills the void, and the cable starts to fall inward.

Again, I'm sucked into my seat because Titus is driving as fast as the car will allow. Northbound vehicles likely heard the noise, but don't know what it was. I see their faces, and they see mine, eyes wide with panic, and they sense something is wrong. I run my fingers along the passenger panel in search of the window. Nowhere. I execute the same exercise on the holopad center console and find what I'm looking for.

Boisterous air enters the vehicle bringing a cacophony of

rushing wind, low rumbling, cars honking, and bridge components whining.

"What are you doing?" Rachel shouts from the back. I ignore her question. I've lowered the window so I can guide Titus to avoid the falling cable. What I witness is more horrific than I imagined. Flailing and shaking, the cables — as big around as a kitchen table — are twisting inward on the bridge. The main parallel and many, many vertical cables will fall onto the road. I shout into the vehicle.

"The cables are going to hit the road; we need to get as far on the opposite side as we can!"

My chest slams into the passenger door with a thud as Titus takes my advice immediately. Once a small orange line across the piercingly blue sky, the cables gather speed, gravity invisibly pushing them down against their will to cause even more destruction on this day.

I can distinctly *hear* their falling: a grandiose ache against the backdrop of other sounds, forming a crescendo until they reach the ground.

"Go, go, go…gogogogogo!!" I scream into the vehicle. Titus is doing his best; the vehicle is maxed out. The main parallel cable is only meters above us.

Now only centimeters.

A hand pulls on my back, bringing my head inside as a northbound van scrapes our paint, horn echoing.

The cable slams on top of it, pulverizing and flattening the hull. Shards of glass and metal and dust leap outward, some entering our vehicle. Behind us, the remainder of the parallel cable and all the attached vertical cables follow suit, crushing any vehicles and roadway underneath. The sound is the loudest thing I've ever heard, the eerie yelp of an injured American symbol.

My stomach travels into my throat as the road beneath us jolts downward. Our tires momentarily lose traction, which is quickly regained. We pass the threshold of the large towers from where the cable snapped and emerge on the other side of the bridge. Titus slows the car to a stop, out of the way.

For a moment, the shaking has stopped, almost as an apology for what it just did.

We'll be lucky to make it out of this day alive, and I'm still not sure what happens if we die.

Chapter 44 – Aiontis
2098 | May 15th | San Francisco

I'm shocked our trip toward downtown doesn't take longer. Titus stays on a dilapidated Freeway 101 and Rachel guides on the best route. Along the way she calls audibles because the navigation path set out by the car's UI is useless in the current predicament.

Receiving another stroke of luck, the shaking has minimized and even paused for minutes at a time. The initial slipping and friction of fault lines has slowed, but only for a moment. Rachel is optimistic. "It should be over now," she keeps saying. I don't have the heart to tell her it's not. I've communicated this to Titus through a side glance, warning him to stay alert. The shaking is going to come back. Hard.

All around there's shocking, cataclysmic destruction. Bodies in the street. Some dead, some bloody and moving with tattered, torn clothing. Rubble is everywhere, coughing up dust and spewing onto broken streets and walkways. Grass fields show massive cracks, revealing the dark dirt layers underneath. Water pipes are broken, causing pools of liquid that desperately search for the next place to flow. Worst of all are the fires. Many blocks have multiple hotspots and, across the span of 20 minutes, we witnessed entire buildings charred and engulfed in angry orange and red flame. They are hopeless to save as firefighters have prioritized saving lives over saving buildings…if they can even reach those who need saving.

Insultingly, the day is beautiful. Any other like it would see San Franciscans spending some of their first "summer" moments outside, having lunch in parks, taking work breaks on corporate patios, and exercising. Today, many are fighting for their lives. Their human instincts have shifted to *survive*. What we are doing feels like the opposite.

"Shit!" Rachel exclaims from the backseat, pulling me back to the moment. Titus' eyes dart back and forth. He glances in the rearview mirror. On either side and in front of us, the streets are impassable, either covered with debris, broken completely, on fire, or some hellish combination of all the above. Smoke billows and its odor seeps into the car's air conditioning.

"We should get out, continue on foot," Titus starts. "If we find your son, we can make a plan from there or even come back to the car."

"*When* we find my son," Rachel corrects him, "We'll do what we need to survive. The car doesn't matter and likely won't be here when we get back."

"I thought you were positive the shaking had stopped?" I counter, contemplating why she's not questioning *our* motives and willingness to help. I would be in her position. There's apprehension within her eyes.

"I do. We're not exactly in the best part of town. Someone's going to take up the opportunity to have a free eSUV."

"So, where is your son?" Titus moves the conversation forward, gesturing at the skyscrapers in the distance.

"I've been trying to figure that out. I have their itinerary, and once this all started, they were likely at Salesforce Park, potentially having lunch."

"Where is that in relation to downtown?" I ask.

"The heart of it. East of where we are now by quite a few blocks."

"I imagine they're no longer there. They've hopefully tried to find shelter." Titus adds.

"I agree." Rachel appreciates the vote of confidence that her son is still breathing. "I just have no clue where, but I imagine it couldn't have been far from the park."

"Does he have a cell phone?" I ask, forgetting what exact form of communication had been established by this time. I glance nervously at my iNsert, hoping she hasn't seen it yet.

"Yes, I've been trying it this whole time." Her eyes begin to water "There's no answer…it just goes to his voicemail." She unfolds a thin piece of translucent glass that displays a screen. It plays her son's voicemail greeting.

"Yoooo dooooods!" A high-pitched childish voice starts, followed by giggling. "I'm doing tons of important stuff at the moment." More giggles. "So, leave a message if you're over 90 years old, otherwise just shoot me a gigchat! Snag at cha' later!"

I have no idea about half of what he was saying, but I want to sooth Rachel, as tears trickle down her cheeks.

"Cute kid. What's his name?"

"Bryson." She replies, folding the phone away.

Collective silence falls over our group for a moment.

"Ok, look." I start. We need to make moves. "The shaking isn't over. There's going to be more – "

"How…?" I cut her off.

"It doesn't matter how, I just know, ok? Going on foot is going to be dangerous, but less so if we move quickly. This is a long shot and we need to agree on something."

"On what?" She asks. Titus remains silent.

"If we get to that park and don't find him within 30 minutes, we keep moving and find safety ourselves."

"Fine." I can tell she won't follow that rule if it comes to it, but it's a start. "Why are you helping me?" She finally asks. Before I can answer, Titus does.

"We don't have anything better to do, do we?"

I smile, "No, we don't."

"Well okay, let's get going!" She starts to go for the door handle when we collectively notice a group of eCycles approaching us from the rear.

"Shit." She shakes her head. One of the stealth-looking vehicles circles to our frontside, easily traversing the cracks and bumps in the road with a large suspension kit. A bulky man sits on the bike's throne as it self-balances. There's a gun in his hand, metal and lethal, that he waves at us. *Get out of the car* it whispers. Titus unlocks his door.

"Titus, don't do anything stupid." I warn, still thinking about what happens if we die here. He glances back, smiling.

"I wouldn't dream of it."

Chapter 45 – Titus
2098 | May 15ᵗʰ | San Francisco

A swim lane of frustration drew itself in spirals through Titus' system. Here he was, apparently with his "master", being bounced around time like a couple of pawns, stuck in the middle of one of the most destructive earthquakes in human history, and *now* this pack of idiots wanted to dance.

I'll show them how we fight in 2477. Then a second thought. *I'll show them how an android does this.*

The gang was off their eCycles by now, except for the apparent leader. Each wore black, dressed eloquently. There was a raggedness to the fabric, as if it was well worn and rarely swapped out, but most wore suit jackets, ties, shined shoes with metal decorations, and dress pants. Each was sporting thin sunglasses with yellow lenses, and Titus gathered enough to identify they were Asian in descent, likely Japanese. *Yakuza perhaps? Were they still active in 2098?* It would make sense they'd set up in San Francisco.

"You look like a big guy." The leader commented nonchalantly. Through his yellow lenses, he measured the rounds in his gun through its touchscreen. "We're going to be taking that vehicle." His eyes leveled at Titus, dark. "And the girl."

"You don't have your priorities straight!" Titus mocked. The bulky leader's eyebrows rose above the yellow glasses, black and bushy. "We're in the midst of an earthquake and you're more concerned with dying? Strange. Most are trying to survive."

"Dying? No my friend, that's wh – " A heated hole bore its way through skin, skull, and brain. Zorex had only needed a single round and Titus' draw time caught everyone by surprise. The other gang members didn't register what happened until the top of their chain-of-command slumped forward on his eCycle and slid off, staining it with crimson pouring from the gaping wound. A well-timed rumble shook the street, compounding the surprise.

Titus released three more shots, the curved metal of Zorex's trigger comforting his finger. *It has been a long time, friend.*

Aim. Shoot. A hole through a chest.

Aim. Shoot. Another headshot.

Aim. Shoot. In and out of a shoulder.

All three victims were down, but there were too many remaining. Beneath him, there was a deep gnarl and a cracking burst of concrete. The shaking tossed everyone to the ground and Titus dropped Zorex, sending it sliding and scraping against gravel and debris.

Another gang member witnessed this, snagging the interesting weapon. Legs wide in a bracing stance and a devilish smirk, he aimed his own handgun and the newly-acquired Zorex at the man who'd killed his boss.

Titus, lying on the ground, couldn't help but smile as he rolled out of the way from the present-day bullet. Zorex fired a reverse round through the head of the man whose biological signature was *not* Titus. A useful feature, especially in a period where that technology was decades away.

Scrambling, arm over arm, Titus was inches away from reclaiming his trusty sidearm. The vibration of the shifting earth rattled his stomach and ribcage as he reached for it. A crowbar thwacked his hand and a surge of pain leapt up his arm, reminding the android that he was *fully* programmed.

"Argh, damn!" Titus yelped as he rolled on this back, dodging another crowbar swipe. His foot came up and hit something solid, shattering the assailant's nose and yellow sunglass lenses. Blood crept and dripped through the man's fingers; eyes wide. Titus found Zorex and another round barked from the chamber, exiting the top of the man's head. For a brief moment, Titus studied his hand. It was red from the crowbar strike and the pain was still there, but the damage wasn't as extensive as it should have been. *Why have I never realized this before? Because I didn't know any different?*

Nearby, a two-story building collapsed in on itself, sending dust across the road. A small explosion leapt from the debris – likely a broken gas line – and fire began to eagerly attach itself to anything that would burn. In the distance, people were running, oblivious of the deathmatch occurring in the middle of this street, and seeking respite from the much more immediate danger of an earthquake.

A knee crashed into the side of his head – on his scar – sending him spiraling. Briefly the world turned fuzzy, but corrected itself. Again, faster than he would have expected. More of the Yakuza had gotten off their eCycles and joined the fight, most of them armed, yet choosing to use a melee weapon. They wouldn't be taking turns anymore…

"C'mon." He huffed, crouching his legs and putting his arms up. A chaotic yell echoed, coming from each of the men, charging wildly with swinging weapons. Black garments and yellow lenses closed in, giving Titus only time enough to put down one with a shot, through the teeth.

Collisions came from all angles. The iNsert in Titus' eyelid flashed red with his heart rate, indicating he was under physical duress. The pain was relentless, annoying given the revelation he'd just had.

With an opportunistic duck, Titus avoided the end of a baseball bat that instead connected with a man behind him. Reacting, his hand grasped the wood shaft, yanking it away. Perhaps channeling his inner samurai, he blocked a ferocious swing from a metal bar and swept the bat across the man's face. It broke into splinters with a thunderous crack – *or had that been the earthquake?* - leaving the man lifeless on the pavement, less a few teeth. An extendable baton slammed onto his shoulder blades, driving through. Titus spun, met with a fat gang member whose sunglasses stretched across his face like a corset about to burst.

He charged at Titus, baton raised, yelping, and received a boot to the chin. The kick did little to slow his assault as he crashed into an off-balance Titus and they fell hard to the ground. As if the earth reacted to the impact, the shaking started once more and grew in severity.

"It's another one!" Cried a gang member, running in fear. The others remained, crouching to maintain balance, but momentarily prohibited from beating the shit out of Titus. All except the fat one on top of him, jiggling and crushing his body. They'd rolled close to the sidewalk, near a corner with a fire hydrant. Fits of crackling concrete played like menacing popping corn, but a lower rumble interested Titus. It was coming from deep in the earth, speeding toward the fire hydrant.

With a heave, Titus rolled the man underneath the yellow city device and pushed upward. The sound reached its exit as the heavy hydrant cap burst off with a plume of high-pressured water behind it, looking for an escape. The sound had been drowned out, but Titus felt it; the fat man's neck had snapped.

Titus' clothes stuck with wetness, his hair drenched, and screaming water filled his vision. As he struggled to lift the limp man off him, a sound like a bomb pushed them both back across the street. The entire hydrant had burst upward, crashing back to earth in a nearby yard, leaving a geyser of city water arcing into the sky, translucent rainbows shimmering in front of the sun.

"Titus!" Aiontis was out of the car, worry etched across his face. The blast had been loud, but the pressure had escaped mostly upward, leaving Titus unscathed aside from road rash and now free of the dead fat man.

"I'm fine, get back in the car!" He shouted over the water-flow and earthquake rumblings. There were still too many gang members. He had to deal with them first. Their path was blocked and on foot was their only option, but not if Rachel or Aiontis were dead. A handful of short, but boisterous claps arose over the other noises.

Three gang members all dropped dead, bloody wounds on their upper chest or head. Their crimson life oozed toward the small lake forming on the street. Aiontis had fired several rounds at the foes nearest Titus. *Hmm. An X-34 model? Nice.*

To their left, one of the men, lacking any yellow-lensed glasses and looking torn to shreds himself, pulled a circular orb from a jacket pocket. Even though it was centuries old technology to Titus, he recognized it instantly. *A fragmentation grenade.*

It left the man's hands, rolled like a bowling ball. The sphere containing fire and shrapnel headed for the eSUV, a crooked smile on his lips as he tossed its metal ring aside.

Chapter 46 – Aiontis
2098 | May 15ʰ | San Francisco

"Aiontis!" Titus barks. "Get Rachel out of the car!"

Beside the vehicle, I spot the grenade roll toward it, disappearing underneath. The door nearly comes off its hinges when I yank, overriding its dreadfully slow electronic opening sequence.

"Rachel!" I reach, fingers splayed and arm frantic, grabbing her wrist and tugging, falling backward onto the pavement. I imagine time slows – or at least that's what it feels like – because of the sparse moments away from death that Rachel and I share.

This woman who I've found in history (three times now, but who's counting?) and I, are trapped with no idea why. A pawn in some higher beings' game. What will happen to us if we die? *When* we die?

Rachel isn't letting that happen, understanding we need to clear the vehicle. She's already on her feet, dragging me upward with a heave, while tossing her momentum away from the car.

A massive shove of unknown force tosses me aside like worthless trash, plunging my hearing into a high-pitched squeal. Heat scorches my back, singing through my clothing and burning hairs on my neck. I take stock of my surroundings, impeded by blurred vision and a sudden headache. Rachel lies beside me, motionless. The eSUV hull is smoking and in flames.

My vision graduates from blobs to edges. Shrapnel litters the roadway and my clothes are scratched and torn in places, with black dirt pressed into my skin. Blood flows delicately from small wounds, but I'm okay. Rachel stirs, thrown a half meter further than I, also blackened with grime. There's a nasty gash on her shoulder to compliment the one on her forehead, but nothing life threatening.

Our eyes meet and she gives a nod, pressing her head almost as if to make sure there's not a dent there, likely feeling the same headache I am now.

"Argghhh!" Her gaze darts behind me. Titus is being ganged up on, with no fewer than five men attempting to beat him, including the one who threw the grenade. My hands scrape the ground, searching for my weapon. I find it, lie on my back, and aim.

I don't have a clear shot. Even hitting one of the men doesn't guarantee the round wouldn't pass through and hit Titus as well.

"Get out of here! I know where we're going." Titus shouts from the pile, a sickening crack following his command. Another man screams in agony. "I'll catch up!"

It's the right advice, but I'm conflicted. I turn to Rachel, who meets me with a raise of the eyebrows that asks, *Well…?* The earth answers for us, supplying a booming shudder that shuttles all of us more than a body length away. Titus and the men collapse for a moment, still fighting and trying to stay afoot.

We've got to save her kid.

"Let's go." I stand, crouched and waiting for an aftershock. The debris previously blocking our original path has shifted and broken down, offering enough room to get through on an eCycle.

Her hand falls into mine, gripping it with trust.

The sensation is not of this world, nearly knocking me down again.

It is a hand I've held before even though I haven't.

It's a trust I've received before even though I haven't.

"What's wrong?" She asks, concern lining her brow.

"Nothing…" I choke. "Nothing." I return the squeeze to her hand, and run to an eCycle. It belongs to the original thug Titus had executed mid-speech, lying several feet away, tossed about by the shaking. The bike stands upright, its magnetic balancers working overtime in this unprecedented situation. As we approach the all-black, fighter-jet-esque machine, I find I'm *too* far into the future to really know how to operate it. My pause and dumbfounded stare put Rachel in motion without a word.

I only see one seat but Rachel reaches underneath it, unlatching a second and pulling, extending it back. It looks flimsy, but is likely made of strong, lightweight metal. Without a second thought, she throws her leg over the chassis, presses the ignition button on its holopad, and revs the engine. It makes a high-pitched whine as if it's about to momentarily explode, and settles.

"What?" She says, patting the seat behind her. "I used to date a guy…" And she leaves it at that as I follow her lead onto the bike, wrapping my arms around her torso.

Again, I feel the pounding of my own heart, tossing *this* feeling around my bloodstream.

It's *her*.

Caroline.

The vizier.

Now Rachel.

We're off, wind scraping at the corners of my eyes and over my hair. Her own hair billows back beside me, catching the sun and giving it back on this hellish day.

I'm on the edge of a memory, frustratingly close, but unlockable. One where, if I just squeeze her closer, I'll remember. It's different than the sensation Odyssian had been creating – a crescendo instead of a guiding light – but there's a single similarity.

It feels bigger than all of this.

Chapter 47 – Titus
2098 | May 15th | San Francisco

Dust plumed behind the eCycle's fat back tire and once settled, the vehicle was gone, along with Aiontis and Rachel.

A boot to the chest sent Titus backwards, interrupting the image.

Five gang members were left, the rest either dead or scattered from the previous aftershock. In the chaos, Titus had lost track of Zorex, pained that he may have lost it forever. He took a moment to bring his breaths from gasps to full exhalations as a thug returned from his bike, carrying a shotgun.

The weapon was long, with a silver fern etched across its night-black metallic surface. Three barrels sought their mark and the other men seemed to lie in wait, thinking this would end the brawl. A nearby eSUV provided cover as Titus ducked behind its pearl white exterior dusted with debris and smudges of disaster from the earthquake. A tight collection of pellets slammed the opposite side of the vehicle, echoing across the street, even louder than the raining arc of the fire hydrant.

A second slam. Titus swore he felt the car move that time.

A third. The pellets sounded closer, making their way through the interior, ending on Titus' side.

A fourth. This one exponentially louder as the shrapnel hit mere inches from him. He wouldn't survive a fifth.

From a distance, a much different sound rumbled, getting louder. Titus couldn't tell what it was, but the gang members were distracted. The noise came to a climax with a primal roar and a police eSUV crashed into the thug holding the shotgun, violently tossing his body a half block away. Beside Titus, a gentle *plop* (one of the softer noises he'd heard that day); a pair of thin yellow glasses, cracked and reflecting flecks of blood against the translucent lenses.

For a moment, there was silence, not even any shaking of the earth. The gang stood their ground, some with scowls and others rocking back and forth, anxious for what would come next. The armored police eSUV's gigantic door flew open, revealing an armed enforcer robot. It was operating autonomously, with janky, but determined movement.

Before any of the men could make a fully orchestrated move, whether it was attacking the metal being or running away, they were all gunned down.

It was over.

A new vibration started in the street, pushing existing cracks further apart. Titus observed the enforcer stabilizing itself. *Is this an early version of me?* A heat built in his chest, partly anger, partly disgust that his "ancestor" was so…archaic.

"Hello?" A voice called out. Titus peered through the window as a flesh-and-blood officer rounded the front end of his vehicle, gun drawn. Titus raised his palms to the air and came out from behind his cover.

"Don't shoot." The officer's gun lowered, minimally. "Thanks for that. I was running out of options."

"Anytime I can get some payback against the S.F. Yakuza, it's worth it. Bunch of idiots they are, doing this kind of stuff today, of all days."

"How did you find me?" Titus asked.

"I've been doing my best to get around on patrol and help. Hasn't been easy but I heard gunshots from a couple streets over and knew Sam and I had to check it out." The officer nodded to the still robot who hadn't moved since firing his last shot.

"Does 'Sam' stand for something?"

"Nope. I just call him Sam."

"Hi! I'm Sam!" The robot recognized his place in the conversation and introduced himself enthusiastically. The officer chortled.

"He's always a little late to the party. He wasn't designed for conversation, obviously." He hesitated, sizing Titus up. "So…what are you doing out here? Shouldn't you be trying to get out of the city?"

Titus weighed his options, realizing a version of the truth was probably his best bet.

"My friend and I *were*, but then we came across a woman and she asked us to help save her son. He's on a field trip down-town."

"Where are they?"

"I told them to take off while they had a moment to slip away during all this." He motioned to the graveyard around him. The geyser from the fire hydrant had stopped flowing a few moments ago.

"I see…and *you* did all of this?" Titus stiffened.

"Yes. It was in self-defense." The officer's eyebrows raised at the reasoning, followed by a subtle smirk.

"It's one of those days where I won't tell if you don't. Quite noble of you though, perhaps you should think of joining the force when this is all over."

"Thanks…I'll think about it." Titus replied, humored that in *this* time period, he had what it takes to be on the police force.

"Well, I'll let you get going." A smaller rumble punctuated his statement. "It's a mess downtown, be careful. Let's go, Sam!" He approached the driver side of his vehicle while Sam got back in. "I hope you find your friends!"

With a quick wave, he hopped in and reversed the eSUV. A glimmer of sunlight caught the splashes of blood on the rein-forced grill. Titus waved back and began looking around for his mode of transportation.

As if the universe willed it, the eCycle nearest him had a shin-ing "L" of metal on the ground beside its dusty front tire: Zorex. In Titus' eyelid iNsert, it glowed with a soft red hue. With Zorex secured in its holstermesh, he commandeered the eCycle and took off in the direction of Aiontis and Rachel, unsure of what exactly he'd find.

My…this day has taken a turn. The earth beneath him replied with a grumpy aftershock.

Chapter 48 – Aiontis
2098 | May 15th | San Francisco

Navigating the horrific piles of debris, floods of broken pipes, raging fires and their smoke, and groupings of abandoned cars is slowing us down. We've come across more bodies than I care to admit and heard cries for help we had to ignore.

It's weird, not having my complete long-term memory, because I must *assume* that I've never seen anything like this before (which I can say for this whole adventure), but I don't know for certain.

I hope I haven't.

We've had to move north and south a handful of times; it hasn't been a straight shot into downtown. Luckily, we haven't encountered any more gangs, but we've seen looting and heard gunshots over the course of the last hour.

The mystery of *who* Rachel is has subsided, if only because of the sensory overload that comes with a once-in-a-century earthquake. I want to talk with her about it, but it's not the time…plus she'll think I'm crazy.

Taking up an equal amount of emotional capacity is feeling guilty about leaving Titus behind. That we *can* talk about.

"I hope he'll be ok." I state near her ear. Her head turns slightly, trying to catch me in her peripherals.

"I would say something like 'I'm sure he will be', but I don't know him. Or you, for that matter." She turns the eCycle to avoid a deep puddle and weaves around some larger fissures in the pavement. "Why don't you tell me about him?"

"I…I really don't even know where to begin." It's the truth. A day ago, I thought he was trying to kill me…because he was…and now I've been granted memories of our long friendship. "We weren't friends, initially." I start. "I thought he, uh, hated me. But we ended up working together and became good friends." I hesitate, realizing my memories are incomplete. "He's funny actually. I know it may not appear that way at first, but…it's there" *His torture from the…Regime likely took that away.* I continue recounting the vivid memory.

"I remember a time where he and I were stuck in an airport, not by our own choosing, but because the government had forced them to detain us. I'd been doing work for them as…ahem…a Historian, and Titus had been along as my assistant and bodyguard. I can't explain why, but he was useful in that line of work." The truth is I really can't explain; I still don't remember fully. "Anyway, we were held in this room for hours, bored out of our minds. They'd deactivated our iNserts and –"

"What's an iNsert?" she inquires. I've slipped.

"It's uh…a type of phone."

"Hmm, never heard of it."

"It's an obscure brand I suppose. We were bored and Titus began to do impressions. Completely randomly, but *very* good ones. He nailed the mannerisms, voice…everything about each one, even females. Soon, the guards who'd been watching surveillance came into the room to take part, making up suggestions as we sat there. Eventually, they were having such a ball they just let us go, tears in their eyes."

"Wow, I would have never guessed."

"I know, right? I later heard a rumor they'd sent a video to the government official who'd detained us and he'd laughed so hard he removed our ban."

"How did he get the scars?" She asks yelling over the wind of the eCycle, but gently enough to show respect.

"I…I think that's his story to tell."

The eCycle hops against the cracked roadway, punctuating our silence. It feels like the shaking has ceased, though it's hard to tell while we're in motion. At the very least, the quakes are aftershocks and not large in magnitude.

We approach downtown to sights that are worse than all we've seen before. Most buildings over twenty stories are skeletons, their glass blown out almost completely. Here and there a window pane shines like a last chink of armor on a dead soldier. The frames look warped and under tension. Some are better than other's – the TransAmerica building seems intact – but many strain as if their structural moans could form a choir. As Rachel slows the bike, this is all but confirmed. There's an eerie echo across the deserted streets as a building wrestles the laws of gravity and physics pressing down on it.

She maneuvers around a blanket layer of broken glass and crushed cars and we're swallowed into the cold shadow of the towers. We're entering south of what I can only assume is the Financial District, with the TransAmerica building (now well over 100 years old) in our rear view. This isn't an optimal approach, but she's doing her best with the eCycle's GPS and the routes actually available to us.

In the distance, a new ghastly sight challenges us. Salesforce Tower, several blocks away, is missing a chunk of its top. The inside of the opening is tilted toward us, leaning against another nearby tower, clinging for life. The injured skyscraper appears like a gruesome broken tibia. Instead of blood and marrow inside, there's smoke and metal.

"Oh my god." I cannot stifle my reaction.

"Bryson…" Her voice shakes. We both know that Salesforce Tower is adjacent to Salesforce Park. I think of ways I could comfort her, but they're all hollow.

Doubt tells me it will be a miracle if her son is still alive.

Chapter 49 – Aiontis

2098 | May 15th | San Francisco

"C'mon." I prod gently. "It looks bad, but that doesn't mean anything. Let's stick to the plan." A tear rolls down her dirty cheek, clearing a thin path from grime. She wipes it and nods, starting the eCycle back up, it's quiet hum vibrating between our legs. After a few minutes, we have to stop again. We've gotten almost nowhere.

"It's no use." She comments, gesturing to the road. "There's too much debris…it's going to be faster to walk."

"Agreed." We get off the bike and leave it behind, gravel and glass crunching beneath our feet, cautious to avoid bigger pieces.

There's a weird smell in the air, frightening and memorable. Underneath the more pungent scents is the tangy brine of ocean air, but it's overpowered by smoke, leaking oil, and – most oddly – stale corporate office spaces. On top of that concoction, you have what I can only label as *death*; an indescribable smell until you've encountered it. It's sterile and metallic, the same I experienced in Japan and the WWI trenches.

So, this is what it smells like when a city dies.

We pass a vehicle, crushed by a large slab of concrete, with an arm hanging out the window, dusty, a trail of blood dripping from its fingers.

"Salesforce Park is right on the other side of the building, correct?" I ask, wanting to distract her.

"Hmm? Yes, it should be."

"If you don't mind me asking, where's Bryson's father? You haven't mentioned him…"

"He…uh…he's dead. Passed away a few years ago." Her voice wavers on the last words.

"I'm sorry."

"Me too. He was a good man, but it has just been Bryson and I since then. He's my whole life." The emotions of the day catch up with her and she releases a sigh that turns into a small sob. I put my arm around her shoulders.

"We're going to find him. Okay? We're so close." She leans into my awkward hug.

"Okay. I believe you." We stand together for a moment, among the graveyard of towers. "Let's get going."

This place is apocalyptic. Destruction is everywhere, fires roar in the distance, glass and paper and random debris blankets the sidewalks and streets. Rachel and I are the only ones around. *I hope that's because everyone else got out.* I know that's not true, but it's worth hoping for. The grandness of the situation settles in my mind once more: I'm *living* history. It's a Hiscon's dream right? I start to wonder if the life I was living before in Omaha – the one I only half remember – wasn't so bad after all.

"Look, through there." We've been walking for ten minutes or so before Rachel points in the direction of the semi-collapsed Salesforce tower. "The road is mostly clear and it'll lead straight to the park." Our gaze tracks upward to the top portion of the broken tower, spanning the length of the street, and leaning on a nearby building. I size up the danger and can tell Rachel is doing the same.

"It's risky." I state the obvious. She doesn't reply and just starts walking. The decision is made for the both of us.

As we approach, shadows of the accidental skybridge create another layer of darkness. There's moaning and creaking a couple hundred meters above, crying out in warning. Paper flutters in the breeze and the smell of iron grows. Lumps on the ground that I'd noticed from afar are now clear: fallen bodies from the tilted tower. Red pools circle their outlines and I avoid studying any further than that.

"Don't look at the road."

"I know. I see them." She replies, head held high to avoid the sights.

For the hundredth time today, a surreal sensation fills me from my toes. I'm off balance and my brain briefly struggles to compute. Rachel's reaction is faster.

"It's an aftershock." Her eyes go wide. "Run!"

The shaking is more intense. I'm crouched, and trying to move forward without falling. Above, there's a heart wrenching scream of metal snapping, a brief silence, and then the audible force of gravity pushing a massive object downward.

"It's coming down! GO!" We're both sprinting as straight and upright as we can, the looming shadow growing smaller. Bits of concrete and glass shower around us, at first hitting like heavy rain and quickly transitioning into painful hail.

We're so close.

The ground vibrates. It feels like the sky is vibrating too. As if compressed, the air feels heavier in this gap between the plummeting section of tower and the ground.

I don't think we'll make it, but then we clear the shadow into pale sunlight. Rachel doesn't slow down, but I yell anyway,

"Keep going! That alley over there!" She hears me and turns slightly, aiming for a gap between buildings that should shield us from the debris wave. A bomb goes off behind me as the tower section disintegrates onto the street, collapsing in on itself. The sensation nearly knocks me over and there's an initial wave of hot, stench-filled air that slaps my back. Rachel's hand reaches from behind the corner, grasps, and pulls me close.

For a moment, I am no longer in San Francisco in 2098. I am in the arms of a woman who looks like Rachel, but is not her…they have the same eyes. The same aura. She holds me tight and I get a brief glimpse at a decrepit world around me. Gray, broken, and hopeless. It's one I don't recognize at all. I *feel* old.

It ends as fast as it began, a reaching arm of purple lightning arcing across the sky being the final image I receive.

The memory…*is that what it was?*…is gone and I'm back in the downtown I came from, watching a wave of debris, fumes, and smoke cascade past our opening. Rachel is against the wall, holding tight, head buried in my chest. Eventually it lifts.

"Did we make it?" She asks, letting go. My mind is elsewhere, gears turning and overwhelmed.

"Aiontis?" She asks. "Are you here with me?" Our eyes meet. *Those* same eyes.

"Yes. I suppose I am."

Chapter 50 – Aiontis
2098 | May 15th | San Francisco

As the dust settles, I roll beside her, my back against a solid wall that has withstood this day. The shaking stops and a cold surge hits my veins while the adrenaline wears off. My chest heaves a huge sigh.

Rachel experiences the same relief. Her eyebrows raise, a smile forms, and she begins to cry. It's only for a moment, and I grab her hand in mine, squeezing with reassurance. I get one in return.

"Let's find your son." I say, leaving our wall and exiting our safe haven. "The park should be just over here."

Navigating the debris takes focus, but at least the shaking has stopped. Within moments, we're clear of its sprawl on the street, the long, thin park in our view. We walk along its concrete section, designed for outdoor dining and gatherings, to find it deserted, and surprisingly intact. There are cracks in the floor and almost every chair and table has been upended, but that's the worst of it.

Looking down the narrow strip of park, I find hope. The lack of damage here echoes what I'm seeing further toward the green spaces. Without many buildings, this might actually be a safe haven on an otherwise deadly day.

"C'mon. Let's go check out the park." I nod to the green area a block away. "If they're still here, that's where they'll be."

Without any quaking, the world is silent aside from our footsteps. It's therapeutic. A gentle draft blows across our skin and the sun, unaware of the happenings on earth, is luminous, warming us. There's something about *right now* that I know we'll find her son. Is it just confidence or do I know something?

Holding onto the railing and with light steps, we follow a half-broken staircase leading to the park. Groups of people stand in the grass. There's the chatter of loud children.

"Oh my God." Rachel's voice catches and she clutches her

chest. She starts running. I follow to keep up.

"Bryson!" It's as if the last, exhausting hour hasn't happened. She's rejuvenated and fast, thrusting her legs against the grass like an athlete.

In the distance, some of the children turn. There are adults with them who look disheveled, weary, and broken. I can't blame them. I can't even comprehend the stress of undergoing the events of today while feeling responsible for the lives of tens of children. They'll never be the same.

"Bryson!" She shouts again. A child, lanky, with glasses, wearing shorts and a cartoon-inspired t-shirt emerges from the pod of students.

"Mom?" The recognition happens almost immediately. "Mom!" Awkwardly, he begins to run and I feel tears sting my eyes. *We did it. Wow.*

Mom and son crash into each other, hugging, embracing, crying. All the fear and sadness and anger from the catastrophic day spilling out into relief. I catch up to their reunion, but give them space, taking a seat in the grass, catching my breath.

I'd almost forgotten this isn't my time. That I'm involved in something grand.

Why take me here? Was it just the easiest event to push us to?
Why her? How is she with us throughout time?
Why all these half memories? What are Titus and I supposed to do?

Bwah….bwahhhhh…bwaaaaahhhhhhhhh

It feels so good to sit down. I could take a nap in this grass, under this sun.

Bwwwaaaahhhhhhhhh

My alertness piques. Is that the rumbling of another after-shock? I don't feel anything from the ground…

BWWWAAAAHHHHHHHHH

It's not a quake. *No, no, no. Not now.* Rachel's teary face looks at me over her son's shoulder as they hug. She can't see the panic that has started in my face, but the image of her calms me. She smiles, hugs her son tighter, and closes her eyes.

BWAAAHHHHHHHHHHHH….

No matter what happens with all of this, that image – a mom reunited with her son – will be one that sticks, comforting me in times of need.

And once more, against my will or understanding, I'm off into the Bulk.

Chapter 51 – Titus
2098 | May 15th | San Francisco

Ground moved beneath the rubber of the eCycle. Slowly, it rumbled some random echoes from the earlier quake. And slowly it was traversed, for the debris that littered the road made it nearly impossible to gather any semblance of speed.

Shifting his weight forward, fidgety, Titus attempted to will the bike and the rubble on the road to move faster. *C'mon…c'mon.* Something about being separated now felt uneasy.

Wrong. Unsafe.

Knowing where he was supposed to be going hadn't helped. He questioned his path's efficiency, wishing he had Rachel to help guide him through the maze of streets. He'd just pointed the bike in a certain direction and done his best to maintain that heading.

It was proving frustrating and time consuming. Eventually, he came to a small clearing facing a bundle of skyscrapers and towers. One of the towers, glinting emphatically in the sun, was broken. Its top third cracked from the base, leaning against a nearby building. It would have been a surreal image if it hadn't echoed what Titus had seen with the Regime in his lifetime. It was surreal now because this was still a society very much in control, enjoying life. But the vision of a war-torn downtown? Commonplace where he was from.

He suppressed bubbling memories; ones he didn't care to relive at the moment. *For another time perhaps…*

Vibrations from the ground pulsed like a cracked whip to the surface, violent and brief. Titus had to steady himself, even with the eCycle's balancing mechanisms. Quiet overcame the earth's grumble until it was replaced by a strange sound in the distance. It was a hollow noise, like a jet taking off, building a crescendo until a sustained peak.

The sound of destruction.

The crooked tower was collapsing. Sliding, crunching,

disintegrating between its original base and the building supporting it. A brown cloud of dust plumed around the debris until a gargantuan *BOOM!* filled the space. After, there were the comparatively silent sounds of falling paper and tinkling glass on the pavement.

The way was now blocked to Titus. He hoped that Aiontis and Rachel had been nowhere near what he just witnessed. *They had to have found him by now...*

He punched the throttle of the eCycle, turning sharply away from the blocked route, determined to get to the park. As he rode, the downtown landscape void of other signs of life, his thoughts wandered to all that had happened...*was* happening.

How did I not know I was an android? Losing his recent memories was an easy answer, but even still...

What's my *purpose in all of this? I thought I was supposed to kill Aiontis but now I only want to help him.*

Is that my coding?

Am I being manipulated?

Annoyance hung around his shoulders. All these time periods were better than the one he'd come from: a world crippled, on the brink of collapse, and full of violence.

The eCycle navigated a left turn, but the road was blocked so he turned right, down an alley. It emerged perpendicular to a road where he could turn left again and continue toward the park. Titus was going through the motions.

Just transport me to a peaceful day. A quiet time. It doesn't matter when. And I'll live out my days there.

He knew it wasn't that simple.

Bwah....bwahhhhh...bwaaaaahhhhhhhhh

The familiar sound started faint, as it always had, fooling Titus into wondering if he'd actually heard it.

Bwwwaaaahhhhhhhhh

He waited for the follow up, louder, to confirm this was happening.

BWWWAAAAHHHHHHHH

What triggers this? He slowed the eCycle and pulled out the portable Warper. It was pulsing its dark glow.

BWAAAHHHHHHHHHHHHH….

No Pulse Sphere, dark and encompassing, emerged. The Warper powered down and Titus was still in San Francisco, sitting on the saddle of the bike. He glanced around, left, right, then down at the Warper again, confused. Nothing – not a *single thing* – had changed.

Strange…he put the Warper back in his pocket. As if it would hold an answer, he looked at his iNsert. Its readout was no different than before.

Confused, but not wanting to delay, he pushed forward with his mission to find the park and hopefully Aiontis, Rachel, and her son with it.

Thirty minutes later, Titus had navigated a route. The landscape of green presented a color he hadn't seen in a while, and the entire scene was a sanctuary, comparatively. As if there was nothing happening, the lush grass showed only slight buckling and the trees, aside from some lost leaves and branches, stood strong with their roots.

And the best sight? A group of children, and several adults, huddled in clusters, some under the shade of the tree, others in the sun. There wasn't any playing among them and it was clear from afar they were shaken, most sitting, picking at grass or staring nowhere to the distance.

Titus left the eCycle on the street and walked the rest of the way, his pace quickening to see if Aiontis and Rachel had made it. As he approached the children, their chaperones eyed him with caution. Here was a man with a frightening scar, large in size, and covered in dirt, ripped clothing, and traces of blood. He'd forgotten this, and the familiar pang of hurt from their concerned gazes slowed him. A voice he knew called out.

"Titus?" He turned to Rachel several meters away, sitting with a boy in the grass. The boy's eyes widened behind his glasses, but gently, with curiosity. "Wow, you made it!" She sprang to her feet and ran to give him a hug. This was a foreign sensation, but he slowly returned it.

"I wasn't sure you'd make it when we left!" She reiterated, breaking the hug. The boy was by her side now, staring up at Titus.

"I almost didn't." Titus returned the boy's gaze. "So, you found your son? Incredible."

"Yes! Once the shaking started, I suppose they were already headed to the park for lunch and decided the safest place was in an open space. They're shaken, especially the teachers."

"I can only imagine. And Aiontis?" Titus noticed his…*friend*…wasn't anywhere nearby. *Had he not made it?*

"I…uh…I don't know." Rachel answered, with hesitation.

"What do you mean, you don't know?"

"We both made it here safely. One minute I was hugging Bryson and smiling at Aiontis."

"Ok. And then?"

"Titus…" she didn't know how to say the next part. "Titus, he just walked away. Terrified, bewildered…as if he had no idea where he was, what had happened, or who *I* was."

Well, this is new.

Chapter 52 – Odyssian

~ ~ ~

Odyssian barreled through his scale of time, frantically glancing forwards and backwards, ensuring all the ends were (or would be) tying up nicely. From what he could surmise, things were fine…for now. He slid a few more centuries forward, did a final check, and nodded to himself.

Something panged him though.

Was it the right move to split them up? It was only one of thousands of thoughts cascading across his brain at that moment, but was the question that rang the loudest. The probabilities he was calculating suggested he'd increased their chances and, at the very least, bought them more time – quite literally – hiding them separately from Ryveliant. *That psychotic bastard.*

Shifting forward a couple millennia, Odyssian revisited when his species had uncovered what Ryveliant was trying to achieve. He was part of a collective that was highly, *obsessively*, focused on furthering the species. Currently, they were beings who could manipulate the fourth dimension, *time*, but there was a widely held belief that there were potentially seven dimensions. This theory was backed by scientific research and even more conjecture, but it was likely true. Even Odyssian believed in it and ventured to guess that as their society's analytical horsepower evolved, seven dimensions would grow to ten. Twenty. Maybe more.

Ryveliant's tactics were something else entirely though. Through his influence, he'd been able to suggest and convince enough members of their species that by removing humans *earlier* in the timeline, evolution would advance faster. Most dramatically, he believed they could initiate the beginning of the evolution into fifth-dimensional beings almost immediately by doing this.

Again, Odyssian had frustrations because he agreed with Ryveliant, *in theory*. But it was a savage thing to manipulate the very evolutionary power they held over their predecessors. Wiping them out without any chance to live their full species' cycle, advance on their own, make mistakes, achieve great things…all the wondrous elements that came with any form of life. It all would be gone so they could speed up their own cycle.

It wasn't right and Odyssian wasn't alone in the belief.

Unfortunately, Ryveliant's plan had already been set in motion by creating and inserting the Regime a few thousand years before third-dimensional beings were originally evolving out. Covertly, Odyssian had been trying to thwart Ryveliant's plan, but it would be complicated and it all depended on one thing:

The woman.

She was the key to avoiding the Regime. She would be the course correction.

The men – one a biological human and the other a synthetic – were integral to her, and thus integral to the operation.

But Odyssian had to buy them more time. He found it a crude and vastly out-of-date metaphor, but time was pliable, like a rubber band. Stretching it along its length would create strain at certain points, but elongate the item as a whole.

His calculations and double-checks assured him that splitting them up had gotten them more time. He had *stretched* the rubber band.

Odyssian just hoped it was enough.

Historian Consultant Report

The Renaissance, Florence, Italy
Summer 1493

The Renaissance was one of the most influential periods in human history largely due to its focus on building a richer culture. Many would associate that to art specifically, with the likes of Leonardo da Vinci and Michelangelo at the forefront of their minds.

Art was just one of many advancements during this time. Significant strides were made in other areas like architecture, mathematics, science and astrology, literature, fashion, world exploration, religion, and philosophy. Not fully responsible – but certainly playing a role – was the invention of the Gutenberg Press around 1450. The new creation improved the ability of European nations to not only communicate, but also share knowledge, skills, and ideas. In many ways, it was the spark that lit the flame.

Renaissance literally translates into "rebirth" (French origins) and this new focus on betterment and progress began most prominently in Florence, Italy. Across the next couple hundred years, this passion and energy would spread over various countries in Europe, creating "mini" Renaissances unique to the citizens of those nations.

Florence was ruled by the Medici family for decades, creating a city of wealth and unique, interesting history. Because of this, the family (and other patrons) had money to spare and spend on artists, encouraging them to pursue and perfect their passions. The funds were bolstered by the emerging concept of "humanism", suggesting that a man/woman was the center of his/her universe and achievements in art, science, music, and many other culture-forward activities were worth pursuing.

Generally speaking, it was a time of peace. Many falsely believe it was a time of total peace (e.g. The Italian Wars still took place during much of the 1500s) but compared to the Hundred Years War (which is exactly what it sounds like + a decade or so), the Crusades, and the Black Death which had preceded the centuries before, most Hiscons feel it fair to call the Renaissance a "peaceful" time in history.

And full disclosure: there's never been a time of <u>absolute</u> peace in history. It is not the way of humans...

Chapter 53 – Aiontis
1493 | Unknown location

"**G**od fucking dammit!" I did not want to leave her. Not then, not after what we'd just been through. The smile she left me with was powerful: a gorgeous, simple gaze while she hugged her son. Her face had been a combination of sweat, grime, and a streak of blood.

It had been the image of victory. A small one in this much more grandiose battle.

This new place is a groggy cloud of confusion. There's the sensation – murky brain function and stiff, unused muscles – that I've been sleeping. My head is pounding too. It's dark in the room, but I can discern details while my eyes adjust. I'm very naked, lying on a disheveled pile of pillows that are the most comfortable thing I've felt in days, only competing with that cushy hotel bed in New York City. For a moment, I revel in their softness. They're made of brightly colored fabric, each a different, muted color in the nighttime.

Around them, several crude, decorated ceramic carafes are strewn about, next to a couple of upright cups. The pillow silk grazes my chest as I reach for one of the carafes to find it half full. I bring the opening to my nose, taking a cautious whiff. *Well, that explains the headache...*it's wine, and my guess is the rest of these were too. Whoever and whenever I am, I was having a party. Good for me.

But there were two cups...

The moonlight provides enough light as I continue to roll on my pillow pile, not wanting to leave its embrace. Across the room is an unorganized pile of easels, and what appears to be paints. Placed crookedly on a taller easel is a canvas with a large hole torn through it, as if someone punched it. Despite the gaping tear in the fabric, I can identify blurry shapes and lines of paint that made it onto the canvas before what I can only assume was the artist quitting in a bout of rage. *Am I the artist? When is this?*

My sight moves on from the painting corner and lands on the most shocking observation yet: a very naked woman asleep on an old piece of furniture – a couch – layered with many of the same pillows. She's on her back, a slender arm hanging, gently resting its knuckles on the floor, apparently oblivious to my small outburst from seconds ago. I study her finer details in the moonlight. Her chest rises and falls slowly, stretched by the way she's laying, and her torso reflects the blueish hue of the night's glow coming from an open window. Her face, softly asleep and beautiful, is not the woman I am anticipating.

She is not the vizier, Caroline, or Rachel.

A swell of disappointment clutches my chest briefly, and I feel alone. Titus is not in this room (which would be awkward) and this woman is a stranger despite the obvious activities we've likely partaken in.

Rachel's worn, but honest smile as she hugged her son echoes in my thoughts and I decide I've earned some rest on this throne of pillows. I let them absorb me as if they were the Bulk.

By the time I wake, it's morning and the woman is gone. Rich, yellow sunlight bathes every inch of the room. The warmth makes me appreciate being in the nude, and my headache is gone thanks to the extra sleep. I rise from the pillows to stretch, elongating my arms, spine, and legs. For just having survived a historic earthquake, I feel great. *But very thirsty.* There's a flagon of water nearby that I chug, disappointed the water is warm, but beggars can't be choosers.

I take time to review my naked body, continuously curious about how this whole process works since I was definitely African American in San Francisco. Here, my skin is olive in complexion, offering a subtle clue. *I'm likely somewhere in the Mediterranean, but what time period?*

Still taking pulls from the water, I visit the painting in the corner and the canvas that I(?) had punched a hole through. My hands meet the textured, thick canvas and I try to smooth and place the triangular tears back toward the hole's center. It's a portrait of the woman from last night – clothed – lying regally in the pile of colorful pillows.

Hiscon excitement stirs in me once more, literally the only wonderful part about this adventure. This painting is immaculate and shows true mastery of lights, shadows, the human form, and how it would interact with the given environment. In my original life, I'm no art expert, but as Hiscons, it's natural to be able to identify most types of art.

This is unmistakably from the Renaissance era.

And I am apparently a *very* talented artist. I have no idea why there's a rage-hole through this piece of art, so I must be a perfectionist too. Without it even being *my* painting (technically speaking), I feel a sadness from its destruction. If only the artist could have known how much this would inspire – and cost – someday. I take a final swig of water and try to find some clothes. Going out into the world will help me determine where I am and [hopefully] find Titus and whatever version of "Rachel" I have in this era.

Strewn about, I find articles of my dress, further confirming I'm in the Renaissance. There are colorful shirts with pillowy shoulders and buttons down their center, pants that flare outward in puffs of fabric, similarly colored leggings, and a red brimmed cap.

My excitement of the time period wanes. *Fuck if I'm putting all of that on.* Instead, I grab a looser – and likely more comfortable – pair of earth-tone pants and a cream-colored tunic with a deep-V. I skip the red cap.

Outside, the sky is a marvelous, cloudless blue. I've emerged into a town square of sorts, with dozens of merchants selling their goods to people walking about. The sandstone colors of roof shingles atop the brown, tan, and white buildings are riveting; I can feel the energy coming from this period.

Unlike so many of the other places I've been on this journey, it is *peaceful.* Focused on growth and evolution versus survival or conquering. It reminds me of my time, 2404.

"Ciao, Leonardo!" The greeting doesn't catch my attention as I continue to soak in the sites. Plus, my name isn't actually Leonardo so…

"Leo-*nardo*!" There's a plump man, outfitted in purple hues of all the clothes I decided to leave on the floor, waving at me. I wave back, awkwardly. "My good man, what *are* you wearing? You may as well be nude out here!"

"Ummm…I was aiming for comfort?"

"You are one strange fool, Leonardo. But a talented one! I'll give you that."

A lightning bolt triggers in my mind. I ask a question without any second thought:

"You keep calling me Leonardo. Is my last name 'da Vinci'?" My heart starts to pound. *It can't be.*

"Good heavens! Da Vinci? Are you mad? I said you were talented; I didn't say you were a genius!" He lets out a heavy chuckle that shakes his gut and my hopes are crushed. He notices and puts a hand on my shoulder. "You are an odd one, Leo, but don't let the da Vinci's of the world discourage you."

"Thanks." I shrug it off. It was a long shot anyway. "Where are we by the way?"

"Where are we?! Leonardo, have you taken ill? You are speaking in tongues!" His eyebrows raise. "Did you have too much wine with the pretty Rossi woman last night?" He nudges me, boyishly wanting to hear of my escapades.

"Ehmmm, yeah that's it. We had such a good time. But still, if you please: where are we?"

"Odd Leo! Odd! We are in Florence, Italy of course." He shakes his head in disapproval. "You best get right before you meet the Medici's later this evening!"

Wow. My heart skips another beat hearing that I'm alive during the same time as this famous patron family of the arts.

"And why am I meeting them again?" The man's eyes widen and his face contorts almost into a scowl.

"You are hopeless, boy. You're showing them your painting this evening. You *did* paint the Rossi woman, did you not?"

"Ahhh yes! That!" I lie. "I did, I did. And it is exquisite."

"Good, good. Stay outside and get some fresh air, you appear to need it. I've got errands, but I will see you tonight." He begins to trot away, waving. "Arrivederci!"

Fuck. I feel like a teenager without my homework done.

Except my teacher is the Medici family who will make or break my (or rather, this person I've assumed) artistic career.

Chapter 54 – Aiontis
1493 | Summer | Florence, Italy

Let's just say the rest of the day was the *best* I've had since getting stuck back in time. It was a quintessential early Italian summer day.

I basked in the sunlight.

I walked along the Arno River.

I ate fresh bread.

I devoured some sugary pastries.

I enjoyed more wine.

It was lovely and, perhaps for the first time, I truly forgot about my predicament. Only as the evening approached did my anxiety kick in. Luckily, aside from sideways glances and a few shaking heads, the citizens of Florence were more than willing to help answer my questions.

The year is 1493 and it's likely early or mid-June. This is indeed Florence (that man wasn't lying, but I wanted to double check). I even found out where the Medici's live, which leads me to right now.

I'm outside the Medici villa, ripped painting in hand under a length of ruby fabric. I have my plan, though I'm not sure the Medici's – those who are paying for my artist lifestyle – will be pleased. Technically speaking though, I'm not the asshole that put me in this position.

It's approaching dusk, and before Florence transitions to a star-filled sky, it puts on a show. I stay outside a little longer, soaking in the lasting warmth from the setting sun, in awe of the purples, pinks, blues, and oranges that act like paint strokes across the atmosphere. Others pass on their way into the villa, ignoring the artist staring into the heavens. It helps that I'm dressed appropriately now, even if I feel like a damn fool.

As the paint strokes on the sky begin to fade, I stroll inside, primarily driven by hunger. Scents tingle my nostrils, wondering several things as I cross the home's threshold:

What will we have to eat?
Is my plan actually going to work?
Will Titus and/or the woman be there?

In this particular Hiscon dreamscape, I'm easily distracted from these most important questions.

The villa itself is impressive, surrounded by lush gardens with rows of green. The main building reflects many others in the city: cream colored exterior with a red-orange shingled roof. It's grander, standing two stories tall, with many windows. Inside, it's adorned with pieces of art: statues, paintings, and busts. Quickly, I'm ushered toward the building's center, back outdoors, to where the party is taking place under the emerging stars.

There's already 30 or more people here, enjoying the perfectly lukewarm evening air. Laughter rings across various groups and there's a buzzy energy among the cliques of chatting groups. Everyone is dressed colorfully, with striking lime greens, bright blues, pinks, deep reds, and sunset oranges. Most men wear a red cap – something I've decided to forego again this evening – and many of the women have pulled back hair, wearing bushy gowns with high waistlines.

No one notices me, so I get to stroll about, soaking it all in. Further out in this courtyard, there's a trio of long tables in a U-formation, and beyond that rests a shallow pool with a gray cherub statue at its center.

Where should I place this damn thing? I question, not wanting to carry the painting around all night. Reminding myself of its presence causes my anxiety to return…I'm trying to get away with turning in a destroyed painting. Even worse, the family hosting this party are the ones that paid me in the first place.

"Ciao everyone, please take your seats at the tables. Dinner will begin momentarily." The crowd migrates to the tables, laughing and conversing. Not sure where I'm supposed to sit, I find an endcap seat on one of the tails of the "U" and lean my painting against the table's edge.

Wine is healthily poured into our cups, the burgundy juice

nearly touching the brim. *Oh, so it's going to be* that *kind of party*. Once more, forgetting all the stress of being caught in a fourth-dimensional war and not knowing where my companions are, I'm having a fucking Renaissance party in Florence, Italy. This may end up being the best night of my life.

"Tonight's first course of ten…" *Ten!* Excitement bubbles within me. "Will be a pear sugar tart, dusted with cinnamon." A few people clap excitedly. Within moments, there are small, square tarts placed in front of us. The crust is golden brown and flaky, with large granules of salt sticking sporadically, while the pear slices rest gently packed in the middle. There's a fine layer of dark brown cinnamon dust on top, so aromatic I can almost taste it already.

I wait for others to begin eating, careful to avoid any rudeness, and dig in. The tart is immensely sweet because at this time, sugar is believed to be a healthy ingredient. The warm pastry also has notes of buttery dough, with salty undertones, and a fresh, almost vanilla-esque flavor from the pear slices. I wash it down with a swig of rich wine, elation filling my bones. I can't remember my last meal, but I know I'm going to enjoy every bite of this one.

Chapter 55 – Aiontis
1493 | Summer | Florence, Italy

We're five courses in and my waistline is tightening, but the food is just too damn good. A rich, creamy pasta was most recent and it sounds like roast turkey, a delicacy, is up next. Wine continues to be filled to my cup's limit and I must remember to pace myself.

People watching has kept me entertained and busy while I've been quiet for most of the meal. The person seated on my right doesn't seem to mind as he's been consistently deep in conversation about philosophy with the man on *his* right. Across the way, I notice the fatter man from before, who's traded in his purple hues for blues, conversing and laughing. Several courses prior, he nodded in my direction and I raised my glass toward him. Now, he seems like the life of the party, telling story after story on the other tail of the "U", just out of reach from my hearing.

I place a final bite of the pasta and its cream sauce on my tongue, savoring the fatty cheese taste. Fermented grape juice follows it and my cheeks flush as I set my cup down. A man at the center table stands.

"Friends!" He exclaims, hands held outward and looking from table to table. "I am so glad we could break bread and entertain each other with our company this evening!"

"Giovanni, the food is delicious!" My larger friend shouts toward the front.

"Ah yes, Bernardo. I can see that *you* are enjoying all of it." Laughter rings out as the man I now know as Bernardo smiles and shrugs.

"Anyway," Giovanni gets back to his main point. "The time has come for a special reveal. Leonardo?" He gestures toward me, eyebrows raised. I feel like a school child being suddenly called on in class.

"Aye! Leonardo!" Bernardo shouts, taking a swig of his wine.

"Yes…yes. Of course." I stand and shift toward the end of the table, where the painting leans. *Here goes nothing…*

"You see…" I begin, wanting to build up the anticipation and entertainment. "An artist is only as good as the *accountability* he has on himself to produce his best work." I see several nods around the table as I pick up the painting. "Why produce anything less than perfect, I ask? Are we put on this earth to produce mediocrity?"

"Here, here!" A random man shouts. I linger for a moment before continuing.

"And so, what I present you with tonight is an example of *my* accountability to perfection." With a dramatic heave, I pull off the ruby fabric, turning to show the captivated audience my damaged painting. "This painting – which has no name – ceased to exist the moment I put my fist through its canvas."

I witness murmurs in the crowd, some cocking their heads at what they can make out, others looking distressed. The man, Giovanni, (who by this point I've assumed is a member of the Medici family) does not look angry *or* pleased. He just…*looks* at the painting. At me.

"I wish I could tell you why this painting does not meet my standards! Is it the muse? Could it be the lighting? The setting? A particular brush stroke?" I list the reasons quickly, with emphasis. This crowd is in the palm of my hand. "But alas! It is a mystery and I must apologize to you, and our gracious hosts. I will need more *time* to reach the perfection which I seek."

Silence. A quaint cough. Most of the crowd is looking at Giovanni, some are still looking thoughtfully at the painting. Finally, he speaks.

"Leonardo, you speak a powerful truth this evening. It overshadows any disappointment I have about the painting and our patronage. You are right!" He looks across the crowd, as if giving a sermon. "We should *all* aim to achieve perfection in our endeavors! For what other goal is there to achieve? I thank *you*, Leonardo, for reminding us of that." I smile at him and nod. "That being said, you *do* owe me a painting. May I suggest a new muse?" He whispers something to one of the staff nearby and they trot into the villa.

A few moments later, with some conversation and drinking having been restarted, the staff returns with a young woman alongside them. She heads to the front of the table, the man putting his arm around her.

Unlike the other women here, her brown hair is undone, flowing gently onto her shoulders. Her face is instantly recognizable and I nearly have to take a seat.

"Let me introduce my daughter, Caterina."

You guessed it.

It's her.

Once more.

Chapter 56 – Aiontis

1493 | Summer | Florence, Italy

I stand in awe – though I suppose I shouldn't be – as our run-ins throughout time are a staple of this adventure.

*Caterina…*The name suits her. She looks truly breathtaking this evening, more natural than the other women around her. There's an authenticity in a time where women (and men) often tried so hard to bolster their appearances. Her green dress is form fitting, but relaxed, letting the fabric accentuate her curves.

The center of my chest is heavy and my throat dry. I'm not sure if my emotion comes from the relief of seeing her, the moment from Rachel that was cut short, or…something else? I cannot help but stare, drinking in the moment.

"Leonardo?" Giovanni asks. "Would Caterina suit your needs?" Bernardo answers for him,

"It would seem she'll be his masterpiece! The boy is smitten!" Some giggles come from around the table at the truth-disguised-as-a-joke. Caterina's eyes have spirit, playfully wondering why I'm so speechless right now.

"Ahem…uhh, yes! Yes! Thank you, Giovanni!" I take a quick swig of wine to get some moisture back in my throat. "She is awe-inspiring and Bernardo tells no lies. I can envision my masterpiece now!"

Caterina smiles, glancing away, embarrassed from the attention. Giovanni claps his hands loudly.

"Wonderful! You will start tomorrow, for I shall have that painting in a month's time." His smile turns stern, without being mean. It is fair given that I [read: actual Leonardo] punched a hole in his last sponsorship. "Perhaps you two should walk the grounds and get to know one another?"

I nod, setting my painting down. By now, the antsy guests have returned to their revelry. I take my wine cup, glancing over to the man seated next to me. He's deep in conversation with tablemates down the way, so I steal his wine cup too, and a carafe off the table.

Caterina notices as I round the corner of the long "U", hands full. There's a devilish smirk on her face as she takes a cup from my arms, pulls a strong swig, and extends an arm toward the dark gardens.

"My lady." I nod, taking a drink of my own. There's a buzz in the air – yes, partially because of the wine – but also the "gut" feeling. Dormant for most of the day thus far, it's strong and brewing now.

Here in Renaissance Florence with this mysterious woman. Caterina.

As we walk, I look to space, swirling with blacks, unsure if that's the right place to be looking. *Odyssian, what are you up to?*

"What are you thinking about?" The question has sincerity. I deflect, confident I should not share my secrets yet.

"Just wondering to the heavens how I've gotten so lucky this evening!" I smile, looking to her. For a brief second, she looks disappointed, having wanted an answer, but it is fleeting and she smiles at the compliment. "I got in far less trouble than I feared for destroying my painting, ate a wonderful feast, drank even better wine, and am strolling these gardens with a woman of ex-quisite beauty. And the night! Look at the moon!"

She giggles at my excitement, but it's true; I'm enjoying my-self.

Away from the villa, moonlight drapes us and the stars shine like pinprick beacons. I am warm in the evening's flawless weather. For a few moments we walk in silence, enjoying it.

Her hand, gentle and light, caresses each bush and shrub as we pass. She's waiting on me to continue this conversation and I'm strangely nervous, like a teenager on a first date.

"Tell me about yourself. What do you like to do for fun, Ca-terina?"

"Hmmm. Well, I actually dabble in a bit of painting my-self…for fun. I'm not very good, but I enjoy it. Perhaps I'll show you sometime."

"I would love that."

"But more than anything, I love to read and write." She pauses, wanting to accurately convey the *why* behind her passion.

"There's something magical about transferring someone's ideas and stories into your mind…into your beliefs and knowledge. Equally as incredible is being the one to inspire others in that way."

"Well stated." I comment, impressed by her eloquent remarks. "Have you published anything?" My mind thinks to the Gutenberg Press invented only decades before.

"Oh heavens, no!" She laughs. "Much like painting, I write for myself. Though I believe I'm better at it than painting."

We both take a gulp of wine at the same time as we round a trimmed hedge that's taller than both of us. Catching each other's eye, we laugh at the unintentional synchronization.

It continues like this for several more hours. We take more laps around the garden. We sit on benches to rest our legs. We finish the wine. And we talk, flirt, and learn of one another.

By the time we return to the party, most of the guests are gone or lingering inside. The table stands uncleared, likely for the staff to finish tonight, with scraps of food and plates strewn about. Glasses of wine are unfilled, a couple even tipped over. As we near the table, I spot one of the pear sugar tarts, completely untouched.

"What?! Who on earth would have left this uneaten!" I step over to the dish and pick up the treat. It has cooled in the night, yet the cinnamon scent trickles into my nose. Caterina smiles, approaching.

"These were the best part of the feast! I stole one from the kitchen earlier."

I do my best to break it in half and give her the larger portion. Her smile continues to radiate, filling me with more warmth than the wine.

"Cheers!" I tap my pastry against hers and take a bite. She looks at me like I'm half mad, half comedian. I realize she's probably never heard that term before, but she takes a huge bite anyway, eyes locked on to mine the whole time.

"Mmmmm awwwmyyy. Issssoooguuud" She mumbles, eyes closed now. Now it's my turn to laugh.

I want to stay here forever.

Chapter 57 – Titus
2098 | May 23rd | San Francisco

Titus felt as if he'd been here…*now*…forever. It had actually only been a little more than a week since the quake, now being referred to as "The Great Faultline Disaster". San Francisco, and a majority of the state of California, was in shambles and disarray.

FEMA, the Red Cross, and the National Guard were out in full force, searching for the injured, collecting the dead, and helping those who were displaced. Daily, Titus would search for some sign that Aiontis was still here (perhaps in another body?) but he struggled to understand what he should even be looking for.

But he knew the truth.

Aiontis was gone. Titus had heard the portable Warper charge and release that day. For some reason, he wasn't taken along for the ride and he couldn't determine why.

Why had Odyssian split them up? Or had this been Ryveliant's doing? Either way, it didn't matter because despite his best efforts to use the Warper, he was stuck. It would not activate, even when he followed the exact procedure as the first time he'd used it.

Frustration and worry mounted, and he was sleeping poorly because of it. Since the 15th of May, he had been staying with Rachel and her son, Bryson. They lived in a cozy, multi-floor townhome in a suburb of San Francisco ten minutes outside of the city. Thankfully, her home had minimal damage compared to what they'd witnessed downtown: some exterior roof cracks, a few splintered windows, a bit of loose plumbing, and nearly everything inside had taken a tumble. They knew she'd been lucky.

To keep busy, Titus helped with repairs, eager to free his mind from the swirl of questions and confusion. It was amusing how simple most fixes were, not only because of his intellect, but also how rudimentary the problems were. Tools and processes were comfortably simple – easy problems for him to solve – and within five days he'd had the place in working order aside from some final supplies that were in high demand.

With school all but dismantled for the time being, Titus had grown close to the boy, who both literally and figuratively looked up to him, aware Titus had played a part in saving his mother's life. Eager to learn, Bryson followed Titus around the house as he made repairs or picked up toppled furniture, helping as much as he could. He stayed mostly silent, asking "why" questions periodically about certain repairs. To his surprise, Bryson never once asked him about his facial scars, a prominent reason why he generally didn't like children; their curiosity usually got the better of them.

For the past couple days, they had shifted attention to helping Rachel's neighbors, most of whom had similar damage. Bryson's lanky, 10-year-old frame was awkward and couldn't do much of the heavy lifting, but he was ok with that and waited patiently for instructions on how to help.

Titus was in awe of the child's youth…reflecting on the understanding of time he now had. This child was technically centuries older than him. His grandchildren several times over would be in the hellscape that Titus was from. But here he was, influencing this boy and making an impression on him, hundreds of years before he would even exist. Much like the World War I sniper he'd gotten killed, Titus wondered if he was altering the current future and *his* past.

Later that evening, Bryson had gone to bed and the news was on the television in the background, acting like white noise. Titus and Rachel sat on the couch, enjoying glasses of wine.

"I really can't thank you enough for everything you've done, Titus." Her eyes gleamed with sincerity. "Both on *that* day and this whole week."

"Don't mention it. I'm just sorry I've been in your hair this long." There was a nagging feeling that he wasn't doing *enough* to earn his keep, even if only for a short time. "I just thought I'd have heard from Aiontis by now."

"Well, if I'm not allowed to mention how helpful you've been, then *you're* not allowed to mention being in my hair." Glass in hand, she made air quotes near the end of the sentence. "I am surprised too. What do you think happened? I've never seen someone look so lost before." Titus let out a small chuckle.

"Only time will tell."

"Did you two have a fight or something? Why hasn't he reached out?" Titus took a gentle sip of the wine. The question was logical, but barking up the wrong tree. He knew Aiontis couldn't contact him.

"No fight. A miscommunication a few days earlier, but a friend helped us clear it up."

Sensing he wanted to move on from the conversation, Rachel decided to go to bed and leave him be.

"Well, I'm sure he'll turn up." Her hand patted his knee in an awkward, endearing way and she gulped the remaining wine in her glass. "In the meantime, you're welcome to stay as long as you'd like." She rose from the leather couch and started toward the stairs. "Goodnight, Titus."

"Goodnight, Rachel." Titus smiled.

As long as you'd like. The phrase lingered like a gnat, buzzing and crashing around in his head.

Problem is, that's not my choice…

Chapter 58 – Aiontis
1493 | Summer | Florence, Italy

After our wonderful introduction under the moon and stars, Caterina and I went our separate ways. She remained at the villa and the last I saw of her, she was helping staff clean up the party, something she certainly didn't need to do. Like a love-sick puppy, I sauntered home alone, enjoying the warm air and the equally-warming wine flowing through my system. Being pushed through time like this – as some part of greater war – was fully a curse I needed to escape, but there were moments of wonder.

Moments I would never forget, or change for anything.

Unsurprisingly, it took over an hour to get home. Once I made my way back into the heart of Florence, the shops, markets, and restaurants all closed, I forgot where I lived. I lollygagged about, eventually finding the town center I remembered from the morning and went up to the room, completely as I'd left it, save for the destroyed painting I'd left at the Medici's.

Now I'm awake, sitting in bed, and it's dawn. I've been watching what started as a millimeter-thin ray of sunlight cascade across the room, its yellow-gold overtaking the black-blue of the evening. I slept as good as I could have, given my excitement for today. Not wasting anytime, Caterina is coming over after breakfast so we can discuss the painting's approach. After how well we got along last night, I'm eager to spend more time with her, thankful this is a much more *normal* circumstance with this mystery woman than what I've had thus far (as opposed to a vizier who believed me to be a curse from a god, for example).

Briefly, I remember that *me* is actually *us*, and there's a pang of worry at the base of my skull that I haven't found Titus yet. The worry turns to guilt, wondering if I should be doing more to look for him. He is the one with the time-travel device after all. *What would happen if it goes off again, and I'm nowhere nearby? It seemed to not matter in 1917.* The inquiry is important, but hard to focus on right now. *It's not like I can control any of this bullshit anyway…what's the point in trying?*

Sun fills the entire space, signaling the transition from dawn into morning. Clothes, pillows, canvas, and paints lay strewn about the floor and on tables and chairs. This is not going to be the best second impression for her to walk into, even if it fits the "mad artist" persona I was selling last evening.

Within 20 minutes, it's clean-ish and the space is at least presentable, warming in the day's light. I'm not sure when *exactly* she'll arrive, so I leave to find food (a pastry sounds delightful, though I am missing coffee in this time period).

I sit on a bench in the center of the same town square that acted as my homing beacon last night, finishing a flaky, sugar-dusted pastry. It will tide me over until I get hungry again in a few hours. Let's be honest, if I'm going to be in Renaissance Italy, I'm going to eat like it's going out of style.

Citizens of Florence pass by, moving along with their errands and duties. Even on my second day here, I've not gotten used to it and my excitement bubbles over into a grin. Sure, it may not be any one, specific event, but people watching during the early Renaissance is something other Hiscons would kill for.

A toddler waddles behind his mother, clutching a piece of fruit, his full determination and concentration focused on performing the two tasks at once. Periodically, the mother turns to glance at him, checking that son and fruit are both upright. She catches my observance and smiles. I return the gesture, amused at the furrowed brow of her son's focus. A thought hits me like a ton of bricks: *This toddler is centuries older than me.* This doesn't come as a surprise, but more a reminder that I'm in a time period in which I don't belong.

Despite the sun on my face, the cold grip of loneliness weighs on my shoulders.

"Hello, good sir!" A light, feminine voice says. I glance around, momentarily blinded by sunlight. "I've heard there is an artist around these parts – mildly talented. Do you know who that would be?"

My hand blocks the sun along my brow and Caterina is

standing in front of me, smiling. Last night's green dress is replaced with a happy yellow one, her brown hair down again, gracefully lying across her shoulders. In the daylight, there are flecks of green in her brown eyes. *The same as Caroline's…*

"Ah why yes! The mildly talented artists actually live another 10-minute walk down *that* way." I point in a random direction. "This happens to be where the *highly* talented artists reside."

"Oh, I see…" She appears crestfallen. Did my joke not make sense to her? *What the hell does banter look like in Renaissance Italy?* "Well in that case, I'll be on my way. Thank you, sir."

She mopes away for a few paces. My heart is racing…is she actually going to leave? Should I follow her? Explain it was just a joke? After a couple steps more, she turns around, smiling devilishly.

"You should have seen your face! It appeared as if the artist was going to cry." She giggles. I'm officially humiliated.

"Caterina," I stand, brow furrowed and hands on my hips. "That wasn't very nice." She's still smiling, sly, with a curl on one end, eyes locked on mine as she walks back over to me.

"Oh, you'll get over it." She pats me on the shoulder and moves toward the center of the square. "So where are we headed?"

I'm stunned by her confidence and that I fell for such an obvious jab. This…version…of this woman is the most playful one I've met yet. She's the most alive, the least weighed down by the world around her. Her spirit is intoxicating.

"We're just over here." I gesture toward my building. "Would you like to discuss what we'll paint inside, or out here in the sun?"

"Inside. I feel as if it's going to be dreadfully hot today."

Leading the way, we head up to my small loft where the sun is bathing the room anyway. But she's right, it's cooler here.

"Cozy." She states, looking around. I'm suddenly acutely aware of how unimpressive the space likely is to her: someone who comes from wealth.

"Yes, well…when I become a famous artist, I hope to upgrade!"

"I like it." She smiles at me, and there's something

mischievous there. "So! What did you have in mind for the painting?" To be honest, I hadn't thought about it. All I could think about was her, but not the painting *of* her. *Shit.*

"I…erm…I like to give my muses plenty of input. Then I can build ideas from there. Does that work for you?"

"Yes." She takes a seat on the pillow-filled couch.

"Would you prefer indoors or outdoors?"

"Indoors I should think. There are too many paintings outdoors these days."

"I tend to agree. Ok then…sitting or standing?"

"Hmmm…I think *laying*. It's more breathtaking wouldn't you say?"

"Yes, it is. All right…from there, what ideas do you gravitate toward?"

"If I'm being honest, I really admired your painting you had at the party. The color of the pillows was playful among a powerful woman and her body, resting on their embrace."

"That makes it easy for me!" I joke. "I've already done that painting before."

"Mhmm." She states, holding something back.

"What is it?" I ask, feeling my heart inexplicably begin to patter faster.

"You're forgetting a final question, no?" Her eyes look at the floor, then directly at me.

"I am?"

"Clothed…or not?"

I gulp like a school boy. *Oh Caterina.*

Chapter 59 – Aiontis
1493 | Summer | Florence, Italy

"*I*...um..." I stammer, knowing full well which option *I* would prefer. "Which would you prefer?"

"Your last painting lacked a punch. It was gorgeous, but forgettable. It would not stand the test of time." She pauses, delivering the harsh critiques bluntly. "You want to be great? You want to be remembered? I can guarantee you that same painting with my nakedness will stop people in their tracks."

"And Giovanni is ok with this?" Her gaze hardens, offended, but I'm simply trying to make sure I don't die in 1493.

"He made me your muse, did he not? His opinion is not important. It is my wish to do this and you can tell him as much." Her flash of anger subsides. "You know I'm right." I've lost the battle, though I'm not exactly fighting hard either.

"Ok, ok. You're right!" My hands go up in mock-surrender. "When would you like to get started?"

"Right now." She states. I watch as she stands, gathering the pillows, and begins to arrange them. There's little rhyme or reason to how she's placing them on the floor, only ensuring that no two colors are side by side.

I can hear my heart in my ears and my blood rushing: excitement mixed with the worry of a specific question.

Can I even fucking paint?! I remember how naturally I was able fight in Japan, or work under the hot sun in Egypt. It seems that I *adopt* the natural talents of these...hosts.

"Well why are you just standing there?" She questions. "Get your paints and canvas ready."

I nod and turn to the nook that houses an empty easel, paints, and a roll of canvas. In the heat of the bloody samurai battle, adrenaline took over, masking the realization of my body doing a thing it hadn't before. Here, it's like a separate piece of my mind – one I've never visited – takes over. Very clearly *me*, but an *unused* part of me. Within minutes I have paints spread across a palette, organized by hues in a rainbow across the top, with my whites, browns, and blacks along the bottom. A canvas has been cut and stretched across a wood frame, eager to absorb and hold whatever creation I put onto it. I place it on the easel and turn the wooden stilts around, so that it faces me and I face Caterina.

My nerves have subsided, even against the thought of seeing this woman – the one who has been following me throughout time – naked. I strongly desire it, but now it's time to paint.

"Can you rearrange those two pillows near the top?" I point to a pair of pillows that have fabric blemishes on them. "Move the tears away so they're facing outward."

Caterina does this in silence, and I move to the windows, playing with the shutters – open, closed – to find the lighting I'm looking for. Via partially closed shutters, I settle on something that would resemble a hazy afternoon, imagining the sun clinging heavy to the horizon, slowly transferring power to night.

"Does this work for you?" I ask, wanting to make sure she's comfortable.

"It's perfect. It creates a distinct mood." She smiles and looks down at her feet. "Are you…ready to start?"

"Yes, are you?" She doesn't answer.

Seeking some element of modesty, she turns away, beginning to undo her sunshine-yellow dress in the back, arms and elbows out gracefully like angel's wings. I watch as the fabric loosens and hangs limp from her bare shoulders. Unusual for this era, she's not wearing undergarments beneath it.

Professional painter or not, my lips go dry and my heart is slamming. I think it could break my ribs…Her bronzed, olive skin contrasts the yellow, the thin line of her spine revealing more and more of itself. With elegance, the dress hangs from her arms and sits, clinging, atop the curves of her hips. Her head turns sideways, bringing tangled brown hair tumbling partway down her back. Out of the corner of her eye, she confirms that I'm watching before the dress overcomes the curves, slides off her arms, and falls to the floor without a sound.

Both because of the Omaha-based memory loss and current loss of focus, I can't recall the last time I've seen a naked woman, much less one from the Renaissance era whom I've been follow-ing throughout time. This might as well be my first because I *know* I've never seen someone as gorgeous as her.

The dim light casts shadows along her curves from right to left, not showing a single scar, blemish, or mark along her skin. She turns, looking down, then directly at me, with her hands by her sides. There's no effort to cover anything, she wants me to see her bare. I swallow hard, trying to concentrate and ignore the butterflies in my chest and stomach, which are remarkably simi-lar to the gut feeling I've been having from Odyssian.

Focus.

"Uhh." I clear my throat and blink slowly, deliberately. That other part of my brain kicks in, the painter's creativity, and the jitters reduce. "Ok. Lovely."

She laughs. I continue.

"Here's what I'm thinking and you tell me if you're comfort-able or not." I point to the pillows. "The obvious part is for you to lie down on them and then we'll work on positioning. Place your head on the end *furthest* from me."

She scoots her dress out of the way with her feet, turns, kneels down, and maneuvers herself onto the pillow pile. The contrast of the greens, blues, yellows, reds, and purples against her skin tone is dramatic. She was completely right: *that's* what this painting was missing.

"Ok. Is this good?" She asks.

"Yes, very good. You were right…the earth-tone of your skin looks special against those pillows." I compliment. She smiles big. "Ms. Medici! No smiling please! You must remain still!"

She looks at me oddly, curious if I'm serious, but I could barely get the jest out without laughing myself and she joins me.

"Just focus on your painting, yeah? Maybe you *won't* punch a hole in it this time."

"Ouch!" She laughs briefly and we both focus.

"I want you to place your right arm…"

"Ok, let's take a break!" I place my thin brush down into a cup of water and my palms on my thighs. Caterina sits in surprise.

"What? We're already done?"

"Done? Oh, definitely not!" I turn the canvas off the easel to show her. For right now, it's not much but an outline of her torso, the couch, and the general blob of pillows beneath her. Confused, a single eyebrow on her face raises.

"This will help the whole process go by faster. Getting the sizing and depth right is critical and I've just done all that. The rest is easy in comparison!"

"Hmmm, I had no idea." She standing now, still fully nude, her arms crossed against her chest.

"Are you hungry?" I ask, hearing the low rumble in my stomach.

"Yes, actually. Very."

"Being a muse is hard work." I joke.

"Lying in a bed of pillows has never been so stressful." She adds, picking up her yellow dress from the floor. "Can you help me?"

My heart returns to hammering against the inside of my ribcage as she steps into the fabric, crouches down, and pulls it up around her. I can smell her sweet skin...*feel* her energy. Some unspoken bond pulses outward from her, crashing into me.

I grab the fabric with the tips of my fingers and bring it upward, as her arms assist in setting the loops on top her shoulders.

"Do I just tie this piece back here?" I ask, my voice croaking ever so slightly.

"Mhmmm." She approves. "Why're you so nervous?" She teases. I finish tying the string of daisy-yellow fabric across her back, accidentally brushing her skin as I do so.

"I'm not..." She turns, challenging my statement.

"Are you sure?" Her eyes look up into mine. I can smell her breath, as sweet as her skin. There are only centimeters between us, the space getting smaller and smaller. Her body is pressing against mine and I feel her face getting closer; I close my eyes.

Strangely, I sense her lips going past my face, toward my ear.

"Leonardo..." I try to control a shiver, but that's fucking impossible. "Let's go get some pasta and wine."

She takes my hand softly and we start out of the room.
My god, I think I'm in love.

Chapter 60 – Aiontis

1493 | Summer | Florence, Italy

Lunch had been delicious, though I was still stuffed from the night before. Caterina was too, so we both ate light, but rich.

The thin-noodle pasta had been luscious, with carrots and chicken. As customary, it had a side of bread, and plenty of wine. It was the latter that Caterina and I enjoyed the most of, establishing a lovely mid-day buzz while we laughed and talked.

Now sitting in the plush grass of a small park, we soak in the sunlight, pillowy clouds, and warm breeze.

"Tell me, Leonardo…why do you paint?" Caterina asks, face to the sky, eyes closed, absorbing the sun. Her brown hair glimmers along her shoulders – almost blonde in some places – as it reflects the light.

"Hmmm." I pause, wondering how to answer. Or rather how *Leonardo* would answer. "Well, for starters, I enjoy doing it! The thrill of creation…it's a powerful sensation putting your mind and hands toward *producing* something. Is that similar to why you enjoy writing?"

"Yes…" She thinks. "I suppose that is part of it. I'd never thought about it that way."

"I also paint because there's the possibility of it lasting the tests of time. Just the thought of that is staggering to me."

"What do you mean?"

I ponder how to explain it to her without sounding like a crazy person from the future.

"Here…close your eyes."

"They're already closed." She says with a small degree of sass.

"That they are! Well keep them closed. Now, imagine about a thousand years into the future. What do you see?"

"A *thousand*?!? How am I supposed to imagine that?" She exclaims.

"That's my point, but let me help. A thousand years into the future there will be buildings as tall as mountains. People will fly in machines. They'll be able to travel to the stars and moon. There will have been times of peace…of war…and of peace again.

"Now, imagine there are places where people can go to look at old paintings and statues. They can study *my* painting from a thousand years before, eager to learn. They'll see *you*, captured forever in a moment, *one thousand years* from now."

"How do you know all of this?" Almost imperceptible, there's a tinge of fear in her question.

"I don't. Who's to say it won't come true?"

"It's a grandiose idea. *Flying machines?* You've got quite the imagination." She loses herself in thought a few moments more. "I like it though. It's a higher purpose."

"Exactly."

Sleepy from the digesting food, the wine, and the lavish discussion, we lie in the grass and doze off under the sun.

A brisk gust of wind stirs me, warm from the day, with a group of sweat beads on my brow. Acting as a visor, I hold my hand and look toward the sky. We've been asleep for about 30 minutes.

Caterina rests next to me, arms lying gently entwined on her stomach, looking elegant, save for her mouth hanging wide open. I try to stifle a laugh, but it comes out as a snort and she stirs, giving me side eye and letting out a frustrated moan.

"How long have we been asleep?" Her voice is groggy.

"About half an hour." I answer. "You must have been very tired."

"I think the wine got to me. Something about drinking in the sun…it makes me sleepy every time."

"Ah, yes. You're not alone there."

She lays silent, with her eyes closed, taking her time to fully wake.

"Are you ready to continue the painting? I figure we can

make good progress before sunset. After that, our lighting will be off."

"Yes." She sits up reluctantly and I brush some grass off her back. "Thank you. Let's get back to it!"

Our sauntering turns to a brisk walk as our bodies realize they have replenished energy to work with. There's also the palpable excitement of continuing the painting and seeing what the outcome will be. Placing myself in Leonardo's mindset, I try to determine how many sessions it will take for us to finish the painting.

"I think we'll probably need five sessions total, including today's." I comment while we round a corner, getting closer to my building. "It could be less…"

Caterina seems distant, distracted.

"Mmm. Ok."

I ignore it and we trudge upstairs in silence. The door closes and I move to the shutters, adjusting the light and accommodate the passing sun. The easel and canvas greet me with the rough outline I left, eager to be filled in.

Looking up, Caterina is still clothed, staring at me intently. A subtle undercurrent of concern lies in her expression.

"Are you going to get out of that dress…or?" *Maybe she no longer wants to do a nude portrait? Did my talk of future generations seeing the painting change her mind?* "If you don't want to be nude, you don't have to!" I add.

"Leonardo, come here." The statement is quiet, but holds power. I'm not sure why, but my pulse quickens significantly. I approach her, an intense aura in the air. Her gaze is locked on mine, but she doesn't say a word. Instead, she slips the dress over her shoulders, and lets it fall, faster than the first time.

Part of me is wickedly confused and the other knows exactly what I *want* to happen. *Does she want the same thing?*

She takes a single step toward me, smolder within her eyes and a thin, excited smile across her lips. My body is an internal gambit of the gut sensation guiding my path, lust, and…love?

Our mouths crash into each other, the pressure of her naked body against my garments. My hands find her back and her bottom as our lips press and open, granting passage for our tongues to dance.

Ecstasy explodes in my mind, a sensation I've never felt before, or at least not one I remember. Past the pleasure and passion of our kiss, it feels like I'm on the cusp of a breakthrough.

Of memories?

Of understanding all of this?

I have no idea, but I can barely concentrate.

Caterina breaks our hold for a moment, grabbing the bottom of my shirt and yanking it over my head. I do everything in my power to assist, but she doesn't need my help to take it off.

Our mouths meet again, almost painfully, trying to release as much passion as they can into one another. The room is warm, both from the sun and our rising temperature.

Her hand slides beneath my pant line, finding my hardness, grabbing it gently. A deep nook of my mind believes this to be fake; that it will all be a dream and I'll wake up heavily disappointed.

Or even worse, the portable Warper, wherever it is, will take me to another era.

God please, just let this happen.

Without words, I feel her guiding me to the pillow-laden floor. I slide my pants completely down, matching her nakedness. Her skin beneath mine glistens with perspiration and her backside finds the comfortable, colorful squares of fabric.

Pausing for air, we stop kissing and stare into each other's eyes. There's something in hers that suggests she feels it too. The reaction *beyond* the lust…something deeper. Mild before, her energy is pulsing loudly now; an entity unlike any I've ever met before.

Slowly, she grabs me again, guiding me toward the place between her thighs, warmth emanating from within. I enter her, hear her luscious gasp, and release one of my own.

Within milliseconds, the memories come flooding, like a cracked dam bursting forth.

Chapter 61 – Aiontis
1493 | Summer | Florence, Italy

I'm no longer lying in a bulk of pillows making love to Caterina. Instead, I'm living key moments of another life. One that I recognize from a distant memory, exactly like the brief sensation I had in San Francisco with Rachel.

I'm stuck between the world(s) I've been living and the one Odyssian brought me to, not fully in control, but with my brain firing memories at me in rapid-fire.

I'm in Omaha again, as a Hiscon, standing on a skybridge, watching the sun sink into the horizon. I'm nervous because I'm meeting a woman for a date. She worked with one of my clients.

There's a tap on my shoulder. I turn.

It's Caroline. The vizier. Rachel. Caterina.

"Hi, Kiaria." I greet her. *Kiaria.* She smiles with the orange glow of the sun against her face.

I'm still in the future…my future…as Kiaria and I are making love, overlooking the ocean. I have no idea where, but I know it's not just a hookup bred out of lust. It's passionate…sincere…real. Just like in 1493.

She's ranting to me about something at work, fiercely attractive when she's worked up. Titus is standing with us, quiet, looking *newer* and without his scar.

"They don't know what repercussions they've created!" From the memory I already know she's talking about Tyme Corp and time travel in general.

"So, what are you going to do about it?" I ask and correct myself. "What are *we* going to do about it?"

"I…I don't know. I need to think."

Kiaria and I are sitting in a doctor's office, overlooking a city.

I'm unsure which one it is, but based on the aesthetics, this is likely an expensive doctor.

"I'm sorry, but it's just not possible."

Kiaria begins crying. I feel myself begin to cry too.

"I know it's not what you want to hear right now, but there's always adoption. It's a very common route nowadays."

I put my arm around her shoulders, feeling them heave with grief beneath them.

We're much older now, in some dilapidated building that looks war-torn. Grief and anger and fear weigh on my mind and I know this world is one that's too far gone.

A weirdly violet sprig of lightning arcs slowly against the darkened gray sky.

Something about *The Regime* drifts through my thoughts.

"Are you sure you're up to this?" Kiaria asks. I recognize her as the same one I was holding in the San Francisco future-memory. This is the same place.

"I'm sure. It's our last chance to do something." A single tear runs down her cheek, but her face reveals no other emotion.

"I know you're right. I'm just afraid of the outcome."

I walk to her, slower in my old age and aching, and hug her close. We stay that way for a while and I watch the purple lightning dance within the atmosphere; the most gorgeous part of a world that seems to have been brought to its knees.

I'm taken back to 1493, upon the throne of pillows, naked, with Caterina beneath me. She looks bewildered, and for a moment, her eyes are wide with fear.

Did she…see the same things?

She must notice the strange look on my face, but mine is one of loneliness conquered. Of meeting the love of my life again. I hug her deep, sex far from my mind for the moment. Slowly, I sense her arms curling around my back, warm against my clammy skin.

"Aiontis?" She whispers. It feels like an eternity since I've heard that name.

"Kiaria." I say back. Beneath me, I feel her shaking as she cries gently. "We've had a beautiful life together."

"Did you see it...*all?*" She asks, pulling away and looking at me.

"Not all...no...bits and pieces, but enough to know our story."

"Me too. I have so many questions. There are other feelings though too."

"Like?" I ask.

"I know that I am in love with you. And that we were trying to save the world. It's like...a gut feeling. That something larger is going on."

I smile. "I've had that same feeling throughout all of this."

"Throughout all of what?" She asks, but then stops herself. "Actually, don't tell me yet. It can wait."

She nudges me onto my back, sits on top, and we finish what we started.

And then I tell her everything; a release *nearly* as good as the sex itself.

Chapter 62 – Aiontis
1493 | Summer | Florence, Italy

Days pass, turning into weeks. The weeks stack into months and I'm still here, blissfully happy and ignorant of the fact it could all disappear any second.

Kiaria and I finished the painting after several more sessions, each coupled with their own lovemaking upon the pillows. Initially, we were slightly disheartened that no *new* memories were granted to us – and we never saw the previous ones again – but we both knew what we'd experienced.

When I revealed the painting to Giovanni, it was nerve-racking. I'd been anxious about how he'd receive Caterina's nudity. I'm pretty certain that's not what he meant when he suggested her as my muse. Luckily, she had been by my side when I tore the red fabric from atop the canvas, revealing the artwork below.

He gasped, eyes big.

"Leonardo…you did *this*?"

I nodded, proud of my work. It was an odd feeling. Although the talent was not *mine*, it had been my effort and creation. This painting would stand the test of time and if I ever got back to 2404, I'd be eager to find and research it. I'd spent some time thinking about that wild paradox now that I'd actually *created* something, coming away confused with too many hypotheses before I gave up caring. It was easy to focus in the present while with Kiaria.

"Why, Leonardo!" Giovanni could hardly get the words out. "It's exquisite! This will surely be your masterpiece." His hand delicately moved across the canvas' surface, fingertips only making contact with the raised ridges of dried paint.

"Caterina, you look beautiful." He turned to her, then back to the painting, shock still plastered on his face. "Nude, yes…but gorgeous. And the way the bright colors of the pillows contrast your skin! It must be a sin to be able to capture an image in this much detail!"

I laughed, bowing slightly. Caterina smiled and winked at me behind her father's back.

"Thank you, Leonardo." His large hand gripped my shoulder, perhaps too tight as my small punishment for seeing his daughter naked. "This is a wonderful painting that our family and the city of Florence will treasure for ages to come."

"You're welcome, Giovanni. I'm very proud of it."

That was several months ago. Now, Caterina all but lives with me (in semi-secret, though her father doesn't seem to mind) and we spend most of our days together. I've found great interest in seeking out many of the epic vistas around Florence – ones where the city melds with the earth's beauty – and have begun to paint those. It's slow progress, but fun work and Caterina often joins me, sometimes posing as a "woman on the horizon" when I need her to. Clothed, of course.

Our lives, smashed together by this confusing adventure, feel like they're being lived within a petri dish of Renaissance Florence. It's not an awful petri dish to be stuck in, but we both have bouts of fear that it'll all come crashing down soon.

"What if you leave me?" She asks, sometimes crying, sometimes calm. "What if I wake up one morning and the man beside me is no longer *you*?"

"I don't know, Kiaria. I wish I did. The thought of abandoning you tears me up, but I've explained how I have no control over this." It's a shitty answer. "We do know that we're eventually together again. In my time."

"Yes, but that's many lifetimes away! How would I cope until then?"

I look down at the floor, unsure of how to answer.

"What if you took control?" She asks.

"What?" The question confuses me.

"You said that you have no control over this. You're being pushed from era to era…what if you *did* have control?"

I hadn't thought of that before, largely because I'd either been so confused or trying to stay alive in each new place. Here, I had the time to think.

"I…I don't know what that would look like. Or even if I

could."

She's frustrated with my answer, turning away, but the thought, now planted, grows like a seed in my mind.

This argument has repeated itself several times throughout our lifetime, but waned in recent years. Forty years, give or take a few, have come and gone, allowing Kiaria and I to build a life together.

She's been my rock throughout it all – and I can't say I've lived a bad life – but she understands that I feel *forgotten*. Coming from a time with as much technology as mine, 1493 was jarring. Exciting at first, sure, but the novelty wears off quickly. For years I had a growing concern of abandoning whatever mission I was on, unsure of what happened between Odyssian and Ryveliant and the fourth-dimensional beings. Did getting permanently stuck here suggest that Odyssian had "won" (whatever that's supposed to mean)? And what had become of my friend, Titus? Stuck in San Francisco? Another era? I'd kept a close eye during the first several years in Florence, but aside from a few, tall doppelgangers, he wasn't here.

So yes, it's been a weird life in Florence Italy of 1493 and onward, but I wouldn't change it for the world.

Kiaria and I got to grow old together.

Enjoy different parts of the world together.

Paint together.

Eat and drink together.

We never had children, unknowing what the consequences would be, not to mention the pain of the future premonitions always sat in our mind. It was a topic we brought up only once and found we were both in agreement.

Now she's sick. Dying. We look much older (can you imagine the guilt I feel, living this man's *entire* life?) but Kiaria's face is sunken…hollow. Her skin hangs loose on her bones and her demeanor is frail. The luscious brown hair has long turned white, swallowing her thin frame when let down. There's still a youthful spirit to her though; a twinkle in her eye.

In a sick turn of events, she's the one leaving *me*, and I'm terrified to be on my own. I don't remember what that feels like and I know death likely isn't far behind, knocking at my door too. What will happen to us? We've seen the future…do we ever get there? Did we trade one life for another when I came here? I find myself crying about these questions often, a toxic mix of fear and grief.

On the day she died, it was one of those crisp, cold fall days. Quiet. The sun may have been out, but the air was signaling the approach of the next season. Leaves clung to trees or littered the ground, crunchy underfoot. Kiaria had been resting in bed, staring out the window with a strip of sunlight against her face, warming it. I'd been holding her cold hand, and felt the energy slip from it. Gently, I kissed her cheek and left to go cry outside. My devastation had arrived, but underneath the hurt, I was strangely at peace.

In her final days, I had an epiphany that I didn't care what happened anymore. It was time to let go. No matter what happened when she died, or when I would eventually die, I got to live a happy life with her in a wondrous part of history. What more could I ask for?

It's colder now, the sun setting early, tears long dried over on my cheeks, and my trip down memory lane waning, so I head back inside. The chill has invaded her room. I close the window nearby. She looks just as peaceful as I'd left her. Bending down, I kiss her cheek softly. *Goodbye, Kiaria.*

We live in her father's estate, who has long since passed away. I want some solitude before having to deal with the body and ceremony arrangements, so I leave to peruse the halls and the extensive art collection this family has gathered.

Many of my own paintings of Florence's views and nearby Italian vistas hang proudly – a lifetime of achievement drawn in colored strokes across fabric – sprinkled with other artists Giovanni had sponsored throughout the years. As I turn one of the grand hallway's corners, I'm struck with grief.

This is a part of the house I rarely come to. I'd forgotten about *this* painting.

I stare at the tapestry of Kiaria nude, lying gracefully atop a mound of colorful pillows. Youthful, happy, gorgeous, and mere *days* after I'd met her for the first time. Tears stream again down my wrinkled cheeks.

The fear comes back.

I miss her.

Loneliness creeps in.

I miss her.

Time is a bastard even as I reminisce on all the moments we shared. Why can't I have the power to go back and revisit them? Why was I sent here in the first place?

It's all replaced with anger, waterworks streaking hot along my face and dripping to the floor. *I'm not going to feel like a pawn. Not after all of this. Not after an entire lifetime.*

"Odyssian!" I bark upward.

Bwah….bwahhhhh…bwaaaaahhhhhhhh

I cannot take my eyes off the painting, trying to understand how I can get back to there. To *then*.

Bwwwaaaahhhhhhhhh

That's right you fucker I think to myself. *You push me back!*
"Push me back!" I scream, spittle cornering my mouth.

BWWWAAAAHHHHHHHH

"I'll be with you soon, Kiaria. Caterina." It's a promise I'm not sure will be kept, but God help anyone who gets in my way.

BWAAAHHHHHHHHHHHHHH….

"Push me back." I plead now, drained of energy, eyes closed. In the final moments of my existence in Florence, I try to remember what the Bulk feels like…

Chapter 63 – Ryveliant

~ ~ ~

"**O**dyssian!"

"Push me back!"

The plea echoed across the Bulk, stained by grief and exhaustion. Ryveliant, scanning the spectrum of time, had finally found the little bastard.

Aiontis. His complex, hyper-advanced mind honed in. *Time to end this.*

Ryveliant's passion for advancing into the fifth dimension was contagious and threatening. All those years ago during his initial studies about how beings, previously humans, had evolved from the third to the fourth dimension of understanding, he'd always been captivated…and angry. The process had taken millennia…frustrating and ample time, coursing by, *wasted.*

Further on in his life, the theory evolved that there was a total of seven dimensions, possibly more, bolstered by the fact they had potentially identified the fifth dimension: *multiple universes.* Multiple *planes of existence.*

Eager to not be stuck in a worthless limbo of being a measly fourth-dimensional creature, he began his life's work to determine how he could expedite the transition into the fifth dimension. He craved the unknown of the fifth dimension…the complete uncertainty of what it held other than one thing: more *power.* Not power in the traditional sense, but more power over time…or multiple times…and a higher understanding of the universe and all the secrets of which it contained.

Followers and supporters happened quickly, relatively speaking. All around their universe, Ryveliant had the backing of important, powerful people, in turn becoming so himself. And then it happened: the key.

For their dimension to further themselves faster (some argued the impact could almost be immediate), they had to sacrifice the third dimension before it. Or at least a sizeable chunk of it. If the third dimension ruined itself quicker, as they eventually did anyway, the process of evolution would begin sooner, thus altering the course of the fourth dimensional beings and propelling them forward closer to (or into) the fifth dimension.

Committees were formed, debates were had, and ultimately the weakness of their species won out, rejecting the theory and the idea. Their argument was that the sanctity of the universe and time should be preserved, leaving the humans to arrive at their own destination. Others argued about how the same thing could be done to their current dimension by more advanced civilizations if they weren't careful.

As massive disagreements between core ideas and morals tend to, it created a war. Ryveliant cared less about the war itself and more about executing his plan. If done right, the war wouldn't matter. By creating the Regime – an ultimate evil, focused only on pure destruction and rule – and placing it far before the actual end of humans, he'd achieve his goal. In addition to the Regime, he'd insert a scientific advancement. One the humans would believe could save them, but would ultimately be their downfall.

Aiontis, Odyssian's pawn, had revealed himself. Just the tool Ryveliant needed.

He was here now, in the Bulk with him, but Ryveliant kept him in the dark. Enough time there and you could make a human go mad, but Aiontis had a purpose.

Ryveliant forced the man – old in his age from whatever era he'd been tucked away in – to the distant future, sliding across the tesseract of time along with him. With little regard for his wellbeing, he shoved him through to the year 2477, deep into an underground bunker. It was here that the android, Titus, was holed up from the Regime.

Ryveliant spoke, plunging his words deep through Aiontis and out his human mouth. This trick had been planned for some time, and his success hinged on it.

"Titus, you must go back before it began…"

Aiontis was annoyingly strong; he'd clearly been to the Bulk before and was familiar with the sensation. *Odyssian…*

Ryveliant compelled the words into the man like a machine press, cold and firm, but they weren't coming out like he wanted. They were confused…mysterious.

"The lines are all different, this isn't what you think. You know who I am. You have to end it."

Aiontis lashed out against the darkness, refusing to speak another word. Ryveliant was shocked at what this human could accomplish here, but punched a final sentence through him, without remorse. Again, it wasn't delivered by this vessel like he'd intended.

"You have to end it…to prevent it."

Angry, he released his grasp on the pathetic creature, leaving him in the darkness of the Bulk, exhausted. As the android slept in 2477, Ryveliant delivered the schematics of the portable Warper to him, uploading them digitally. If there was one other constant outside of time, it was that 1s and 0s make up the entire universe in some way, shape, or form. Manipulating them was easy. In that same vein, he provided Titus a clear objective, to make up for Aiontis' lack of…*cooperation.* The android now had instructions to kill his master.

Ryveliant assessed the timeline anew, hoping his deception had taken effect despite the puny human's pushback. The motivating factor for Titus was a risk, but set well enough, now with a new, destructive technology being taken back in time with him. There was some unknown about *when* the portable Warper's impact would take effect throughout history, but once it did, the human race would consume it so aggressively and irresponsibly, as they had with so many technologies before, that their existence would become a catastrophe, practically begging for the creation of the Regime. If the Regime was the hammer, then the portable Warper was the nail.

But what to do with Aiontis?…He has outlived his usefulness.

Ryveliant didn't care about the pawn, sending him somewhere that almost ensured his death. With a final thrust across the chasm of time, he threw Aiontis, hurtling toward the destination, believing it would be the last he would see of him.

Historian Consultant Report
9/11, New York City
September 11th, 2001

When Historian Consultants refer to a "D-Day", or a defining day in history, of course we mean actual D-Day – the World War II storming of Normandy Beach – as one of those days.

Perhaps an unspoken secret however is that if you mention the phrase to a Hiscon, almost certainly their mind jumps to September 11th, 2001. It's possibly the most *significant D-Day event since the end of the two World Wars and was the catalyst for the direction and behavior of the world for centuries afterward. Some of its ripple effects were obvious – a prolonged war in Afghanistan – while others were more subtle – a distinct period of racism. It led the world, first with the United States, then others, to trust each other less and for a time, the most distinct evil in the world was the threat of terrorism.*

There were other attacks in the years leading up to it and following, but none more significant (even to this day) as 9/11. It was the prime example of what happens when nearly everything goes right for the bad guys, an event so shocking that many described it as "surreal" while they watched it unfold.

At 5:45am that morning, the North and South Towers of the World Trade Center stood tall at 1,368 feet (417 meters) and 1,362 feet (415 meters), respectively. They reflected the morning sun brilliantly off their metal and glass hulls. Similarly, the Pentagon was waking up to the same sun, undamaged, sturdy, and ready for another day.

In Portland, Maine, their attackers were boarding a plane to Boston, where they would transfer to the vessels that would introduce the day's demise.

At 7:59am, American Airlines Flight 11 took off from Boston. 16 minutes later at 8:15am, United Airlines Flight 175 took off from the same airport. At 8:19, the hijacking of American Airlines Flight 11 began and one minute later, American

Airlines Flight 77 took off from Washington D.C. By 8:42am, United Airlines Flight 93 had taken off from Newark following a delay and all four flights used that fateful day were in the air.

Not for much longer...

4 minutes later, at 8:46am, American Airlines Flight 11 began the horror, crashing into the North Tower between floors 93 and 99. The thunderous collision and ball of flame left a gaping hole in the structure, sending debris showering hundreds of feet below. For a time, people – now watching the breaking news – believed it to be a terrible mistake.

Less than 20 minutes later, at 9:03am, the nation (and parts of the world) watched in horror as a second plane, United Airlines Flight 175, came into view, cornering tightly, and exploded into the South Tower's floors 77 through 85, with an amount of violence that could not have been imagined before actually seeing it.

It was in that moment where many realized this was no accident...and the world had changed. It would only get worse.

Slightly more than a half-hour later, at 9:37am, American Airlines Flight 77 flew fast and low into one of the exterior walls of the Pentagon, creating a massive canyon of destroyed building and rubble. Within moments, the FAA grounded all flights in the U.S. immediately, an unprecedented move. Similarly eventful, the Capitol and White House were evacuated while the United States government did its best to protect and hide its most valuable members.

One minute before 10:00am, the South Tower began collapsing in on itself. Its top quarter sunk into a growing cloud of brown and gray dust as it plummeted, sending streaks of larger debris and chunks hurtling toward the ground. Within 10 seconds, something that took 9 years to build had been destroyed, trapping and killing hundreds as it did so.

Minutes later, at 10:03am, the final hijacked plane of the day was obliterated when it crushed into a random Pennsylvania field due to heroic passengers nearly taking it back from the Al Qaeda extremists. For a time after the attacks, this bravery was celebrated as one of the few beacons of hope from that day. It is believed the ultimate target had been the U.S. Capitol Building.

At 10:28am, the day's final horror unfolded as the North Tower, having burned for 102 minutes, collapsed similarly as the South Tower. What had once been two iconic structures among a vast New York City skyline had now been reduced to rubble and a plume of smoke that could be seen from space.

The remainder of the day was lived in shock, sadness, and fear. A visibly shaken George W. Bush, President of the United States at the time, addressed the nation, full well knowing the events of the day were ones that would be in history books hundreds, if not thousands of years from now.

In totality, 2,996 people were killed while another 6,000 were injured. 19 terrorists committed murder-suicide. Outside of civilians, 344 firefighters and 71 law enforcement officers were also lost. Over the years, 1,400 rescue workers who worked through the debris died as a result of illnesses related to World Trade Center dust and wreckage. It is believed another 1,140 citizens who either worked or lived downtown contracted cancer from those same fumes.

The impact it would have on the world was nearly as gargantuan as the attack itself. Ushering in an entire era deemed, "Post-9/11" and setting the world stage for generations to come.

And it all happened within less than 5 hours...

Chapter 64 – Aiontis

2001 | Unknown location

I feel like I've been hit by a train. Part hangover, part adrenaline rush, I'm fatigued and trying to make sense of what just happened. In my eyelid iNsert, my heart rate quickens as if I'm exercising.

There's a gross sensation coursing through me. Not my *physical* self, but mentally…*I've been used*. Close after, the icepick headache and flash of itchiness that I'd long forgotten about hits like a slap to the face. *How could I still be having Jinx withdrawals?*

Ryveliant found me and forced me through time, fucking roughly I might add, leading to a conversation with Titus that was not my own. It was odd…words that didn't seem to make sense, even when Titus had mentioned them previously. The entire phenomenon kept piecing together in my mind. *I took control…Ryveliant's words didn't come through me like he wanted.* As shitty as I felt, I was at least proud of that small victory.

What else was there…?

My memory now spans more than an entire lifetime and has faded.

The portable Warper! I'd had no part in that, but Ryveliant sent the instructions for this tool shortly after I'd visited, or so Titus claimed. It must have been how he captured the urge to kill me too. They were each equal parts to a puzzle that began all of this.

The sun is bright and I have a lasting headache, having been catapulted from higher brain function back into this new body, strangely youthful. My physical, emotional, and mental sensations are foreign. Caterina…Kiaria…is gone after a life and love well enjoyed, and now I am in a new body, in a new time, alone.

A wave of dread strikes, the hardest I've received during this whole journey. How long will I be stuck in this *fucking* game? In this…loop? I am exhausted and without any end in sight, unaware of where Titus ended up after San Francisco, and back to square one in determining if there is a Kiaria "version" in this time. It's a chore just remembering all of this.

My body is shaking, almost revolting from the helplessness. Sweat gathers on the back of my neck and rolls down my shirt. I realize I have sunglasses on, darkening the exuberant morning sunlight. I may feel like shit, but it sure is a bright, gorgeous day in this city.

What city is this? Where and when *am I?*

Pedestrians walk on the sidewalks and slightly overlarge business suits are common, many with muted earth tones. Yellow taxi cabs mull by, honking more than they need to. This downtown has a specific vibrancy to it, a very real energy among the dense buildings, many of them are skyscrapers. By my best estimation, I'm in New York City, generally around the late 20th or early 21st century.

I believe it's early morning because the air has a chill to it, and a strong call for coffee hits. Whether it's my own affinity for the beverage or the person's body I'm in, I don't know, but I'm here for it (is that the saying in this time period?). A shop's window reflection reveals a rather uninteresting man, Caucasian, short but with broad shoulders, and a decent head of brown hair trying to fight back against a receding hairline. In my hand is a briefcase and I'm wearing one of those bulkier suits, in black.

Disappointed, yet realizing it doesn't matter much, I set out on my quest for coffee: the timeless beverage.

Rounding a bustling corner, the resulting image sends a new wave of dread – and pure fear – surging through me.

Against the cloudless, brilliant Robin-egg-blue sky stand two, identical skyscrapers. They're boxy and powerful and very close together, almost like one solid pillar of concrete, glass, and metal:

The World Trade Center towers.

And suddenly, I know exactly *when* and *where* I am.

Chapter 65 – Aiontis

2001 | September 11th | New York City

Ryveliant either sent me here to die, or to witness one of humanity's worst days. Probably both. I'm only a hostage in his overall quest and for a fourth-dimensional being like him, he couldn't care less about what happens today.

My nausea and terror subside into an awkward feeling of the surreal. Seeing these structures standing so tall and free of all the smoke and flame and debris they've come to be attributed with is…eerie.

"Jesus! Get out of the way, asshole!" a rushed businessman chirps as he strides by. I'm gawking at the towers, probably looking distinctly odd (or lost) to everyone else. I'm sorry for them…they don't know how their lives will change or the things they'll see today. Sidewalks host all the bustling people, some headed toward the towers, some going elsewhere, and I wonder how many of them will die today.

How many are headed toward their cubicle or office, on an otherwise forgettable Tuesday morning, never to return again?

This layer of preemptive grief weighs heavy; there's nothing I can do. My warning would fall on deaf ears until it was too late and, if anything, they'd think I was one of the terrorists.

A heavy sigh escapes. The bulky fabric in the suit's shoulders heave up and down. My briefcase feels like 100 pounds.

I'm lost.

I'm alone.

I'm helpless myself and helpless to help these people.

I think I want to die.

That sentiment cascades across my mind like a calm ocean wave, undulating, coming in, going out. The path forward has never been clear on this trip, not since I woke up in Omaha, my memory shot to shit.

But what came before that?

It doesn't matter. Let's just die.

I move away from the center of the sidewalk and lean against a red brick building, staring at the World Trade Center. I begin reasoning with myself.

Death isn't so bad. You've probably *lived a good life and you've certainly had an adventure.*

The other side rebuttals.

You don't know where you are and Odyssian, Titus, and Kiaria need you. You may not know why, but you shouldn't abandon them.

Again, more reasoning.

Who cares about them? You lived a fulfilling life with Kiaria in Italy. What more do you want?

beep-beep!

I glance toward the tiny sound to find an aged watch that looks straight out of the 1990's. It's the top of the hour: 8:00am. Another sigh. We're about 45 minutes out from the start of it all. I'm scrambled, unsure of how to proceed.

So, I listen to my body. My body wants coffee, and honestly? That sounds like a great way to start my (potentially) last few hours alive.

Without much drive, I meander across streets and along sidewalks looking for a café. I pass a Dunkin Donuts and almost go in, but there's no seating. After a couple minutes and a few blocks, I find a cozy little café with outdoor seating that faces the Towers, feeling like destiny.

I lay my briefcase on the last empty table outside before I go in. Probably crazy to leave my briefcase unattended by New York City standards, but hey! It's not *really* mine and I'm not going to need it soon. Inside, a man with crossed legs reads the newspaper in a corner, the black and white pages covering his face. From a distance, I verify the date: September 11th, 2001. It's small among the rather mundane headlines, which won't be the case tomorrow morning.

The howl of an espresso machine brings me back to the moment. I'm next in line.

"Good morning!"

"Morning." I force out, failing to match the barista's energy.

"What can I get you?"

"Can I get a large drip coffee?"

"Certainly." She grabs a cup near her and writes something on it. "Any room for cream or sugar?"

"Nope. Black is fine, thanks." The cup goes under a carafe and she presses the plunger. Another barista behind her unhooks an espresso handle and dumps its contents in the trash. I take notice of the greenery and plants hanging from the ceiling and walls. This is a lovely shop and I hope the coffee matches the atmosphere.

"Here you go, sir!" She slides the cup toward me, complete with lid and sleeve. "That will be $2.32."

I scrounge around in my pockets and find a wallet, and an old, wrinkled $5 bill inside, handing it to her.

"Keep the change."

"Thank you! Have a nice day!"

"You too." I lie, knowing it won't be. For anyone.

As I emerge outside, the sun soothes my face the same way the coffee cup warms my hand. I sit at my table, partially under the shade of their small awning, leaving my briefcase on top. Steadying my hand, I remove the lid and blow on the steaming liquid. Aside from small, tan bubbles around the edge, it is definitely a dark roast, rippling outward under my soft breath. The darkness reminds me of the Bulk. I imagine jumping into my cup of coffee and existing in there like I existed in the Bulk. It is a preposterous thought and the first one to make me smile since I'd arrived.

Dipping my lips onto the liquid's surface, I take a cautious sip, placing the lidless cup on the table, hoping it will cool down.

Damn. That's some great *coffee.*

Its warmth gives *me* warmth. I am still in a black hole of existential thought, but at least I have a small life comfort to enjoy.

My watch reads 8:13am.

I have another taste, staring at the Towers. It's too hot to take a worthwhile gulp, but the excitement of getting a full swig of flavor gives me at least one thing to look forward to.

Could this time maybe be different? What if I sit here and 9:00am rolls by? What if it doesn't happen at all?

I think back to the oddity of the female vizier in Egypt, how I was almost *certain* that didn't line up with my knowledge of the time period.

Another sip of coffee, this time taking more.

"Excuse me?" A gravelly but smooth male voice interrupts my train of thought. "Do you mind if I sit? All the other seats are taken and I'd like to enjoy the weather."

I glance upward to see a normal looking man, with dark skin and sprigs of gray peppering his beard and hair, smiling.

"Sure." I answer, removing my briefcase from atop the table, placing it by my side.

"Thank you!" He sits and reaches across the table to shake my hand. "James. Pleased to meet you."

"Aiontis. Same."

"Ha! Sounds like your parents were into Greek mythology!" His laughter and energy feel…different.

"Perhaps. Where I'm from, names like that are more common."

"Oh?" His eyebrows raise as he takes a sip of his own coffee and crosses his legs. "And where are you from, Aiontis?"

I'm not sure what it is, but something about this man brings back *the* sensation. The gut feeling. Being part of something bigger. The one that's been missing for a long time.

I lean into it, and I tell him everything.

Chapter 66 – Aiontis
2001 | September 11th | New York City

"After she died, I was angry…scared. Alone. In a moment of frustration, I called out to Odyssian and it ended up that fucking Ryveliant found me.

"He pressed me through time, forced me to trick future-Titus, then discarded me here, today, like a used-up toy. And that basically brings us to the present moment."

I glance at my watch nervously and have kept a steady eye on it throughout the course of my story.

8:32am.

I told James everything aside from revealing my weapon and iNsert, fearful he'd immediately call the authorities. For a person who's just been told he's speaking with a future-man who's being forced through time, he's taking it remarkably well. He probably assumes I'm just crazy.

"Well then…that's quite the story." He leans back in his seat, allowing sunrays to bask his face. Slowly, he sips his coffee and I do the same. It has cooled considerably during my story.

"And so, you truly have no idea how old you are, do you?" He asks, looking out to the street.

"No…I suppose you're right. I could very well be over 100 years old, but obviously I've been placed back in this younger body."

"And you've no idea where Kiaria is in *this* era?" I'm surprised by his genuine interest. It's a relief he takes me seriously…or he's indulging me.

"Not a clue."

"And why *this* era exactly? Why today?" His question has the lingering pitch of worry. "You keep checking your watch…what happens?"

"Do you really want to know?"

He nods and takes another sip. I check my watch: 8:34am.

"In 12 minutes, a passenger airline will fly into the North

Tower of the World Trade Center."

"That sounds bad."

"Yes, well…that's just the start. By noon, another plane will have hit the South Tower, another at the Pentagon, and a fourth will crash in a field in Pennsylvania. In just a few short hours, those Towers will no longer be standing. All planes have been — or *will be*, I suppose — hijacked by terrorists. It's one of the most significant and horrible days in human history."

Once calm, his face can't mask the shock. A hand, quite large, covers his gaping mouth while he stares at the Towers. He looks back to me.

"You're not kidding, are you?" He asks. "About any of it?"

"I wish I were, but I am not. I'm…sorry."

"Wow. Well then..."

For a moment, we sit in silence, drinking our coffee and watching the sun bounce off the Towers.

"Thank you for telling me your story." He says quietly.

"Thanks for listening. It felt good to let it go." I answer. A respite of silence punctuates us. "What would you do if you were me? I'm…lost." I feel vulnerable, naked, asking the question to him.

"Hmmm." He considers for a moment, coupling the thought with another swig. "I'd stop worrying so much."

"Excuse me?" The answer surprises me.

"I'd stop worrying so much about the past, the future, or what part you play in these gods and their games. Before you know it, you'll be 400 years old with nothing to show for it except for a single well-lived life in Renaissance Italy."

I remain silent, considering his poignant words as he continues. "By almost every measure, you've been given a *gift*, Aiontis. You get to travel through time! You get to see things in a way that no human being *ever* has. Out of the billions of people who have ever lived, you are *special*. Don't you dare waste your time doing anything but *living* the way no one else has, even on days like today."

There's passion in his voice now…it's not frustration but rather a wiser man trying to open the eyes of a lesser one. I'm listening.

"Even if you're only here today, for a year, or five years…live in the present. You've the tremendous gift of foresight now; how can you use it to help others?" He pauses for a moment and looks from me, back to the Towers. "Stop feeling sorry for yourself and take control of the situation."

Across the table from him, I'm sitting there numb, flabbergasted. Not only did this man believe me enough to listen to my story, but he's providing me tough love. And he's right. I have no control over the inner workings of where I'm going next, or how long I'll be there; I need to make the most of each situation. The rest will work itself out.

"What time is it?" James asks. I glance down, feeling my stomach constrict.

"8:44."

"Hmm. Well then, let's see if times have changed." He stands briefly, turning his chair toward the Towers. Sitting, watching, waiting. My body tenses, not sure I want to watch, yet equally unable to look away.

After a few moments, a deafening roar fills the air like the howling wind inside a tornado. A shadow passes overhead for the briefest of seconds and the roar turns into a mechanical screaming. We both watch American Airlines 11 rip through the air and disappear into a hole on the North Tower, immediately regurgitating a ball of flame and smoke. There's a booming thud that echoes off other buildings and vibrates through them.

It's the vibration of fear and horror.

"Oh my God." James states, shaking his head. "I…I can't even…" A tear runs down his cheek. Nearby there are screams. Murderous screams. Dark smoke billows eagerly from the hole and debris floats in the air, sinking slowly.

"James, you need to get out of here. Get out of Lower Manhattan. You don't want to be around for this, it gets very bad."

He sits in silence, transfixed by the horrific image. Not looking away, he asks, "What will you do?"

His advice inspired something in me…something deeper. In my gut, as well as my heart…my soul.

"I'm going to go try and save as many lives as I can."

Still in shock, he nods at the sentiment. I need all the time I can get; I've only got about 15 minutes until the second plane hits. I stand to leave.

"Thanks for the advice, James." And I turn to go.

"Aiontis." He says calmly, turning to look me in the eyes. "You have infinite possibilities. Live them."

And with that final parting advice, I toss my bulky suitcoat aside, loosen my tie, and sprint toward the disaster unsure of what will happen or if I'll live, but knowing that it was my choice.

Throughout the day, I save anywhere from 300 to 400 lives. Knowing when things are going to happen and which people to prioritize getting out was an invaluable key. Part of me wonders if these people died (or would have died) in the 9/11 *without* me…or if I've always been here all along.

I'm careful to keep my eye on the clock and make it out of either building before the collapses start, safely distancing myself from the smoking Towers. Even amongst all the horrific imagery and death, I'm proud of myself and filled with renewed energy.

Eventually, the North Tower collapses, similar to the South that hadn't lasted as long under the stress and fire. The plumage of smoke and debris swallows the structure while I hear the familiar low rumble of time travel, distinctly different from the bass of the collapse itself. It starts faint, as it always does, and becomes more intense.

Without the Warper, I'll be pressed through time again, similar to how Ryveliant sent me here. I just hope for my sake that it's Odyssian come to get me this time. Whomever and wherever it is, I commit to remember what James told me: to *live*.

Chapter 67 – Titus
2098 | June 20ᵗʰ | San Francisco

A month had passed, almost in a blink (or so it felt), and Titus was beginning to believe he was a permanent resident of 2098. In that span, not a single thing had happened with the Warper, or any messages from Aiontis or Odyssian.

I've been forgotten.

It didn't sadden him. If anything, the sentiment gave him a weird comfort. This life he'd started settling into wasn't bad…it was easy, especially compared to where he'd originally been.

Even a month later, Rachel and Bryson were more than happy to have him stay with them. There was no romantic connection between he and Rachel – neither of them had hinted toward it yet and he figured it best to not go down that road – but there was a strong friendship forming. With the boy too…Bryson had been attached at his hip for most of the past few weeks as they continued repairs around the neighborhood.

Anymore, as he and the awkward 10-year-old walked the surrounding blocks, neighbors would wave and laugh at Bryson's oversized toolbelt. Many had taken to thanking the boy with candy or cash, while others brought food and much-appreciated booze to Rachel and Titus. Given the fresh trauma, there was no neighborhood gossip about the man staying with Rachel, they were accepted as their own little happy family.

Throughout the San Francisco area, there was an energy and a passion to rebuild, better than ever. The deep scars of a natural disaster that had killed thousands was fresh, and there were tears often, but Titus was excited every day to interact with humans who just wanted to get better and live for something. A far cry from the era he'd left behind, where the population was submissive, defeated, and cold.

I could build a life here.

Though he knew earthquake repairs wouldn't last forever, in his moments of pondering the future, he wanted to be a handyman. The gap in technology meant nearly everything he came across was simplistically basic and he found solace in the tasks. He could repair almost anything.

"Power drill." He stated, like a surgeon asking for his tools. A bulky plastic touched his palm, and he took it from the child, his other hand holding a screw in place.

"Can I try one?" Bryson asked, with a slight crack in his voice.

"Sure. Let me get it started for you. That's the hardest part." They were putting a shelving unit back together that had dismantled in the quake. Certain boards had broken and they'd spent the better part of yesterday cutting, sanding, and staining the wood. Titus tapped the trigger of the drill and the screw spun around the wood's surface for a brief moment, then pierced it.

"Okay. Come here." He scooted to the side and Bryson took the drill in his hands. "Now…the trigger is sensitive. You probably just need to tap it and apply slight pressure *toward* the wood. Otherwise, just let the tool and physics do the work for you."

"Okay." Bryson replied, his tongue out for added concentration. He tapped the trigger and a loud rotation of metal against metal popped from the drill bit. It had come out of the screw head, colliding against it.

"That's ok. Happens all the time." Titus explained. "Why do you think that happened?"

The boy thought for a moment. "I probably wasn't pressing in enough, right?"

"Exactly. Your pressure not only tells the tool where you want the force to go, but it also creates the connection point with the screw. Try again." Titus encouraged.

Tongue out once more, Bryson lined up the bit with the screw, pressed in, and lightly pressed the trigger. The bit, snug in the screw's grasp, turned slowly at first, then faster. Like a professional, the screw spun inward and Bryson let up just as it became flush with the wood surface.

"Wow! That was really good." Titus was impressed.

"Woah cool. That was fun." He held the drill up and pulled the trigger quickly, pulsing the roar of the motor and getting a short blast of air from the fan. Titus laughed.

"Ok there, secret agent. Don't get carried away. I'm going to get these other screws started for you to finish. Sound good?"

"Yep!"

Once he'd readied seven more screws, he let the boy go to work, standing back to watch him. He was slow, and knocked a couple screws out, but was learning. Titus had noticed he picked up things quickly and this was no different.

Leaning against a wall, overseeing the repairs, his mind wandered to the talk he needed to have with Rachel. Without being able to pinpoint why, he felt nervous about it. He wanted to stay…potentially with them. There was comfort here and a future he liked, but he wasn't sure if her hospitality would run out. Or, if she said yes, would she be comfortable with it three months from now? A year? Obviously, he could always get a place of his own, but then he'd be alone again. And he didn't want that.

I'm definitely an advanced *android if I'm afraid of being alone.* The thought ran across his mind with humor, but left a wisp of mystery. *Incredible.*

"Ok, I'm done!" Bryson stood beside the shelving unit, smiling, power drill leaning against his shoulder, evidently proud.

"Nice. It looks great. Help me tip it back on its side and then let's head home to your mom."

With a heave (and an overzealous grunt from the boy), they pushed the cherrywood furniture right-side up, helped Ms. Knudsen place her knickknacks upon its shelves, said their cheerful goodbyes, and trekked the steep sidewalk home as the sun crafted purples in the sky above the healing city.

"He did good today." Titus informed Rachel while they enjoyed a full-bodied, red wine on her front porch. It had become their nightly tradition, and one of the key contributors to their emerging friendship.

"Oh really?" She smiled. "Those legs and arms didn't get in the way?"

Titus laughed as she sipped her wine with a wry smile. "No, they certainly did, but I let him work with the drill at Ms. Knudsen's. He got the hang of it quickly."

"He always seems to. He's a smart kid."

They both took a gulp of wine and let the moment sit in silence. The air was warm, accompanied by a salty ocean breeze. Damage from the earthquake was readily visible all around the street, but it was nice to forget it had happened, even if only for a second.

"Rachel…I…" Titus stopped, trying to gather his thoughts. He wanted to ask if he could stay. Indefinitely.

He'd caught her in the middle of a drink which she cut short, eyebrows raised, and wiped a dribbling bead of wine off her chin. "Yes?"

"I wanted to ask you something."

"Okay…" She lingered. "What's going on? You're being weird."

Titus had his mouth open, ready to speak. Ready to ask if he could stay, but a sound caught his ear. A low, quiet hum. All his attention shifted toward listening.

Did I really hear it?

The sound got louder, confirming his fear.

"Titus? What's going on?" Rachel was sitting up now, wine down, looking at him with concern. He debated pulling the Warper out of his pocket to check if it was indeed going off, but didn't want to reveal it to her.

Maybe it will be another false alarm?

Maybe it will bring Aiontis back?

"Titus!" Rachel raised her voice just as the humming upped its ante.

"Listen, I'm sorry. I didn't mean for it to be like this and there's a lot I haven't explained. I wanted to stay here with you and the boy…I enjoy this life."

A louder hum cascaded from the Warper, drowning out his own speech. He wondered if she could hear it. She could see the rush in his eyes.

"I have to leave. And it's going to happen right now. I just need you to trust me."

"What the fuck is going on?" She snapped.

"Rachel! Just…trust me. And thank you for everything." A tear rolled down her cheek and Titus wiped it with his thumb.

"Can't you say goodbye to Bryson? He'll be heartbroken." The question stung Titus, already knowing the answer.

The bass-filled sound felt like it was vibrating in his pocket. It would be any second now.

"I…I can't. I'm sorry. Tell him I love him."

Without a moment more, the warm touch of Rachel's cheek under his palm disappeared. Cold. As if it had never been there.

He only had one thought in the darkness.

This had better be good.

Historian Consultant Report
The Cuban Missile Crisis, Washington D.C.
October 16th, 1962 – October 28th, 1962

Not all "Defining Days" within history are laced with death, but almost all are connected to the potential *of it. Disturbingly, events that would/could shape the course of human history are often intertwined with some amount of suffering.*

The Cuban Missile Crisis is one of those situations. An event where only one official death was ever recorded – a U.S. U-2 pilot shot down over Cuba at the height of the dilemma – but could have ended beyond catastrophically.

Even to this day, the majority of Hiscons believe the world was closest to nuclear annihilation during this 13-day, tension-filled period. There have been close calls since, some of which the public isn't privy to, but by and large this "battle of egos" was the primary showcase to the world that decisions that could affect the entire world were in the hands of a few men.

The Crisis had a long path leading up to it, though it really came down to three drivers:

1) *A botched (and humiliating) Bay of Pigs invasion from the United States in 1961 that empowered and fueled Castro's alignment with the Soviets (buoyed by an economic blockade of Cuban goods)*
2) *U.S. nuclear missiles stationed in Turkey, within distance to many key Russian cities and targets*
3) *The storied and extensive war of ideologies between Communism and Democracy*

In 1962, the Soviets moved their own nuclear missiles into friendly Cuba – just 90 miles from U.S. shores - ready to fire at key cities like New York, Washington D.C., and Miami if the need arose.

As most moments in the Cold War were, the movement of these missiles were captured via spy-work: a U-2 plane flying at high altitude over Cuba took the iconic photographs of missiles being assembled, organized, and readied in the jungle. By October 16th, President John F. Kennedy had been briefed on the photos of the Soviet SS-4 medium-range ballistic missiles he knew could cause massive destruction to his country. In response, he formed EXCOMM to bring together ten of his most trusted advisors and find a path forward. It included Lyndon Johnson (Vice President), Robert McNamara (Secretary of Defense), Robert Kennedy (his brother and Attorney General), and John McCone (Director of CIA), among others.

Together, they determined there were several options ranging from "doing nothing", invading Cuba with Operation Ortsac ("Castro" backwards), or creating a naval blockade of the island. In a serious and solemn address to the American people on October 22nd, JFK announced they would be placing a blockade to quarantine Cuba from receiving aid.

The next several days were packed with tension around the world. Citizens in both countries could hardly concentrate for fear that the Cold War turning hot might finally be coming to fruition in an apocalyptic way. The Cuban leader, Castro, egged on Soviet leader Nikita Khrushchev to fire the missiles should the U.S. invade or attack. Meanwhile, in the surrounding ocean water, a nuclear-armed Soviet submarine frequently "buzzed" American warships, causing more anxiety.

Unknown to many, the "height" of the Crisis came early in the morning of October 27th. Unbeknownst to the Pentagon, U.S. pilots at Eilson Air Force Base in Alaska were still doing routine flyovers in the North Pole to gather air samples. The samples were used to determine if the Soviets were doing nuclear testing.

Shortly after taking off at midnight, the pilot, Charles F. Maultsby, was blinded and thrown off by the aurora borealis in the night sky. He was unable to orient himself on the stars which acted as his map. Eventually, he crossed into Soviet territory and pinged on their radar, resulting in two Soviet Migs scrambling to intercept him.

As a counter, the Alaska Air Defense Command sent two of its own, F-102 interceptors, to guide the pilot home and deter the Migs. The F-102s were armed with nuclear warheads.

After 10 hours and 25 minutes – the longest recorded U-2 flight ever – Maultsby, gliding on fumes, returned to base in Alaska, and the ultimate moment of the crisis was averted. The very next day, the Cuban Missile Crisis came to a close with Khrushchev agreeing to remove the missiles from Cuba if the U.S. would stop the blockade. In secret, the U.S. also agreed to remove their nuclear arsenal from Turkey and the Cold War returned to being just that: cold.

In a memo to Kennedy on October 28th, Khrushchev emphasized how easily the intruder in Soviet airspace could have been mistaken "for a nuclear bomber, which might push us to a fateful step."

And what a fateful step it would have been...

Chapter 68 – Titus
1962 | Unknown location

An odd weight hung along Titus' ears and nose as he oriented himself within a bland room adorned by ugly, green and brown carpet. He took the glasses off to find an aged gold, wire-rim frame with smudged lenses. Almost subconsciously he grabbed a corner of his button-down shirt, wiping the lenses clear, and placed them back on his head.

The room lacked any technology other than a phone. Various papers and manilla folders were scattered across a long, walnut table. It smelled of smoke, there were several ashtrays strewn along the length of the wood, with trails of gray seeping from the ends of some cigarette butts.

Frustrated, Titus checked to make sure Zorex was still with him; he'd been close to leaving it behind in San Francisco. It was in its holstermesh, secure. Aside from the smoke, something felt…intense in this space. The wood paneling could have almost screamed about what it had seen. Recent perspiration, body odor, and stress was in the air, lingering.

Behind him, a door opened and a young man, no older than thirty, entered and discreetly shut the door behind him. His frame took a half leap at the sight of another person in the room.

"Oh…uhh…sorry, I…" His eyes narrowed on Titus' face. On his scarring. "Titus?"

A jolt hit Titus in the stomach. He knew this feeling; it was his biometric sensor.

"Aiontis?"

The man didn't reply, but nearly collapsed to the floor, grabbing the tall leather back of a nearby chair to stop himself. He clutched his chest and tears began to stream down his face.

Titus studied him. "Is it really you?"

The man, wiping his tears, nodded.

"It's been a while, friend." He approached with arms open wide, and hugged Titus fiercely.

"Jesus, Aiontis. What's happened to you?" He patted him on the back awkwardly. "It's only been a month…"

"A month?" Aiontis threw himself backward from the embrace, eyes wide and brow contorted.

"Yes…?" Titus was confused. "We were in San Francisco, I heard the Warper go off, and then you were gone. I stayed with Rachel and her son for about a month."

Aiontis took a seat this time, stabilizing himself as he collapsed into the chair, his stare a thousand miles away.

"Why…?" Titus was starting to piece together that their journey had not been the same. "What happened to you?"

"I…" Aiontis throat closed. He could barely get the words out. "I…I have lived an entire lifetime, my friend."

"What? How?"

"I do not know. Apparently when we were separated, time didn't flow at the same rate for us."

"Where did you go? What happened?"

Aiontis smiled at the questions.

"Perhaps we should go on a walk. I have a lot to tell you, and the story isn't *all* bad." He placed a hand on Titus' shoulder with a squeeze. "It is really good to see you again."

"Same." Titus smiled. "And where is here, exactly?"

"Oh, right. We're in the White House, in the midst of the Cuban Missile Crisis."

"Wow, really?"

"Yeah, pretty wild. People are running around like mad; it's very intense." After a brief moment of silence between them, Aiontis motioned to the door. "Let's go on that walk now, get some fresh air."

They made their way around the halls and exterior pathways of the White House – seemingly allowed to go most anywhere they wanted – and Aiontis told Titus everything.

How he'd traveled back to the Renaissance, met Caterina. Painted her portrait, bed her, and how Caterina had become Kiaria. How they'd lived a lifetime together, in love, before she got sick. How he'd cried out to Odyssian, but instead been forced by Ryveliant to deliver the spark for Titus to start down this path with him. And then how he'd been dumped on September 11ᵗʰ, only to get some sage advice from a stranger, and save many lives, despite all the horrors of that day.

"That's…a lot." Titus instinctually removed his glasses to clean them once more, even if they didn't need it. He removed the portable Warper from his pocket, glancing quickly to see if there was anyone around.

"I have many questions," He started, "But the biggest one is why does this thing matter? Obviously, the fact there's a *portable* Warper is huge, but we can't even control it. So, what's the point?"

"I'm still confused on that point as well, but it could be as simple as Ryveliant just wanting to send you back to kill me, knowing you'd lost access to your memories. Looking back, he very nearly succeeded."

"True." Titus was puzzled. "There're still so many unanswered questions. I imagine you feel the same, but I feel like a puppet in all of this."

"The feeling is mutual. That's for damn sure. I've started to make my peace with it…we can only control what we can control and it's clear this war is much bigger than the both of us." Aiontis glanced around, contemplating his next words. It was as if a spark had hit him. "Come to think of it, we may be puppets, but we're still in play."

"How do you mean?"

"We were both brought here together, weren't we? That's got to count for something. And, I think it had to have been Odyssian. Ryveliant tossed me into 2001 like I was garbage, expecting me to die."

"Fair point, but how much longer is this going to continue?"

Aiontis let out a small laugh. "You've got me there."

"What do we do *here* then?" Titus asked.

"Again, you've got me, but given the complexity of this particular event, I'm wondering if we can do some good and help ease tensions or guide the conversation in the way history intended."

They made their way back inside to an eerily deserted hallway. A buzz hung in the air.

Something was happening.

From the bathroom, a man sprinted across the hall, wiping his mouth and looking pale.

"Hey!" Aiontis called out. The man glanced toward the two of them, one young and another tall, with glasses and a long facial scar. "What's happening?"

"Who are you?" He stopped to look closer.

"Does it matter right now?" Aiontis replied calmly.

"I suppose not. I'm busy." He turned to leave.

"*Hey!* What's going on?" Aiontis reiterated.

"One of our pilots in Alaska accidentally flew into Soviet airspace." He paused, contemplating if he should reveal the rest.

Before he ran off, he muttered, "The Soviets have declared war."

Chapter 69 – Aiontis
1962 | October 27th | Washington D.C.

My overwhelming excitement and relief from finding Titus – my long-lost friend (although apparently not nearly as long for him) – is cut short.

"War?" By the time I ask the question, the hustling man is gone, having run off into another room, slamming the brown wooden door behind him. My gaze catches Titus' raised eyebrow.

"That doesn't happen originally, does it?" He inquires.

Sunlight pours in from a window behind us, warming the hallway, making me stuffy and hot in its noon-time presence.

"No. Things were always on edge, but war was never officially declared." I pace about, with my brown leather shoes drifting across a strange carpet design consisting of squares. *This is definitely the 1960s...*

"I do remember the pilot entering air space though..." I explain. "He was on a routine recon mission that started in Alaska. Given the tension at the time, it was strange the U.S. didn't put those on pause, but either way, he ended up getting lost in Russian airspace and intercepted by their jets."

"Really?" Titus was surprised. "That does sound like enough to light the fuse...but in our version of the story...what? The Russians just escort him home?"

"Basically. A couple of our fighter jets come to help, but all in all, it's a smooth transaction."

Something doesn't feel right. The perpetual gut feeling is present, likely because I'm standing side by side with Titus, but this is the biggest departure yet from any historical reference point I have.

And I know I'm right.

"We need to get in that war room." I point to the doorway the man had disappeared into.

"That's going to be easier said than done."

"I'm not so sure…if what he said is true, it's going to be mass chaos. We may be able to blend right in."

Titus turns his whole body to me, arms crossed.

"What? Look at us! We look the part."

Looking over one another, we're both dressed in slacks and rather itchy 1960's business attire. My sleeves are rolled up, while Titus' hair is combed *quite* tight to one side.

I cock my head, "Do you ever wonder why I seem to change bodies throughout all of this but you're still…you?"

"My clothes keep changing." Titus counters.

"Yeah, sure, but you're still you underneath. I've changed bodies completely."

"Add it to the list of questions, I guess."

We're both frustrated with my distraction.

"Ok, never mind. Not important right now. Just…act like we belong there. Follow my lead."

We head for the door and I reach for its ostentatious circular brass handle. Boisterous noise escapes its confines as I pull, showing off the expectedly strong noise proofing of the White House.

Yelling echoes back and forth.

Papers rustle.

We enter to see grown men shouting, some calm, but all fearful. There's so much going on that it's hard to take it all in. I was right, unfortunately.

A phone rings perpetually on a boardroom table made of walnut, shiny with varnish oil. It smells of body odor, sweat, and stale, poorly circulated air.

No one notices us and I pull Titus to the side to stand in a far corner, observing the pandemonium.

I don't know how to comprehend this. It's a different fear than New York City on 9/11. This is more…*real?* If that's even fucking possible. At least with 9/11, I knew what was coming and what I needed to do.

This is uncharted territory.

Anything can happen.

For these men, the fear is acute. Based only in their linear experience of time and the consequences to actions. Titus and my fear is more whole, coupled with the knowledge of what's *supposed* to happen.

The phone stops ringing for a moment – a breath – and begins once more. It sounds louder, trying to get the attention it craves.

"Men!" I hear a faint shout, unsure of where it's coming from.

"Men!" A little louder, still barely able to break over the other conversations.

A loud, old-fashioned whistle rips atop the ceiling, gathering everyone's attention immediately. My sight locks on the man who issued it, removing his fingers from the side of his mouth. He's a stoic individual, with slick combed hair parted just left of center, and wire-rim glasses.

The Secretary of Defense, Robert McNamara.

He doesn't say anything to the silent room after his whistle, but instead shifts the audience with his eyes to another man.

"Thank you, Robert." I hear the thick Boston accent as I trace the sound of the voice, seated in the middle of the room.

It's a younger man – by comparison to most of the room's other occupants – with a tall coif of dark hair and narrow eyes, complete with heavy bags beneath and wrinkles on the side. He's handsome, but the disheveled flow of hair and distant stare suggest he's tired. And afraid.

Still, it's moments like these that take my breath away.

I'm in a war room for the Cuban Missile Crisis, staring at John F. Kennedy.

Chapter 70 – Aiontis

1962 | October 27th *| Washington D.C.*

"Gentleman…" His voice is iconic and I can barely comprehend watching his lips move as sound leaves them.

Titus is a statue next to me, worried if we're supposed to be in this room. I observe the Commander in Chief's tired eyes glance around his consort of men. There's a subtle look of sadness…of failure…etched in the young lines of his face.

It is dead quiet, except for the ringing red phone that sits in front of him.

"Gentleman. I understand this is a trying time. What we wished hadn't come to pass just crossed our doorstep."

He takes a deep breath.

The phone stops ringing for a moment, as if waiting for him to continue.

"We are the leaders of this nation. We are the *servant* leaders. In perhaps the most crucial moment in our nation's history…in human history…we must remain calm. It is our job. It is our duty. It is the *definition* of leadership."

Silent nods cascade around, some small dips of the chin, others deeper, but the understanding is the same: this is *their* leader.

For a moment, my mind drifts to the original path this man's life takes. One where this crisis is avoided and his diplomacy is looked back on throughout time as a masterstroke of control and resolve. And then, just over a year from now, he's brutally assassinated.

How will these events change that one?

How will one of America's darkest days – a Presidential assassination – observe the ripple effect of this branch?

Branch…the term feels right as it spins in my thoughts, but it implies something I'm not sure is scientifically accurate. Odyssian would know, and I'm eager to find out should we ever meet again.

If we ever fucking meet again.

James' comments push the thought out quickly.

"You have infinite possibilities. Live them."

My mind focuses back to the room and the *now*. JFK is speaking again.

"Men, I understand this is a distressing moment. You're scared. Scared for your families. Scared for your countrymen. Scared for yourselves. I am too. For now, I'm asking that you keep this declaration of war within the confines of this room."

The controversial ask lingers in the thick, odor-filled air.

"You're all aware of the tension we've been through in recent days. Let us determine if this can be solved with diplomacy before ever alerting the citizens of our country to our…to *my* failure."

Shame bleeds across some of the men's faces. Unsure if they could have done more themselves, and embarrassed their leader has to take the full brunt of blame.

Someone coughs quietly.

White noise seeps in from somewhere. Either that or the silence is so loud it's ringing in my ears.

In front of Kennedy, the red phone rings, rattling between its plastic stocks. The sound makes several men jump, including myself. Reluctantly, the man's hand, cracked and dry, grasps the device and brings it to his ear. He glances at McNamara as if to say *Get Ready* and answers.

"This is the President."

A moment goes by.

"Yankee. Zulu. Eight. Six. Two. Romeo. Romeo."

He's listening intently. I glance at Titus and he at me. The look on our faces is similar: *worry*.

Kennedy closes his eyes…deeply. His free arm places an elbow on the table and pinches the bridge of his nose. I can practically see the gears of control turning; he's trying to keep it together.

Whatever news he just received is not good.

"Understood." The receiver claps back onto its stand as he looks around the room.

"The Soviets…" His voice cracks. He starts over. The tension in the room is like thick syrup. "The Soviets…have launched nuclear weapons toward our mainland.”

Sighs tear through the void of the room, some more like cries. Chaos erupts as the men…fathers…brothers…husbands process the news.

I'm in shock. This is *not* how history goes. If I was ever certain about being in my own reality before, that concept has been shattered. Titus lays a hand on my shoulder, confirming his friendship but also kinship in fear.

Throughout the room, a few men cry. Others are observably losing it. More than a couple move for the door but before they get there, a boisterous Boston accent yells out.

“DON'T YOU FUCKING DARE!” The anger in his voice scares me. A swath of hair matches his fury and drops in front of his face, forcing him to run a hand up and over his head.

He slams the table with his fist.

Again.

Once more.

McNamara and the other men look pale, but calm themselves. He has their attention.

“We are the LEADERS of this country, GODDAMIT! FUCKING act like it.” He points man-to-man. “This is the most important hour in all of history and you will not want it looking back at you weakly.” A rigid anger laces his voice…vicious and mean. Necessary.

“We will move to the bunker from where I will address the nation. They have been prepping for a moment like this, but it will be chaos. I will permit each of you to call your loved ones and tell them to hunker down and seek shelter.”

Fear courses cold through my veins, this man's assassination now the furthest thing from my mind. We'll be lucky to survive the next few days.

“Our radar indicates these missiles are coming from Cuba and submarines in the surrounding area. We also shouldn't ignore the fact that several could be coming on the west coast, but that's uncertain.

“I want our best defenses deployed to try and shoot as many of these out of the sky as possible. If that means our planes shoot them out of the sky, so be it. We've prepared for this scenario.

"I will be transparent with you men. A nuclear weapon will make U.S. landfall. We won't be able to stop all of them and we will retaliate in kind. I want our strategic targets in Soviet Russia fired upon immediately. If we find that a target did not make its mark, we'll fire another one."

The silence is deafening.

"Rise to the call men. We can't afford to perform any less at this moment and time is short. Pray to your gods. It's time to face adversity, whether you want to or not."

Many men turn for the door as Kennedy stands.

"Sir?"

"Yes, Bill?" Kennedy replies with less vigor and more empathy.

"How long do we have?"

"10 minutes. We need to hurry."

Chapter 71 – Aiontis

1962 | October 27th | Washington D.C.

Given the crazed initial reaction, I'm impressed by the orderly cadence with which the other men gather their papers, folders, pens, and archaic leather briefcases and file out of the room.

As if it had been any other meeting.

As if the world wasn't about to be set ablaze.

The open wood door lets in a welcome draft, exchanging warm, stale air for a cool replacement. A distant smell akin to a men's locker room remains, our bodies all reacting in various ways.

"What should we do?" Titus asks, hoping I'll know.

"I think our only option is to follow them." I nod toward the exiting crowd. The last few stragglers make their way out to the hall. Several have lit cigarettes to calm their nerves. "They're probably going to pack as many people as they can in a bunker and ride out the storm."

"We should be in there."

"I agree."

A nuclear weapon will almost certainly hit Washington D.C. Both the Cubans and Soviets have it painted as a key target and now we wait to see which missiles break through the defenses. Titus' fingers curl around my goosebump-peppered forearm and he pulls me toward the door.

"C'mon. The more we stay in the crowd, the less suspicion we raise if we're not supposed to be here."

"I think we're far past whether or not we'll be allowed in, but good point. I'd rather not test my theory."

Rushing into the hall with the ugly, square carpet, the group of men turn a corner, cigarette smoke trailing like wispy fingers behind them. We jog to catch up, doing so easily. Far in front of us, JFK and McNamara hustle from door to door, checking to see if they have any occupants, telling them to drop everything now and join the group. Given the events of the Crisis thus far, I imagine when the President knocks on your office door accompanied by a worried crowd telling you to come with him, you listen.

I am uneasy. Not just about the impending nuclear doom, but the calmness the scene paints. Not quite sure what I would actually expect, I attempt to put myself in the shoes of some of these men.

With families. Wives. *Children.*

Are they abandoning them?

Do they have a choice?

On autopilot beside Titus, our group's mass makes turn after turn in the halls, expanding size considerably, forcing us to reside in the center, the width of our blob slowing us down as we try to squeeze through the halls.

Secret Service, uniformed in black suits, black ties, and old-tech ear pieces sprint past.

"We have eyes on Lancer. Copy that."

Kennedy knocks on a closed office ahead of us to our left. "Mr. President!" With a waving hand he flippantly shoos them away.

"Mr. President. We need to get you to safety immediately. Please come with us."

"Alright boys, fine. One of you escort me to the bunker. The other needs to ensure all these people get to that same bunker, and quickly. Radio in and find Jackie too. Don't take no for an answer from her."

Even in crisis, he has control.

"Roger that, sir." The agent presses his hand against the President's back, coaxing him forward. As he departs, "I have Lancer, headed toward the bunker. I need someone with eyes on Lace to get them to the bunker immediately. This is not a drill."

The urgency of the Secret Service to whisk away the President has forced the group to quicken their pace. With more intensity than the President had used, the remaining agent races from room to room, commanding anyone still left inside. By now, our crowd creates enough noise that many have opened their doors and joined already.

Once again, several people cry.

Murmurs echo across the top of the crowd.

More cigarette smoke blossoms and drags behind us.

The air returns to a stale, stenchy state.

How many minutes have passed? Panic bubbles in my chest. I know we don't have long and this will be a lot of people to fit into a bunker…a scenario forms in my mind I'd rather not think about.

"People! Let's go! We need to pick up the pace! The bunker is just through this doorway." A different Secret Service member ushers us into the room off the hallway with his hands. The room is small and discreet. I'm unsure what you'd use it for otherwise – *a reading room perhaps?* – which means it's probably the perfect place for an underground, high-security bunker.

Although the crowd is slow like cattle, there's a focused urgency driving people to move faster into the stairwell that has risen from the floor in the ground. Titus and I approach the edge of the stairs in a single file, he stands aside to let me go first and I oblige.

The brightness of the reading room disappears when I turn an immediate corner from the stairs, now facing a long, concrete hallway with dim lighting. The walls warp in my mind, nearly closing in on me as I – and tens of people ahead and behind me – shuffle forward. This would be a very shitty place to die.

This hallway, which seems to double back into the core atrium of the White House, finally ends (or at least widens a bit), introducing a larger set of concrete stairs downward. Still, the lighting is sparse and my eyes are adjusting, but the air is warm and thick with humidity. I would have expected it to be colder, but it's the other panicked 20-30 crammed human souls driving the temperature up.

I cannot get a sense for how long the staircase goes downward, but I've counted at least five flights of stairs thus far. If we're hoping to survive a nuclear blast, I hope it's at least ten more. Our footsteps echo loudly in the stairwell chamber, like a mini stampede, punctuated by the remarkable lack of voices. Once we entered the stairwell and began the descent, something clicked in the crowd.

It all became very real.

A sneaking sense of claustrophobia comes over me, briefly imagining being entombed with all these strangers – some on top, some on bottom – and hundreds of feet of concrete pounding us together. Under my armpits and at the back of my neck, I feel slick. Sweat dews and my hand grips the red iron railing tighter.

The downward spiral marching has become monotonous. Our human line accepts a plodding cadence, with one half of our minds focused on subconsciously moving our feet while all the others are generating worst-case scenarios.

Finally, a huge whirring sound emerges from down below and within seconds, the air is cooler and more tolerable. They must have reached the bottom and turned on the cooling system. After three more staircases, each of which look exactly like the last, Titus and I reach the bottom too, greeted by Secret Service ushering us inside.

"There's plenty of room, get comfortable. Please sit on the floor and make room for others behind you." One says with a circling arm motion.

A quick glance reveals the bunker has many different rooms, each with their own brand of wood paneling and ugly carpet, but similar to any room I would have seen several stories (are we *that* far down?) above us. The lighting is different – artificial – but otherwise this is a remarkable bunker that seems well outfitted.

I'm not sure why I'm surprised that a Cold War-era White House has this impressive feat, but I don't get long to think about it.

Far above us, like the distant growl of an angry dragon, a rumble begins. It echoes through the stairwell, rattling the handrail and creating small plumes of concrete dust trailing downward.

"It's starrrtttinggg!!" Someone yells nervously from above. Two or three screams from different places reverberate off the stairwell's walls and the crowd begins moving faster.

Disorderly.

Titus and I don't take time to observe, quickly pushing further back into other rooms.

A loud, deep clap shakes the ground and almost causes me to fall over.

That's when the lights go out.

Chapter 72 – Titus
1962 | October 27ᵗʰ | Washington D.C.

The abnormal sensation crept across the underside of the bunker's carpet. A rumble so deep it suggested that it came from below. Titus, only a month removed from the Great Faultline Disaster…from the future…noted how the two events felt similar.

For now.

Groping air and stationary objects around him, he eventually found Aiontis' shoulder, squeezing it as a signal. His friend's hand lay over top of his for a moment.

"This is fucking crazy." Aiontis started. "This isn't supposed to happen."

"What do you think it means?" Titus asked without a clue of the answer himself, their discussion masked by the surrounding commotion.

"I…really don't know. Not even a damn guess." He had to shout over the noise of screams and talking and crumbling facades. Titus, who was not prone to *fear* often, had it surging through his body.

His *android* body. The realization had reached a state of awkward acceptance during his time with Rachel and Bryson in San Francisco. Even still, he'd lose himself in thought from time to time. Right now, it was a helpful distraction.

What does fear look like? Is it simply 1s and 0s going to my brain? Do I have an adrenaline equivalent? A racing heartbeat? Tunnel vision?

A new loud thump shook them, definitely coming from above, and smacking a deep pulse of bass through their bones. Across the room, a hubbub amidst the normal sobbing and prayers. With a different noise than all the others – an electronic whirr – the rooms and hallways lit up, bathing them in fluorescent, but welcomed, light.

At a distance, Titus heard others talking about a back-up generator or some sort of failsafe. Now, he could finally begin taking stock of the situation. From the sporadic looks and faces of those around the room, they were all doing the same thing with their newfound sight.

As if disconnected from the gargantuan moment of history above them, the rooms that held them did not resemble anything catastrophic. There were cracks in the ceiling, sure, and many people crammed together, but any sign that a nuclear weapon – and likely the beginning of World War III – had just been dropped was sparse. Beside him, Aiontis stood, nervously glancing across the rooms, but focusing primarily at the one deeper into the bunker. Where the President had gone.

"What do you see?" Titus asked.

"Not much. They have the doors closed to where JFK is…or at least where I think he is."

He sat down; a mild look of bewilderment etched in his eyes. His gaze pierced the dusty carpet. "What the *fuck* is going on? Why are we here?"

"*Now* do you think this is Ryveliant? It would make sense if he's trying to kill us…"

"I agree, but something doesn't add up."

"What doesn't?" Titus wasn't tracking.

"You and the portable Warper."

"What about it?"

"If that was part of Ryveliant's plan…the portable Warper…why send us to a timeline that deviates so greatly? We already know he set you up to kill me, so the portable Warper had to have been a different play completely. It makes no sense he'd send that technology to a world like this."

"I suppose." Titus stated. "But we've never known either of their plans, have we? For all we know the Warper could be a distraction."

"Fuck! I don't know." Aiontis leaned his back against the wallpapered surface behind him. Hard. Knees to chest, his eyes darted sporadically.

Titus gave him some space. After closing his eyes in a meditative state for a few moments, a whimper whispered from across the room.

There were others in the office-like space with them. An

American flag hung loose downward from a pole stuck in a decorated ceramic pot in the corner, there was a deep cherrywood desk near the center, and several orangish office chairs faced the desk.

Again, a small whimper. Like crying.

Others were distracted with their own thoughts and hysteria. Some had since left the room all together. To where, Titus was not certain.

Getting on all fours, he crawled, hands pushing into the scratchy carpet, toward the desk. It was a heavy piece, made of solid wood, with baroque woodworking detail along its edges. Titus came round to the backside of the desk, the whimpering more obvious now.

There, in the desk's kneehole, was a small child.

A girl.

Crying and alone.

Her eyes glanced upward, saw Titus (and likely his scarring), and darted back into her huddled body.

"Hey, hey…" Titus' voice was light and sympathetic. "It's okay."

A choking sob came out, shaking her rounded back. Titus guessed she was seven or eight years old, wearing a school uniform of sorts.

"It's okay. I'm really scared too." That earned Titus a half-eye raise. Tears glistened on the edges of her brown eyes. "It's true. This is *really* scary. Do you mind if I hide under here with you? It seems like a safe spot."

Her head was fully raised, streaks of the crying apparent against her reddened cheeks, with strands of auburn hair stuck to them. She cocked her head slightly, confused by Titus' ask.

"I don't…think you'll fit?"

"Oh, that's ok. I'll leave my legs out here. Don't need those anyway!"

She giggled, a smile emerging. "Yes, you do!"

"Oh, you're right! Well…they'll be ok out here."

Titus situated himself so he was mostly under the desk, leaning on his arm, facing the girl. Providing a smile to match hers.

"What's your name?" He asked.

"Bekkah." The response was warm, but faint.

"That's a nice name!" Titus said enthusiastically. "Where are you from, Bekkah?"

"Here. Washington D.C."

"Oh? That must be fun! And are you here with anyone?"

Tears welled in her eyes. She wanted to give an answer, but she'd been separated from whoever it was. Titus followed his question with a gentle hand on her shoulder.

"It's ok. I'm sure they're safe and we'll find them."

"You think so? When the booming started to happen and the lights went out, I lost my mommy's hand."

"What's your mother's name, Bekkah?"

"Julie. She works here in the White House."

Titus wanted to help this child desperately, but briefly realized that in this situation, "worst-case scenario" was a very real possibility.

The two talked for a few minutes more about Bekkah's favorite colors, animals, and ice cream flavors. Titus had calmed her down.

"Bekkah!" A questioning scream came from several rooms away. "Bekkah! Where are you!"

"I'm sure she's ok, mam. Let's look in here." JFK's unmistakable accent assured the woman.

"Mommy!" Bekkah jumped from under the desk with Titus slowly emerging behind her.

"Bekkah!" The woman ran from an attached room, gripping her child in a tight embrace and picking her up off the floor. President Kennedy sauntered in behind her, acknowledging Titus with a nod.

"Well, see? There you go! Smart girl, hiding under a desk!" The President smiled at her then addressed the mother and Titus. "If you'll excuse me, I'm going to go make sure everyone else is accounted for."

"Thank you, sir!" Tears gently trickled down the mother's cheeks.

As Kennedy exited the room, her gaze shifted to Titus. For a moment, he noticed the flicker of her reaction to his facial scar.

"I'm sorry. And who are you?" She asked, without spite, but

full of motherly concern.

"This is my friend, mom!" Bekkah chimed in. "He found me crying under the desk and told me everything would be ok. He was right!"

Ready to reply, Titus instead chuckled at her enthusiastic description in agreement.

"Is that so?" The mother, Julie, beamed at her daughter, giving her a soft bump on her arms. She turned to Titus. "Well thank you very much, sir. I'm sure she was as scared as I was."

"It was no problem at all. I was scared too and she helped me." Titus explained, the little girl blushing in her mother's arms. "And you know what? Chocolate Chip Cookie Dough is *my* favorite ice cream flavor too!"

Julie laughed. "I see she's been explaining to you all her theories and love of ice cream."

Bekkah giggled too, followed by a short silence. Eventually, Julie placed her daughter back on the floor and positioned herself to sit down too. Bekkah went back under the desk while Julie's back was to the hardwood wall facing her. Titus copied the motion and noticed that Aiontis had made his way into the room, looking anxious.

Maybe it's a good thing for us all to spend a little time getting our minds off what just happened up there.

"Aiontis, this is my friend, Bekkah. And her mother, Julie." Titus motioned for his partner to come over and greet them. Aiontis grasped what Titus was trying to do and came over with a warm greeting.

"Nice to meet you."

"You as well." Julie stated from the floor. Soon they were all sitting in a row, facing the desk. Despite the pleasantries, their faces all appeared morose.

"Hello!" Bekkah waved enthusiastically from her kneehole.

Aiontis smirked. "Hi! That looks like a pretty cozy spot you got there!"

"It is. You can come in if you want!"

"I may just take you up on that, thank you!" Bekkah smiled and leaned back inward. Aside from the small sounds coming from other rooms, silence took over once again.

"Do you guys know what's going on?" Julie asked quietly, pivoting her head on the wall toward them. Aiontis and Titus exchanged glances.

"It sounds like a nuclear weapon was fired at D.C." Aiontis explained.

"Yes, but why? I mean I know things were tense, but…" She trailed off.

"This whole situation was a tinder box, ready for the right spark." Aiontis started, losing himself in thought. "But this wasn't supposed to happen."

Titus shifted uncomfortably.

"What do you mean?" Julie had picked up on the slip.

"I…uh…just all the analysis we've run. It wasn't supposed to go this way." Aiontis tried to cover his tracks.

"Oh…so you're an analyst? You must be pretty high up if you're working on this stuff." She commented, impressed. "What *was* supposed to happen?"

"The blockade was supposed to work." Titus interjected, trying to prevent Aiontis from revealing them. "Eventually the tension would dissipate enough to give Kennedy and Khrushchev the ability to converse and come to terms."

"Well, what about Castro? Isn't he the one that sent the missiles?"

"No. Castro is really nothing but a minion of the Soviets, trying desperately to earn their allyship. At the end of the day, this was always a showdown between the U.S. and Soviets."

"Hmm." Julie acknowledged Titus' explanation, her gaze returning to her daughter under the desk. "Her father was away on business to Denver this week." A pause. "Do you know…" A trail of tears trickled from her eyes, ones she quickly wiped away, "Do you know if Denver was hit too?"

Neither man answered immediately, but eventually Titus did. "We don't, sorry. I know about as much as you at this point."

The radiation of several nuclear missiles would undoubtedly affect Denver, but now wasn't the time. Aiontis rested a supportive hand on his leg.

Julie closed the conversation. "Well, it's no longer a showdown now, is it? It's a war."

Chapter 73 – Aiontis
1962 | October 31ˢᵗ | Washington D.C.

It's Halloween as Bekkah has reminded me several times today. We remain in the bunker per order of…well…I don't actually know who. My best guess is the President and whoever he's speaking to on the outside.

Things are bad up top, and we're trapped down here. A high-yield nuclear missile directly hit Washington D.C., among several other targets, and there's not much left of the nation's capital. The concrete tunnel and staircase partially collapsed, killing a handful of people who were scrambling to reach the bunker.

Inside, we're not packed too tight, but tensions are high. My assessment indicates there's plenty of food and water, probably enough for a month. But people are scared. Many are devastated from what they lost on the outside. Guilt runs rampant, sending several individuals to very dark places. They were just "at work" but their families didn't have the same luxury. Now, their husbands, wives, sons, and daughters are likely all dead.

Eviscerated.

Titus and I do our best to help where needed, but I can tell we're shaken too.

Is this the world we're stuck in now?

How long will we be here?

Trying to plan a Halloween for Bekkah helps distract everyone, including Kennedy. She's a sweet girl whose innocence acts like a bright light in a place that desperately needs one.

Throughout the day, I've been making rounds from room to room, checking with others for gum or candy to give during Bekkah's planned trick-or-treat path. Many do not, and several are too distraught to even give an answer. Cowering in their corners, their unwavering gaze bores holes in the wall. I can't blame them, and make note of which rooms to avoid.

After an hour, I'm partially successful, securing only a handful of future treats. I head to the kitchen pantry, under watch by an armed Secret Service member.

Even the disaster above cannot make their dedication waver. Impressive or blind?

"Hi, Michael." I wave, entering the room.

"Afternoon."

"Can I take a look in the pantry for anything we could give to Bekkah? She wants to trick-or-treat tonight. It's Halloween."

He grimaces briefly. We're supposed to be rationing portions, but it's also hard to deny a child this small luxury amidst horrors.

"Sure. Just check-in with me after so I can record what you take."

"Will do." I walk past him, entering the densely stocked cabinets of food. For a while, there's nothing. Just cans of vegetables, meat, and soup. In a past life, I would have been fascinated by this; the labeling, the nutrition (or lack of it), and the food itself. In 2404, our food is much different. The novelty has somewhat worn off after a lifetime in the past and I've more pressing concerns right now.

My shoulders loosen when I finally find a wall of cookies, Oreos. It's not much variety, but at least it's something. Emerging from the pantry, I find Titus speaking with Michael, the Secret Service agent.

"Ah. Found you." My friend comments. The agent says nothing.

"Hey."

"Find anything?" Titus asks, the agent turning to me so he can take inventory.

"There's some cookies in there that will do the job."

"Why don't you have any with you?" The agent asks.

"How would you feel about giving them to her yourself? Tonight." I'm hoping he's willing to help make it special. Surprisingly, he returns a big smile.

"I have an idea. Come back tonight for the cookies."

"Ohhh…kay?" He can hear the suspicion in my voice.

"Just trust me."

"All right, we'll see you later then."

Titus and I walk away, meandering through the halls-turned-living-quarters.

"How'd you fare?" He asks.

"Okay. A few people have some gum or hard candy. I think she'll like the cookies too. More importantly, I learned who to avoid."

"Hmm. Makes sense. The general mood is quite…depressing."

"Would you expect anything else?" I challenge.

"No." We turn a corner away from our "rooms", consciously extending our walk to continue the conversation.

"What were you talking to Michael about?" I ask.

"Getting filled in on what's happening with the world." Titus starts. "Apparently, there's a perception I'm a senior analyst, so they trust me with this information. Plus, I think they're aiming to provide transparency and not sugar coat what's going on."

"So, what *is* going on?"

"It's not good. We at least have communication with the outside world and they know the President is alive." His voice lowers. "Nukes hit Miami, New York City, Chicago, and LA. Millions are dead and the entire nation is dealing with fallout and radiation." His gaze darts around to see if anyone's listening. "We struck back, basically obliterating Cuba. Moscow is wiped out, as is St. Petersburg. The rest of the world is begging for both countries to stop, which they have…for now. There's no going back from this though, and now we're hearing chatter of World War III starting."

We stop walking, I'm shaken, my head racing.

"I know not with what weapons World War III will be fought, but World War IV will be fought with sticks and stones." I let the Einstein quote linger before Titus responds.

"It would indeed seem that way."

Chapter 74 – Aiontis
1962 | October 31ˢᵗ | Washington D.C.

"Ok Bekkah!" I can't tell if Julie or her daughter is more excited to go trick-or-treating. "Are you ready?" Her mom's joy is overflowing and, truthfully, we're all eager for this small chunk of happiness after being stuck for days.

"Yeah!" I'm sure Bekkah's smile stretches from ear to ear, but her eyes are the only thing any of us can see. "Do you think people will like my ghost?"

"Absolutely!" Titus answers. "You're quite scary!"

Bekkah giggles. Even though "ghost" was the only option down here, her spirits remain high.

"So, where should we begin?" Julie asks, looking at me, trusting that my earlier survey should guide her daughter.

"Well actually," A familiar voice enters the room. It's President Kennedy. "I was hoping I could kick things off and come with you?" He kneels down to Bekkah's level. "Would that be okay?"

Julie's eyes are wide. Bekkah nods enthusiastically.

"Do you have something to ask me, Bekkah?" His tone is playful.

"Hmmm? Oh yeah!" She holds up a periwinkle pillow case we found. "Trick-or-treat!"

"Wonderful! Well, let's see what I have here…" The President rummages through his pockets dramatically. Out comes a normal sized candy bar – probably the only one in here – and he plops it in her bag. "Do you like that kind?"

"I…think so? Thank you!"

"Oh, I'm not done yet." Kennedy responds, pulling out a small metal object from a different pocket. "This here is a Presidential pin. Only the President gets one. But now it's yours and you'll be the Ghost President!"

Bekkah chuckles so hard I think she may pee her pants. Her mother's eyes glisten, in awe of the President's kindness.

Carefully, Kennedy secures the pin on the front of her costume, the black and gold Presidential seal as a striking contrast to the white sheet.

"Ok!" Kennedy stands up. "Shall we continue?"

The group moves slowly through the bunker, much to the benefit of everyone. It gives Bekkah time to try out her candy and show off her costume while also allowing Kennedy to check in on everyone and give them attention.

Nuclear bunker or not, you respond when the President asks how you're doing.

Thirty minutes have passed and the mood room to room fluctuates from pleasant (with an undercurrent of dread) to outright somber with occupants trying their best to not imprint their moods on Bekkah, and show Kennedy their better sides. Either way, it's working to keep her excited about candy and most rooms are left with subtle smiles.

Next is the pantry, supposedly hiding Michael's surprise. Bekkah will love the stash of cookies too. For most of what she's scrounged up so far, she's being polite. Oddly, the pantry lights are off and the Secret Service agent is nowhere to be found.

"Oh my, Bekkah!" Kennedy sells the drama. "Where did my Secret Service go?"

Bekkah tenses, clutching her bag of candy tightly, walking slowly into the darkness. A single flashlight beam turns on facing upward beneath someone's face.

It's Michael's, his eyes wide in false horror and minor bloody scars on his face.

"Bekkkkkaaaaahhh!" He gargles. Bekkah relaxes, knowing it's part of the act and giggles some more. "I hear you've come for cooooooookiiiiiess!" Unexpectedly, some soft music, light rock, starts further back in the room. "But first, you'll have to get throoooooouuuughhh usssss!" Michael's glances side-to-side, "The daannnnnncing zommm-bieeeeess!"

Julie audibly laughs and Kennedy's chuckle fills the room.

On either side of Michael, two other agents turn on their flashlights, outfitted with the same makeup, and start a small choreographed dance to some catchy hit from the 1960s.

They're laughably out of sync, lifting the tension like a helium balloon floating in an open sky. Each agent is on the verge of bursting out in laughter and now I'm certain Bekkah might pee her pants as she's belly laughing next to a similarly keeled-over Kennedy.

Eventually, the music ends, the agents stop their uncoordinated dance, and each walks over to Bekkah with a package of cookies in their hand. By the time all five have delivered her the Oreos, she can barely hold them all, emphatically stuffing all but one in her pillow case and ripping one open. Pausing briefly, she offers an Oreo to Kennedy, to the horror of her mother, but Kennedy smiles and gladly takes the cookie, unscrewing the top licking the cream, and then eats the entire thing.

"Everyone eats an Oreo differently!" He explained. "That's half the fun!"

Bekkah copied his approach underneath her costume, likely unaware that she had just made friends with the President of the United States.

Several weeks pass in the bunker and tensions run high among everyone. Even the information Titus had been getting has turned into a mere trickle. The only things he knows about are the abysmal conditions up top (which is obvious) and that a rescue mission is underway, but it's difficult. We'll all need hazmat suits which, at best, will only slow the radiation amounts on the surface. Getting to the bunker has proven the greater, nearly insurmountable challenge, because of the depth and collapse of the stairwell.

Good news finally came this morning however: the rescue operation will arrive tomorrow, and we'll all be out of this literal hell hole within 36 hours.

I've secretly been keeping stock of the Oreos as a mechanism of measuring our pending descent into madness and the rescue comes at the perfect time.

There's only a single pack left.

I am beyond disheartened when I make contact with the first rescuer. Bags hang dark and heavy under eyes that hold a stare so distant and haunting I'm not sure I'll ever forget them. He doesn't speak and manhandles us like products. The colleagues he brought along are no different while they hook us one-by-one to the ascending pulley to the surface.

They look dead, but living.

Full of motion, but not thinking.

Dread weighs like a brick, churning my stomach and pushing on my shoulders. *These men look like they will kill themselves once this task is done.*

My rescuer with no name attaches a carabiner to the hazmat suit I've carefully put on.

Is this one of the last acts he will perform?

The thick metal oval clacks, attaching around its brethren on the pulley rope. As an instinct, I grab the man's arm, startling him, and look him in the eye.

I hug him.

I'm not sure why.

I'm not sure if it will help, but it can't hurt. The embrace ends after a few moments, without him looking back at me, and he gives the pulley rope two tugs downward.

My hips jolt upward as I launch into the tunnel, unable to notice anything other than dark blurry walls and a dull, hazy light above me. A light that *feels* as if it should be much brighter.

Even after the things I've seen on this journey, nothing could have prepared me for this.

The pulley system is hooked to a metal arm that stops raising me a few meters above the hole's entrance. A landscape once full of gray and white historic buildings, lush trees and greenery, and blue skies, has been replaced with the apocalypse.

The White House is nothing more than a random collection

of toothpick wood and debris around me. Charred, disintegrated, and in flames. Further out, the landscape gets bleaker, with black and gray and brown shades dominating everything I see, especially the sky.

Strangely, I feel as if I can *smell* the death and smoke through my suit. It's pungent and reminiscent of 9/11 and the Great Faultline Disaster, but more…vibrant. More *severe.*

There's a collection of seven aid workers below me, their bright yellow hazmat suits being the only distinct color on the horizon, and they latch a long hook to my rope, pulling me closer to the side of the hole. Similar to the no-name helper in the bunker, their eyes betray them.

The world is a different place and they've seen the horrors.

We're only just being introduced to it.

Titus comes up after me, looking just as bewildered. Once unhooked, he walks over, his mouth agape. There are so many things we could say to each other…something like *So this is what the end of the world looks like?* comes to mind. Instead, we stand in silence, slowly taking in all 360 degrees of the destruction.

Through the haunting silence – only pierced by infrequent, but fierce wind gusts – a familiar deep rumble seems faint. A wave of thoughts sends electricity up my spine.

Bwah….bwahhhhh…bwaaaaahhhhhhhhh

What? Now?

Bwwwaaaahhhhhhhhh

Titus hangs his head, having recognized the sound too. He reaches in his suit, likely not as susceptible to radiation as a synthetic creature, and holds the miniature Warper. Sure enough, a blackish glow surrounds it.

BWWWAAAAHHHHHHHH

We exchange glances, unsure of what will happen. Will both of us be moved to a new era? Will we remain in this unknown history? There's a high degree of uncertainty now that we're in uncharted waters.

BWAAAHHHHHHHHHHHH....

The noise, deafening, yet invisible to others, swallows us whole. Instantaneously, we travel from one blackened, cold environment to a much darker one.

Chapter 75 – Aiontis

~ ~ ~

I know this place.

Even if it's not…a place.

Across every type of sensation imaginable, I feel new and lost and…in the dark. *Absolute* dark.

My mind itches. On prickly fire with an entirely new realm of functionality. I'd say my synapses multiplied by a trillion, but I've got no fucking clue if that's scientifically accurate.

I'm in the Bulk.

I'm back in the fourth dimension.

"Titus?" Once again, the conversation feels both as if I'm having it now, already had it, and am going to have it at some point. Everything is revealed at once, leaving my intricate mind to decipher it.

"Yeah. Aiontis?" The response seems distant at first, but then right next to me…if I had a physical presence.

"Good, we're both here." For a nanosecond, my mind pictures a sigh of relief, but the sensation is measured in kind across a small part of my now-vast neurological network.

"Aiontis. Titus." Odyssian's voice is foreign; I've not heard it in over a lifetime, but also immediately recognizable.

"Where have you been?!" My statement is laced with hurt.

"I am sorry. To both of you, but especially you Aiontis." The sentient being pauses. Seeking remorse? "My plan has taken longer than I would have presumed and, as you'll recall, time does not…*flow*…the same way for both of us. I can only hope the life you lived was a good one."

"It…it was." I release my anger. Apparently, these advanced brains are more forgiving. "How did Ryveliant get to me first?"

"He was faster than I and…" Could I sense a sigh? Did fourth-dimensional beings actually sigh? "It was part of the plan."

"How so?"

"Ryveliant capturing you was something we already knew was going to happen, correct? Titus mentioned it the first time we met in the Bulk."

"Sure, but…"

"Think!"

With minimal effort, the strategic bullets snap together.

"We knew his plan. If you'd prevented it, he would have changed it, and we would have been one step behind."

"Precisely. Good."

"What have you been doing this whole…time?" I'm unsure if that's the right word.

"My people and I have been building toward the end. We think the moment has come. It is why I've brought you here."

"The end of…what exactly?" Titus questions. I wonder the same thing.

"Ryveliant, primarily. And the Regime." He pauses, recognizing we're confused. "Apologies. Let me fill you in."

Odyssian carefully explains how Ryveliant seeks to eliminate third-dimensional creatures like Titus and myself, *sooner*, in order for the era of the fourth-dimension to begin. That speciocide likely brings the start of the fifth-dimension right to their doorstep. It's a sinister scientific argument for their time and, even with the extra brain power, is nearly lost on me.

Sometimes this time travel bullshit is too much.

"Ok, let me make sure I have this." I start, sensing that we have plenty of time with Odyssian, as opposed to our rushed first meeting.

"Ryveliant created the Regime in order to wipe out…humanity…or the 'third dimension' sooner. By doing that, the fourth dimension, *your beings*, would instantly be further along in their development?"

"The term 'instantly' is only relevant to a certain flow of time, but otherwise, yes. That's correct."

"Ok then, I have a big question for you."

"Why us?" Titus breaks his silence and beats me to it.

"Why *not* you?" Odyssian challenges. "In all great moments throughout time, there always has to be *someone*."

I don't really accept his answer, nor can I think of a follow up question to ask. He's right, but dodging.

"Tell me," He starts. "What do you know about Infinitude?"

"Infinitude?" I repeat.

"Isn't infinitude just…infinity?" Titus challenges, seeming as confused as I am.

"Yes. It is." Odyssian answers. "But do you recognize what *infinity* really is?"

"It's endless. Boundless." I reply.

"Yes…now use your minds. Think about that…"

All at once, my mind bounds in a million, trillion different directions. Calculations, observations, feelings from every reach of its organic fiber. If my head itched with capability before, it's now downright engulfed in power.

I can feel it pushing to the brink.

"Come back. Let me explain." Odyssian comments. I can hear myself breathing from the exertion. An odd note in total nothingness, I know.

"Infinitude is a concept that us fourth dimensional beings hardly understand and third dimensional humans certainly don't. Yes, you get the concept of infinity, but only at a surface level. I believe you would refer to it as…'a lot'?"

I chuckle. "That's fair."

"Infinity is just that. It never ends. And when we speak of Infinitude, we're referring to time. Specifically," He pauses, "time*lines*…"

"Is that what we just experienced? Infinite…timelines?"

"A small portion, yes. That was your first experience sliding along time – and thus various timelines – as we do."

"Holy fucking shit." It comes out as a gasp.

Odyssian replies. "Holy shit indeed."

Chapter 76 – Aiontis

~ ~ ~

Conceptually, I can only scratch the surface when I start to think about Infinitude. The moment my brain recognizes the idea of it, it's mentally exhausting to control the connections that begin to fire. Absorbing the conversation is like the hardest form of meditation I've ever had to do.

"What does Infinitude have to do with us? With this war?" Titus pushes.

"It is equal parts problem *and* solution." Odyssian starts. "You both come from a period where 'time travel', as you understand it, is a commercialized experience. Correct?"

"Yes. It's expensive." I add, half wondering if Odyssian and fourth dimensional beings have any concept of money.

"Perhaps shocking, but you're not actually traveling *through* time when you use Warpers. You're traveling *across*. Put simplest: you are changing timelines every time you utilize your form of time travel."

"There's no way." My retort comes immediately. "Wouldn't people have noticed that by now? Missing persons, family members, etcetera?"

"Ahhh. That's you failing to grasp the concept of Infinitude. Because there are *infinite* timelines, the degrees of change are sometimes infinitesimally small. Non-existent to a third dimensional being.

"As an example, suppose a man travels back 10 years for a business purpose. He's crossed to one other timeline by doing so, but one with changes perhaps as minimal as what someone across the world wore as an outfit that day.

"After his business, he travels back to his original timeline – the Warper process can accomplish that much – none the wiser to having visited two distinct timelines."

"Wouldn't that create a lot of problems?" I challenge him. "Things like missing persons in timelines that are radically different than ours? People coming back with misunderstandings of history? I'm sure there are more I'm not thinking of…"

"Are you so sure there aren't those examples? Tyme Corporation is a powerful and wealthy company…" Odyssian's suggestion is fair. "And there's the rule about traveling back before a certain point, correct? The year 2377, I believe?"

"Yes, that's true…"

"That's a falsity. There's no physical limitation to traveling whenever you'd like – as you've well experienced. It's to control the narrative with a narrower scope of world history. The less time available to travel from, the less likely for drastic changes to be encountered. Eventually, it would have been uncontrollable for them to police."

"Hmmm. Okay…" I'm skeptical, still confused. "But how does this play into Titus' question? What does Infinitude have to do with everything else?"

"Yes, sorry. I'll cut to the facts. Infinitude is the problem as it has allowed Ryveliant to create a Core Event on timelines accessible to humans."

"A Core Event?"

"I believe you refer to it as a D-Day in your profession? This is less a single day and more an endpoint of your time."

"What's the Event?"

"The creation of the Regime."

"Wouldn't Infinitude argue that there are both infinite timelines *with* the Regime and infinite timelines *without* it?" The enormity of my question makes even my own head spin.

"Ah." I sense Odyssian is smiling through the nothingness. "You're catching on. And you're right. Keep in mind that even as fourth dimensional beings, we struggle to comprehend the gargantuan nature of this statement. Because of that, we've only been able to access so many timelines ourselves. An arguably infinite amount by most any measure, but still with infinite ones undiscovered."

The silence indicates we're confused.

"Think of horizontal time, in other words *timelines*, as an infinite ocean. Sure, we've explored large swaths of it, can map just as much, and been to some of its deepest depths…but if it's *truly* infinite, will we really *ever* see all of it?" Now I get it.

"I suppose not. You're using my own point against me."

"Merely to prove my own, but that is why Infinitude is a problem: Ryveliant has mapped a Core Event of the Regime to our known timelines. We haven't been able to determine a way to undo that action."

"You mentioned Infinitude was also the solution…?" Titus is asking the important questions.

"Yes. I have a feeling you know what that may be already."

"The infinite timelines without the Regime." I answer.

"Precisely. We've been able – with much sacrifice – to extend past his reach."

"How many timelines have you found without the Regime?"

His answer lands like a bullet between my eyes.

"Just one."

Chapter 77 – Aiontis
~ ~ ~

"One?" It's a question that is released as an exclamation. "We have our limitations as a species too." Odyssian explains.

"Ok…so, what's the plan?" I ask, with an immediate follow up. "And what timeline is the 'one'?"

"It's the timeline we just came from." Titus answers for him. "That's why it deviated so much from reality."

"That's correct. That's how we were able to find it."

"So, the timeline in which the Cuban Missile Crisis turned into a full-blown nuclear war is what we're going back to?"

"Yes, but you're going to the year 2477. Though, I should warn you," Odyssian's tone seemed heavy…distant. "The world never really recovered from what you saw."

"What do we need to do?" I ask, already not loving this plan.

"Infiltrate the beginnings of the Regime and take it down. From the inside."

"What the fuck? I thought you said there was no Regime?"

"There isn't. Yet. As the Core Event is spreading horizontally across timelines, we found this single one that it hasn't hit. We can go there and ensure it never happens."

"Meaning?" Titus presses.

"Meaning that this timeline will extend past the point at which the Regime destroys humanity and third-dimensional creatures, extending your time and place throughout history."

"All the timelines with the Regime are unsalvageable?" My gut aches, if that's even possible. And my head spins. *I've been in the Bulk for too long.*

"Yes, we believe so. If we can stop it at this timeline, we can stop the spread. Like removing the rot from a piece of fruit."

"Jesus." I think for a moment, now getting nauseous. "And what will you be doing?" There's an obvious undercurrent of anger in the question.

"We'll be killing Ryveliant. If we can stop him here *and* you can stop the Regime there, it'll be done. For good."

"Wow. This is it huh? It all leads to this?"

"It all leads to this." Odyssian responds, more confident than he's sounded since we began chatting.

He wants us to believe this will work.

Sounds that I've never heard before echo elsewhere. Almost electronic, pulsing. Other voices?

"I'm sorry. I have to go…the moment is upon us." Odyssian says with haste. "Aiontis. Titus. You can do this. We all believe in you. Do not fail us."

No pressure.

"Wait!" I shout into the endless dark. "What about the girl? Who is she? And why is she never here with us?"

"Yes! The girl!"

His reply sounds distant, rushed. He doesn't answer my questions but leaves us with an instruction.

"Find her!"

Historian Consultant Report
Unknown
2477, Unknown specifics

!OUTPUT ERROR!
[Report could not be completed]

!DATA ERROR!
[Data for time period not available]

!MASTER ALIGNMENT ERROR!
[Event mapping failed at 32%]

Chapter 78 – Titus

2477 | Unknown location

"Fucking 'ell, they're finally here." A gruff, weirdly Australian accent accompanied the statement. Australian mixed with some unknown dialect…Irish?

Titus opened his eyes, accepting golden hues of sunlight that poured through uncovered windows into the dilapidated room around him. It felt like he'd been in the Bulk for ages. Perhaps an entire millennium?

No…that wasn't possible.

Was it?

Aiontis sat up beside him. They were both on medical beds with tubes inserted in their arms. Titus' looked like electrical cords while Aiontis clearly had medical fluid within his.

"God, I have a massive fucking headache." Aiontis rubbed the back of his head and neck. His hands moved to opposite arms, scratching furiously.

"Happens." The Australian replied. "Get him some coffee and pump in a dose of Zingers." He yelled somewhere behind him. "And for the android, check his systems. Let me know if anything's off. If he's been hacked, we put him down."

Titus constricted, ready to run. The Australian's gaze diverted to him briefly.

"Nothing personal, mate. You're likely fine, but don't even think about it."

"What are Zingers?" Aiontis asked, barely able to keep up with the situation around him. A half second later, he was vomiting beside the bed, away from Titus.

"They're just there to flush you out, mate. You were in the Bulk a while."

"Can I have some water?" Aiontis swung his legs off the bed as he wiped his chin. Still itching himself, but at his chest now.

"Take some coffee first boyo. Water after. The caffeine will help. Plus…you love coffee."

"How did you know we were in the Bulk?" Titus asked, very confused.

"He's clear!" A voice echoed from a far-off place behind the surly man with crossed arms.

"Good. Titus, you can unhook your cords."

"Ok, thanks, but I asked you a question." Titus reiterated. "Where are we?"

"We've known you'd be coming from the Bulk for a while now. It's complicated, but it's just the way this stuff works and I don't have time to walk you through it. And I don't think you mean where, but *when*."

"We're in 2477." Aiontis contributed. The Australian looked mildly surprised. "Odyssian told us."

"Ahh. Of course, he did. Well good. Less for me to explain."

"So, where are we?"

"You're in the Egyptian desert, mate. Just outside Cairo."

Titus unplugged the cords from both of his arms and stood to stretch. For the briefest of moments, the sensation of having a body again was absolutely foreign, and he staggered, but his programming kicked in, catching him.

Someone, much smaller than the Australian, came out with a yellowed mug filled with steaming coffee. Horrifically, their mouth was seemingly fused shut, aside from one small hole. Gingerly, they handed the cup to Aiontis and scurried off to the darkness.

How many people are back there watching us? Titus wondered, one of the many inquires floating through his mind.

"Why Cairo?" Aiontis questioned, followed by a careful sip of coffee.

"Look. I don't have all day to explain this shit to you. And half the time, it still confuses me. That's what she's for." His frustration was apparent, with his weight impatiently shifting on his heels. Probably a soldier made a temporary errand-boy.

After a brief pause, punctuated only by the sipping of Aiontis drinking his coffee, he continued. "Just take a couple more sips of your coffee and let's get going. There's lots to do. You can unhook yourself."

Aiontis glanced down at the cords coming out of his left arm and unhooked them gingerly. Avoiding the vomit, he stepped off the bed on the opposite side, coffee in hand.

"Who's 'she'?" He asked.

"Kiaria."

Aiontis and Titus exchanged glances.

"What? He didn't tell you about *her*?!" The Australian belted out a hearty laugh as the three men left the dirty makeshift hospital room, unsure of what they were about to see in the timeline built off disaster.

Chapter 79 – Titus
2477 | Egypt

The exterior of the building "just outside of Cairo" was as worn and broken as the interior, covered in a thick layer of grime and windswept sand. Titus had to shade his eyes while the brown desert granules and sun blasted him. His first indication that something was different in this timeline was the temperature.

Wind swirled a vortex of scrappy grains of sand around the trio while they walked, though regardless of its speed, Titus was surprised to find the desert heat palatable rather than insufferable like he was used to. Most likely a side effect of the nuclear war from 500 years ago.

Had there been another altercation more recently?

The sand required thick punches from his feet to gain traction and push forward. Thankfully, they'd only had a few meters until the Australian's vehicle. Aiontis was going through the same struggles, both of them hastily getting into the back seat. Aiontis was coughing, wiping his face and eyes, while Titus was similarly trying to clear sand from his face and hair.

In front, the Australian gripped an interior handle and pulled himself inside, fitted with a thick, woven scarf and goggles. Titus watched him peer over his shoulders into the back seat and he let out a massive laugh, more Irish than Australian in nature.

"My bad, boys. I should've given you these beforehand. It's a bit of a windy day." Titus grabbed the scarves and goggles – both as well-worn as the building – and handed Aiontis a pair. They stayed silent, wrapping the scarves several times around their necks and sliding the goggles atop their heads. The Australian's forgetfulness felt intentional.

Letting it slide, Titus studied the vehicle. Outside of minor interior lighting, it was eerie and dark as the sand's wind walls grew thicker. *It's really raging out there…* The car was organized and constructed like a typical vehicle, but felt awkwardly different.

For starters, it was clear automotive technology had been stunted in this timeline. 2477 featured ATVs – air transport vehicles – where this was still a ground-bound craft. As the Australian pressed a couple buttons on the dash, Titus noticed two things: the car rolled very differently than the experiences he'd had in 4-wheeled vehicles thus far and there was no steering wheel. Intrigue begged he watch the driver, who's gruff, cracked hands held two separate levers. As they reversed, turned slightly, and pulled away, Titus noted that one handle controlled forward and back, while the other registered adjustments to a right and left axis. The severity with which each handle was pushed correlated with the speed or the degrees of turn.

The strange roll attributed to the large, half sphere residing in the middle of their trio. Initially, Titus assumed it was just a design of the car's console or some type of storage, but it was obvious now: the car had a single, gigantic ball at its center. There was a low hum underneath the metal composite where Titus held his hand. He could almost feel the *direction* of the monowheel's spin.

Fascinating.

Otherwise, the console was completely digital, one massive screen, that wasn't all that dissimilar from his own timeline. In front, the Australian swiped a few motions onto a portion of the touchscreen and began to speak.

"Tell her we have both of them. They're ready to go." A moment of pause was followed by a quick recourse of his side profile. "Fuck if I should know?" His face turned to agitation. "Yeah, yeah, yeah. Aight, I'll fucking ask him."

The Australian pressed a button – likely an autopilot – and turned to Aiontis.

"Hey, boyo. You remember anything from this time period?"

"What?" Titus could see the confusion on Aiontis' face and he shared it.

"Do. You. Remember. Shit?"

"We're not from this time period. We're not from this time-*line.*"

"Yeah, I get that, but the body you're in right now belonged to another Aiontis." His gaze narrowed. "I'll tell em' you don't know shit."

He turned around, pressing the same button as before, and gripped the handles once more.

"He doesn't remember shit. That what you wanted to hear?"

"Why didn't you ask me?" Titus inquired.

"Because you're traveling different, guy. Plus, you're an android. Aren't you supposed to know everything already?"

"Traveling different?" *What did he mean by that?* "Do you even have actual Artificial Intelligence in this timeline?"

"Pfffft. Yeah, sure. And flying cars too." There was thick sarcasm in the Australian's reply. "You, my friend, are officially the first fully-functioning, AI android in *this* world's history."

"What were you saying about trave – " Aiontis was cut off as the vehicle took flight, disconnected from the ground beneath them. The cabin flooded with light and the wind's grip of the sand outside faltered.

Or we're above it.

"Woooooohoo hooo hooo ho!" The Australian yelped, pulling one lever hard and pushing the other forward. Light remained in the cabin, but they slammed down hard, barely cradled by a tall dune of sand. "I fuckin love the dessert. Sorry, gents. Wanted to get out of the storm, so I took the quickest path."

"What was?"

"Cleopatra's Dune."

"Cute name." Aiontis retorted. The Australian glanced at a reflective surface of the dash toward him but remained silent.

"When are we getting there?" Titus asked, becoming increasingly uneasy.

"We're here. Thank the gods." The Australian commented, pulling hard on the handle in his left hand, throwing Aiontis and Titus faces forward from the abrupt shift in momentum.

Titus glanced out the window, caked with tan dust and dirt. Through the grime, a swath of memories from early in this adventure greeted him.

Outside the window were the Pyramids of Giza, half destroyed, but still gargantuan.

Things really do come full circle.

Chapter 80 – Aiontis
2477 | Egypt

I cannot fucking believe where we are.
The Pyramids…thousands of years after I built them.
Did I build these?
This is a completely different timeline…
My mind concludes I didn't touch these specific ones, but I'll be damned if this isn't the most surreal thing that has happened yet.

Of course, the pyramids look different now. There's some battle or war of old that damaged them. The smaller one has been reduced to a sad mound of rubble, rock, and sand while the remaining small pyramid resides miraculously intact, aside from a few chips missing from the stone blocks.

I stand before the massive central pyramid, once again enamored by its size. Half of it has been blown away by some massive bomb strike (or at least, that's what I assume, given the extent of the damage). Replacing the hole is a set of modern, square hulls built into the structure. It's a blend of future tech with one of the most advanced and ancient buildings throughout history.

The white, square compartments zigzag up a crack, contrasting the golden hue of the ancient bricks. Through massive glass windows I see people inside.

Strange. What is this used for?

"Ayy! Boyo, let's go. Get inside before the wind makes its way over here!"

I'm gawking outside the strange vehicle we arrived in. Though I'm not a fan of this asshole, he's right and I follow, closely behind Titus.

"This is wild." I comment, out of earshot from the Australian. The sand rests dense and hard under our feet.

"Agreed. I can only imagine for you. You helped build these, right?"

"Well, not *these*, but yeah. Either way, still incredible."

"What's your take on him? On all this?" Titus inquires in a hushed tone, nodding forward.

"I haven't figured it out yet. He's an asshole and this world is clearly…different from ours. I never actually make it to 2477, I'm from 2404. It's hard to believe the world would crater *that* fast."

"From what I remember of my 2477, things are better here, but just barely. By the time I left to come back and find you, things were…dire."

"That's so fucked up."

"The Regime is not a conquerable thing. Odyssian referred to it as a Core Event and I get it. They are the end of the world. Period." Titus makes a slashing movement with his hand.

We continue in silence. The Australian parked further away from the pyramids than I'd perceived, once again underestimating their size on the nearby horizon.

"I wonder if it will really be her. If it will really be Kiaria?"

"Why wouldn't it be?" Titus challenges.

"Don't know. Just…I just hope it is. I've missed her." My tone is somber, reliving all the fun memories we created together in Italy.

Titus places a hand on my shoulder. "I'm sure it will be. And I'm sure she knows who you are."

We arrive behind the Australian (read: asshole) to a sizable bunker door made of thick steel. It's cut into both the pyramid's stone and the updated architecture, creating an eerie gateway into past and present.

After opening slowly, it closes behind us at a similar pace. If I was impressed by the exterior, I'm downright flabbergasted inside. It has been hollowed out and reinforced. Even the stone portion has backing underneath it, creating the false impression that this structure might be weaker on one side.

The tech is no frills and old compared to my 2404. Screens around the atrium are covered with a thin layer of dust, there're stairs and an elevator, and the design is straightforward: this is a bunker. A military bunker.

The Australian leads without speaking, nodding grunts to

people he passes. Some give Titus and I weird, almost excited glances, but we don't have time to linger or ask why. His heels press down with purpose as the brisk walk continues to an elevator at the pyramid's center.

"Get in, get in." I can tell he's antsy as he waves us in.

With a few, quick button presses on a wall-mounted tablet, the elevator starts upward. Several seconds pass and the rising altitude observed through the greenish glass walls is replaced by darkness, save for the tablet's light.

We come to a stop and I shift my weight, preparing to exit. Instead, the compartment moves laterally, sliding along some hidden track. To my surprise, it heads back down, seemingly the exact same way it came. Titus and I tense, turning toward the Australian. As if on cue, he answers.

"Hidden track. No one in this building 'cept you two and myself know about the basement. They think we all hang out up top, elevator has a hidden shaft where they don't see us come back down and go below."

"Why?" I inquire.

He taps his toe once, and sighs. "Just in case, ya know? If someone gets captured and interrogated. Or if the enemy takes a lucky guess and fires at the top of the pyramid, we'll be fine. In fact, they'll think we're dead. Even better."

"Hmm." Titus sounds. "Not an awful idea." He sounds genuinely impressed while the Australian continues to be an asshole.

"Thanks. Glad we 'ave yer fuckin approval."

Our compartment jolts when we reach the bottom, finally, and the doors slide open with a greasy screech.

We're in a hallway that spits out to a collection of mundane rooms.

Some with long tables, similar to a boardroom.

Others with lots of screens and keyboards and tech I don't recognize.

Down the very short hallway, there's a larger room – one with high ceilings, round walls, where the shots are called – and I see a woman standing there.

Her brown hair isn't across her shoulders, but in a high pony. She turns and faces the elevator. I ingest the image in slow motion. My heart catches in my throat and a vast, pummeling wave of emotion explodes warmly behind my ribcage. Tears well in my eyes.

I stare into hers.

I'm not close enough to see them, but I know what color they are.

Brown, with green flecks.

The tablet in her hands gets dropped carelessly on a table and she's walking toward me, angrily.

Once she's close enough, her gaze shifts to the Australian along with a pointer finger.

"Took you long enough." He has no response.

Before I have time to contemplate what she means, her hands grip my face and her lips are pressed to mine.

My world is complete for the first time in over a thousand years.

Technically speaking, of course.

Chapter 81 – Aiontis
2477 | Egypt

Against my deepest desires, she pulls away, palms still cupping my face, and stares into my eyes. Deep within – far back, in the green flecks – there's a sparkle. No new "visions" come to me during the kiss, but there's recognition back there.

I could cry. I want to hold her, forever.

"We don't have time for sexual tension." She says, still looking deep into my eyes. I hear the comment, but am confused by it. "I'm not the Kiaria you fell in love with. At least, not the exact one as you know her."

"I…I know?" I'm unsure how to respond. The Australian and Titus are silent, avoiding eye contact.

"You don't know, but that's ok. We love each other, across many times. Including this one." She smiles briefly, melting my insides all over again. "But we don't have time for it here. Got it?"

I stammer, trying to find words, finally pushing out, "Got it."

"I need you focused."

I nod into her palms and she lets go, providing the slightest nod back. She steps away to look at the three of us.

"I trust you have both reacquainted with Track?"

"Track?" Titus questions as Kiaria extends an arm toward the Australian.

"I never properly introduced myself. Forgot…to us here you're not exactly new." Behaving better now that he's in front of his leader, he extends hands to both Titus and myself. I shake his calloused grip with a squeeze. He doesn't seem to notice.

"What's your accent? It sounds like a mix between Australian and Irish." I ask, now more curious.

"Those things don't fucking exist anymore, boyo. The world is just a group of loose governments and cities. Ireland, Australia, hell even the United States aren't functioning entities anymore.

"So, to answer your question, I have no idea what my accent is. I just know this is the way I talk." Now he seems annoyed, back to being an asshole again.

Asshole.

"What do you remember?" Kiaria asks, pointing at me.

"From when?" I'm not sure what she means.

"From this timeline, this year, before your current-self took over your past one."

"Woah, what?"

"Remember what I said? I need you to focus. I don't have time to explain, just answer the question. What do you remember?"

"From this timeline and year, nothing." I say, much like a pouting child.

"Okay. That's what I figured." She responds, unbothered by a response I thought would be disappointing. "What about everything else. What do you remember from all the other timelines?"

"Everything." It's the biggest I've seen her smile since we got here.

"Amazing." She gets right into her next set of questions. "And what did Odyssian tell you?"

I think back to the host of information he provided and try to piece together what's relevant.

"It sounds like the time for action is now. The Regime has not become a Core Event on this timeline yet, but the spread is like a cancer. It's coming."

"Got it. We have a plan for that. And Odyssian?"

"He's going to confront Ryveliant and end it. He didn't provide details and I can't picture what that looks like for fourth dimensional beings, but…yeah. That's his strategy." I finish, strangely feeling like I didn't provide much valuable intel.

"Good. The plan is in motion then."

"And what's the plan?" Titus speaks up again, an undertone of protectiveness there.

"Follow me." Kiaria walks back toward the tall room she came from, turning left into a private office. The Australian,

Track, shuts the door behind us.

"Sit." She motions to the chairs in front of a black, unadorned desk with a keyboard engraved into its surface with red lights. After a few keystrokes, a holographic screen emerges. Her hands move in the air, making the screen larger and bringing it closer. I glance back, suddenly nervous in the dark room, to find Track leaning against the wall next to the door, watching us.

"The Regime of this timeline isn't all that powerful yet. At least not how you may remember them." She looks at Titus. "They have money and resources, but not nearly the manpower they need to take over everything left of this world."

A handful of pictures swipe through, showing a collection of men and women of all races and sizes congregated. Some pictures feature weapons I don't recognize, in others there are similarly unknown vehicles, except for those that have the single large ball in their center.

"Unfortunately, given what has happened in this timeline, their ascent to power would be quicker than most any others."

"You mean the Cuban Missile Crisis going south?" I clarify.

"Precisely. The world has tried for hundreds of years to recover…gotten close a few times, but it's never stuck. Governments are weak and disorganized, or abandoned altogether. People fend for themselves which means they're vulnerable more often than not, and to be honest, there aren't a whole lot of people in the world. We estimate 1 billion worldwide. Something like the Regime would only take a couple years to blossom and there would be no coming back from it."

"Ok, so what do we do? You seem to have the resources here…" I sense she's burying the lead and stalling.

"We're going to wipe them all out. Every last one of them."

How's *that* for a straight-forward objective?

"And you're sure that will work? It won't be like pulling a weed and ten more grow in its place?"

"The future Regime contains the only people on the planet, outside of this room, that know about time travel and the next phase of dimensional life. If Odyssian does his job and we do ours, while also erasing any Warper tech they may have, I do believe that any other 'weeds' would be simplistic in their objectives, comparatively."

What she's saying actually makes a lot of sense. "And what's the objective of the Regime exactly?"

"Evil. Rule. Death." Titus interjects, head down.

"Wrong." Kiaria responds. "We've found something worse. They want to use Warper technology to nuke the world…thousands of years in the past."

I'm confused. Odyssian never told us this.

What does that even mean?

Kiaria can see my confusion.

"They don't want to just shorten third dimensional beings' existence; they want to eliminate it all together."

Chapter 82 – Titus
2477 | Egypt

"Jesus Christ." Aiontis gasped across the table while Titus tried to recall if *his* Regime had a similar endgame. Despite his best efforts, it didn't sound familiar. By the time he had left to kill Aiontis, the Regime had a stranglehold on his world anyway.

What did it matter?

"Ok, so the plan is simple: elimination." Titus began. Track shifted in the background. "What are the finer details?"

"I'm getting there." Kiaria answered curtly. "But first, one thing. You have to understand that this is your one shot. If we fail here, it's highly likely the Core Event of the Regime spreads infinitely and Ryveliant's goal is accomplished."

"We're ready. We get it and we…I've…been trapped in this for a long time." Aiontis explained. "It's time to end it."

Kiaria nodded and motioned with her hands, moving some more holographic images around. Eventually a globe appeared and she zoomed in on a massive island, then near the center of that mass.

"Their compound is here, east of center in what used to be Australia."

A massive gray set of structures got larger and stopped. It was a series of broken concentric arcs that made a larger campus in the shape of a solid circle. Even from satellite imagery, the walls appeared high and thick. Titus could only assume all the important targets were in the center.

It was on the edge of a desert, close enough to where greenery could be seen at a distance to the right, but still wholly surrounded by orangish, red sand. Not all that different than the fortress they were in now.

"In case you're wondering," Track commented from behind, "It's as impenetrable as it looks."

"Yes, thank you, Track." Kiaria responded. "Which is why we're going to hit it with everything we have."

"You're going to nuke it then?" Aiontis asked.

"No. We already know it's protected against nuclear attacks, not to mention they have an air defense system that would likely shoot any missiles down." She paused for a moment, sensing the confusion in the room. "We're going to go in with stealth, straight to the center, and work our way outward."

"The schematics for all Warper-based technology is housed in the compound's center, naturally." Track added more from behind them. "If we can take it out first, all that's left is to kill everyone else."

"How would a stealth option work, exactly?" Aiontis inquired. Titus wondered the same thing given how much security was present.

"Cloaking." Kiaria replied simply. "I know it may come as a shock in comparison to the timelines you're from, but we do have *some* technology in this world, and cloaking is one we've perfected."

"Cloaking by itself is not a plan." Titus commented, growing increasingly worried they'd been sent here to do nothing but die.

"Cloaking and a betrayal then." Track spoke up, pushing off the wall and approaching the desk.

"Betrayal?" Aiontis questioned.

"Yes," Kiaria began. "We have an ace in the hole when it comes to the Regime."

"Who?"

"Me." Track answered, standing with arms crossed. "I used to be in it."

"No wonder you're an asshole." Aiontis whispered under his breath.

"Can we stop fucking around please?" Titus was assertive and frustrated. I realized how rare it was for him to curse. "What's the plan without all the smoke and mirrors?"

Kiaria exchanged glances with Track. "Fair enough. The plan is straightforward, but has years of planning behind it. We've broken it into three parts: Infil, Tech, and Erad.

"Infiltration, Infil, has already started. Our spies have established contact with the Regime and whispers of Track have begun to spread. The Regime believed him dead by our hand, so they'll be eager to get him back. Keep in mind they're not as established as you may know. It makes them more susceptible to double agents.

"We will transport Track and the three of us down to Australia where he'll meet them outside the compound, be swept for bugs, explosives, etcetera, and transported inside the facility. We'll be fully cloaked and it is imperative that we make it in with him."

"How do you suggest we do that?" Aiontis challenged.

"Not everything can be planned. We'll have to improvise."

"Improvise? The fate of, well…everything is on the line." His voice full of nerves as opposed to anger.

"That's why we've trained for so long. You may not remember it now, but the second we start this mission, your instincts will kick in."

Titus observed the gears in Aiontis' mind turning, likely harkening back to when he was a Renaissance artist. He'd described how painting had felt natural in that era. Kiaria continued.

"Assuming Infil goes on without a hitch, which is a fairly big assumption, we will end up at the compound's core, thus beginning the Tech phase." She swiped a few more images across the screen, blurry ones of a lab and massive Warping room. "Tech is simple, but the most important: destroy all technology in the lab. Hardware, software, notes, holoboard calculations, you name it. If it's within the vicinity of the Warper, it goes.

"Track will have both an EMP device and a DVL. He'll use the DVL first to wipe any computers connected to their network, which will then trickle out to any other device that has had any sort of handshake with their network, again and again and again."

"What's a DVL?" Titus raised his hand slightly to ask.

"Sorry, Digital Viral Load. A death sentence for your stored memory."

"And wouldn't the trickle-out-effect of this DVL eventually affect every computer on earth? It sounds like it just keeps replicating…" Aiontis followed.

"Correct. It's a sacrifice we're willing to make, but that's a safe bet. Much of the world's digital memory will not exist if we do this right, but obviously there's bigger things at play and we have to be sure."

"What's the EMP for then?" The question came from Titus once more.

"Think of it as either insurance, assurance, or both."

Track gave an "ahem", indicating that question time was over. Kiaria took the hint.

"Again, moving forward under the assumption that Tech goes right – another fuckin biggie – then we come to Erad. Obviously much shorter version of *eradicate*, but I'm sure you can guess what it is."

"Kill everyone." Titus said as a near whisper. Kiaria's fingers snapped and pointed at him.

"You got it. By the time we've done the first two phases, I'm hoping to have a small army surrounding the complex. Between them on the outer perimeter and us working our way out from the center, there's not much place for Regime members to go."

"Are there any escape shuttles or aircraft they could run to?" Titus thought this sounded too easy.

"Yes. Our reports tell us there are vehicle bays at various spots around the compound. If they run, which is likely, you must stop them. Their escape only *delays* their plan, it doesn't prevent it."

A silence overtook the room that was dimly lit by the holographic images. Kiaria didn't need to ask for questions because there wasn't really a choice.

"And then we all come back home, chummy as fuck!" Track clapped Aiontis on the back shoulder and nodded to Kiaria. She mysteriously nodded back, signaling for him to leave the room. The light hit her just right and his memory flashed. Titus was taken aback by just how much Kiaria looked like Rachel in this moment. A pang of regret swept him; he missed the simplicity of their month together.

"I need to know that you've told me everything." Her weight was supported by her hands as she leaned forward on the table. With a small motion the holoimages disappeared.

"What do you mean?" Aiontis asked.

"I mean what I said. I need to know this is everything. There's no time for playing secrets right now."

"What about you?" Titus started. "What aren't you telling us?"

"You know everything you need to. Anything you don't, doesn't matter." The declaration came with a calm, yet harsh authority.

"Who determines what we *need* to know?"

"Me." She jumped back. Aiontis kept quiet, but Titus attempted to press and she cut him off. "Why me? Because I'm in charge here."

Chapter 83 – Aiontis

2477 | Egypt

It has been several hours since our testy meeting reviewing the Infil-Tech-Erad plan. The conversation ended once Kiaria emphasized her authority. I explained there was nothing else Odyssian had divulged to us in the Bulk, and she dismissed us to our quarters.

We leave first thing tomorrow.

Tonight, I'm supposed to get sleep. I've just exited a refreshing shower where I was able to think. As I stare at my *true* self in the mirror – the actual physical image of the real me – I'm surprised nerves aren't getting the best of me.

This is the end. Or at least it's supposed to be.

I gaze across my reflection. The brown and gray stubble along my jaw. My nearly shaved head. Tanned skin with signs of past injuries as scars. Green eyes. My chiseled shoulders. Less chiseled chest. My arms and hands feel like they could be lethal, but I remember I'm new *here*. I know how to use them, but there hasn't been a moment yet.

I am exhausted, tired of being in a stranger's body. Even this one that is supposedly "me". It's "me" from a timeline I don't recognize. I'm tired of running around in circles, even if I do have purpose from my epiphany with James in 2001. Most of all, I'm just tired of the mystery…the games…being the pawn.

If this all ends tomorrow, so be it. Images of Italy with Kiaria bounce around in my mind. Kneeling next to her death bed as she peacefully took a final breath nearly breaks me again. *I've lived too long, but I've had a good life.*

There's a knock at my door and before I can reply "Who is it?", the dull metal frame slides back and Kiaria enters, closing it behind her. I abandon my thoughts and the mirror, leaning out of the bathroom, keeping my distance.

We both just…look at each other. Taking the other person in. Something seems wrong. This bold, hardened Kiaria is suddenly timid. Sad?

"Sorry, I'm not dressed. If you just give me a second I can put some cloth – "

"No." Is all she says.

"Okay. What did you need?" It's as if the question itself jump-starts my nerves, my stomach. An ache in my chest.

"I need…" She's lost, not quite sure how to say it. So, she just does. "You."

"Me? How…" Kiaria strides over to me slowly, removing her ponytail, and letting her brown hair cascade across her shoulders and down her back. The resemblance to the Kiaria I grew old with is enough to well tears. One dribbles down my cheek.

Her hands reach around me and across my back, her face against my chest. The hug is warmer than my shower and I return the squeeze. For a while, we stand in each other's arms. I'd forgotten how much like home – amongst all this craziness – it feels. Time is complicated, but it feels like forever since I've been here. Her head moves to look up at me.

"I've missed you. So much."

"I've missed you too. It's been so…hard." I try to explain.

"I know."

"I grew old with you. I watched you die."

"I know."

"But weren't you with the Aiontis from this timeline? This body?"

"Yes, we were together, though it's not the same. He's the same person, but a different version. A different soul."

"And you?" I imagine she must be a different version of *her*.

"It's hard to explain, but I'm me. The same one you had in Italy. I lied earlier."

I have so many questions, but right now I just trust her. It's like having *my* Kiaria back.

She is my *Kiaria.*

"Why such a cold welcome then?" We kissed, sure, but then she treated me just like any other soldier.

"I'm sorry…I…I needed us, me, to stay focused. And I was apprehensive. I didn't know what it would be like to see you again." Her palms on my lower back press tighter. "What we're doing here is so big. This is *it*. The end of it all. I'm scared."

"I'm scared too." I reply with honesty. It's refreshing to see this Kiaria be as vulnerable as the one I fell in love with.

We spend a moment gazing silently into each other's eyes. Hers are like a long-forgotten poem where I remember the words once lost, and the emotions that came with.

Our lips press into each other with a ferocity I've never known. Hundreds, thousands of years that separated our last kiss, felt all within this moment. My body trembles, my hands swimming all over her. Hers find the towel wrapped around my midsection. It falls to the floor.

I grab her shirt and pull it over her head, her hair following it like an umbrella until it comes off. She removes the athletic bra underneath before I even notice it.

For several more moments – or an hour, time means nothing right now – our tongues and lips find each other, over and over. The sensation of her hair through my fingers sends a fresh round of shivers down my spine, reminding me of the day I painted her in Italy.

She plants what feels like a final kiss on my lips and then traces down to my neck…my chest…my stomach. On her knees, she takes me in her mouth as passionately as she was kissing. I can hardly stand my legs are shaking so badly.

"Let's go to the bed." I say, barely able to concentrate. She stands, grabs my hand, and takes me there.

What happens for the next several hours is a blur of ecstasy as we rekindle our love in position after position. Much like our first time, we end on the floor in a tangle of pillows and sheets. A comforting wave of sleep hits as I hold her. I notice she's drifting too.

"I love you." I tell her.

"I love you too." She kisses me. "Now get some sleep. Tomorrow is going to be the biggest day of both of our lives."

"That's saying something." Is all I can muster before I drift off into a Bulk of my own making.

Chapter 84 – Aiontis
2477 | Australia

We're screaming across the sky in a cargo-plane-jet-hybrid, impressive in both size and speed. It's becoming apparent that nearly all technological advances went into warfare as opposed to anything superfluous, like consumer goods. This aircraft is so quiet I bet you could hear birds chirping outside.

Last night's sleep was deep, tangled in the sheets and embrace of Kiaria and my re-introduction to one another. Now however, my nerves tingle; frayed edges scratching against the inside of my skin. The first time I ever felt like this was upon a hill in Japan, readying to enter a samurai battle, a memory from so far ago it's a wonder I still have it.

"Here," Titus hands me a drab protein bar. "Eat something. No telling when we'll be able to next."

"Thanks." I grab the bar, reluctantly mashing its dryness in my even dryer mouth. On cue, Titus sits beside me in the cargo bay and places a slim canteen of water in my other hand. I repeat the exercise of getting the protein bar to a paste and washing it down with water until I finish.

There's a lot we could talk about, but it's nicer just sitting in the silence together as friends. My mind travels backwards; I recall when there was a time we believed we were enemies. I was being hunted by *this* Scarred Man.

What a wild trip we've been on.

Eventually, Kiaria enters the cargo bay from the front of the plane with Track in tow. He looks distant…ready, outlined with a shadow of fear. He'll be the only one uncloaked so, at least initially, he'll be at the greatest risk.

"We're 10 minutes out." Kiaria mentions with some small form of vigor as our leader. "Let's gear up."

We stand and follow her to the front of the bay where the equipment is stored, glistening like medieval contraptions in the fluorescent light. She continues speaking.

"I wasn't sure if these would be done in time, but we've now got our best bet at following Track's transport." She holds up a slim metal 'V' no wider across than my shoulders. "Jetpacks."

"Excuse me?" I stammer. "*That's* a jetpack?" It's too small, there's no way.

"It is. They use thermal fusion propulsion which is quieter and more discreet than what we've had in the past."

"And you *just* finished them?"

"Yes. It's why I didn't bring it up earlier on the off chance our engineers couldn't work out the kinks."

"The *kinks?*"

"Ay! Boyo! Suck it the fuck up and listen to the lady!" Track snaps.

"Anyway…" Kiaria starts again. "The jetpacks will allow us to fly and hover cloaked above Track while he's transported to the compound. We'll have to get very close once the gates open, we'll not be able to go over. Again, I'll reiterate that we may need to improvise."

"What about the fuel tails?" Titus inquires. "Won't they see flames dangling in the air?"

"I'm glad you asked." Kiaria smiles. She's very impressed with herself. "We've also created a cloaking attachment to these. It's carbon fiber, wrapped in the cloaking material, that snaps onto your pack and overhangs the jet tails far enough to mask them. The only way someone could see them is if you were directly overhead and they looked up."

She tosses one to Track, myself, then Titus.

"Put these on each other once you're geared up. They'll lock into place on the back of your stealth suits. As for those," She turns and opens a longer locker, "They're here. You should have already been fitted, make sure there are no loose clips and that all pockets are closed. The cloaking can't hide carelessness."

We nod in silence. The carbon fiber jetpack is impossibly light in my hands, the material cold as ice. I'm in disbelief at its efficiency.

"For weaponry, we'll find many in there that we should be able to use. Your gloves will have biometric overrides, allowing you to use their guns. Before it comes to that – which hopefully it won't – we're going in quietly with these."

In her hands is the sleekest firearm I've ever seen. It's a handgun, average in size, with a square-edged silencer all crafted as a single mold, black as night.

"Each Nightfire has a silencer built in and the radiated microbullets explode internally once they hit a target, killing them instantly from nearly any shot to the torso or head. Appendage hits only give them minutes. These bullets are small to cut down on noise and improve mag size; you should have 50 in here now and 300 spare on your suit.

"If your cloaking is active, the cloak will extend from your suit to the gun, masking it as well. I've programmed each of these for all of our biometrics in case we'd get in a situation where we need to use each other's weapon, but they will trigger an explosion to all bullets inside should a Regime member try to fire them. I'd suggest you're not around if that happens."

Kiaria shifts her gaze to Track with a quick nod that he returns, then to me. There's no sign of the love we experienced last night. She's shifted entirely into the mission.

I should too.

"Any questions?" She's met with silence. "Good. Suit up and get ready. We'll drop Track and the Roadrunner off first, then we'll jump out shortly after. Track, you go in three minutes."

"Copy." He begins getting into his suit, inspecting his Nightfire and jetpack. Kiaria does the same and I figure Titus and I should get a move on as well.

Among us, there's a frightening silence. No quips from Track. No small chatter. The lack of engine noise. All vacant, with only the sounds of rustling clothes and weapon checks.

Beneath me, the cargo bay's floor shifts. We're decelerating for Track's drop. He finalizes his stealth suit, and stores the Nightfire in the holster, pressing a button on his upper chest. I gasp as he completely vanishes.

"Cloaking check." I hear his voice from an ether.

"Check." Kiaria calls back. Track appears again.

"Wow…you weren't kidding. This tech is incredible." I say, but I'm ignored as Track gets into the Roadrunner.

"We'll drop you low, but landing will still be rough. Trust we're above you. We've got this." Kiaria says to him through the vehicle's front window. "Follow the route and stay off comms until we're inside."

"See you on the other side." Track replies as the aircraft's cargo doors open. All at once we lose speed and altitude while rushing, screaming air enters the cabin. The single-wheeled vehicle begins to slide backwards out of the metal and polymer hull, eventually dropping off into the brilliant blue sky. The bay doors shut and silence consumes us once more.

"You two ready? We've got seven minutes." Titus replies by sitting back down and staring at his feet.

After four minutes, we all do cloaking checks and pass with flying colors. I expected something to feel different when I turned the cloak on, but there's no sensation aside from a soft, small blue light around my wrist to indicate it's active.

"Sixty seconds!" Kiaria shouts while the cargo doors open for our departure. I imagine her blood is pumping because mine is too. Aside from the exhilaration of jumping out of a plane with a jetpack, there's also the prickling anxiety of ending this once and for all and saving an infinite number of timelines in the process.

"Remember! Jump, fall, count to eight, then engage your pack! Your suits will directionally vibrate as you approach another cloaked individual. Use that and comms to keep tabs on each other!" Together we walk toward the edge of the ramp, the outside air challenging us to jump. Swirling around us, almost mockingly.

"Cloak up!" Kiaria shouts, disappearing from view. I press my chest and notice the blue wrist light turn on. Immediately, I feel vibrations along the right and left of my ribcage and arms, indicating the positions where Kiaria and Titus are standing.

Her disembodied voice shouts, "Go, go, go!"

Inhale...Exhale...Fall.

There's no turning back now I reason as I leap into the beginning of the end.

Chapter 85 – Aiontis
2477 | Australia

1...
2...
3...

The air is unexpectedly scorching as it flows around me, gravity heavy on my backside. Much different than the coolness of Cairo.

4...
5...
6...

Kiaria and Titus are nowhere around. The cloaking technology is flawless and I wouldn't be able to feel the vibrations from my suit if they came close. A split-second vision of a mid-air collision materializes, but I refocus.

7...
8...

I pull out the small, horizontal tablet that's been in my sleeve, tied around my wrist. Briefly, it flaps in the wind until I grip both handles. The screen comes alive with the pressure of my touch, simultaneously booting up my jetpack.

For several seconds, I'm still falling, wondering if something is wrong. Below me, the barren brown and reddish land meets the verdant forestation in striking contrast. It's far beneath me, but I'm no fool.

I've only got seconds.

The screen displays the jetpack boot-up sequence at 99%...100% complete, transitioning to read: "Air Dive Sequence Initiated". Instantly, my shoulders and back lurch, painfully, and my falling slows momentarily.

The pack cycles off and on through this dramatic slow fall to save fuel and not burn it all overcoming my momentum at once. I'm thankful the painful tugging is lessened throughout.

"Comms check." Kiaria is in my ear.

"Check." Titus follows calmly.

"Check." I answer too. "You might have warned us about the jetpack initiation?"

"Sorry. Rougher than I was expecting, but this is their first time being used live in the field." I remain silent because her statement doesn't make me feel any better.

We're 30 meters off the ground, low enough to see the details we need, but high enough to avoid detection. That's good because I begin to wonder how audible our jetpacks are, despite Kiaria's assurances. The propulsion comes out like a dull roar, but I'm not sure how badly it echoes below.

Out of caution, I double check my wrist for the sacred blue ring, relieved it didn't turn off in the fall. I'm still cloaked.

Now we wait for Track to reach the desert. Kiaria has never called it the Outback. *Where along their history was that name abandoned?* The Hiscon in me is fascinated by the potential volume of inconsistencies, though equally shaken by the delicate fabric of history.

I once thought it was infallible.

Written.

Now I know there are infinite histories.

Infinite presents.

Infinite futures.

The scope of Infinitude makes my third-dimensional head spin so I return my concentration to the tree line.

Where are you, Track?

We hover a few moments as I scan the border where green and red landscape meet. There's a pale brown strip sprouting from the vegetation that appears to be the only road in and out. I turn to assess my entire surroundings, noting the compound in the distance. It's larger than I could have imagined from the photos, both taller and more daunting against the landscape. Striking black against a blue sky and red ground.

"Track should be coming into view any minute." Kiaria mentions. On the brown strip are stationary vehicles — three of them — with a host of black dots outside each. They're ready for him.

Titus sees him first, "There."

The Roadrunner busts forth from the foliage, pluming dirt along its side. The swirls of translucent red diminish as the vehicle slows down.

"Approach. Slowly. 20 meters altitude." Kiaria instructs. "Remember, don't get directly above anyone. They could see you."

My back senses the jetpack cut off fuel to adjust my height while the black dots take more shape into soldiers with guns drawn. I check my blue wrist out of anxiety. The tension of the moment is immediately palpable, as if a switch was flipped.

Track hasn't emerged from the Roadrunner yet and there are no fewer than eight weapons trained at him. There's no yelling, or if there is, I can't hear it, and all parties are motionless. Slowly, the door opens from Track's vehicle and he steps out, hands in the air. There are normal clothes over his stealth suit.

"My jetpack is acting odd." Titus whispers into the comms.

"Shhh. Cut comms right now." Kiaria snaps.

"I would, but something…ugh…" It sounds like he's struggling. Is he trying to take his pack off?

"What's going on, Titus?" I ask. Kiaria remains quiet.

Beneath us, Track approaches the Regime members he will betray. They're talking, but I can't hear what's being said. Titus still hasn't answered my question.

"Patching Track's comms through." Kiaria says.

"Heyo boys! I'm unarmed. Let's be civil." There's tension in Track's voice.

"My jetpack is broken. It's sputtering." Titus comes back on.

"No! Of course I'm not dead. You can't kill Track."

"I'm gaining and losing altitude wildly. I think I need to reset."

Kiaria barks into her comms. "Don't reset! We're too low."

"Then what the fuck do you want me to do?" *Uh-oh. Titus cursed again.*

"I…just deal with it. Hold tight."

Track is trying to explain himself. "Listen boys. You've been instructed to bring me in. Don'tcha think you should do that?"

I'm sweating. We're barely into this mission and it's degrading.

"I'm losing altitude. I think the engine is about to go." Titus is trying to keep his cool.

"Fuck!" Kiaria yells in a whisper.

"On who's authority? I don't know! I've been dead, so you tell me!" Track lectures them. "All I know is if you kill me out here, you're in trouble with *said* authority."

"Resetting my pack!"

"Don't fucking reset, Titus!"

"Titus," I start. "Turn your stealth suit off for a half second. They're all focused on Track, they won't see you."

I expect pushback from Kiaria, but none comes.

My eyes frantically scan the space beneath me.

In a brief flash, I see Titus' black suit hovering in the air, looking up aimlessly for one of us.

"Got you." I inform him, swerving my jetpack over to him quickly. "Raise your hand."

"My pack is going!"

"Raise your fucking hand!" We're both whisper shouting.

"It just cut off. I'm falling!"

The moment he says it, my left hand explodes with vibration up to the shoulder and I close my grip around something solid.

"I got you." I strain. My arm is barely able to keep hold and my pack moans from the extra weight. Our close call, no more than three meters off the ground, sent a plume of sand upward from the propulsion blast.

"You two have lookers." Kiaria states, fear in her voice. "Titus, reset your pack now and do it fast."

My brow tingles with beads of sweat rolling diagonally across. Track and several guards are distracted by the plume of sand that has since dissipated. Two other soldiers are at the ready, weapons pointing around in the sky and toward the forest of vegetation. They haven't seen us.

Yet.

"Resetting. 25%." Titus is whispering again, his legs dangling invisibly above their heads. Below, I hear Track.

"Huh! That's wild, must have been a dust devil!" his attention returns to the tall Regime soldier who's been doing most of the talking. "You gonna take me in or not? C'mon boys. I'm back!" He says it with a laugh. "Don't piss on my parade."

My arm is on fire and the sputtering on my back tells me my pack could go at any moment too.

"Titus…" I murmur through gritted teeth. "Hurry the hell up. I can't hold you – " I try and readjust my grip. "Much longer."

"Almost there." He promises.

My grip is slipping. *Shit.*

"Don't engage your thrusters to full power right away. They'll hear it." Kiaria warns.

"Kiaria, tell Track to move this circus along." I command, feeling like my fingers may rip off.

"Track, we've got a situation up here. You need to get the group moving. Now."

"75% complete." Titus tells me.

What the shit! I still have 25% longer? I'm not sure my pack will make it.

"It's moving faster. 90%!"

Thank the heavens.

"Guys, I'm getting annoyed and I outranked all of you before you thought I was dead. Keep wasting my time and you're not going to like me very much." Track explains. My curiosity distracts me. *I wonder* how *high up in the Regime he was?*

A short, outrageously bulky – even from up here – guard approaches the taller one. He shows him a tablet, gives what looks like a nod, and returns to his vehicle, which looks like an offroad version of the Roadrunner.

"It's your lucky day then. Nothing on thermal or infrared except for you. You're to follow us, dead center of the group." He points a long, bony finger at Track. "Any bullshit and I'll execute you myself."

"Fair enough." Track obliges and starts back toward his vehicle. The soldiers part ways to do the same.

My grip officially slips on Titus, his fingers dripping between my grasp.

"Shit!"

"100%!" Our exclamations come at the same time. There's another plume of red sand tossed into the air, but I don't observe any crater. Titus must still be airborne.

"You good?" I ask.

"Barely. Thrusters are at lowest possible setting. I'm only a meter off the ground."

"Get higher now. We need to follow the group." Kiaria orders.

"Already on it."

Track's vehicle rolls forward to meet with the soldiers, burying and blowing the particles of sand – our only sign of a near-catastrophe – back to the vermillion floor.

Chapter 86 – Aiontis
2477 | Australia

Flying to the compound was thankfully uneventful, as much as something like this could be, and the three of us (four, including Track) didn't speak a word.

What had once been a thin black strip in the distance, was now massive, muted in its darkness and free of shine save for the forceful sun hitting a few angles just right. It was a daunting structure, as I'm sure it was intended to be, largely because of its contrast from the environment. By now, the lush, tree-peppered horizon is a hazy line behind us and this hulking, half-spherical mass battles against all the reds and browns of the arid landscape, vying for the attention of everything around.

Strangely, but well timed, the epic gut feeling is back and I think of Odyssian. *What is he doing now? Is he still…alive?*

I assumed we'd be flying *over* the compound's walls, into a deeper level near the center, but given the height – reminding me of the Salesforce Tower from San Francisco – we'll need to get in through the same gate Track does.

Our packs have kept us higher than I'd prefer (I'm having a hard time seeing exactly what's happening below), but I trust Kiaria. At this altitude, it would be nearly impossible for anyone to spot us.

Unless…

Phew. My blue wrist light still shines brightly and I recognize my dependency and obsession with it has passed the point of prudency.

"Heads up." Track mutters. "I'm approaching the gate. It's heavily guarded, work your way downward from high altitude."

"Copy." Kiaria responds. "Titus, Aiontis. There are going to be structures on either side of the gate, multiple stories high, with open-air exposure. These men are there to prevent airborne attacks, provide distant cover, and scan for threats.

"Titus, you'll take the left. Aiontis, take the right. The killing starts now, do not give away our position." She finishes explaining, both Titus and I remain silent.

"Good luck boys. We got this." Track encourages. Normally something that would have surprised me, his last-minute support provides the fire I need.

Our packs decrease their altitude with smaller thrusts and I release the tablet that provides finer control, switching over to manual-motion mode, allowing the pack to take cues from my muscle movements for thrust direction.

I'm near the top of the tower-like structures Kiaria described, continuously impressed by how massive this entire compound is. Titus's side is at least half a football field away, if not more.

Focus…

Descending slower, I gently wrap my fingers around the grip of my Nightfire, the dense weight reminding me that it's time to kill.

And this version of Aiontis is very good at it.

Below, a guard leans on a railing, equipped with a massive backpack sporting a miniature, spinning satellite dish on its back. His focus peers through the scope of a sniper rifle, matte gray and long, pointed downward toward Track and the Roadrunner.

His weight against the railing means I can't shoot him right away in case he was to plummet over the edge. Navigating the jetpack, I approach from above, diagonally downward. With a whir, the satellite spins wildly, then trains directly onto me and emits a quiet ping.

Shit.

His attention shifts, but pulling back from the scope to investigate is all the delay I need. I cut the thrust of my pack, freefalling and crashing into him. The Nightfire presses against his helmet.

I fire.

No blood exits out the other side, but there's a "Click!" and a gasp as the miniature radiated bullet explodes inside his brain.

One down, likely hundreds more to go.

I've made too much noise here. Below me I hear, "Paul. Check-in. Paul." The same voice echoes from the radio of this dead guard. I can only pray this is on an individual line and not broadcasting to the rest of the men in this tower.

With skills unfamiliar to *me*, but very common to *this* Aiontis, I leap and gracefully backflip off the platform, my jetpack picking up thrust as I lift my knees, facing the floor below. The soldier calling for Paul is looking me dead in the eyes, he just doesn't know it, and I squeeze the trigger on my Nightfire, sending a single microbullet into his chest cavity.

There's a moment of shock, a jolt, and he crumples to the ground.

My core rotates to look across the gap toward Titus's side. I have to squint and zoom-in with my iNsert. There are four dropped bodies along the interior platforms.

Damn, I need to catch up.

Shifting around, I press through my heels, signaling to the thrusters to cut power. For a moment, it feels like floating, almost as if gravity is trying to decide if it wants to imprint its force on me. Then I begin the fall.

My Nightfire points toward the tower of exterior platforms, held by both hands for stability. Adrenaline bubbles and I breathe deeply to focus my vision as I plummet parallel to the side.

Pvvvvt!

The hollow, quiet sound leaves the chamber as fast as the bullet. A soldier grabs his neck reactively before a twitch that sends him to the floor.

Pvvvvt! Pvvvvt!

Neither of the men have time to react to the other's demise as microbullets hit them in the nose and mouth.

Pvvvvt! Pvvvvt!

There's only a single man on this platform, but he's further back from the edge and looks more heavily armored so I send two shots his way.

His oversized weapon, a bulky LMG by the looks of it, clangs to the metal floor loudly.

I'm dropping very fast…my legs kick to re-engage the thrusters. I'm closer to the ground than I realized and they'll have to blast in order to overcome my momentum.

Pvvvvt!

I put a shot through the teeth of the man on the final floor of the gate's tower, a commander by the looks of his ensemble.

All at once, my legs hit the hardened dirt ground while I drop to a knee for stability. A soldier on the ground whirls around, gun pointed at the mystery thud. His eyes go blank and his body limp as I watch a spray of blood exit out his ear. To the side of where he stood, Track holds his weapon, looking at me, but *through* me.

Several other Regime bodies drop to the floor in rapid succession and Kiaria appears near Track, her cloaking turned off. Titus also appears by my side and I decide it's safe to disable mine, even if it makes me wildly uncomfortable in this hostile environment.

"You're all a bunch of bloody showoffs? Ya know that?" Track whistles as he says it.

Kiaria's face relaxes beneath the hardened determination. "We're in."

Half a moment passes in the hot sun, without any breeze to embrace us. We wait to hear if more soldiers are on their way. For the inevitable alarm to blare…announce our presence…make our lives much harder.

It doesn't come.

Kiaria's right. We're in, and no one is the wiser.

Chapter 87 – Titus
2477 | Australia

This felt too easy. The thought kept jumping around in his mind like a fly caught in a glass jar. *I can't be the only one who feels this way.*

There had been the close call with the jetpack failing, sure, but in terms of resistance they'd encountered, it had been more than manageable.

This isn't YOUR Regime. Not yet. This memory from infinite timelines away gave him some solace in the baking desert sun.

"Track, get what gear you need from the Roadrunner. Leave the vehicle here." As Track did what Kiaria instructed, she continued. "We're about to enter the compound. It's a winding, confusing maze, but we know where we're going."

"The core." Aiontis stated.

"Exactly. *Extreme* stealth is the key here. The further we can get through this mission without any alarms raised, the higher chances we have of pulling it off. Keep in mind we have reinforcements ready should things get loud. I don't want to use them until we're absolutely certain we can contain and eliminate every last member of the Regime."

Titus nodded enthusiastically and inspected his Nightfire. For him, this was personal. *Beyond personal.*

The Regime had taken his life from him.

Given him these scars.

Taken his memory.

Made him forget he was an android. Forced him to discover that shocking truth all over.

And those were just the things he knew about. He thought of all the friends who had gone missing in his timeline. The way of life that no longer existed. The relative peace that had preceded the Regime's reign.

All these feelings of anger, revenge, and bloodlust had been boiling beneath the surface their whole time here, but now he had killed a few of them. It felt powerful. Unstoppable. In a way, he *felt* so much right now that he hardly believed he wasn't a true human being.

Beside him, his friend Aiontis read his mind, bumping Titus' shoulder with his own.

"You good? You ready?"

"You have no idea." Titus replied, cocking his Nightfire to prep it for death.

"Oight. Ready to go!" Track returned to the group. Without instruction, he pressed his stealth activation, held it for a moment, then released it.

"You're good." Kiaria told him. He moved on to checking over his own weapon, cocking it similarly. "We go in, horizontal spread. Keep weapons facing forward so there's no friendly fire. I'm adjusting the calibration on our suits to have a dampened stealth covering. We'll be able to see each other – just barely – but that means that if the enemy is looking hard enough, they will too. This will be better for tight spaces indoors. Got it?"

They all nodded, eager to start.

"We still have comms so call your shots, just do so quietly. Use your jetpacks only in extreme circumstances or to get higher quickly. It's likely they'll make too much noise indoors."

She had no sooner finished her sentence and the metal double doors that led into the compound swung open with a clang. Ten soldiers, guns at the ready, fanned outward, suspicious why the exterior squad was not checking in.

Instincts and training had all four of them in activated cloaks within a half second of the first *THUD!* from the opening doors. It was likely that some of the soldiers had seen them, but so briefly their brains didn't register it.

"Stand still." Kiaria warned. "Sand is soft enough they'll see movement."

Titus hadn't thought of that, thankful for her reminder. He pivoted slowly and carefully; gun aimed toward a cluster of the unaware enemy guards.

"Left to right, each take three. I have four." Kiaria explained in a succinct whisper. The tension in her voice echoed the thickness of it over the entire situation.

Titus mapped out his trio, each walking crouched and hunting. Getting closer.

"Hold." Kiaria's word barely came out through gritted teeth, then an airy, breathless command, "Kill."

Titus pulled the trigger three times, quicker than he ever had. *PvvvvtPvvvvtPvvvvt!*

A fourth silent breath followed: Kiaria's extra.

All ten men died within the span of a second, none aware of the four concealed warriors in front of them.

Four that would save the world.

And all other infinite worlds.

"Nicely done. Let's go inside." Titus noticed the footprints of Kiaria in the sand, until they reached the concrete slab that extended from the entrance. Minor traces of blood were already drying brown and soaking into the gray surface.

"I'll take rear." Titus told the group, receiving no acknowledgement but knowing they got the message.

Two other pairs of tracks made imprints in the sand and stopped on concrete. Titus followed them, Nightfire at the ready.

Into the darkness of the compound.

Onward to its core.

Into the belly of the beast.

Chapter 88 – Titus

2477 | Australia

Even past the vast doorway, darkness flooded the majority of the interior. Titus wondered why; it made him uneasy.

Like they were walking into a trap.

"I've heard rumor there's not as much energy availability down here these days. Fuel's running scarce." Kiaria explained, on cue.

"I remember it being this dark most the time." Track continued with an accent-laden whisper. "They pump as much of the juice as they can into the core where all the Warper tech and network servers are."

It's disconcerting Titus answered in thought.

The first room was an abnormal thing to see when first entering a building of this size: a gym facility. There was plenty of battered, worn equipment organized haphazardly, but it appeared deserted. No lights. No windows. No people.

On their left, sharing the floor with the workout space, was a garage. Tens of vehicles – many similar to the offroad Roadrunner variant – were lined in orderly rows.

Still absent of any enemies.

Just shadows dancing across the rare bits of light that belonged to distant hallways. Even the air smelled vacant. Overly clean and oxygenated. He wondered if they were playing mind games with them.

Where was everyone?

"Anyone else smelling something off here?" Titus pushed it to the group. Almost immediately Aiontis responded.

"Fucking yes. Something's up."

"Do they know we're here? They have to, right? Otherwise, where is everyone?

"If it's a trap, it doesn't matter. We're here to kill them all so until it's time to go loud, we stick to the plan and stay quiet." Kiaria interrupted. Her wavy outline glistened around the edges in the darkness. Completely invisible unless you knew where to look.

A minute passed with the group slowly floating their way across the workout facility and garage, to a series of hallways of concrete walls and ceilings, higher than the average man would need. Four were scattered along the back wall of the garage, two that appeared well lit and two where the black shadows went even deeper.

"No splitting up, we stick together." Kiaria instructed. "We're taking the middle right one."

"With the lights off?" Aiontis questioned.

"Yep. We move in the darkness."

Soft shadows transitioned into curved blackness entering the hallway. Titus wished they'd come prepared with some sort of night vision capability then remembered his eyelid iNsert, activating the function with his retina.

"Aiontis, use your iNsert to see. Let us go first, we have night vision with tech from our timeline."

"Damn, I'd nearly forgot." Aiontis answered. "Good call."

"Acknowledged. Track, you take rear. I'll take three spot. Keep contact with left wall as we move forward." Kiaria led the group once more.

"I'm at two. Aiontis, let me lead." Titus suggested.

"Copy, moving to two spot."

Titus observed Aiontis' outline lean heavier into the left wall and stop walking while he passed. Even with the extra light pouring in, this deserted, curved hallway was giving him second thoughts.

The length and the curve continued, deeper and deeper. What had been an unnoticeable downward slope at first was now gradual and oddly steep. The whole affair seemed to stretch on forever, even if it had only been minutes, and Titus was instantly reminded of the White House bunker from this *exact* timeline.

Wild. That event essentially produced *this compound.*

Cough! Cough!

Titus' gently spoke to his comms, "Hold."

Ahead, two guards leaned against opposite walls of the hall, caught in the middle of a break. Thin, gray smoke trailed from a lazily held cigarette (*They still have those in this timeline?*), dissipating before it hit the ceiling.

Both men had some sort of personal lighting device that filled the majority of the hallway section they occupied. Either that or they wore sensors that triggered hallway lights as they moved along, Titus was unsure.

It didn't matter.

Two microbullets left the inky barrel in quick succession. Both men were hit in the neck and could only provide wide-eyed shock for a quickened moment before slumping along the walls.

Kiaria whispered to the group. "There's bound to be more as we move deeper. Stay alert." She was right.

As the hallway continued – and claustrophobically became narrower – patrols increased, many of them much more active than the deceased smokers.

Titus killed them all, swifter than his opinion thought they deserved. *A radiated, exploding bullet that kills you almost instantly? Too nice.*

After 20 dead soldiers in their wake, give or take, they approached a massive opening more akin to what they expected when they had first entered.

Titus understood why a bomb would have hardly touched this place.

"We're here." Track added. "This..." He gestured as he moved closer to the front of the group. "Is the core."

A weird energy surrounded Track when he passed Titus, one that made his internals prickle with anticipation. Call it intuition or call it advanced programming of his algorithm, but something was...off. The Australian hybrid of a man turned to the group with a smile,

"All right boys! Take em in!"

"You fucking asshole!" Aiontis' reaction had come instantaneously.

Kiaria remained strangely silent.

Titus couldn't believe it. They'd been betrayed, dooming them all.

And dooming the infinite remaining timelines to an existence infected by the Regime.

Chapter 89 – Aiontis
2477 | Australia

"**Y**ou stupid piece of shit!" I growl under bated breath. Somewhere in the back of my mind, I'm anticipating a wall of bullets cutting us down any second.

"Oi! Shut the hell up, boyo." That sack of shit (I have many superlatives for him), Track, attempts to calm me down.

"Aiontis. Stay calm. We're not out of this yet." Kiaria cautions. She's more stoic than I am so I listen.

Down the long, sloped tunnel, eight Regime soldiers flank us, guns aimed at our backs. Soldier after soldier emerges in the grand core. I take a quick count. We're outgunned 7:1 by my estimation. Actually, make that more like 9:1…I forgot to remove the heaping stack of shit from our count.

We're not going to make it out of this alive.

The realization is a terrible fear. A dark and *very* deep one.

All of the historics and historical moments I've been part of sprint through my mind. All pointless, about to be wiped from the map, so to speak.

I don't fear the death that is coming.

I fear the failure of our mission more than anything I ever have in my life.

"Why don't you all make your way over here, now?" This man's drawl is awkward. Far different than Track's…more Southern meets British.

Track emerges from the tunnel first, hands raised. Kiaria, Titus, and myself feel the gap closing on our backside so we push further into the huge room, shuffling like shackled prisoners.

Despite how hot I was on the surface, I'm suddenly very cold, as if coolant surges through my veins. My forearms are chilled and icy beads of sweat glisten on my brow. It's fear in physical form.

"As promised," Track begins. "The head of the resistance and her time-traveling sidekicks." The gloating bastard presents us like cattle for slaughter. Like a child seeking a father's approval.

I smile when he gets none. The Southern-Brit merely glances toward him, then back at us.

"Search him."

Four soldiers approach Track and roughly pat him down. There's a gleam in the dull light when his Nightfire is removed and pocketed by another soldier.

"So, where oh where have you two been?" The twang is so strange and I can't get past it. Titus and I remain silent. Kiaria, finally, does not.

"What do you want Ryveliant? If you're going to kill us, stop pussyfooting around and get it done."

Ryveliant?! There's no way.

"Ahhh. I'm not *the* Ryveliant, now am I?" *What?* "I'm his earth-bound, loyal follower. I like to think of myself as Ryveliant II. But that brings up a good enough reason as any, no?" He glowers at Titus and I. "I want to know what they know."

"He's clean, sir." A soldier who'd been thoroughly checking Track interrupted. Ryveliant II continued.

"It seems not everyone is who they say they are, hmmm? Ain't that the pits?" Again, with that *weird* accent! It's fucking infuriating.

"I'm sure you know everything you need to. Or…at least…everything your overlord would want you to." Kiaria taunts him. "Does he make you call him daddy too?"

What is she doing?

Track slowly circles the perimeter, finding a seat. Odd. Our gaze connects for a moment and his is filled with intensity. Not an anger or passion from the betrayal, but a…warning? Almost yelling at me: *keep it together!*

Eventually, he sits at a generic desk, one likely used by whatever form of a receptionist they have here. *Why is he acting so strange?*

"Hahahaha!" Ryveliant II's laugh is moronic and cartoonish. I really hate this fucker. "The famous Kiaria! Just as stubborn and *stupid* as the stories tell." The '*stupid*' comes out decidedly British.

"I aim to please."

"Yes, I'm sure you do." A slimy tongue licks his bottom lip and he points at her, shifting his weight. Like a sleazy cowboy. "Tell me, how does it feel to fail? And so spectacularly!"

My attention jumps back to Track. He kicks his legs up on the desk near a holoscreen. But it's…? The image is dim, and the device is doing something. He keeps checking it periodically. Nervously.

Holy shit.

The Digital Viral Load.

Track is uploading the DVL.

Does that mean he didn't betray us? But he did.

He sold us out.

Kiaria practically answers my questions for me in her reply to Ryveliant II.

"Oh, I don't know. I wouldn't count us out quite yet."

That earns a queer look from him; a cocked head to the side.

"Fair enough. I'll get this over with then."

Immediately there's a tightness in my chest from the visual my eyes absorb.

No.

Ryveliant II levels his weapon – a gun much smaller than our Nightfires – at Kiaria and fires. No hesitation whatsoever.

The round hits her in the chest, pushing her to the ground.

Did he just kill her?

Chapter 90 – Aiontis
2477 | Australia

The echo of the gunshot bounces across the tops of the high, boring, concrete ceilings, gradually dissipating.

"No!" I scream, lunging. Immediately, I'm hit in the stomach, *hard*, by a guard.

Beside me, Titus is calmer, standing stoically in the face of betrayal.

As quick as he shot Kiaria, Ryveliant II shifts his aim to me. He's an ugly man.

An evil one.

In an instant I *feel* the same hatred for the Regime as Titus.

A cancer spreading on our timelines.

And we failed. After all of it!

Fuck! Fuck this!

I attempt to squirm free and am greeted with a weapon butt to the side of my head, sending a warm stream of blood along the contours of my cheek.

What happens next is a wild series of events, all quick, and vividly intense.

My gaze catches Track once more. Up from his seat near the computer, he looks back, nods, and activates his cloaking.

"Move, you imbecile! Or I'll shoot you too!" Ryveliant II shouts at the hovering soldier who hit me. Even across the room, I can see the dark tunnel of the weapon's barrel.

Where did Track go?

My question is answered instantly as a massive, thunderous boom goes off in the center of the soldiers. It's accompanied by a blue orb of light that erupts into tendrils of similarly colored lightning around the room. The shockwave hits against my own body while soldiers closer to the blast are tossed backwards.

Track appears several meters away, crouched. His cloaking is deactivated…

That was the EMP.

This was always part of the plan?

During his time of brief invisibility, he's stolen a guard's weapon, aimed at Ryveliant II's head. Close by, the guard who searched him and confiscated the Nightfire aims it at Track.

"Track…!" Is all I have time to get out. The man pulls the Nightfire's trigger before Track can fire his weapon.

Once black as onyx, the Nightfire is encased in a burning, bright burst of flame as it explodes. The security measure disintegrates the man's arm in a shower of blood and gore. The rest of this body doesn't fare much better.

Soldiers nearby are pummeled with microbullet fragments, shredding their skin and organs.

Track's weapon discharges around the same time, thrown off by the explosion, missing his target.

Mass chaos ensues.

The DVL has been uploaded.

The EMP went off.

A Nightfire exploded.

We might just win this after all.

"Get him out of here! Now!" A deep growl from one of the men echoes, referring to Ryveliant II. "Kill the rest!"

A group of soldiers, panic on their faces (you have no idea how satisfying that is to see), circle around Ryveliant II and leave out a different door. The rest quickly orient themselves on Track, Titus, and I.

There's a large hand on my right shoulder, thrusting me forward. It's Titus. The soldiers that had been around us are all on the floor, dead. He's been busy.

"Go! Get Kiaria!" He barks, laying down cover fire, as the Nightfire whispers several quick shots in succession.

Snap out of it. Focus.

My legs move before my mind. This version of me has had good training. Within seconds, I'm at Kiaria's side.

Her face is pale, her brown hair scattered and sprawled on the ashen, cold floor. She grips her lower chest in the center; there's dark red blood seeping through clasped fingers.

She smiles as I come into view. We're low enough that several pieces of furniture protect us from gunfire. It's just us now.

The green flecks in her eye twinkle a little more brightly.

"Aiontis." She struggles. A bloody hand comes to my cheek and I grab her other one.

"Kiaria. We have to get you out of here."

She whispers. "No."

She can see the confusion and pain in my face. I've only known this Kiaria for a couple days, but we're both the loves of each other's life.

"This was always the plan." She talks calmly and clearly. "Only way to gain surprise. Track was the only one to know. Couldn't risk you finding out."

In case I would have done something stupid, I'm sure.

"We all know about Warper tech too." She continues. I see where this is going. Damn. "We all must die. Can't risk it in this timeline."

It's like a gut punch. I'm losing her. And I'll have to die too? At the end of all of this? I'm hurt. Angry.

"We'll find each other again. In a different timeline." She smiles then coughs. Blood layers the insides of her lips.

"I've played my part." Her gaze is deadly serious, locked onto mine. "Go play yours. One last time."

The green flecks dim and the light disappears from her eyes.

Chapter 91 – Aiontis
2477 | Australia

The weight of her head is heavy in my palm, her lovely coffee-colored hair entwined around my fingers.

I'm not sure why I had to lose her.

Again.

It doesn't seem fair.

Somewhere, in a far-off land, a battle is raging around me. Bullets and microbullets and smoke and fire all within the confines of a concrete base. But here, now, I'm just staring at her.

"Go play yours. One last time."

I think back to how I nearly lost her in San Francisco's earthquake.

Or how I watched her die, peacefully, in Italy.

And now again, so close to the end.

Damn.

Fuck this.

A good friend who understands my pain is yelling at me. There's no time for delicacy.

"Aiontis, she's gone! We have to end this!"

Titus has always been good at the killing part, but I suppose this version of me is too.

For the last time, I look at her and slowly lower her head to the ground.

Goodbye.

In a rush and blur of sound and sensations, the battle around enters my life. I can't tell how many soldiers there are, but it seems like Track and Titus have made a dent in their volume. Bodies lie strewn about on the floor as both of them rise and duck from cover, incessantly laying down fire.

I press the button on my chest to activate cloaking. There's no blue on my wrist.

Oh right. The EMP.

I shift my knees and calves to a more athletic stance and eject upward, eyeing the enemy positions over my cover. Fire *ratatats* my way and I duck back down.

"We need to follow Ryveliant! Everyone has to die!" I shout, hoping Track and Titus can hear me.

"Whatd'ya think we've been trying to do, boyo? Nice of you to join us!"

"We're not all going to make it." Titus is shouting. "Someone needs to stay back and distract this group!"

Shit. He's right.

"What about the backup?" I try to ask it quietly to avoid spoiling the surprise for our enemy friends.

"They're on the way, but too far out to help now." Track answers.

I stand to release a dozen microbullets. One of them connects in a shoulder and I come back down. By the time we've eliminated all the people in this room, Ryveliant will be long gone.

It's now or never.

Reading my mind, Titus answers the call. "You both go! Let me stay back and finish this." I remember this is personal for him. Not *his* Regime, but close enough to take revenge.

A wave of fear attaches to his statement. Several bullets zip above me. If I leave now, will I ever see Titus again? I don't want to lose him too.

I see no other way. One of us has to stay and Titus is stubborn. Track knows this place and likely where Ryveliant went.

"Go!" Titus erupts from cover, firing two weapons. Some other gun from a distant memory…long, squarish, and barking loudly. Definitely not using microbullets.

Why do I recognize that gun? I remember my own X-34, long retired during my life in Italy.

"Aiontis, just go!" Titus growls at me. I focus. So many memories – painful and nostalgic – at once. Time to live in the present.

My Nightfire spits out several more rounds above to ensure my cover is laid and I twist out of my protection, running past Track.

"Let's move!" My gaze remains ruthless toward Track, a part of me still blaming his "betrayal" for her death, but we both know that's not true. With a nod, he falls in line behind me, armed to the teeth with several other weapons hanging from his body.

This place is a maze and the hallway Ryveliant II ran down feels no different than the one that brought us here, except that it slopes upward.

"He's trying to escape the compound." I yell back to Track. I slow to let him catch up and pass. He knows more about this place than me.

"We can't let him get in the wind. We're too close." He's somber, likely saddened by Kiaria too. I forget they were close friends.

"You uploaded the DVL, right? That's what you were doing?"

"Yep. The killin' is all that's left." He cocks a long, assault rifle that looks akin to a sports car; sleek, black, and full of angles and vents. "Your boy gonna be ok? He'll have to last a while without backup."

"Honestly, I don't know, but he's capable. Either way, does it matter? We're in the endgame."

"True." We run along the hallway in silence. "I think there's a hangar up here that spits out the backside of the compound. If I were him, that's where I'd be headed."

The words no sooner leave Track's mouth than gunfire pummels into the walls around us. Reacting, we both skid to a stop, Track pulling up his weapon first. The assault rifle shouts, sending bullets back toward the two soldiers ahead. We press forward as they fall to the ground, their wounds more obvious and bloodier than what the Nightfire produces.

They had been the first line of defense for the hangar Track mentioned, their now-deceased bodies guarding a wide opening into a massive, dark room with cathedral-high ceilings. Hundreds of vehicles rest organized in neat rows, most of which are similar to the off-roading Roadrunners. Others appear to be akin to massive tanks, not like any I've ever seen.

Far away, there's a sliver of golden light, stretching from floor to ceiling, getting wider.

"They're opening the bay doors on the other end!" I urgently inform Track.

"Yep, I see it. That ramp goes out the back and into the desert. C'mon!"

We run faster through the rows of cars.

It's a foolish move.

Bullets slam across the sides of vehicles near our heads. They're so close, the air density changes.

"Shit!" I skid behind a vehicle to my left. Track goes right.

There's an odd sound among the gunfire: prolonged metal scraping against a concrete floor.

Grenade?

Several metal disks the size of my fist slide past us, emitting a dark smoke.

"They're pressing forward!" Track warns. I think there's more to it.

"No…they're covering their escape." My comment is met with silence. We don't have time to wait for the right answer.

"Fine! We keep moving." Track speaks quickly. I can't see him through the thick film of smoke. "Keep your eyes open, go forward on the *outside* of your vehicle's row. We'll meet back in the middle."

"Got it!"

"Do *not* wait for me. I won't for you. Ryveliant is the priority!"

Our conversation ends there. I peer my head along my own path. The smoke is so thick I can't even see the light from the opening bay door anymore.

Queerly, my mind thinks of a poem:

Into the mist I go
To my death, I do not know

Chapter 92 – Odyssian

~ ~ ~

Odyssian gazed across the battlefield where he'd lost so many comrades. The one upon which he'd lost so many *friends*. It had been violent and cruel, but necessary.

To describe the battle with words was impossible, not only because of the inability to describe the use of time, and time as a weapon, in a battle of fourth dimensional beings (though that was certainly impossible), but because words could not capture its scope.

Its meaning for the universe.

For sentient beings both present, past, and future.

There was too much weight in it, but it was over now. At least *his* piece was.

Ryveliant, the bastard who had started this whole thing, lay scattered in gory pieces across time. More dead than dead can be. Odyssian had been the one to put him there.

His followers were mostly destroyed, killed in similarly beyond-permanent ways, and the ones still alive would be banished from society in every possible manner. It was a sentence that might as well *be* death.

Still, Odyssian had an uneasy feeling. One that sent his brain into overdrive through calculations and scenarios.

Ryveliant was dead. He had finished the deed on his end, but that was just one side of the coin.

The rest lay in the hands of Aiontis, Titus, and Kiaria.

The single timeline to stop the spread.

For all his understanding of time and Infinitude, he still had a hard time wrapping his head around the smallness and exactness of this plan, but their math had checked out, a thousand different ways.

Odyssian just hoped it would work.

There was no backup plan.

Chapter 93 – Titus
2477 | Australia

Track and Aiontis had run through a passage and were gone. Titus was unsure if he would ever see his friend again, pain made worse given they'd just been reunited. There was a somberness there, and grief too for Kiaria's death. Titus didn't love her the same way Aiontis did, but she reminded him of Rachel back in San Francisco.

A time when he'd been at peace.

Helping others.

Building a friendship with her and her son, Bryson.

The dull ache of sadness in his chest shifted to a fiery, tingling anger, blazing across his arms and scalp. The Regime was responsible for all of this. They had put his world to ruin, separated him from his friend in *that* timeline, scarred him permanently to look like a monster, tortured him tirelessly, made him forget important memories and who he *was*. Maybe not this Regime – not these men here and now – but they were all the same.

Evil bastards. They all needed to die.

With pleasure.

In the grand complexity of being an android, Titus pushed all his 1s and 0s to build a coat of steely resolve. Behind cover, he returned to the monster they'd created:

The Scarred Man.

From the amount of gunfire and shouting and feet shuffling in the room, he calculated there were no fewer than 30 men. If more showed up, it wouldn't be a surprise.

Good. Let them come.

Titus checked to see if cloaking was working again, by some chance of dumb luck, but the blue wrist light was absent. That was fine. This way they could see him coming.

Claps and pangs of bullets ricocheted off his cover. The tall column (*what was with all the concrete in this place?*) had several pieces of larger furniture pressed against it – desks and computers, chairs, etc. – ensuring he wasn't in danger until someone flanked him. With that extra comfort, he took time to check his Nightfire's ammunition. Microbullets were lodged in several tight stacks, more than enough for the men present several times over, not to mention the extra ammunition on him. The gun had no electronics so it was unaffected by the EMP.

In his other hand rested Zorex, the weapon from another timeline. He'd dealt plenty of death with it elsewhere; it was a trusted ally. Loud and heavy compared to the Nightfire, but able to do just as much damage. The grip felt at home in his hand, encouraging him to take from these men what he wanted.

From his L-shaped cover, Titus rose with wild speed, each weapon finding a target's head in milliseconds. Both shots erupted at the same time, Zorex's overtaking the Nightfire's, and the rippling kickback along Titus's arms, shoulders, and back felt familiarly pleasant.

Just as quickly as he'd risen, he spun round the concrete column, briefly glancing at the hail of gunfire that littered his previous cover. These stupid Regime soldiers focused too much on where he'd been…not where he was going. *A far cry from the geniuses they bred within my Regime.*

Halfway across the grand room was an oddly placed metal barricade, likely set up before the Nightfire and EMP had exploded. There were bodies – and pieces of bodies – scattered in pools of deep red around it. It was his next destination. Without taking a second glimpse, he bolted toward it.

The Nightfire was held extended in his left arm while Zorex faced the same direction in his right, stretched across his body. Titus ripped off shot after shot, experiencing the kickback perpendicular to his core as he ran.

Zorex bullet: took half a soldier's face off, spraying those around him with his warm, now lifeless blood.

Nightfire microbullet: entered a man's throat, triggering its small explosive and blowing his neck backward.

Nightfire microbullets: three entered a woman's stomach as she sent a line of bullets behind Titus. Blood coughed out her mouth as she hit the floor.

Zorex bullet slammed into the right thigh of a soldier wearing a helmet and blew out the back. They were still alive, but wouldn't be for long; the femoral artery was severed.

A combination of several more bullets found their marks as Titus slid along the concrete slickened with gore. He put on the brakes, almost passing his target, and hunkered down. This new cover was loud; ricocheting bullets hammered its hull with boisterous twangs. A sting of pain entered his mind. He'd been grazed deeply by a bullet on his ribcage. One or two were likely broken.

The rageful determination that burned and *itched* along his appendages was now coupled with a racing mind, needing to problem solve. His plan had only extended to this piece of cover. His objective was to kill them all. Now he needed to connect the dots.

Immensely solid against his back, this obsidian metal cover wasn't going anywhere. It had auto-screwed itself into the floor and could take a beating. Unfortunately, it was exposed, with nothing nearby he could transfer to. Popping out in either direction would be suicide and there was little room for diversion.

"Push, push, push! Blindeye tactic!" A gravelly soldier's voice shouted from back in the room.

"Flanking left!" An equally gravelly female voice rang out from further to the side of the room. "Left" was a diversion, he figured, as a flank from the right actually approached. Either way, they were pressing and he needed to think fast.

His gaze frantically scanned the ceilings, walls, and floor. Drab gray everywhere in this hell hole. Titus shifted his aching leg muscles and felt a knob in his back, bulky and certainly not built in to the cover. How had he not noticed it yet? Carefully, he turned – his blindside now facing the flank coming from the right – and found his solution.

Hanging from a hook within the cover was a bag of grenades and leather satchel of knives, with a much larger sword-machete hybrid. The latter object was wildly out of place, and he figured it must have been ceremonial weaponry for a high-ranking official. Either way, it could still kill.

The grenades were unique and dark gray, shaped like disks, with one side flat and another with three rollers. This disk in particular had a simple piece of art in black ink, indicating some sort of explosive. Titus assumed there were different types, but he had no time to check each one individually.

Now how to activate the damn things…

There was something intuitive about the disk and Titus went with his gut. First, he pressed down on the art, hearing a click that depressed the outer rim of the grenade. He twisted the outer ring, and heard a click. It was all he needed. Ignoring the rollers that made it easy to travel along smooth surfaces, he chucked the device toward his right.

"Grenade!" A mere half second after the exclamation, a powerful, deep thud sent a hammer of vibrating bass throughout the room. A couple small screams escaped, cut short, and a disconnected arm shot across Titus' view.

"Shit! He's got grenades!" A shout further back, almost from the tunnel exclaimed. Titus knew they'd be pushing aggressively, and the commands would stay silent. There were only moments to act.

His pulse quickened, he frantically reached into the bag – a net-like material – for another grenade that was marked with an explosive tag. He removed the knives from the dark brown satchel and shoved them in the bag. Many poked through, but he didn't care.

*That's the point…*comically the pun came to him while he placed the last knife. Same as the first grenade, he activated the one he'd singled out, put it in the bag, cinched its top, and threw it over his shoulder.

A flurry of gunfire slammed too low into the barrier, missing the bag of grenades and his hand by centimeters. There was a brief pause and the gunfire picked back up, aiming for the soaring target. Their hesitation would prove costly.

Titus plugged his ears with barely enough time.

For a brief moment, the impenetrable compound that wove deeply into the earth, shuddered and shook.

Chapter 94 – Titus
2477 | Australia

Even with plugged ears, the blast disoriented Titus. For a few moments, he was nauseous, but it passed. Silence infused the room, aside from crumbling rubble. Somewhere, someone coughed. Likely their last breath.

A pointed, black scorch mark stained the concrete floor as Titus rose to assess the outcome. There were downed bodies scattered across the room along with body *parts*.

Crouched and cautious, Titus waited for any movement. There was none. He holstered the Nightfire and Zorex on the stealth suit and grabbed the machete sword; his tool to put any survivors out of their misery. Making his way toward the room's center, he felt awkwardly exposed, but he'd done more carnage than intended.

The closest body was wide-eyed, with a ghostly gaze aimed at the ceiling. In his torso was a massive cavity. *Oh my word. What happened here?*

Behind the man was a spurt of blood and one of the large knives, soaked in gore. It had travelled through his body, like a gust of wind passing through a field.

Other bodies were strewn about in various manners of death. Titus found the other knives lying about the smoky, hazy room. Several hadn't hit anyone. One was lodged in the neck of a woman, accompanied by a dramatic pool of blood along the column she was slumped upon. And then there was a poor soul who'd taken two knives to opposite shoulders and lost both of his legs at different spots.

Jesus…

But Titus held no remorse. He'd long lost any empathy for Regime bastards. They hadn't shown him any.

The room suddenly felt very big, as if it had been growing. Aside from the ringing in his ears, calm continued like an eerie fog on this battlefield. Titus was very alone and he felt it.

Aiontis and Track went chasing after Ryveliant.

Back-up wasn't here yet.

They weren't needed because everyone was dead.

Everyone? Titus questioned his own luck. His own *dumb* luck. Were they really *all* dead? *Should I follow after Aiontis to help?*

Still nakedly exposed in the center of the room, there was a scuffing of gravel against concrete. The answers to Titus' questions had been answered: he was not completely alone. Startled, he twisted on the spot, only to witness the flash of some silver metal alloy zip past his head, trimming hairs with it. It clanged against the hard floor across the room, and Titus was introduced to his final challenge.

A man, taller than he, stood with no evidence of scratches or damage. His black-gray tactical pants and vest were crusted with aged sand while his tanned, exposed arms encased bulging forearms, biceps, and triceps laced with intricate black tattoos. A gruff and misshapen beard, with sporadic gray hairs, tapered off to a bald head. Titus noticed both the man's ears had thin trails of blood running into the beard. There was an expression of anger and hatred etched across his brow and jaw.

"Who the fuck *are you?*" He asked.

Titus thought for a moment, "The Scarred Man."

The man's gaze was blank, half registering that Titus had spoken, half waiting on a response. It slowly hit him that his eardrums had ruptured.

"Ha!" His huge laugh turned into a near fit of laughter. Titus wasn't sure what was so funny. "I don't need to hear you to cut you up. Let's go!" Spittle caught on his beard when he growled. He reached behind on either side and grabbed two lethal weapons, shorter than swords, longer than knives. They twirled in his hands while he rocked back and forth on his heels, their space-black metal not reflecting an ounce of light.

Swifter than Titus would have expected from such a large specimen, he tossed one of the tactical knives into the air, and grabbed a smaller dagger from his vest, chucking it at Titus. Without any misstep, he caught the tactical knife again while the thrown weapon passed within inches of Titus' crotch, instead going between his legs.

The distraction worked. By the time Titus looked up, the savage beast was charging toward him like a rhinoceros. Every muscle in Titus' body contracted and pushed toward the right, but it wasn't enough despite his inhuman speed. Head down, the gargantuan man's arms wrapped around his waist, driving him backwards into the rubble-strewn concrete floor. A loud thud filled the room as Titus' head smacked the floor, followed by the scratchy sliding of Zorex and Nightfire across the floor, both far out of reach.

"Ugh…fuck." The beast had failed to keep a grip on Titus while he ran through, scattering along the floor as well. Dazed, Titus stood quickly and gripped the machete-sword, sharp and smooth on one side, serrated and jagged on the other, with a slight curve to a lethal pointed tip.

Covered in dust, rubble, and blood that wasn't his, the man sprung up, quickly hurling another dagger with the full force of his bulging arm. Its aim was true and the machete-sword swung around, cracking against the dagger, sending it off to the side with a *TWANG!* that echoed multiple times in the walls of the great room.

Both men stood still, weapons ready, and vengeful eyes unwavering from the other. This time Titus would make the first move, racing toward the Regime bastard with aplomb, and bringing the cold metal of his blade toward the man's face.

His dual knives blocked the strike, and the several that Titus followed with.

CLANG!

TING!

CLANG! CLANG! CLANG!

Both men were furiously locked in a ballet of metal strikes and blocks. Titus recognized the stalemate and feigned a slip of the blade, leaving his left side exposed. His enemy took the bait with a growl while Titus stepped and spun on his heels, catapulting the serrated edge of the blade into the man's meaty shoulder.

With a rip, he pulled the blade through, destroying skin and muscle on the way out. A yelp followed, and the contest paused while the man studied his new injury and Titus caught his breath. Blood snaked in tendrils down his bicep and forearms, dripping to the floor. No signs of agony were on his face, but he could no longer lift that arm at the shoulder. The beast across the room dropped one of the knives to the floor with a single *CLACK!*

Something peculiar broke the man's gaze with Titus. A flash of something in his peripheral and straight back to Titus. *Was it a trick to distract?* Titus gave in and glanced to the same spot: Zorex. It lay cold, lethal, and unused on the floor only a hair closer to the man.

He used Titus' acknowledgement of the weapon as his window to make a play for the firearm. Titus' reaction was swift, but not enough. He made a run for the gun, but the giant made it first, having placed his knife on the magnetic holding along his back and diving for the weapon. For the first time in his life, Titus was staring down the barrel of Zorex, but he dropped and slipped feet first before any shot escaped.

Sliding, with the sword above his chest, the blade struck upward underneath Zorex.

Underneath the man's forearm.

Titus' feet smacked into the man's chest as the sword sliced through his radius and ulna bones, cleaving the arm off just below the elbow. The disconnected appendage dropped Zorex while it fell, blood already pooling.

Now was the moment to end it. The rhino was stunned from the amputation.

Titus wrapped his fingers around the textured grip that scanned his biosignature, the weight of his familiar friend comforting. His core braced as his obliques brought his arms around, aiming Zorex between his legs.

At the other end was the bewildered man. The savage, tattooed beast who knew he'd been bested.

At the other end was the *end* of the Regime.

At the other end was the end of all this for Titus.

Like it had many times before, Zorex took a life, thunderously applauding itself as it did so.

For a long while, Titus sat in silence among the carnage. Slumped against a column, he pondered what was next. He was too far behind to catch up to Aiontis and wondered if they'd been successful.

If this had all been for everything, or if it had all been for naught.

Eventually, the footfalls of soldiers, incoming backup, marched eagerly down the long, barren tunnel toward this room of death. Closer and closer they came; here to put a pin in an operation that was no longer in any of their control.

Titus felt a familiar pull and let it take him. He closed his eyes to blackness and opened them to a darker variation back in the Bulk.

So, this really is the end…

Chapter 95 – Aiontis
2477 | Australia

*I*nto the mist I go
To my death, I do not know

I'm unsure how many vehicles I've passed in the hangar thus far.

Four?

Five?

The surrounding smoke is so thick I can only feel the machines, and it's putrid…smelling like burnt rubber. I just hope I'm keeping pace with Track.

So many sounds echo in the distance that I have a hard time decoupling them. Vehicles and machines, roaring to life. Distant yelling of Regime soldiers. They sound frantic, yet measured. I think I hear Ryveliant II's grating voice. There's the soft, wispy release of the smoke from the disc grenades.

Footsteps?

I pause, a subconscious reaction along the entirety of my spine. My grip around the Nightfire solidifies. Among all this smoke I truly wish my cloaking hadn't been disabled by the EMP blast. I try to listen harder.

Definite footsteps. Light, but quick, and multiple pairs of them. I lean hard against my machine, scanning for places to hide. Thanks to the single, large roller at its core, there's not much of an undercarriage to conceal myself, but I try anyway. Unless they have thermal vision equipment, it'll provide some element of surprise.

My legs curl along the frontside of the rolling sphere, smooth and feeling as if it's made of a polymer unfamiliar to me and my time. The top half of my body is mostly hidden underneath the vehicle's overhang, but it's a tight squeeze. A pattering of footsteps comes closer, probably only a single row away.

Somehow, even after several minutes – *has it been that long?* – the smoke is just as dense. The smell might be getting worse.

A pair of legs, with heavy black tactical boots runs in front of my hiding spot, unaware of my presence. I can't see if they have thermal equipment. Two soldiers follow, slower. They're searching harder. Finally, a fourth soldier takes up a slow, methodical rear.

That's my target.

Without a noise, his boots – pressing and rolling carefully along the hard floor – pass before me. I roll to my side, between two vehicles, trying to mimic his silence as I stand. I startle as he calls out,

"Dom, what do you see?" A strange pause.

"Nothing!" The voice feels further away, likely the first man. There's no visor or goggles on his head, so I assume that "Dom" is the only one who may have thermal vision. He was moving too fast through the smoke to notice me. My lucky break.

Theirs? Not so much.

I strike the final soldier, covering his mouth with my hand, pressing Nightfire just under his collarbone, and sending the poison microbullet down through his body like a missile. I feel the life leave him and I catch his weight under the shoulders to drag him out of view.

"Not sure where he could have gone!" The voice calls back. "You there?"

They're on to me, so I've already moved over a row. Turns out *both* Track and I were correct: they were pressing men *and* escaping. Guttural engine noises in the distance disappear, all but confirming what I cannot see. The bay doors are open, and they're making a run for it.

I catch the pair of men who passed earlier, quietly discussing. Tense. Scared.

"I fucking told Dom to slow down. Can't see shit in this smoke."

"Doesn't matter. As long as we give the Master time to escape, we've done our job."

"I ain't trying to fucking die today, man!"

"Not even for the Regime?"

I press Nightfire against the neck of the soldier who's having second thoughts about his Regime tenure.

"What the–" a microbullet through his throat cuts the phrase short and enters the female loyalist in front of him. I toss the dead one aside and put another round in her back.

"Hey!" Ah…the infamous Dom. I catch her limp body before she falls to the ground and turn, placing it between us. Some sort of shotgun round erupts, filling the grand hangar with yet another noise, and her body is racked with its scattered discharge.

I drop her and attempt to bring Nightfire up, but Dom is there and knocks it aside.

"You bastard!" He yells while attempting to bring the shotgun barrel to my chest. My gloves grip round its lethal cylinder, pressing away with every force of my might. Another shot fires from it – I feel the vibrations rattle through its metal – and the heat escapes just clear of my abdomen hitting a vehicle behind me with a shower of sparks.

We're in a dead lock. His hidden eyes staring into mine. I imagine he can't see the finer details of my features, just the red and orange heat emanating from my body. My grip on the shotgun holds as he fires another round into the ground, blowing a cacophony of concrete debris into the air.

Across the hangar, there's an explosion. I spot the dull glow of the fireball through the hazy smoke. That's where I'd expect Track to be so I hope it was his doing and not the other way around.

I capitalize on the distraction, headbutting Dom in the bridge of his nose. There's a satisfying crack when it breaks and he reactively releases the shotgun. I swing it beneath my arm and against my core, finger on the trigger. His goggles are knocked to the side and blood is streaming from his nose.

"No, no, nonononon – " The plea gets cut short because I empty a round into his upper chest. There's an explosion of fabric and blood as he flies backward between the vehicles, swallowed by the smoke.

Quickly, I find the Nightfire, holster it, and take the shotgun with me. I've got to escape this goddam smoke and get a vehicle.

Now.

I'm thankful to emerge from the haze, both from the smell, and to finally orient myself within the hangar. My pleasure morphs into dismay as several vehicles climb the orange dusted ramp out into the desert sunlight. The bay door is wide open, and I have to squint to let my eyes adjust, small tears pooling in their corners. One after another, noises of engines hitting the ramp and getting further away echo like a repetitive chorus into the huge atrium.

My footfalls are light and fast toward the openness. I seek a Roadrunner near the edge so I can skip maneuvering about all the rows and columns of other vehicles and just drive. More than ever, there's a sensation around me: that epic message to my body, from some other dimension, that what I'm doing *now* and *here* is pivotal.

It fuels me.

I'm nearly at the final row of single-roller vehicles when a much larger machine cuts me off. It's one of the tanks, built like a hulking rhinoceros. Instead of two metal treads, this one adopts the rolling polymer technology to new heights. There are hundreds of smaller spheres underneath, each with their own motor function. Above them sits a squared hull that only resembles a tank due to a massive cannon pointing out of the center. Two turrets flank the central cannon, barely comparing to its length, and a cockpit sits above both, able to turn and pivot independent of the cannon's direction.

My awe is only superseded by my defeat.

My weapons are no match for this desert-painted behemoth and even if I hide, that's wasting precious seconds and minutes I can't afford.

The best I can muster is a steely gaze at whomever is in the cockpit, defiant against my imminent death.

I will look it in the face.

Chapter 96 – Aiontis
2477 | Australia

With a creaky crash, the cockpit's hinged door swings open, a man leaning out.

"Let's fuckin' go, boyo!" The death that flashed before my eyes fades and I've never been more relieved to see Track (to be fair, I've *never* been relieved to see Track).

As I'm scrambling up the vehicle's sand-crusted edges, he has already put it in motion. I nearly lose my footing and reactively grab hold of a random crossbar.

"Holy shit!" The vehicle accelerates far quicker than any tank I've ever seen, though I wonder if we'll be able to make up ground and catch Ryveliant II's pack. Some more maneuvering gets me to the cockpit door and inside. There are holoscreens everywhere with four seats in total.

Track slams into the divide of flat ground and outward-bound ramp, shaking the contraption. It's remarkably solid. Beneath me is the growl of the mechanisms and engines. This thing is an absolute beast.

"Good choice." I nod, taking a seat.

"Thanks. Got dicey over on my side so I said fuck it and grabbed this beaut."

"Will we be able to catch up?"

"I think so. The number of rollers this has beneath it is ridiculous." Track explains. "I'm more worried about energy."

"Meaning?" I'm not sure I like the sound of that.

"In order to hit top speed, acceleration, etcetera, I've got to use a bloody lot of power. These things only have limited range when topped out."

"Shit." It's a distant problem on the horizon, but one I see sitting ominously in our future.

"Chin up, boyo. We'll be fine." Track's voice is confident. Sure.

"What makes you so certain?"

"Because we have to be." His answer is stoic. "For Kiaria, mate."

The ramp ends and intense sunlight fills the cabin before the glass can turn the auto-shaders on. There's an immediate transference of heat in stark comparison to the coolness off the deep, underground bunker.

The distance is a vast, barren landscape of small maroon and vermillion rocks, tan dirt paths, and red-brown swirls of dust jumping in the air, all layered beneath a cloudless blue sky. Centered on the horizon is a translucent plume of the sands, ebbing and flowing in a gentle breeze.

It is the last of the Regime, making their escape.

Track pushes upward on a bulky lever and a mid-pitched whine crescendos and peaks. A smaller, mechanical dial near him gets turned and I'm subsequently sucked into my seat. A distant memory of the MagRail train pulls from its deep caverns.

"Holy shit!" Track exclaims. "I don't think I've ever done full power in one of these before. Incredible!"

With this much speed and the litany of rollers along the bottom, it's like we're gliding over a frozen lake. Even after only a minute, the plume beyond has grown in size. I glance behind to find the equivalent of a sandstorm in our wake. Out front, our cannon and flanking guns glisten like proud steeds in the sun, directly aimed at their future targets.

"How do we monitor power consumption?" I ask loudly over the noise.

"On this screen." Track points to a holoscreen centered between us. "If we can catch up to them with 50% remaining, I think we'll be in good shape. Luckily, I picked a fully charged Sandscrapper."

"Sandscrapper?"

"That's what we're in now. Tis' top of the line tank warfare for the Regime and one of their most feared technologies."

Given how fast we're traveling, I can see why.

"Should we shoot the cannon from here? We may hit something."

"No! It'll only waste energy. At the speed we need, we gotta wait until we're right on their arses."

"Got it." I watch the power meter dip below 90%. It's draining fast.

Aside from the whir of the engines and the rattling of the cockpit, we sit in silence for several minutes. A healthy dose of fear and purpose has overtaken both of us. It's that wild, knotted pit in your stomach that knows you *have* to do this, but may not succeed.

I busy my hands by checking both weapons. Nightfire has more microbullets than I would hope to need and I replace the spent shells in the shotgun's surprisingly deep mag. Both are ready, should I need them, though I know the distraction is what I was truly after.

There, still on the horizon, is The Plume. Our enemy trying to escape, with us on their heels. I've refrained from watching the power gauge too much to manage my own anxiety, but it now reads 70%. My peripherals catch Track nervously checking it too, while holding the steering levers on his side in place.

Our silence continues a few moments more (65% power) until I notice two black specks between us and the slightly-larger Plume.

"Oh really!" Track exclaims. "They're tryin to slow us down." He's giddied for some reason and senses my confusion. "We're closer than it looks if they're sendin these assholes after us!"

"Could they be running low on power?"

"Not sure. Wondering the same thing."

The specks are now clearly defined as off-road Roadrunner, hustling toward us with vigor.

"Smoke these fuckers." Track instructs, nodding toward a holoscreen and panel near me. Loud smacks start peppering our glass cockpit and the bulletproof material holds, leaving no trace.

"Use the guns, not the cannon yet. Less energy."

"Got it." I grab the yoke on the panel and press two black buttons that sit comfortably under my thumbs. The controls are intuitive and almost immediately a stream of hot yellow lines beam across the road, spewing sand into the air. My aim is off, but I quickly adjust.

A flurry of bullets, brightly burning against a hot desert, pummels – *one.two.three.four.five.* – into the front of an enemy vehicle. It practically implodes, shooting up into the air and crashing in a mass of blackened debris.

"Press the button in the middle." I do as Track says and the yoke separates in two. The weighty motion of the guns aims separately like a chameleon's independent eyes. I instruct the right-hand yoke toward the remaining enemy and draw a line of bullets along them, shredding it to mangled pieces. Through the window I observe blood spray.

"Nice job." Track compliments.

"That was rewarding."

"Yeah…well, don't get too excited." Track nods in front of us. The Plume has shrunk, but not in the way I'd expect. Ryveliant II and his remaining Regime loyalists have slowed to let us catch up. Their army of black and gray vehicles standing out like a sudden mountain range against the landscape. In the center is a Sandscraper like ours, black as coal. Nearly metallic. Perspiration prickles under my arms and my tongue is sticky.

It's them versus us. For the fate of everything and everyone…no pressure.

Chapter 97 – Aiontis
2477 | Australia

A percolating eeriness fills our cockpit cabin as we slow to match their speed. Our hulking mass and their bulbous group all pressing forward into the previously-known-as-the-Outback desert. My new formed habit kicks in…51% power.

At least we've caught up.

"What are they waiting for?" I question. Track's answer is nothing short of incredible.

"Better question, boyo: what the fuck are *we* waiting for?" He leans over to my seat, grabbing a maneuverable stick, flips open a yellow lid atop, and presses the similarly yellow button revealed underneath. For a moment, nothing happens aside from a small whine below us, and then I notice our central cannon.

Glowing blue.

"Holy shit. Is that a –" Before I can finish, our cabin shudders and vibrates, deeply, and the cannon presses a massive blue beam into the environment. It's deep cobalt, laced with white lightning, contrasting against the red ground and robin-egg sky. Narrowly missing Ryveliant's Sandscrapper (*Fuck!*), it hits a group of Roadrunners further back, sending them catapulting, aflame, into the sky.

"A railgun?" Track finishes my question. "Why yes, yes, it is."

It doesn't take long for their response to fill our cabin with boisterous noise. The bullets are like torrential hail, never ending and numbing to the senses. Track's reaction time is just as fast, and we're already maneuvering toward one side of the group at a blistering pace.

47% power indicates we spent quite a lot on that railgun round, but it was so fucking worth it.

"Ay!! Quit gawkin and start shootin!" Track yells at me, sweat glistening along his forehead as his hands manage several driving tasks at once.

I grab the separated yoke, heart pounding like a prisoner trying to escape my chest. Streams of bullets cross and zag and zig in front of me. There are so many targets, I barely have to aim to hit something. After I carry several lines of death across the mass, I zero in on specific Roadrunners, ones that are causing the most noise to our hull. Their bullets haven't made a dent in the glass, but I don't want to test the limits.

Meanwhile, we've collectively sped up. Track calls out his angling and turns beforehand, allowing me to accommodate the changes in direction.

Vehicle after vehicle dismantles grotesquely from my torrent of bullets. Once they explode or crash, the carcasses tumble past us. In a few, I can spot the gore entombed within. Engulfed in a fireball, a vehicle wrecked to our side features a soldier running around outside, ablaze.

"Why aren't they shooting back?" I ask, clearly meaning the Sandscrapper since it's the only silent participant in this battle. Once the mayhem began, they pulled away.

"I don't know. Looks like they're still trying to escape, but I'm thinking their power is dangerously low."

That's music to my ears because ours isn't much better. Below 40% now.

"How long do we have once the power runs out? Is there any backup?" I pry, hoping for a good answer.

"It looks like there's a diesel backup, but that tank will only last us 10, maybe 15 minutes at most. And the railgun will be offline."

"Let's make sure we're not the last ones with a railgun round then."

"Agreed."

For several more kilometers, our pursuit against the red desert brings fire, death, and carnage, leaving a peppered trail of it behind us. I've thinned their herd, and Track's driving has been masterful.

Along with the familiar gut of purpose, an excitement burns along my body. *We may actually have a chance at this. Things are looking up.*

As if my optimism is cursed, there's a parting of Regime vehicles while our tank comes closer to the center of the road. I only have a moment to notice it, but Ryveliant's Sandscrapper has a familiar blue glow – laced with white lightning – along the cannon.

"Oh fuck!" Track screams, seeing it too. Hard enough to break the levers, he yanks in the opposite direction, destroying our momentum and throwing me to the floor of the cockpit. Our entire hull creaks and moans, angry at the driver for such a direction change, but beneath us, the rollers are aggressively shifting their course.

We lurch toward the new direction, exactly at the moment the round of sapphire energy releases from the enemy tank. Track's decision has saved our lives, but Ryveliant II still caught us off guard, and there are consequences to comfortability. From the floor, I'm shouting as a corner section of our cockpit's roof rips off in a cataclysm of blue fire and energy. Shards of metal travel with the beam behind us while others sprinkle onto me, white hot and burning through my sweaty cloaking suit.

Airstream noise fills the cabin, rushing in with a warm, oddly comforting breeze. Windswept grains of sand find their way in.

As I'm trying to brush off the hot debris, a noise louder than anything we've heard thus far crashes into the glass. My eyes connect with Track's, bravely at the helm and steering as if our lives depend on it (because they do). There's a deep panic etched along his face. I piece together that the sound is the flanking guns on Ryveliant's Sandscrapper. Track's reaction tells me the glass won't hold back *those* bullets very long.

"Aiontis." He states, peacefully, despite his fear. "Get up. End this."

The noise has gotten louder, and breaking glass accompanies it now. I remember that Track *has* to die. He knows about Warper technology and those are the rules. Knowing that doesn't make it any easier as I glance the massive rounds slamming into his shaking body before I turn away, tears in my eyes, huddling on the ground out of sight.

It's all on me now.

Chapter 98 – Aiontis

2477 | Australia

The full range of the tank's controls are on my side of the cockpit too, though I'm unsure how well-versed this Aiontis is at managing steering, speed, and shooting simultaneously. It's not exactly like I have a damn choice.

I stand, trying my best to ignore the bloodied mess of Track's body that has fallen to the floor. The massive vehicle is still speeding away at the angled direction he input, separating us from the main pack of remaining Regime members.

Air rushes into the cabin, cooling from its flow, but bringing in too much sand. I can see okay, but I'll be useless if I get grains in my eyes. On the wall at the back of the cockpit is a host of useful items like medical kits, rope, and, thankfully, goggles. I put them on, sensing the sand and dirt-grime that has crusted to my face from sweat. It's thick in my hair too and my cloaking suit has been colored sand camouflage as opposed to its original black.

Thankfully, the shooting has stopped from all parties. I'm hoping it's a combination of the perception we're dead *and* being low on energy, though I recognize I lose one of those elements once I make a maneuver. There's enough sturdy glass in front of my seat to take a few beatings, but the structural integrity has been damaged. I'm not going to be able to take the same heat we did before.

I assess the controls methodically. I need to be ready to fight the moment I make a change in direction.

Okay. Let's do it.

My mind remembers our own energy.

33%

Yes, you're right: it's going to be close.

I pray Ryveliant is in a similar situation.

My initial inputs are tweaks, just to make sure I understand the workings right. They'd only be visible someone paying close attention. With that final check, I make my move, pulling hard to the right, back toward the traveling pack.

Within a few moments, I'm close enough to lock the speed and direction, and I grab the separated gun yoke. There's no hesitation to my thumbs pressing the hard black buttons, releasing a new stream of vengeful rounds. My concentration, a dangerous mixture of anger and adrenaline, pulses as highlighted targets in my mind. I shred several to bits.

A Roadrunner explodes upward in a furious, violent fireball, thrusting a body upward, into the stream of bullets where it disintegrates into a mist of red. The machine bounces noisily off my own, tumbling along the road behind me. The total count of Regime enemies has dramatically plummeted since we started. Their group is sparse, with only three vehicles maneuvering alongside Ryveliant's quiet tank.

My hopes are all but confirmed: his tank must be incredibly low on energy. He's neither sped up or fired any guns, much less the railgun. I'm energy-rich over here sitting at 25%. Almost.

Shit. 25%. I need to act fast.

I have a plan, but it's dangerous and risky (as all good plans are). If it's botched, that's it and Ryveliant II will get away. If it goes smoothly, I can end this now.

It's a risk I must take.

I lay off the guns, likely to the surprise of the leftover Regime soldiers. With a few lever adjustments, I alter my speed and begin cutting across the middle of the group.

I'll have one shot at this.

I grab the railgun joystick, and press the yellow button of death. I take half a second to ensure the cannon is facing directly in front of me, anticipating where Ryveliant's tank will be as I swing across its backside. The hum of the charge feels quicker this time. Likely my anticipation. Along the cannon, the familiar caerulean energy pulses and releases with the same tremendous vibration. With an open cockpit, the resulting sound hits so hard I nearly vomit.

There's a thud a half second later as my railgun blast eviscerates the bottom of Ryveliant's machine, destroying at least half his rollers and ability to navigate.

10%

Let's do this.

I slam forward on the throttle to cut off the arc I've made across the group.

Full speed ahead.

There's a small peppering of gunfire from the remaining Roadrunners. They can tell what I'm going to do, but they know their gunfire is useless against this Sandscrapper.

7%

My acceleration continues and I'm gaining ground on the damaged tank.

5%

I've still got some fuel if I need it, but I won't. This ends now.

3%

2%

1%

My cannon, raging hot from its last round, makes contact with Ryveliant's own like two jousting sticks. Our hulls crash together as the cannons twist and bend and break with loud pops and moans. I'm thrown to the floor immediately, and I curl up, hoping to avoid any lasting damage.

I'm bucked along the dirty surface, slick with blood and sand, as metal crashes around me. Sunlight is purged from view, replaced with dark, burning smoke and a metallic tomb.

Finally, the vibrations cease as the violently conjoined vehicles lose momentum and speed, slowing to a halt in the middle of the once-Australian desert. I'm sore as shit, but miraculously okay. Getting out of this beast will be a challenge, but I'm relieved.

The risk paid off.

I can only crouch among the jagged, bent steel, and I grab the shotgun and Nightfire.

It's time to confirm a kill, or put the bastard down myself.

Chapter 99 – Aiontis
2477 | Australia

As I finagle out of the totaled tank, smoke billowing around me, a rhythmic pulse of purpose appears slowly. They're the drums of some far-off music thundering one smack at a time…building toward the end.

Thum…

Thum…

Thum…

The butt of my shotgun catches on some hot, sharp debris so I unhook it. I hope I can actually *get out*, though if not this path, I could always engineer another.

Within a few moments, there's a light boring through the smoke. It's dense, and while I'm thankful for the goggles, I don't have anything around my nose or mouth. After a coughing spell, I shove the bend of my arm against my face and head toward the potential exit.

Thum…

Thum…

Thum…

I wonder about Odyssian, and, more acutely, Titus. Has their portion of this mission been successful? Are they still alive? What does "alive" even mean for Odyssian? I have to assume everything rests on my shoulders…anything less and the crushing mental blow would not bode well if there are Regime soldiers still alive.

The vibrant desert daylight pokes through the mangled wreckage. Instinct takes hold as a Regime Roadrunner passes in front of me with a soldier leaping from the flat roof, arcing downward for the kill. Without a thought, my hand shifts to the shotgun, slinging it under my arm and moving both hands to its length. The crook of my finger pulls the trigger, there's a kick, and with a spray of red mist, the man's momentum and trajectory shifts away from me.

Crouched, with the shotgun firmly wielded, I run further into the desert. There may be enemies left and I need a better vantage point.

Thum…

Thum…

Thum…

These ethereal drums are deafening, but pulsing me forward vigorously. A quick scan reveals no other enemies, and the Roadrunner's driver is still in play, out of view. The best place to observe is my own tank, atop its burning heap of scarred material. Adrenaline pulses from head-to-toe and my feet are moving wild while I sprint to clamber up the sides.

Thum…

Thum…

Thum…

Unless there are subtle, strategic places to hide, my plan worked better than I could have imagined. In the distance, the Roadrunner that buzzed by makes a wide turn, probably shocked at the violent departure of his fellow soldier. Otherwise, there's no signs of life.

Ryveliant II is apparently buried in his tank (hopefully now a tomb) and the other Regime vehicles crashed on their own among the chaos. My brain feels light, ecstatic. A smile turns on my lips.

I've done it. All that's left is a final soldier.

Scorching metal and burning smells remind me of the smoke I encountered in the hangar. When I close my eyes, I hear the remaining vehicle, maneuvering among the debris, turning around…likely to check on his very dead comrade. I'm at a disadvantage without any explosives, but they can't reach me up here.

Still, I have to kill them.

I have an idea.

Carefully, I hustle to where the airborne man met his untimely demise. There's a jagged edge of various vehicles, part Roadrunner and part hull of my own Sandscrapper, conjoined together by fury, providing some semblance of cover.

Sure enough, the Roadrunner whips around into view, pressing sand and dirt away along the sides of its massive, central roller. I grab my Nightfire, not by its grip, but by its prolonged barrel. It's awkwardly light when I handle it like this.

Below, the hum of the offroad vehicle quiets as it slows to a gradual roll, looking for the other soldier. Through the windshield, the driver is frantically searching, confused. I'm not positive where the body landed, but I use the distraction to my advantage.

I heave the Nightfire toward the vehicle with a mighty, full-shoulder throw. It lands with a 'plop!' in the dirt, next to the vehicle that has since come to a rest. The driver has not seen it – better for me – so I take the proper time to aim the shotgun at the resting weapon, full of minorly radioactive microbullets.

My first shot echoes loudly against the quiet horizon.

No explosion comes, but the sand around the gun blossoms with the impact.

Fuck! The spread is too wide!

The driver's gaze snaps to me, both of us startled by the other. I clamber over my cover, frantically trying to rush closer for a better shot. I'm focusing on the gun and where I should put my feet, hearing the door to the Roadrunner open. He doesn't know the Nightfire is in the sand, but he'll shoot-to-kill regardless (and probably thinks I have awful aim).

I press the shotgun into my shoulder and let out another booming round. Still nothing, and the makeshift explosive has only burrowed further into the soft ground.

God fucking dammit!

The Regime soldier takes aim from behind the cover of the vehicle's front half, clearly confused why I'm shooting at sand. Nearly off the wreckage, I leap from its edge, ignoring how I may land, instead pointing at my target. I have to be close enough now, right?

My third round screams from the jet-black barrel and connects with the Nightfire, exactly as my shoulder lands. The weapon's discharge is superseded by a bass-laden explosion that lifts the undercarriage of the Roadrunner, tossing it and the soldier hard against other debris.

I roll away as hard as possible, covering my face with my arms. I want to get clear of not only the fireball, but any microbullets that scatter like fireworks. Several meters away, the carcass of damaged transportation crashes with a dull thud in the sand.

I'm okay. No sharp pains, nothing where I felt impact. Adrenaline has been like a river through my bloodstream for the last couple hours though, so I thoroughly check myself for any silent wounds. Aside from deep bruises and small cuts, I'm fine.

Is this over?

Did I just save…humanity?

An infinite number of times, no less?

"AIONTIS!!!" The scream is barbaric, an odd accent lacing the exclamation. Vengeful. Revengeful.

I roll and twist on the scalding sand, looking over to the towering combination of collided Sandscrappers. A man stands atop, wielding a sword – a thick, Arabian-like, scimitar – in front of his face. There's an aggressive twist of the handle, and a curved blue shield emanates from both edges of the sword.

Fuck. This is definitely not over.

Chapter 100 – Aiontis
2477 | Australia

"AIONTIS!" He repeats, foaming at the mouth and projecting spittle. "You FUCKING coward!"

I remain silent, and stand up like an old man. I'm beaten and tired, sure, but I want him to think it's worse than that.

"We're at the precipice – for the first time in history – of having a single ruling body around the world! You would get in the way of that?"

I laugh. "You think the Regime is an accomplishment? You're a group of thugs taking over a broken world."

"LIES!!!" He's slowly walking down the tank toward the road. "I've been given visions! Visions by a god. A *master*." The Southern drawl element of his accent is prevalent now.

"Let me guess, his name is Ryveliant?"

"YES!" His eyes light up, aroused at the sound of the name. "I am his disciple, and we will make the world whole again!"

This guy is fucking crazy.

"I hate to break it to you, but you're just a throwaway piece on the board. In a massive, *massive* war. Bigger than you could possibly imagine."

"You BASTARD, you LI – "

I cut his tirade short, yelling over him. "I was shocked when I found out too. It's the truth." I pause, thinking. "You know my name. What have they told you about me?"

There's a raised eyebrow. He answers, finally stepping onto the crimson, dusty ground. "That you are a key leader of the rebellion and one of the final insects I must crush."

Perfect.

"Did they tell you I'm a time traveler?" My question is met with confusion. "And not only traveling time, but across time-*lines*?"

"You've used the Warper tech?!?"

"Many times. The timeline I come from has seen the technology commercialized." Hard as he might to cover it, there's astonishment in his reaction. They haven't perfected the technology yet.

"Where I come from, the nuclear war between Cuba, Russia, and the U.S. never happens."

I debate telling him all about Core Events and Infinitude, remembering that he's nothing more than the last body I need to drop. I'm not trying to convince him of anything.

"Blasphemy!" The sword's shield hums with a soft buzz. "I've seen the truth. Ryveliant is the Regime and the Regime is the Way!"

I let out an audible sigh, not surprised, though disheartened by how much Ryveliant has poisoned these timelines. The Regime is his product – all because of his quest to hasten the dimensional-evolution process.

Without much warning (something I don't have time for these days) I heave the shotgun to my shoulder yet again, and fire a round. I'm too far away. My real goal is to test the shield and potentially expose a weakness.

The sound of the blast startles him, but the shield holds steady, only providing small ripples where the spread made contact. I move closer, gaze aimed down the barrel, and pull the trigger a second time. Another eruption cascades into the cloudless sky and more ripples shake along the shield, Ryveliant II bracing this time. They disappear quickly. There is no weakness or brief retraction of the shield.

I'm caught off guard as the crazed wannabe-prophet storms at me, scimitar raised high. It's an opportunity to fire another time – *how many rounds does this thing have again?* – but the sword swoops down and blocks the blast. In a smooth motion, Ryveliant turns the shields off, and swings the laser-sharp edges upward.

I slip to the right as the point of the sword nicks my cheek. We both spin to face one another, positions in the sand reversed. A hand to my cheek reveals a smeared stream of blood. The bastard is smiling, twirling the sword.

He takes two steps forward, taunting me, and begins releasing a flurry of slashes and swings. I've since put the shotgun along my back to be more agile, and I desperately try to maneuver around the death blows. There's not much else I can do.

I've fallen to the ground, dust blanketing my goggles, and roll several times to avoid quick slashes that slice the sand. There's a distinct fury and rage to his style, though also a lot of finesse and talent. Some distracted part of me wonders about his story…where he came from before the "visions".

A strike thuds between my legs, showering sand onto them.

Focus, Aiontis. Get your shit together.

I roll hard another time, the sand's heat trying to penetrate the stealth suit, and am finally able to stand. Ryveliant II pauses, exhausted from his failed swings. I use the only weapon I have and grip the barrel of the shotgun like a bat. Another thin smile slinks along the top of his chin.

Somehow still possessing energy, a new wave of attacks comes. I maneuver around them, waiting for my moment to use the shotgun without it getting sliced in half.

Slip.

Duck.

Slip. Slip.

He's getting tired.

I roll out of a dodge with my grip firm against the metal of the shotgun, letting my momentum carry most of the power. The club-like butt of the weapon hits the broadside of the sword hard, with a thunk, nearly knocking the weapon from Ryveliant's grasp.

I wish it had.

Not sparing any time, I throw the shotgun back against my shoulder, find the trigger and fire at this son of a bitch. He's quick though, and in the second I took to position the weapon, the sword appears in front of his face.

At the last possible moment, coupled with the thunder of the gun, the shield pops out from the sword's edges, catching the projectiles.

But I got to him. Behind that shining azure energy is a face laced with surprise, shock, and now fear. He knows I was *this close.*

I press the barrel closer to the shield, unsure if I should actually touch it, and pull the trigger.

CLICK!

Now worry is etched across *my* face, but I had subconsciously been anticipating this. I press the barrel into the shield hard, then the entire length of the gun, and soon my whole body. We're running backwards and there's no mobility for him to move the sword.

Combined, we gather enough speed that his feet tangle. My body, the empty shotgun, the shield scimitar, and his body fall onto the dusty brown-red earth. The shield turns off, acknowledging the sword's sharp edges are now a danger. There's not much room for either of us to move, and that's how I want to keep it. I'm searching for an opportunity to steal the sword.

Grunting, yelling, and struggling ensues. The shotgun eventually falls out between us, no longer an element in play. I squeeze my knees against his ribs to break them, while my hands search for the hilt of the sword, finding his sweaty fingers in a death grip around it. I pull hard, accomplishing little more than readjusting the sword between us. Once vertical along his body, it's now diagonal, with the dangerous edges facing our chests.

This is a delicate game of tug-of-war.

Ryveliant is strong, but tired from all his wasted energy. I'm exhausted as well, but driven.

My lifetime and a half…

The understanding of what kind of war I'm in…

How important killing this man is…

Even with all that, my mind wanders to Kiaria. The various versions of her I knew. The one I grew old with in Italy. She's been the gut feeling all along. The driving force behind all of this. The *reason.*

The sword edges closer to the man's neck and I shift a hand, one around the hilt, the other now gripping the sharp edge facing me, pressing downward. Stinging pain surges and adrenaline and warm blood follows, but it provided the leverage I needed. My deep red lifeforce contrasts the colors of the desert as it drips onto the sand and Ryveliant's cheek, eye, and mouth.

There's a clarity that came coupled with Kiaria's memory. A distinct path forward, and I follow it.

My hand atop his own grip of the hilt tightens around his knuckles and bones fiercely.

I twist the handle.

The sting in my palm along the blade turns to fire as blue energy hums and cackles against the flesh, muscle, and bone of my fingers. I brace as three of them fall off, bouncing off Ryveliant's body onto the ground.

The other side of the sword hosts a grimmer picture. My twist of the handle came with a final, painful shove. With his head and neck against the ground, it had nowhere to go…and neither did the emerging shield.

Ryveliant's head holds a blank stare and a snarled expression, separated from his body with the smoke of burning flesh silently twisting upward into the sunlight from blackened edges.

Now…it's done.

Finally.

I stand, nursing my damaged hand that's been cauterized by the shield's burns. It still hurts like hell.

For a brief moment of respite, I'm in the unknown. I hadn't thought this far and I'm unsure of what happens next.

Do I live here? Do I need to die too?

How do I get back to civilization?

The moment transcends into darkness quickly, answering my call. Pain disappears and my mind begins clicking in a familiar way.

Of course.

This would all end in the Bulk.

Chapter 101 – Aiontis

~ ~ ~

I'm not sure if it's possible to feel *relief* in the Bulk (or what the equivalent of relief for a fourth-dimensional being would be), but that's the sensation I'm filled with at the moment. Again…don't focus too much on the word "moment" in the Bulk.

My metaphorical shoulders feel lightened and, looking back at this journey, positive energy rushing throughout my essence reveals another impression: pride.

Thinking to the future, I am unsure and unsteady, though half expecting the next step to be death. And I'm okay with that. My life(s) has been good, adventurous, and spontaneous, even if not always by my choosing. To think this all started in Omaha, craving some obscure drug.

Wild…

Similar to the first event that led me into the Bulk, I *feel* other entities around me. A rush of emotions, understanding, and conversation hit my heightened mind at once, as they normally do here. Despite this complication, I believe I've gotten quite deft in describing what happens in this place.

I'll do my best to achieve that now: recounting my final time in the Bulk.

"Odyssian?" I question into the infinite darkness.

"Aiontis?!" It's Titus' voice.

"You made it!" I exclaim, wishing we had bodies or some way to hug in this space. "Tell me what happened!"

Titus explains how he violently destroyed an incredible – and nearly impossible – amount of Regime members. I sense it in his voice, the exercise had been cathartic. Revenge, but revenge that actually accomplished our goal…helped us succeed.

"Wow." I start. "I wondered the whole time if splitting up was a good idea."

"What about you?" He gently asks. I believe he already knows the answer.

I tell a similarly violent story as his, about the chase, Track, the crash, the sword, and Ryveliant II's grisly death.

"So, it's over?" His question is the same as mine.

"Yes," A commanding, non-human, but familiar voice answers. "It's over."

There's a long silence between us, basking in our success, remembering the shared losses.

"Ryveliant is deceased and scattered in my dimension. You've prevented the Regime, the portable Warper technology, and their plan. And we've stopped the spread of the Regime as a Core Event across Infinitude."

"I don't...know..." I stammer.

"What happens next?" Odyssian answers, somehow always knowing what's on my mind.

"Yes."

"It's simple." The ethereal voice pauses. "You both go home."

What does that even mean anymore?

"What if I don't have a home?" Titus presses. "I came from a Regime-ravaged world. You already told us those timelines are unsalvageable. I don't want to go back there."

"Hmmm. Yes, that's hard." Odyssian thinks. "I could put you in a specific time period, if you'd like?"

"I'd like to go back to 2098. To San Francisco."

"Titus...I...can do that, but you'd be going back for Rachel? Her and the boy?"

"It was the first time in a very long time that I was happy." He explains.

"You should know the chances of me getting that *exact* timeline where Rachel knows you is nearly impossible. She'll be in many of them, but only remember *you* in a single one."

"The chance alone is better than where I'd be going back to. I understand."

"So be it." Odyssian concludes. "As for you Aiontis..."

"Omaha, 2404?" I guess, confident in my answer.

"Not…exactly. You must trust me; I'll be sending you to your *true* home."

"I…erm…ok." I know arguing is pointless by now.

"This is it." Odyssian announces. "This is goodbye, hopefully for good. Though I've enjoyed our time and experience together, we'll never cross paths again."

There's a brutal finality in his statement. Grief and loss well up within my consciousness.

"Thanks for everything, Odyssian." Titus mentions.

"We couldn't have done it without you. Literally." I add.

"The same is true from where I sit." He pauses. "I will give you two time to say your goodbye's. When you're ready, you'll both arrive home."

That's the last I ever hear from Odyssian, an equally alarming and comforting thought.

"Titus…I…" I suck at finding words right now. "Thank you for everything you've done. Both on this adventure, and the many we had before. It's crazy to think we started this with you trying to kill me."

Titus laughs. "Thank you, friend. I will miss you too."

Among all this, I'd nearly forgotten he is an android. An advanced AI. I seriously doubt that, given I love him like a brother.

"I hope you find peace where you're going. I love you." They are my final words to him.

"I love you too, Aiontis. May the rest of your days be pleasant ones."

Gradually, the sensation of other beings fades from my grasp in the Bulk and I am alone.

The adventure is done and I'm going home.

With a strangely organized chaos, the blackness begins to recede and I see the light of an image far in the distance, gradually getting closer and sharper.

Only time will tell what mystery remains to be revealed ahead.

Chapter 102 – Titus
2098 | June 21ˢᵗ | San Francisco

Departed from his dear friend forever, Titus' heart hung hollow, or at least his programming and behavior pattern algorithms suggested as much. True AI or not, he would miss Aiontis.

Around him, the blurry image cleared as his feet attached themselves to his consciousness and found solid ground.

A concrete sidewalk, jagged and cracked, alongside a park of green grass with chunks of ground sitting atop others. A pale blue morning sky, speckled with wispy cirrus clouds met a horizon of sloped stacked homes. Damaged apartment complexes, townhomes, and smaller business offices stood brown and gray in contrast. Between some of them, clear gaps of demolished brick, timber, and other debris.

This was clearly a San Francisco rocked from the Great Faultline Disaster, but there'd been some time since. No fires smoldered or produced smoke, debris was cleaned out of the streets, and no sirens or screams wailed. Instead, birds chirped pleasantly in the warm morning sun.

The road ahead of Titus was dramatically unclear, something that terrified and excited him equally. There was no Regime, but he was utterly alone in this timeline.

Except for a chance…

A nearly infinite chance against him, but Odyssian had said he'd try. Titus had faith in at least that, so he got his bearings and proceeded across several blocks toward Rachel's home. The same one he'd shared with her and her son, Bryson, for a month after the disaster, helping to repair countless things, and eventually moving on to helping neighbors in need.

Peaceful. Full of hope.

He wasn't sure if he was in love with Rachel, at least not in that way, though he didn't want to completely rule it out. Instead, he knew she was a comfort. A light in a life where that had been extinguished long ago. Bryson too. There was something *safe* about the two of them and, after the life he'd had, *safe* sounded like the best way to spend the rest of it.

After half an hour, a familiar block of homes appeared around a corner. One stood out among the rest, all showing signs of some damage, but intact.

Strangely, nerves were not present as he approached the door. Excitement, maybe, but anxiousness was absent. Something in his gut told him *this* was the right place. He was sure of it.

He rapped on the faded paint of the door, dusty with residue from the outdoors and constant construction of the rebuilding neighborhood. From inside, he heard a soft yell.

"Be right there! Bryson, finish your breakfast!"

Footsteps tapped behind the door and it swung open with a slight creak halfway through.

The look of surprise and confusion could have said it all, but Rachel said the one word he'd wanted to hear:

"Titus?"

Chapter 103 – Aiontis
2477 | Unknown location

From the darkness, I've arrived into a lesser version of it, off-set by a faint light above my forehead. Comfortable pressure lines my heels, legs, back, and neck.

I'm lying down?

I couldn't describe it if I tried, but something feels *different*. Across a distant sea, this body is an island of a memory, slowly sailing back to the shores of my consciousness.

This is…my body

Dull aches are present in my knees, my hips, and my shoulders. I've not moved yet, but I sense the age of this vessel. Having been old once before, it's a recognizable feeling.

My core tightens as I sit, with more struggle than I'd care to admit. A small tug along my forehead informs that I'm attached to something, my fingers feeling the cold metal links on my temples. They peel off without much resistance and I sit the metal band from my forehead on my lap, reviewing my shocking surroundings.

I'm in an old, dilapidated, and damaged building with no light. The ghost-white medical bed I'm on emits a soft glow, and there's a tall machine next to it, beeping softly since I took off the headpiece. Across the dusty, bare floor, a window is open and there's the recurring pitter-patter of rain along its cracked pane.

I'm taken aback when the room lights with a bright purple hue, bouncing off every wall and surface. Outside, a long, gangly trunk of violet lightning reaches horizontally across the sky, several other branches arcing outward. After half a minute, the image fades against the night sky.

Where…where have I seen purple lightning before?

A collection of memories dance across my mind. I've seen this before. With Rachel. With Caterina.

With Kiaria.

Just then, there's a crash and a gasp behind me. My whole body turns, feet dangling off the bed's edge, and the thin metal headpiece on my lap falls to the floor. I go to stand, but my legs struggle to support my weight. Before I fall, there's a lift beneath my arms and I sit back on the bed.

"You're…you're awake?" I stare into the deep brown eyes with flecks of green I know so well, glossy with pending tears.

"Ki – Kiaria?" I choke. She's old. Weathered. There's defeat in her stance, in her energy. I'm all those things too.

She crashes into me like a youthful lover all over again, arms wrapped tightly around my neck. I wrap mine around her back, soft sobs cathartically releasing from both of us. The embrace breaks, she grabs my face, and kisses me with all the purpose I've felt across my long-lived life into one moment.

"I thought you were lost. I thought we'd failed." She cries after the kiss.

"What…what's going on? I'm so confused."

"We sent you back to save everything."

"We?"

"You and I. Odyssian."

"Odyssian is real?" He feels like a long-lost dream.

"Yes, very. And so is the Regime. And Ryveliant. All of it."

"Why do I feel so different this time?" I ask, accepting that all of it was real because there's no way I could have dreamed it up myself.

"What do you mean?"

"I feel like I know *this* body. It's mine." I explain. "All of the previous ones, I was a different person."

"Ah yes…that's because you were not using Warper tech to travel through time. You've been using a safer technology: Conscious Embodiment."

"Why?"

"It guarantees you can return to your original self and time. You're not physically traveling through time, just mentally.

"Doesn't Warper tech return you to the same time?"

"Not after multiple jumps like you experienced." She begins to explain. "We mapped you to your younger self and had to hope you'd find your way."

"Why just 'hope'? Why couldn't I remember anything?" I ask, thinking all the way back to the start of my journey waking up on my apartment floor in Omaha.

"It was all we had. Conscious Embodiment doesn't take the core user's short-term memory with it."

"Okay." I've learned to accept answers at this point. "How long have I been…under?"

"A little over three years." Her gaze is downcast.

Jesus Christ.

Something else bugs me. "What about the Jinx? Why was I craving it to start? And having withdrawal symptoms whenever I'd go from one place to the next?"

"Oh…interesting. That must have been an unintended side effect. It's the sedative we used to put you into your coma."

"Huh." Another pressing question pops in my mind. "And how are you here?"

"It's…complicated." She shifts away and she wrings her hands.

"Try me. At this point I believe pretty much anything."

"I'm a fourth-dimensional being…" She lets the revelation bathe for a moment. "…who elected to live a third-dimensional life."

My heart wrenches like a wringed cloth.

"What? Why?"

Why would she demote her evolution?

More tears glisten in her eyes. "Because I love you. I've always loved you."

Something's not making sense to me. "But how did you know you loved me *before* you made the decision to become…lesser?"

"Odyssian sure didn't teach you much." She smiles and my body shivers. "'Before' is a concept of normal time flow. We don't experience the tide of time the same.

"When it became apparent that Ryveliant had created the Core Event of the Regime, I experienced a whole host of emotions and memories at once. Odyssian and I knew it meant we'd found something *special*, something Ryveliant wouldn't have: a strong connection in the third dimension.

"There was little time, so we made our plan the best we could, and I found you all those years ago as a talented Hiscon, working with a client of mine. You asked me out, and it led us here…"

"But what about all the other…" I search for the right word, "…*iterations* of you?"

"Part of the package becoming a third dimensional being: I experience *all* time. Egypt, San Francisco, Italy, the *other* 2477…I only knew you in that last one because Odyssian told that version of me everything and Aiontis – a version of you – already existed there."

"This is…a lot." My head is spinning. There's a dull ache along the sides.

"I know, I'm sorry. I'm sure Odyssian explained, but even we haven't perfected everything, despite the evolution. A lot of this war was fought stumbling in the dark."

There's an awkward silence between us. I'm elated to be with her again, though struggling to understand where we go from here. My gaze holds, downtrodden, on the grimy floor.

"Hey." She lifts my chin and presses her soft lips against mine. They feel 30 years younger than they are. "We *did it*. It may not look like it here, but we stopped Ryveliant. The Regime. Everything."

"I know. I just…" The right words are hard to find. "I was hoping for peace. For home. This doesn't feel like it after everything I've been through, aside from you being here."

"Well, that's why we made a retirement plan." Her smile is devilish and there's a twinkle in her eye. She walks over to a decrepit and crooked desk, the wood splintered and aged. A dramatic slash of plum lightning fills the room with an obscure hue. Kiaria opens a drawer and pulls out a small sphere and two small discs: a miniature Warper and what I can only assume are memory implants similar to the one I used at the start of this adventure.

"Where would you like to go?" She asks.

"But what about…?"

"This timeline is unsalvageable. The Regime infected it and it will end soon."

That's tremendously sad, so I try not to dwell on it.

"Let's go home." I finally answer. "2404. When we first met."

Her smile agrees and she plugs the date into the dial. I stand from the bed and she hugs me, head resting against my chest. There's a deep pounding of bass and together, for the first time, we enter the darkness as one.

Epilogue – Aiontis
2404 | *Omaha, Nebraska*

Something about the air is different here. Healthier. Free of war and cataclysm. It's fresh and a warm sun bathes us. I release my hold from Kiaria, looking around. Memories and thoughts of 2404 Omaha, deeply locked away after so many years, tell me this is where we're at.

This 2404 is a lot like the one I lived in. The one I was sent back to at the beginning. We're high atop a walkway among the layered levels of skyscrapers, near a west facing railing. Behind us, there are a series of benches, holo-ads, and greenery.

Is this my *2404?*

Kiaria answers for me. "You know the chances of this being the timeline you came from is infinite, right?"

"I…suppose."

She gives me a squeeze and turns to the railing, leaning against it, observing the horizon. "It's ok. It's peaceful here. We can grow old together."

"We're already old." I joke.

"Oh! We are?" Looking back at me, her grin is devilish. "So…what do you want to do?"

The question – one I hadn't considered – overwhelms me. It's the most hopeful respite I've had in a while. For several moments, I'm unsure of my answer, my mind racing with the possibilities.

With enormous clarity, as it was *sent* to me, an idea comes.

"Out of all the things we could do," Kiaria begins, "and you want to go to an *art museum?*"

"Just…trust me. I think." I drag her hand as we enter the ornate, organized hallway, lined with paintings. The ceilings are high and the rooms large, with hosts of artwork along them.

In my timeline, Omaha was known worldwide for its art museum, an interesting direction for the long-ago farming town to take during its artistic reinvention.

Hall after hall and room after room pass by, decorated with pieces of art worth adoring, worth studying. We skip them all, practically jogging through the exhibits.

My heart pounds.

I'm sure of it.

It's here.

Finally, we turn a corner and all but skid to a stop. Onlookers stare, confused. I don't care.

At the far end of the room is a painting. One I'd recognize anywhere.

It's a woman, the most beautiful one in the world, lying naked on a collection of colorful pillows, her gaze soft, and the room's light a dull afternoon glow.

Caterina, la donna
Unknown Artist, Renaissance Era, 1493

Beside me, Kiaria gasps. "Is that…?"

Tears well in my eyes, and drop delicately to the floor. I'm frozen in place. My heart balloons in my chest. *This* is home.

For a time, an unknown amount of it, we stare in awe, transfixed by the infinitude of the universe.

Acknowledgements

2023 | *Denver, Colorado*

Writing *Infinitude* was like no other project I've had in my life. It started off as a much different idea, but slowly morphed into an equally concrete and ambiguous one. Per usual, I like to begin "with the end in mind", but the journey there required a lot of research, plot mapping, and critical thinking. It was fun, frustrating, challenging, and incredibly rewarding.

And it didn't happen alone.

The first person who deserves thanks is always the teacher who instilled in me an interest to write at a young age. She may never read my novels, but Mrs. Littleford was one of those teachers you remember; it was her "write anything!" prompts that kicked off this lifelong passion.

It's also worth mentioning all the *other* artists that inspire me, which are too many to list here. At this point in human history, stories are but reflections and fragments of other stories, told in unique ways. And across many books, movies, television shows, and videogames I have gathered a broad arsenal of *stories*. And to the artists that work on those things, I am grateful because they inspire me.

My wife, Molly – who was not my wife at the beginning of writing this! – is a steady rock and always a strong supporter of my pursuit to write. Whether it's my career someday, or just something I like to do, she's always there and willing to listen to ideas, read my content, and provide loving feedback. And throw surprise release-day parties…those too. I love you, Peach!

My editor, Lexi is utterly fantastic and professional. This is the third time we've worked together and she is always able to push my novels to be clean and error-free, but past that…just *read* better. Her additional thoughts on the story and the excitement she had for this one was infectious and came at a critical time in the writing journey. Thank you!

To the brilliant designer of the cover, Christian Storm: it was downright awesome to work with you. This is the first time I took this avenue with one of my books and it was thrilling to see the ideas you were able to come up with and learn more about the process. This book at least looks fantastic because of you!

To all of my "virtual" beta readers: Mikey, Samantha, Ayan, Jodi, and Keith. I appreciate your feedback a tremendous amount, especially because we're arguably strangers. A lot of times, it was your critical eye coupled with praise that gave me even more hope *Infinitude* would and could find a home outside of my family/friend circle. I hope you enjoyed the final product that you helped build!

Thomas, Bekkah, and Gary – my three friend beta readers: I value your input a tremendous amount and I was so excited to gather, read, and apply your feedback, not to mention, hear about your reactions along the way. I know that you went through it with extra love and care and this book is a reflection of that. A special mention to Gary who continues to be the best cheerleader-I've-never-met and fellow writer. You build my confidence up, and I am grateful!

And then there's the most important thank you of all:

YOU!

Reading is a dying art (I won't get on my soapbox), and the fact that you picked up a book I wrote and trusted me to take you on an adventure is a tremendous honor. It's the reason I ultimately keep doing this. So…**thank you** for the support and I sincerely hope you enjoyed your time with *Infinitude*.

About the Author – J.T. Rath

J.T. Rath has had a passion for writing since he was in the 5th grade. In high school, he was given an opportunity to write a 5-page short story that ultimately turned into 20 pages and the prologue of sorts to his first novel, *Agents & Angels*. That action-packed story, set in the world of spies, had an even more exciting follow-up, *Agents & Angels II: The Wolfpaw Initiative* that concluded the tale. Both can be purchased on Amazon.com

Infinitude is J.T. Rath's third novel, but certainly not his last. He also has a recently published short story, *The Mask of a Marriage*.

J.T. Rath lives and works in Denver, Colorado with his wife Molly and their Bernese Mountain Dog, Barley.

He loves hearing from fans and fellow writers and encourages anyone interested to reach out to him at his email j.t.rath.author@gmail.com, Facebook, Instagram, and Goodreads pages, or via his website, www.jtrath.com.

In his free time, J.T. Rath reviews movies and videogames that can be found on his blog: www.raths-reviews.com

www.ingramcontent.com/pod-product-compliance
Lightning Source LLC
Chambersburg PA
CBHW032111310726
48972CB00001B/177